# HOUSE PARTY

## A NOVEL

### edited by
# justin a. reynolds

joy revolution

Compilation copyright © 2023 by This Just In, LLC
"The Actor" copyright © 2023 by Angeline Boulley
"The Artist" copyright © 2023 by Jerry Craft
"The School Paper Editor; Knower of All Tea" copyright © 2023 by Natasha Díaz
"The Wannabe Rapper" copyright © 2023 by Lamar Giles
"The Popular Girl" copyright © 2023 by Christina Hammonds Reed
"The Influencer"; "The Cool Mom" copyright © 2023 by Ryan La Sala
"The Jock" copyright © 2023 by Yamile Saied Méndez
"The Class Clown" copyright © 2023 by justin a. reynolds
"The Emo Band Kid" copyright © 2023 by Randy Ribay
"The New Girl" copyright © 2023 by Jasmine Warga
Jacket art copyright © 2023 by Kelsee Thomas

All rights reserved. Published in the United States by Joy Revolution, an imprint of Random House Children's Books, a division of Penguin Random House LLC, New York.

Joy Revolution is a registered trademark and the colophon is a trademark of Penguin Random House LLC.

GetUnderlined.com

Educators and librarians, for a variety of teaching tools, visit us at RHTeachersLibrarians.com

Library of Congress Cataloging-in-Publication Data is available upon request.
ISBN 978-0-593-48815-7 (hc) — ISBN 978-0-593-48816-4 (lib. bdg.) —
ISBN 978-0-593-48817-1 (ebook)

The text of this book is set in 11.75-point Adobe Garamond Pro
Interior design by Michelle Crowe
Blueprint design by justin a. reynolds

Printed in the United States of America
10 9 8 7 6 5 4 3 2 1
First Edition

FOR EVERY KID FIGURING OUT WHO THEY ARE
AND WHERE THEY FIT IN. THIS PARTY'S FOR YOU.

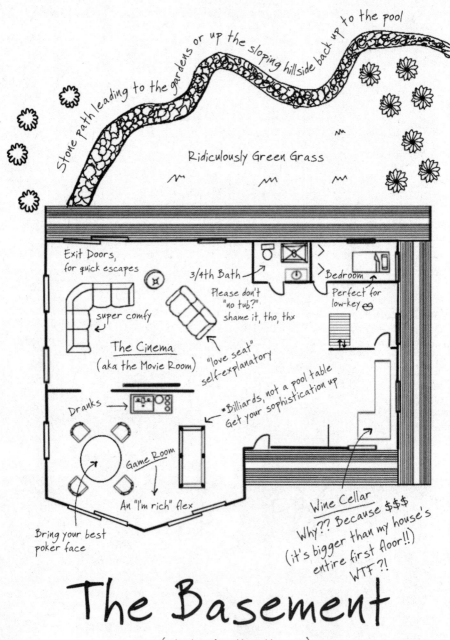

Stone path leading to the gardens or up the sloping hillside back up to the pool

Ridiculously Green Grass

Exit Doors, for quick escapes

3/4th Bath
Please don't "no tub?". shame it, tho, thx

Bedroom
Perfect for low-key 😴

super comfy

The Cinema
(aka the Movie Room)

"love seat" self-explanatory

Dranks

*Billiards, not a pool table
Get your sophistication up

Game Room

An "I'm rich" flex

Bring your best poker face

Wine Cellar
Why?? Because $$$
(it's bigger than my house's entire first floor!!)
WTF?!

# The Basement

(Starting from the bottom...)

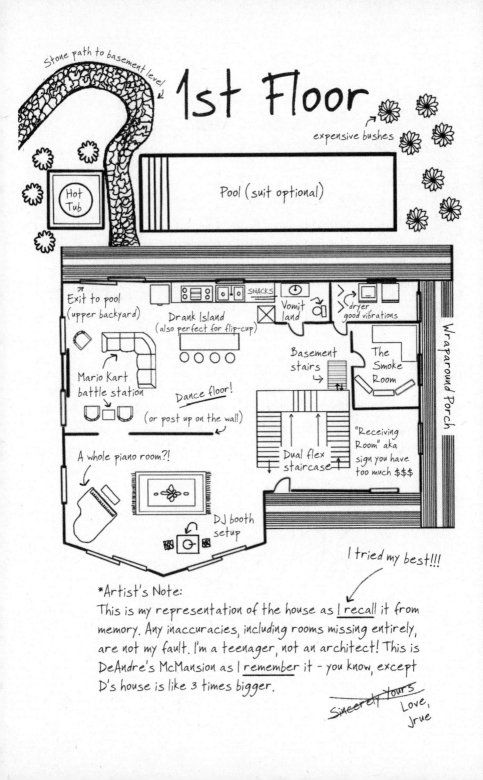

Stone path to basement level!

# 1st Floor

expensive bushes

Hot Tub

Pool (suit optional)

Exit to pool
(upper backyard)

SNACKS

Vomit land

dryer
good vibrations

Drank Island
(also perfect for flip-cup)

Basement stairs

The Smoke Room

Mario Kart
battle station

Dance floor!

(or post up on the wall)

Dual flex staircase

"Receiving Room" aka
sign you have too much $$$

Wraparound Porch

A whole piano room?!

DJ booth setup

I tried my best!!!

*Artist's Note:

This is my representation of the house as I recall it from memory. Any inaccuracies, including rooms missing entirely, are not my fault. I'm a teenager, not an architect! This is DeAndre's McMansion as I remember it – you know, except D's house is like 3 times bigger.

Sincerely Yours
Love,
Jrue

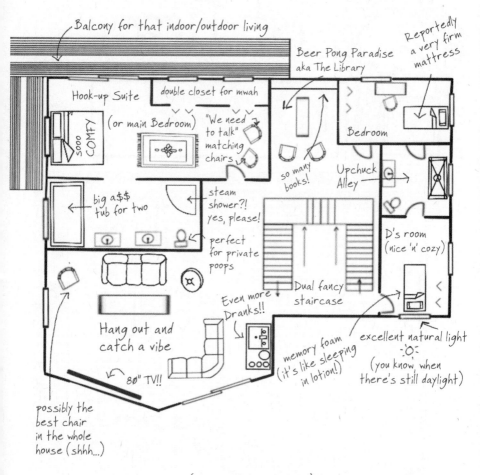

Balcony for that indoor/outdoor living

Reportedly a very firm mattress

Beer Pong Paradise aka The Library

Hook-up Suite

double closet for mwah

(or main Bedroom)

SOOO COMFY

"We need to talk" matching chairs

Bedroom

so many books!

Upchuck Alley

big a$$ tub for two

steam shower?! yes, please!

perfect for private poops

D's room (nice 'n' cozy)

Dual fancy staircase

Even more Dranks!!

Hang out and catch a vibe

80" TV!!

memory foam (it's like sleeping in lotion!)

excellent natural light

(you know, when there's still daylight)

possibly the best chair in the whole house (shhh...)

(... and now we're here!)

# 2nd Floor

# JRUE EDWARDS
## THE CLASS CLOWN

**PART I**

IT'S FRIDAY, AND YOUR BOY'S ON A MISSION. OUR main objectives, in no particular order, are as follows:

### PREPARTY

☐ Get invited to DeAndre's house party.
☐ Convince Sadie to go to said party.

### AT THE PARTY

☐ Confess feelings to Mia.
☐ Maybe make out with Mia?
☐ Secure GOAT status.

ACTION ITEM #1: Convince Sadie to go to the party.

Trap sprung, I throw the kitchen island spotlight onto the intruder and yell, "Yo, you jacking my strudel?!"

"Dude, no," Sadie says, shielding her eyes from the accusatory halogen. "Just no."

I grab a rolling pin from the nearest drawer and slap it into my palm a few times, like a nightstick. Except this nightstick is still caked with dough. Man, our dishwasher sucks.

Me, I suck. I'm the dishwasher.

I scowl at my best friend since second grade. "What, you think you can just waltz into my home, broad daylight, and cherry strudel jack me with impunity, Sadie Bernbaum?"

Sadie cuts her eyes, unfazed. "Ha, you wish I'd jack your little nonpopped cherry strudel, but I'm on a strict no-corny-dude diet, sorry."

"Wooow, for real?" I put the dirty rolling pin back, then pluck the last frozen pastry from the box. "And you didn't put the box back in the freezer? You're savage."

She winks at me, smushing her last bite of my all-time favorite breakfast treat into her mouth with the ferocity of a world-champion eater. "So they say."

Except her mouth's full so it sounds more like: *Schlo dey shay.*

"Hmph," I say, locking my *Trust me, you don't want this smoke* eyes onto hers as I rip open the last packet of strudels with my bare hands.

"Hmph," I say again, eyes still locked, as I . . . as I . . . *Damn you, kidproof packaging!*

Sadie holds out her hand. "Need an adult?" she asks, reading my mind when I wish she'd mind her own.

"Why, you know one?" I elevate my package-ripping mission to my mouth, setting the plastic onto my canines to open it with my teeth, but there's a gap between my top and bottom teeth from not wearing my retainer back in middle school, so yes, my parents paid thousands for an under-overbite, *Thankssss, guys.* The retainer made my cheeks even bulgier than normal, like I was having a permanent allergic reaction. Or stashing acorns. Plus, I couldn't talk with that thing; I sounded like the love child of Donald Duck and that teacher from Charlie Brown, so every morning, the second I got on the bus, I ditched the retainer.

I pull a knife from the block like it's the Sword in the Stone and slice the wrapper's corner clean off, one swipe, mission accomplished. Almost. "Hold up, where's my—" I upside-down the box, but it's still empty. I eye-sweep the floor, nope. I'm about to search the freezer when I spy Sadie trying to slide something under her island-flattened palm, on the low.

I lift an eyebrow. "Well, that's not suspicious."

Sadie shakes her head. Twists her face into her version of *I'm innocent.* I try to lift her hand, but she's stronger than she looks. So I booty-bump her off-balance, which she exaggerates, flailing extra dramatically like LeBron pretending to take a charge. I wave the evidence in the air, two used-up glaze packets.

"The hell, Sadie? You used *two* icing pouches?"

She laughs, casually licking leftover glaze from her fingertips. "You know there's never enough glaze in one package."

I throw up my hands. "Now I gotta eat icing-less strudel," I whine. "Again."

"Oh, boo-hoo," Sadie says, making that super-weird universal gesture for fake crying when you put a fist on the outside of either eye and twist like you're gripping the handlebars of your invisible motorcycle.

I sidestep her one-woman performance to scribble "strudel" onto the family grocery list magnet on the fridge, adding it just beneath "condoms," scrawled in Mom's handwriting—as usual, she turned her "o's" into smiley faces.

"Wait, why is Deborah buying condoms; she having issues with her IUD?" Sadie asks, resting her chin atop my shoulder and reading the list, like we're two wily raccoons peering out of a hole in a tree.

I fake vomit. "Please never say my mom's name in the same sentence as 'condoms,' 'IUD,' or any other popular forms of birth control, okay, thanksss. Besides, how do you know those aren't for me?"

Sadie stares into my soul and cackles. "Yeah, the thought did cross my mind, considering the great abundance of intercourse you're having, but the drawn-in smiley-face 'o's' in 'condoms' gave it away. Your 'o's' would've been sad."

"Whatever." I roll my eyes. "I choose to abstain."

"If by choose, you mean set your sights on unattainable humans, then yes, you are the poster child for abstinence." She makes a weird flourish with her hands, like they're a butterfly, then adds, "The More You Know."

"Yasmine Kalouria isn't unattainable."

Sadie blinks at me, hard. "Dude, she has been your international pen pal since fifth grade. If after seven years of you translating 'So, how's the weather there *now*' in Spanish you haven't hooked up, it's not happening."

"Hey, I begged my parents to fly to Honduras. Not my fault they're haters."

"Right. Because your parents were clearly the problem in that can't-miss plan."

I shrug. "What about Mia?" I ask, except the name Mia drops off my sentence like an anvil, so it sounds like *What about me-oooow?* But leave it to Sadie to catch every vowel and consonant.

"Mia?" Sadie double-bops her fist on the island, punctuating both syllables, like *Mee Uhh*. "The same Mia who is one of the five most popular kids in school? The Mia who broke up with QB One and Student Body Co-President DeAndre six weeks ago, and yet you, after crushing on her since preschool, have barely spoken a word to, despite the fact she lives right next door to you?"

I pause to make sure she's finished and then I go in. "Okay, one, it hasn't even been four weeks since the breakup. Two, Mia wasn't even in Florence Hills for preschool. Three, she lives two houses down." I clear my throat. "And four, today is not only the day I, Jrue Edwards, pour out my heart to Mia, but it might even be the day I find out if she's wearing lip gloss or colored ChapStick."

"Eww," Sadie squeals as the napkin she uses misses nearly all of the strudel remnants clinging to her chin. I, not very helpfully, direct her efforts to the cleaner side of her mouth, where a cherry glob is not glistening in the kitchen skylight, and she diligently wipes there, too. "Never say anything about what's on someone's lips again, creeper," she says.

"Easy there, Minecraft," I say, but if she catches my joke, she doesn't let on; she's too busy crumpling the barely soiled napkin into a ball and chucking it at my head. Direct hit. Two can play that game . . .

"Thanks, but I think you need this more than I do, looks like you missed a spot . . . or three," I say, pointing at my own face like it's a handy reference guide to the regions of her face still covered in strudel crumbs, before flinging her napkin ball back at her, aiming for where her heart should be; Sadie, diving to the other side of the island, unable to control her grinning.

And now it's a full-on napkin-ball war. I wish I could tell you this was new for us, but we've been trading napkin grenades since your mom.

When the dust settles, I rock on my cardinal-red Jordan 3s, which is normally a big NOPE for an aspiring sneakerhead like me, but I'm nervous. "Listen, Sadie, about tonight? I was, uh, sorta thinking we could shake things up a bit and maybe, uh, you know, check out a party or something . . ."

Sadie peeks over the top of the island. "Hold on. What's happening?"

I shrug. "Nothing."

| SADIE | JRUE |
|---|---|
| "Something's definitely happening, and I can't believe I . . ." | "Omigod, nothing's happening. Why would you even think that, that's what's really . . ." |
| ". . . almost thought tonight wasn't gonna turn into some Disney quest to save the world with one kiss from your OTL. I should've known something was up when you sent me that squirrel gif this morning." | ". . . weird . . . you . . . thinking . . . that . . . I can't believe you'd even imply that I'd have an ulterior motive for this party. It's absurd is what it is. Absurd." |
| "I see right through you. Like, maybe I'mma start calling you Lingerie because that's how see-through you are to me." | "If I'm Lingerie, then you're . . . Negligee . . ." |
| "Wait. Huh?" | "Yeah, because you're so *negligent* when it comes to looking out for your friends . . ." |
| "One hundred percent not how that works." | |

I shake my head. "Look, I didn't want it to go down like this, but you leave me no choice . . . Sadie Bernbaum, you owe me."

"What?" Sadie scoffs.

"Tommy Pilgrim's coed seventh-grade sleepover, Sam Dreyer's bat mitzvah, Devon Lyle's birthday party . . ."

"Dude, that last one happened in third grade. Move on."

"Point is, I'm always there to support you."

"Oh, and I'm not there for you?" Sadie shoots back. "Fernanda Manning's quinceañera, Memi's theater road trip, Gregg's mini-golf course takeover party. Should I keep going?"

"Okay, okay, you support me, too. Damn. I'm just saying—"

"One word for you, Jrue," she interjects, waving her finger in the air, the way she sometimes does when punctuating her point. "Goat."

I shake my head. "Excuse me for including you in Florence Hills High history. My bad."

"You hear yourself? Why do you give a fuck what these people think about you?"

"Um, maybe because I'm a human with complicated feelings and irrational emotions and sometimes I want things that are inherently unhealthy and occasionally bad for me, what can I tell you?" I toss the empty strudel box back into the freezer. What? The freezer's infinitely closer than the trash can.

"Listen. When we look back in twenty years, we're going to think—*Damn, that night really meant something.*" I turn to a still-skeptical Sadie, deciding to take one last shot at convincing her. "All I'm saying is wouldn't it be cool if for once we went to a party where you weren't investigating everyone for the school newspaper and we just, you know, had regular fun?"

Sadie sighs. "Regular fun? First of all, that sounds boring.

Who wants to be regular? And two, fine, whatever, maybe, okay. I'll think about it."

I hop up and down, clapping my hands like I'm jumping on someone's couch. And then I'm chanting, "Reg-u-lar fun. Reg-u-lar fun. Reg-u-lar fun," admittedly for a few beats too long, but whatever because Sadie's gonna *think about it,* which usually when people tell you *they'll think about it,* it means they've already decided but they're gonna wait to tell you no. This is one of my parents' go-to moves; they are masters of the "tell you no later" move. But not Sadie; if she says she's gonna think about it, she will.

We're halfway out the front door when Sadie whirls around with her *Holy fucking shit* face. "Omigod, what if your parents got pregnant again?"

I fake vomit all over our shoes.

ACTION ITEM #2: Get invited to DeAndre's party.

DeAndre Dixon's locker is directly above mine, which means five things:

Thing #1: I'm constantly asked: *Yo, you see that ass?* To which I reply, *Boy, do I,* even though it's hard to know which ass, seeing how in our school hallway somehow everyone walking by seems to have a seeable ass, thus making everyone a candidate for *that ass.*

Thing #2: I speak fluent bro. Every school day, DeAndre and I "interact" for three to nine minutes, via a series of coded grunts and barely perceptible head nods, that run the gamut in translations from *What I wouldn't do for a fistful of tots right now* to *Yo, but did you just see THAT ass?* To which, again, I'd awkwardly smile and reply: *Boy, did I.* To be fair, DeAndre isn't *strictly* a bro; admittedly, he behaves better than most, gets good grades, volunteers at the food pantry on weekends, but still, the bro is strong with this one.

Thing #3: I smell like DeAndre. How could I not? Dude one hundred percent does his part to support the perfume + cologne community. Thrice daily he spritzes his neck, chest, and both biceps—his perfectly smooth, dark brown cheeks beaming as his trigger thumb detonates one last misty blast, forming a woodsy-citrusy cloud for him to step through, and for me to get a secondhand hit, as if smelling like an oak tree that fucked a tangerine makes him feel whole.

Thing #4: This—me, standing off to the side, while DeAndre fist-bumps and bro-hugs nearly every standing member of the Jock-and-Popular Kid Consortium (JPKC)—is undoubtedly as close to being *cool* as I'll ever be.

And last but definitely not least, the crown jewel of them all, Thing #5: Every morning, before first bell, I get a daily dose of Mia McKenzie. Which makes her sound like a multivitamin, I know—but that kinda fits, too, because Mia McKenzie's got everything you need. Obviously, she's gorgeous, but honestly, that's the least interesting thing about her. She's wicked smart but not an asshole. She's crazy passionate about the environment; last month, she organized a student walkout for fifth period, to bring awareness to ozone depletion. Plus, she's got the most adorable laugh. Like, you get her going and her whole body convulses; it sends me every time. Mia McKenzie's the whole deal.

DeAndre grins. "What up, Mia?"

"Sup, D," Mia says, returning his smile.

Question: Is it strange they still talk despite their breakup?

"Hey, J," Mia sings as she floats by, sprawled on a bed of roses sprinkled across a long puffy cloud. No, this is not that kind of situation where every time your crush walks by, it's a slow-motion, gospel-choir-backed fantasy.

No, Mia is really lying on a rose-covered cloud—something to do with drama club.

"Huh? Oh, hey, Mia, um, hi, hey-ho, hiyaaa, sup, whaaat'ssss uppp," I say, cycling through every variation of the popular greeting because I'm spicy like that.

Mia laughs and shakes her head as if I'm the funniest person she's ever met—which she actually did say, at a beach bonfire three weeks ago, right after I decided to moon the moon, because I'm crazy clever, but also uncoordinated, leaving me falling on my thicc, bare ass. Not my best night. I shook sand outta my crack for a week. Mia McKenzie, seventeen and three-quarters years old, Black, witty, stunning, smart, perfect—is one of the cool kids.

"Wait, wait," Mia says suddenly. "Stop the float!"

The float halts abruptly, its engine, three theater kids wearing all black, slamming on the brakes—which is to say, they discontinue walking. And I assume Mia wants to confirm her attendance at DeAndre's party, maybe she'll ask if she should bring anything, you know, because she's classy. Oh, should *I* offer to bring something, too? My parents and their friends are always asking each other *What can I bring, what can I bring*—is that how high school parties work, too?

"Hellooo? Earth to Jrue," Mia says, in a voice that implies she's repeating herself.

I wag my head and approximate a casual smile.

Mia stares at me for another beat, then chuckles again. "Sooo, is that a yes?"

Yes what? Omigod, Mia asked me something, and I don't know what. FML. What do I do? What do I say? I smile wider, like I'm the one waiting on her answer. "Yessss what?"

"Can we talk later at the party?" Mia asks. The thought already has my heart thumping, except it ramps up even more when she brushes my wrist—fine, it might've been her attempt to steady herself on the float, but we can debate that later—and adds, "There's something I need to tell you."

Okay, so technically what just happened was not actually on our list of objectives, but I feel like it should've been, so I'm including PREPARTY ACTION ITEM #3A: LET MIA KNOW YOU NEED TO TALK TO HER AT THE PARTY.

Even though, technically, *she* asked *me*.

Which feels very . . . significant.

So of course, I act cool, leaning against my locker all casual. I say hella aloofly, "Yeah, wasn't sure I was going, since *somebody* didn't exactly invite me yet—hint hint—but uh, yeah, maybe you'll see me there." Except DeAndre's not even paying attention, missing my hints entirely.

And Mia, still smiling, shakes her head like, *Um, okay?*

And then Savoy, our resident influencer extraordinaire, looking runway-ready as usual, and their unholy trinity (Grant, Mirage, and Effie) materialize alongside the theater-kid-powered chariot and the six of them usher Mia away.

In conclusion, late addition ACTION ITEM #3A? Check *and* check.

Yes, 3A is only one action. No, I do not know why I needed two checks.

Gregg "Double G's" Fox whistles as Mia's float disappears around the hallway corner. "Damn, Mia could get it." Feeling DeAndre's eyes snapping him in half, Gregg adds, "You know, if she wasn't completely off-limits because of bro code."

All you need to know about Gregg "Double G's" is:

1. He only rocks Adidas tracksuits, ever.
2. He's basically the Uber of high school party promotion; he never throws parties at his house, but he's happy to throw a banger at your house for a nominal fee.

Except DeAndre's face is smoke-free. He even cracks a smile—not full DeAndre wattage, but still. "Dude, Mia's free to date whomever she wants. As are you."

Gregg's face morphs from confusion to mad excitement. "Wait, for real?!"

DeAndre shrugs. "Whatever, dude," he says, turning to me and offering me a . . . a . . . fist bump. Which, no, this is not my first cool-kid fist bump. I've had plenty. It's just that normally they come after I've made some dumb-ass joke in the middle of a school assembly.

"Heard you got a killer fake ID," DeAndre says with an authority that makes me forget that I, in fact, do not have a killer fake ID. That I, in fact, don't even have a student ID anymore; I'm pretty sure it's at the bottom of Lake Michigan. Also, does this mean DeAndre Dixon talks about me . . . with other people?

"You heard wrong," I say, shaking my head, and I see it, the flash of disappointment across his athletic face. And I think to myself, *Damn, that could've been your in, Jrue, why didn't you seize the day, man?* And that's when I hear myself say, "Because I've got *two* killer fake IDs."

DeAndre laughs, claps me on my back as he turns to walk away. "Dude, you're so funny. Definitely bring beer and jokes tonight, yeah?" DeAndre nods at Gregg and Gregg hands me a sheet of paper. A quick glance confirms it's a party flyer, which is wild because (1) it's an actual piece of paper, who knew people still used *real* paper, and (2) not only am I going to the party tonight, I was officially invited by the host himself.

And then I watch DeAndre step out into the center of the hall, the sea of upperclassmen instantly parting, bending at his will. And then, glancing back over his shoulder, meeting my eyes, he adds, "But mostly beer."

I laugh too loudly because I'm extra. "Right," I call out after him, barely able to convince my voice not to crack. "If it somehow comes down to me bringing jokes or beer, obviously I'mma go with the jokes, haha. *Kidding.* I'm kidding. Beer all the way. Beer, beer, beer. Have no . . . fear . . . the . . . beer is . . . here . . ."

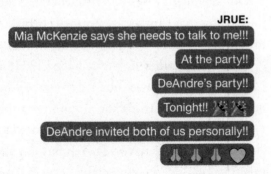

JRUE:
Mia McKenzie says she needs to talk to me!!!
At the party!!
DeAndre's party!!
Tonight!!
DeAndre invited both of us personally!!

Sadie explained to me that there are two kinds of texters: those who send you *one* text with all the info and thoughts neatly condensed, and us.

And that, my friends, completes phase one of our mission.
See you later, *party-gator.*
. . . I hate myself.

I PULL UP early to the party flexing my seven-year-old,
old-man-tan-colored Town & Country, sitting on nineteens
and fully loaded, duh.

Plus, I come bearing gifts, bringing with me two out of the
three necessary *final party of our high school lives* things.

THING #1: Alcohol.

I know you were probably expecting some wild story
whereby the cops are staking out the liquor store as I, wearing a
not-so-convincing disguise, try to convince the burnout behind
the counter that I am a thirty-year-old baby-faced redhead from
Iowa, but nope, sorry. The alcohol's yawningly easy to acquire.

You know earlier how it sounded like I'm an only child?
I actually have an awesome sister-mom, who spent much of
her teenage years carting me around to tap dance lessons and
Power of the Pen practice sessions, and who just celebrated her
twenty-ninth b-day last week. Yep, my parents are old enough
to retire and drive a golf cart full-time. It hasn't been a normal
week until someone mistakes my mom and dad for my grand-
parents. Which the *Are they having another kid?* thing is sounding even grosser now, right?

Anyway, older sis, after a moderately lengthy lecture on the perils of underage drinking and making me swear I won't drive after the party, drops off a backseat full of booze—*Love you, Lauryn!*—all of which is now sitting atop DeAndre's crowded kitchen island.

Now, THING #2? Well, that takes a bit more coaxing to get out of the ole minivan.

"Does she bite?" DeAndre asks, only seconds after exclaiming *Holy shit, are you serious,* as I pushed the trunk power-gate button and we stood at the rear of the van, watching its ass flap open.

I shrug, masking my slight disappointment that Mia isn't here yet, and also unable to tell whether DeAndre thinks Brenda the Goat possibly being a biter is actually a good thing. "Not so far she doesn't, but the night's young."

DeAndre claps his hands, his eyes lighting up like a Fourth of July sky. "Bro, this is unreal. Seriously, Bayside is gonna lose their shit when they realize she's gone. This is so good. Do you have any idea what you've done? This is their good-luck goat. They've won fifty games in a row since the old goat croaked and they brought in Brenda."

"I know," I say, grinning. "They're the only school who's beaten us almost every time we've played them all four years we've been at Florence."

DeAndre's face deflates. "Dude, ouch. *I* was playing in those 'L's."

"Right, sorry." *Duh, Jrue, way to insult your host.* "Anyway, thanks to an anonymous tip, Bayside's football team knows Brenda's here."

DeAndre's eyebrows slide up. "Wait. Here? As in Florence Hills, right?"

"No, *here*. As in your house."

"Dude!" His face twists. "You trying to go to jail? That's possession of stolen property."

"You really think Bayside's gonna call the cops? If they stole our mascot, would we?"

DeAndre's face scrunches in confusion. "You know our mascot's a human in a costume, right?"

"For real? You mean there are no five-foot-eight falcons?" I grin. "My point is, we wouldn't call the cops, right?"

DeAndre nods. "Nah. We'd just show up to the party, get back Flo, and then get even."

"Bingo," I say. "Give this man a prize. Except when they show up, that's when we're gonna show . . . out."

DeAndre cheeses, daps me up. "I love it. I feel like it's my birthday, I'm so pumped right now. When Bryson finds out she's missing, dude's gonna lose his whole shit! Whoo! Tonight's gonna be the best party ever!"

We high-five violently over the enemy QB's distress, and I only mildly dislocate my pinkie.

And okay, maybe we can't cross ACTION ITEM #5 (Secure GOAT status) all the way off yet, but we're close enough to sniff that shit.

Wait, no, my bad, that's just Brenda dropping a megadeuce in the middle of DeAndre Dixon's immaculate four-car garage, next to a sparkling-new G-wagon.

I laugh nervously. "Got a shovel?"

And I know what you're thinking. How exactly does one class clown procure his school's fiercest athletic and academic rival's most prized pet and luck-toting mascot?

With help, duh.

Aka the one of my three major party necessities still not here yet.

Sadie Bernbaum.

A horn blare at the end of the long driveway as a huge U-Haul truck grinds to a halt. I turn to DeAndre, his eyes still glued to Brenda's pile of magic poop pebbles. "Sooo, is this a *moving-away* party, or . . . ?"

DeAndre doesn't answer.

I scratch my arm. "It's just that I kinda have a severe allergy to cardboard boxes."

# DEANDRE'S GROUP TEXT—FHHS TRENDSETTR

## PRIVATE CHAT
### [THE SQUAD: MIA, PENNY, FERNANDA, KRIS, GREGG]

**DEANDRE:**
yooo, party's gonna be crazy tonight, i can feel it, best night of our lives

**MIA:**
umm question, when have you ever NOT felt sumthin you were doing, D?!

**PENNY:**
😆 cuz he always doin the most

**FERNANDA:**
bahahaha facts!!!

**DEANDRE:**
Jokes but u know you don't wanna b the 1 to miss a DD party 😄

**KRIS:**
Wrap party's tonight!! I'll come thru after

**GREGG:**
there might be a cover charge, fyi

**DEANDRE:**
stfu gregg

# SAVOY

## THE INFLUENCER

### PART I

THE OTHER KIDS HAVE THIS JOKE ABOUT ME THAT goes: If Florence Hills was on fire, Savoy would take a picture in front of it.

And you know what? I would. Do you know how costly it would be to ignite my own homemade studio? Just for a few photos? No, bitch. I'm hot, not dumb. If I see a fire—or any natural disaster that I don't actively need to be running away from—you can bet your thrifted Gucci slides I'm taking advantage of Mother Nature's fury, striking a pose, and getting my shot for free. Because if there's one thing I love more than drama, it's drama I don't have to manufacture myself.

That's why I decide to take DeAndre up on his invitation to attend his end-of-year pregraduation party, or as he called it, "the Met Gala of Florence Hills, except more beer." This is also why, when unofficial party promoter Gregg texted me with The Plan (his capitalization, not mine) to truly make tonight quite the rager, I was like, yes, DeAndre, I would love to attend your sticky Met Gala, let me pick my outfits accordingly. And I'll make up my own theme, too, because *beer* and *sticky* aren't—how do I say this in the most derogatory way possible?—*inspirational* or *elevated,* two words that my looks must always achieve.

So I shirk DeAndre's casual theme and simply decide to look amazing, which, let's be honest, was never not going to be the case.

I love parties. The energy, the authenticity that can't help but bubble out of people, the clothes—they're the ingredients I need for the backdrops of these massive photo shoots my friends and I have been planning forever; outfits we've been designing forever; video shoots we've been storyboarding forever. God, I love the way parties make dreams matter. I love how they make you feel like everything hinges on just one night. And I guess in a way, everything does. At least for me. And for sure tonight.

Me and my crew show up fashionably early. Part of the Plan is to get some early posts uploaded showing some of Florence Hill's elite already present at DeAndre's. This will do two things: one, lock in the attendance of anyone who was on the fence about showing up, because if Savoy et al. are there, it's gonna be a wild time; and two, show people they gotta look good. Peel off their mom or dad's Lululemon leggings and oversized tees and put on a dress for once, you know? This is what I'm good for. I show people where to go, and what to wear there. I influence, as they say. Hence, Gregg tapping me for The Plan.

And sure, I have my own plan (lowercase "the plan," for discretion). Tonight, at the final party of my final year of high school, I lock down my legacy as the Baddest, Most Fashionable Bitch this school has ever seen, and launch my post–high school career as a full-time content creator. A fantasy career, I know, but I'm good. I can do this. And one day, my razor-sharp aesthetic is going to get me an invite to the *real* Met Gala. But first I need to pull off tonight's plan, which will require so much more than just gorgeous clothes.

My plan begins the second we pull into the already crowded cul-de-sac.

Picture this: me, Savoy, stepping down from the back of a rented U-Haul, the June sun scorching the last clouds in the sky above the illustrious Ellison Estates. I'm dressed in a clingy cropped top—an original There Is No Kevin in Team band T-shirt, tie-dyed black and blue—and shiny, olive-green track pants, the bottoms flared wide to focus the shot on a pair of chunky thrifted boots. Black, angry clompers, cluttered with girly charms strung into the neon-green laces. The camera's point of view is low, nearly on the ground, its eye zipping up my extended leg, making me look way taller than any human, way more powerful than just a high school fashion blogger. And in the photo behind me, in the dark of the truck, the camera's flash catches on the white of several toothy smiles—fake paparazzi made from oversized painted masks, breathing down my (very fashionable) neck. The paparazzi are holding up boxy cameras we stole from the photography club. Altogether, the image is sleek, eerie, and a little cartoonish. Perfect for an arrival, and we nail the shot in record time.

I land on the asphalt, and my friends rip away their smiling masks.

"Wonderful work, Savoy."

"Genius, per usual."

"The camera loves you."

Effie, Grant, and Mirage. My crew. My hype team. Their praise is half sincere, half sardonic. When they praise me, they're praising themselves because what we create, we create together. And what we intend to create tonight will be epic.

I grin up at them in the truck.

"Shut up and help me unload this equipment," I say.

While most people arriving at DeAndre's appear to be carrying in coolers, or cases of smuggled beer, we're hoisting in boxes of lighting equipment, garment bags, and cameras. All of it stolen from the school's tech lab and theater department. *Temporarily* stolen. We'll have it back before Monday, and we didn't take anything they needed for their show, although I was tempted after they axed my offer to do the costumes for this spring's *Romeo and Juliet* (barf). That rejection hurt, especially after I pitched resident theater geek Memi Matson my idea to let me do up their production in streetwear instead of the typical stuffy brocades and ruffly sleeves (double barf). But no, they went with . . . "another vision" (barf everywhere). A worse one. A vision I very publicly tore apart on last week's vlog, posted within minutes of the cast taking their opening-night bows. Not my noblest moment, I'll admit, and a potentially incriminating one if they figure out who took all this techy stuff. So we were careful to not take anything they'd miss immediately.

See? Again, I'm hot. Not dumb.

Here's another example: I may be posing around DeAndre's front lawn looking like a model drunk on golden hour, but getting here early gives us all the time we need to set up for our other shoots. DeAndre knows I think his place is nice but . . . darling, the lighting. Evil. Gulag-inspired. I won't stand for it, and I don't have to, because with DeAndre's permission we're rigging up enough flashbulbs to communicate with deep space via Morse code. Track lighting, too, for a runway segment. Maybe even some waterproof neon lights for the pool, if there's time and we haven't blown a fuse by then. Even if we do, I made DeAndre check and, yes, he does have a backup generator in the basement, but in his own words the thing is: "Ancient, man. Like, I think it's from the nineties, so maybe we don't attempt to use it?"

The one thing I haven't quite worked out is where I'm gonna get changed between shoots. DeAndre, bless his heart, has been very lenient with me on account of our childhood-friend status, but I don't think he'll be psyched if we commandeer his bedroom. He might need that later, I think as I spot his former bae Mia laughing over a bowl of chips inside. I end up directing Grant to set up in the primary bedroom. Someplace out of the way of the party's center, which I'm betting becomes the pool. Plus, DeAndre's mom loves me. She'd want me occupying that room over the alternative (drunk, sticky teenagers). If anything, I'm doing Mrs. Dixon a favor.

Smart, I know!

We get the track lighting wired up in the entryway (god bless the architect that put in this double staircase) and I keep a tally of who's arriving. Gregg did some damage—it's beyond even DeAndre's usually large group. Like, what's Merrill doing here? Why is she trading glances with the stoners, piled up on the stairs like sluggish von Trapps? And is that . . . Jrue Edwards?

If Grant sees Jrue, he'll blush—he's got a thing for the goofy type, which is probably why Grant and I have never even thought about kissing. It's strictly business between us. And speaking of boner-killing ambition, I register that there's no sign of Miranda or her posse.

Yet.

My blood turns to ice. Miranda. The also-kinda-internet-famous, also-queer witchy bitch of Florence Hills High, and my sworn nemesis in fashion and fame for the last three years. The second I think of her, I halt, her name freezing up the logistics of my ever-whirring brain. For the first time, standing here in the bubbling chaos of the party, tonight's plan becomes real. She'll be here tonight, she'll bring her own crew, she'll be doing her own shoots. Our ever-escalating rivalry is about to come to a head at the party of the year. Ever since some-one started a rumor a week ago that there'd be some sort of showdown between us tonight, people are expecting just that. A show. Two shows! Competing! And neither Miranda nor I ever back down from a challenge.

So that legacy I mentioned? The prophesied Baddest, Most Fashionable Bitch one? Miranda is after it, too, with just as many dreams on the line, and in the world of fashion, the most memorable takes all.

Whatever people are expecting tonight, they're not really ready. This is about to be some gay-ass chaos.

"Savoy, give me a candid!"

On the stairs, I spin. I pop out my tongue, throw up a peace sign, and manage a wink. Effie gets the shot on her phone and, as we slip through the crowded upstairs hallways, she narrates her caption:

"How 'bout . . . 'No party animals were harmed in the making of this photo shoot,'" she shouts over the music as she types. "Or maybe: 'It's not my party, but I will cry if I want to'? Is that funny?"

"Too cheesy for Savoy's voice," Grant shouts back. "Just use an emoji?"

"The fire emoji?"

"No. The sensible little sandal."

"What? Why?"

Grant rolls his eyes and grabs the phone. "'Cause you got Savoy's boots in the shot. The sandal is sensible, but Savoy's shoes are not. It's ironic."

Grant is our brains. He wants to study marketing in college. He treats my social feed with precise, thoughtful professionalism. Effie is our voice and eyes. Half art director, half loudmouthed Italian, she wants to become a nightlife producer, which she insists is a real job. Mostly, it just sounds like an excuse to go to parties and get paid to post about them. And Mirage—she's . . . wait, where is Mirage?

"Getting look number two ready," Grant answers my confused expression as we break from a clot of people waiting in line for the bathroom.

Oh, right. Mirage is our hands. If you ever need her, check a sewing machine. Or beneath a fallen bolt of fabric. She can make clothing out of anything. She's a vanisher, too, hence the nickname.

Together, we operate as the elusive, fashionable internet icon SAVOY. In all caps. I happen to actually be Savoy, the Body. But we're all integral to the illusion that is SAVOY, the star. All of us have some stake in watching this star rise.

And rise it has! Just this year, we've accrued a following of close to half a million, with hundreds more flowing in each time we post. Brands are starting to notice. People listen to me when I talk about anything, listen to us when Grant, Mirage, and Effie talk through me about what to wear, where to thrift, and how to cultivate a personal style without dropping bundles on overpriced designer clothes.

It's wild and surreal and so unlike the life I thought I'd have when my mom and I moved in with my grandmother a few years ago, dumping me into the rich soup that is Florence Hills. The kids on this side of town—they've got money for college, for European spring breaks, for ski trips in Cali. I don't have any of that, but I've got fashion sense, and confidence, and enough delusion to bet everything on the two combined. It's paid off.

Effie and I met on my first day at Florence Hills when she complimented my self-made jacket (recycled denim, acrylic paint stolen from my niece's art kit, and safety pins). Effie introduced me to Mirage. I poached Grant from the nerds. We quickly became our own little family. And then our found family founded my identity as SAVOY. The result: I love our scrappy fashion house. And I'm totally dedicated to the group project that is my life.

Except, not really.

Except, maybe not at all.

But I can't tell my friends that. They'll be crushed. There's no SAVOY without Savoy, after all.

"Initial stats are up," Grant says as we get to the primary bedroom. Mirage helps me into my next outfit while I blink away my momentary doubt. Time to be SAVOY, Savoy.

"Have you seen the app yet? Oscar did a great job," Effie says as she scrolls through both my phone and hers at once. She shows me a litany of messages and emojis pouring into the online hub. Oscar Graham—coding kid genius to the stars—set up the party app at my request, but Effie glows with pride like it's her own, which makes sense; setting up a self-destructing app for tonight's party was her idea, just like enabling anonymous posting. Like every SAVOY project, it has a few purposes: first, we need a place to collect votes for tonight's competition between me and Miranda in real time, and second, it's cool to have a secret message board just for one night, where gossip can be mined from one source. Like the party, the app is a temporary flex in the matrix, a place where anything that might happen must happen, because by sunrise, it won't even exist.

"Oscar gave us some admin privileges. Damn," Grant whistles, squinting into the glow of his phone. We're all logged in as me, on all my accounts, so we all benefit from this. Grant reads aloud the header: "'Two of Florence Hills's finest seniors, the fashionably industrious SAVOY and the diabolically regal Miranda, have announced competing photo shoots at DeAndre's End of the Year Bash. Vote below for your Fiercest Fashionista!'"

"Fierce." I spit the word out. "I hate that word. This is about so much more than just being fierce. And what's the gender-neutral version of 'fashionista'?"

"Attention whore?" Effie guesses.

"*Couture* whore," Mirage offers. "It rhymes."

"Semantics." Grant waves away our laughter. "Oscar gave us the ability to upload photos. Videos, too. We should cross-post whatever we're putting on social, and make sure to link out to our other accounts."

"I'm on it!" With a whoosh, Effie uploads the entrance-look photo, the one with the truck and the ghoulish paparazzi faces. It takes only seconds for the comments to start rolling in, way more than the attendees at the actual party. Looks like news about Oscar's app is already going wide.

"Great," Grant says, his eyes aflame with the growing metrics. "We can shunt this into a follow-spree on your socials, Savoy, just in time for Monday's merch drop. And then Tuesday, we'll post the monthly thrift haul vlog, and Wednesday we'll upload the video covering next season's trends—"

"Swamp-green velour," Mirage pipes up. "Children's art as graphic tees. Ironic argyle."

"Right, that one. Thank you, Mirage," Grant barrels on. "Oh, that reminds me . . . Savoy needs to do a few partygoer spotlight interviews. Does anyone know what Penny's wearing? And what about that guy dressed as a cowboy? Also, unrelated but related, we need to track down Jade. She's DJ'ing and she said she'd put together a runway mix so we could tag her. I checked and industry standard for runway music is about a hundred and twenty-five to a hundred and twenty-eight BPMs, so up-tempo but not too quick, allowing—"

"Okay, okay." I cut Grant off. "I get it, you've got a list, Grant. I trust you. But don't you think we're getting a little lost in the details? We want to capture the vibe of the party, and parties are about fun. And chaos. Not . . . beeping M&M's? Beepy-ems?"

Grant frowns. "BPMs. Beats per minute. And any DJ would disagree."

"Whatever." I press on. "My point is, our content is gonna be better if it feels authentic and not so controlled, right? Can't we allow ourselves to have, like, one night of actual fun? Even for the sake of good content? Have any of you taken a sip of beer tonight?"

The three blink at me, the glow of their phones lighting up the undersides of their faces, making their wide-eyed stares look alien and uncomprehending. As if to say: *Fun? Us? Never.*

"I can't," I laugh. "I simply cannot. But I will, on the condition that you guys actually try to have fun. This is a party, remember?" I dig into my bag and out comes my handy-dandy bottle of Grey Goose (thank you, Grandma). There's a lot of eye-rolling from the group, but everyone swigs some. Then again, for good luck. Eye-rolling turns to grins, and we shift into go mode once again.

"You've got this, Savoy," Grant says, grabbing me by the shoulders and marching me out of the bedroom. Mirage trails after, still working on some pins in my collar. "Tonight's big for us. The perfect launch for our summer season of content and our transition into the big leagues. We're all counting on you. It's our last chance to best Miranda, once and for all."

"I knoooow," I grumble.

Effie pipes up. "She already styled the cast members for *Romeo and Juliet*. Now she's creating a whole series on Tik-Tok about those costumes for *Playbill*. If she wins tonight, it's over."

"I gueeeeeess," I huff.

"But if we win," Grant says, "we win for *good*. Who cares about a stupid school play? Tonight is the real show, and it's about time someone upstaged Miranda in the theater of public opinion."

"Jesus, Grant, what is this? AP Bad-Mouthing?" I slur a little. The vodka's got me a little flustered, and this pep talk is remarkably unpeppy. "I'm gonna nail it. I always do, don't I? But can we please stop talking about her? I'm afraid she's gonna manifest or something."

"She would manifest. She is one spooky bitch," Mirage says. I agree.

The chill stays with me as we bustle back down the stairs.

The house is filling quickly, with barely enough space on the stairs to place each footstep. In the family room, someone has distributed Jell-O shots, and there are fingerprints smeared into the wallpaper. The kitchen island is crowded with busted bags of chips, bulk orders of fries and dipping sauces, and stacks of red cups. I grab a fistful of chips and a few cups, as props. Someone, somewhere, is smoking something potent, and I swear the air is getting hazy.

The sun is barely down, and we're already rocketing toward debauchery, but it doesn't feel out of control yet. No, the energy is good. Electric. And loud. Jade's whipping the crowd into a frenzy with some synth-laced ABBA, and even the quiet corners of the living room and office are thick with laughter and shouting and so much life. Trying to capture all this chaos in a still photo feels futile, like . . . how can a single frame ever do an entire movie justice? But SAVOY can pull this off. I know we can. And I relax, thinking of the glorious final product.

We've got this.

Grant directs. Mirage artfully moves people—yes, literally people in the background—around for a better composition, then plucks at my outfit until it's just right. I take my position based on their direction, and Effie lifts her dad's huge, ancient camera. It's so big, I can only see the sly smile on her lips as she depresses the shutter, and then Pop! Pop! Pop! The lights flash!

Picture this: Me, Savoy, leaning so far backward I'm nearly falling, my body a frozen slash of white against Technicolor pandemonium behind me. The look: bleached denim tailored into a full-body, bone-white catsuit, racing stripe of reflective tape swerving down my legs, my arms. The effect: The camera flashes and I flash back, a neon filament against the static storm of people jumping, cheering, laughing, screaming, taunting, flirting. The party. Electric life, arrested in a blur that will never clarify, never sober, never end.

And we snap pictures again, and again, and again, all over the house. We get shot after killer shot out by the pool, and I consider it a major success I don't let the crowd push me into the open water, especially when something—probably a couple already getting handsy—crashes into the nearby hydrangeas. We get sweeping videos, too, roping nearby guests into our shenanigans. Jade comes through with the runway remix, and some button on Grant's phone irradiates the ceiling of the living room with laser lights as we coax guests into stomping it out, one by one, down a makeshift runway that ends with Effie's cameras. Other people are recording, too. Grant spots each lifted camera and makes sure to give them my username to tag me. He even hands out little business cards.

Mirage helps me shrug on a long jean duster barnacled in beaded appliqués, all of them white, making me look like a frosted alien amid the riot of color around me. We take a few more shots, these ones full of harsh, boxy poses. Inaccessible fashion shit. You get it? No? Good, that's the point. I glance at a few raw images on Effie's camera, and it's just as I pictured. Contrast, turned all the way up. The unfiltered life of the party is the perfect backdrop to the highly manufactured model.

But.

Oh god, there she is. In the last shot. Just behind me, a face floats in the blur of motion, a vampiric smile lilting her lips.

I recoil from the camera, but it's too late. She's already cut through the crowd, her friends flanking her shoulders like unfolding demonic wings.

Miranda. She's swathed in a clingy black dress, studded choker, and long patent leather gloves that flow like oil from her elbows almost to her fingertips, where they cut off so her coffin-shaped nails can shine malevolently. Florence Hills's very own Black trans goth Barbie has come to suck my blood.

"Savoy," she says, scanning me from my eyes down to my outfit, her face showing how unimpressed she is with the avant-garde look. Her eyes never rise back up, never meet the cool fury I keep in my stare, just for her. Instead, she surveys our setup and gives her posse an embarrassed smile, like she can't believe she used to be friends with me back in middle school.

"This is cute," Miranda says. Her shoulders are exposed, the brown skin glistening with the oil I know she applies for a shimmery, supernatural effect. "Must have taken you all evening to put up, let me see, three? Yes, three flashbulbs. The devil works hard, but the SAVOY circus works even harder."

"We're not a circus, we're a fledgling fashion house. We just did all this in a few minutes," Grant fires back.

"That's the joke, nerd." Miranda and her friends cackle. Demons, all of them.

"And this," she says, turning back to me. "So . . . brave of you, showing up in something so . . ." She draws it out. "Well, 'brave' really is the word for it, I guess?"

"Oh, sweetie, that was a really, really admirable effort at sass, but unfortunately the adjective you're looking for is *fucking iconic*," I correct, pitying, like I'm letting her down as easy as I can. "I thought you would appreciate this, Miranda. I know it's not a designer Spirit of Halloween–esque knockoff, but it's got your sense of . . . romanticized confusion. Except, you know, done well. You don't approve?"

Miranda's eyes narrow. "Oh no, Mirage's beading is lovely, absolutely praiseworthy. But Savoy . . ."

A pause as she readies the punch.

"You must be exhausted. It takes such a strong back to wear someone else's work with so much pride."

Ah, that one stung. I lift my chin. "Mirage did the beading, but I designed it. And styled it."

"If by 'styled,' you mean you took something nice and, per usual, trashed it up with an assortment of ironically ugly accessories and digital filters so saturated that the FDA won't approve them, then, yeah, you certainly did that, Savoy."

I stand taller, thankful for the extra inches in my boot heels. "Would it be better if I just wore the same crusty fishnets and black lipstick for the hundredth time, like you, Miranda? You must be running low, and I hear it's been hard to get your hands on that much tar since the US re-signed the Paris Climate Accords."

"Fuck you," she says. "You couldn't afford even a sample of this lipstick, not with your willfully tragic thrift store penny-pinching. Yet the brand sent me a PR kit with a tube in every color."

"How many shades of black can you pretend to see, Miranda? And how embarrassing that you only seem to look good in half of them."

Miranda laughs, but it rings false. She's pissed.

"Like I'd take notes from the Tom Daley of dumpster diving," she hisses.

"Mall goths should take whatever they can get," I fire back.

"That's rich," she says, "coming from someone with platinum status at Florence Hills Galleria Auntie Anne's pretzel shop."

I gasp.

"Well, you're just . . ."

I've got nothing. I'm choking. She grins.

"You're just a rich . . . bitch" is all I can come up with.

"Actually . . ." Miranda savors whatever wicked retort she's got brewing. "I'm *that* bitch. See?" She hooks a manicured nail beneath the dog collar she's wearing as a choker and jangles the little metal heart charm at me. Sure enough, where a dog's name should be engraved are the words THAT BITCH.

*Damn*, I think. *She's good.*

I just now register Miranda's friends filming our little fight. People are watching. What started as an attempt to create a cool photo shoot has evolved into petty name-calling, which is my cue to leave. I'm about to back out of this when she catches my shoulder.

"Savoy, Savoy, Savoy," she whispers. "It was a risk to wear white. I thought you'd know better."

"I look great," I spit back.

*"Looked,"* she corrects, and with that, she dashes her drink across my chest. I see red. Literally, red. All down my jacket drips a slick ruby stain.

I scream, pushing her away. She shoves me back, and suddenly, we're tangled in a fight. Red is everywhere, smeared across the clean white of my outfit, the fine beading ruined. Miranda laughs and her teeth are stained red, too, and for a second, I'm afraid I actually hit her.

"Fake blood capsules," she says, thumbing a drop from her lip and wiping it on my shoulder. "Even the stains look real, I hear."

Cameras are lighting up around us. Not just ours, but everyone's.

Imagine this: Savoy in ruined white. Red stains, rosy cheeks. Fury in the face, the eyes, the body as they stand, frantically twirl, and carve a way out of the crowd of gawking partygoers. Miranda, covered in (fake) blood from the busted capsule in her mouth, the party backing away from her as she laughs, and laughs, and laughs.

I run upstairs to the bathroom, the one off the primary bedroom. I push inside and strip. I'm rushing, breathing hard. There's a knock and Grant tries to enter, but I tell him I need a minute. He leaves, and for the next six minutes, I'm completely focused on shoving my entire bulky jacket into the steaming sink. DeAndre's parents have all sorts of fancy soaps and I try every single one, but I know it's pointless; these stains are forever. And then . . .

The door opens, but it's not Grant. Or Effie or even Mirage.

In slips Miranda, smile still glossy with fake blood.

She closes the door and locks it, trapping us in a cell of silence.

I'm frozen. She joins me at the mirror, using a sopping sleeve of my jacket to clean her lips and chin. Then she spiders her long fingers over Mrs. Dixon's serums and makeup, like she's a witch selecting the next ingredient for her potion.

"Hi, Savoy," she says, all casual.

"Hi, Miranda."

"That was some show," she says.

"Are you pleased?" I ask.

"I'm about to be," she says, her eyes finally meeting mine in the mirror.

We break character at the same time, both of us smiling. The next moment, we're kissing. My hands dash backward over the sink, toppling faceted bottles of perfume, twin electric toothbrushes, things so expensive I'm not sure if they're ointments or heirlooms. I'm arching my back against the mirror, anything to push myself against Miranda, not because I want to get away but because I want to be closer, as close as possible. Finally, after all this waiting and acting, we're alone. We're together.

I break the kiss and Miranda's lips are marching down my throat, leaving little drifts of syrupy red in their wake. She's already got my bodysuit halfway off. If I don't stop now, I won't stop at all.

"That was good," I say, referring to the fight.

"I know," she murmurs.

"Just as you planned. I bet the red on white looks amazing."

"And," she says, dragging herself upward to look me in the eye, "they don't suspect a thing. Our biggest and best charade yet."

We never kiss for long, Miranda and me. We're together so infrequently that we always get down to business right away. As Miranda takes out her phone, I feel the new rawness of my lips, my throat. I want her back—I want her attention on me again. But she's already scrolling.

"See. Perfect," she says, showing me snaps of our altercation. The red is bright. The anger looks real. We nailed this fight. It'll be all over our little fashion corner of the internet in mere seconds. Maybe this one will go viral, too, like the time we wrestled at the roller rink dressed in competing fake mink. Or the time I tipped a tray of chili dogs down her back as she posed on the high school's bleachers at homecoming after she was crowned queen and used her speech to exile me. From our public high school.

I glance at the comments.

> Savoy should have kicked her ass.

> Miranda is a psycho, but damn does she look good terrorizing us unfashionable peasants.

> Wait but like, these candids are actually so cool??? Way better than the posed pics Savoy posted earlier imho.

> You guys think this is real? Please. These aren't enemies. These are lovers. Oldest trope in the book.

We pause, both of us focusing on that last one.

"Someone knows," I whisper.

"It's just a guess," Miranda says, too quickly, though.

I scramble to think of who could know that, beneath the bluster and rivalry, Miranda and I are secretly together. Sadie Bernbaum comes to mind as a possible suspect—she'll make a great journalist one day, but right now she's simply a great pain in my ass, writing all sorts of nonsense in that little school paper of hers. She even tried to review a series of self-portraits I did a while ago, as if she has the range!

Miranda puts her phone away, but we don't start kissing again. A new tension slips between us.

Because someone knows our secret.

And then, as if manifested by the thought, someone knocks on the door.

"One minute!" I shout. But Miranda shouts it, too. The knocking halts, like the person on the other side can't believe what they just heard.

Savoy and Miranda, hiding in a bathroom together.

The knock comes again.

Miranda drops her voice and in an unrecognizable baritone she groans, "Don't come in! I'm gonna need a minute. Or ten!"

We rush to the window. Thank god it faces the next house over, not the front or back lawns. And thank god the primary bedroom's balcony wraps the corner of the house and is only a foot from the bathroom window's ledge, because otherwise Miranda and I would not only have plummeted to our deaths, but we would have been exposed. This little charade of ours would have ended, and all of it—the crackling spicy rivalry, the drama, the content, the contempt, the hype—would have vanished. Poof. Crushed, like the azaleas we nearly fall into.

But we don't fall, because I manage to swing a leg over the balcony railing and pull us to momentary safety. I badly want to creep around to the bedroom's window and see who almost caught us, but Miranda holds me still. Kisses me again to shut me up, her laughter flowing into me. I can't help but kiss her back, feel the thrill of what we have. A secret, coiled and precious. Ours.

In the bedroom, a door slams shut. The spy, fleeing. Then there's relative silence until a few minutes later the door opens again, a whole parade of people flowing in. It's my friends, calling my name and cursing Miranda's.

We're trapped.

I peek around the corner. A duo of stoners sits on the far side of the balcony, smoking, blearily staring through a cloud of vapor at the pool below.

I back up, pushing Miranda behind me. We can't go back into the bathroom, and we can't stay here. So where do we go next?

"Up," I whisper.

"Savoy, I'm in heels."

"And I'm half naked," I fire back. I am. My jacket is still in the sink, which is probably overflowing by now since we might have accidentally left the faucet running. And my bodysuit is around my waist.

"Up," I repeat. Using the railing, I manage to get my hands into the eaves of the slanting roof. If not for a strange corner caused by the bathroom, we'd have nowhere to go, but with some silent grunting and a few heart-pounding seconds where I literally have to hoist Miranda straight into the sky, we make it up. Just in time, too. The stoners are on the move, but they don't see us because we're already crawling over the shingles like two very clumsy, very fashionable arachnids.

We end up on the highest edge of the roof, facing the cul-de-sac, shielded by treetops from any would-be stargazers below. The entire party vibrates under our asses, rhythmic and urgent and accelerating, like the house itself is about to have a heart attack. But it's peaceful up here. Private. The night is clear and fresh on my sweating skin, and we can see all the way to the HILL-IONS Amusement Park. The Ferris wheel stares us down, our only witness for the time being.

"What now, mastermind?" Miranda asks me, but the sarcasm in her words is playful. She slips her hand over mine where I clutch the roof.

"I'll text my friends and tell them I need a bit. You do the same."

"And then?"

I give an innocent shrug. "We make out as much as possible before you reapply your lipstick."

She smiles, and in the night she glows with an inner warmth.

She leans in, sharing her warmth with me, and at her touch I light up, too.

But I can't help thinking: *Someone knows.* Our little fantasy is unraveling. If I want to secure our secrecy, now's the time to stitch it back up.

But what if I don't?

What if I want it all to come undone, so we can finally just be real?

# FERNANDA MANNING

## THE JOCK

## PART I

"THIS CAN'T BE REAL!" I MUTTER, MY PATIENCE undone like my outfit. This is the third one I've changed into tonight. My favorite yet.

Problem is, I can't zip up my cream-colored dress with the nail tips I got this afternoon. The turquoise polish and the glued crystals look like a dream against my medium-brown skin, but beauty has a steep price. I'm not used to long nails, not because I don't want to wear them, but because in sports they're a nuisance, bordering on a distraction.

But in my years as an athlete, I have learned that you dress with the proper attire to win, and tonight? Tonight, I'm going to win. Or at least, I'm going to score.

Not being an expert in fashion, I took some inspiration from the ultimate influencer, Savoy, whose photos and stories on Trendsettr I'm obsessively following. Hence the nails, and the outfit changes.

My crystal high heels sink into the shaggy carpet of the hallway as I shuffle to my mom's room to ask for help.

"Mami!" I call out. But she's not in her room. Weird. My parents should be back with my car by now. Maybe they're downstairs.

The FOMO (or more accurately, the certainty that I'm missing out) after seeing Savoy's posts is killing me, even though the party's barely started.

"This is what you get for offering to drive, Manning!" I say to myself as I carefully walk downstairs without falling. I'm not *that* used to four-inch heels, either, but my poor feet have been through worse torture on the field. I don't want to take them off in case I can't get them on again the minute my dad arrives with my car. Once he's back, I'm out. Well, after zipping up the dress, of course.

The sky outside the living room window is completely dark. How did it get so late? How did I lose track of time? I should've been at the party ages ago.

The words of Travis from *Clueless* echo in my soul: "Tardiness isn't something you can do on your own. Many, many people had to contribute, and I'd like to thank my parents . . ."

Or something like that.

I usually don't mind being "fashionably late" to a party, but this one? This one's special, and my time in high school is already running out. I feel it slipping through my fingers, like the final seconds before the buzzer goes off.

People measure time in different ways, especially athletes—and people with a crush. Like me. I am people.

For soccer players, a game is two halves of forty-five minutes each, plus stoppage. Runners count in seconds or kilometers. Basketball players must keep track of multiple clocks, but they have the luxury of time-outs to reassess their game plan. In softball, there are runs and strikes.

Throughout my life, I've counted my progress in all of the above. Now the timeline of my high school years is winding down, no matter how I measure it, and I can't even call for a time-out.

As I step into the kitchen, I remember the night before soccer tryouts (a month before eighth grade officially started). I was so nervous and excited that I couldn't sleep. When my dad found me in the kitchen surrounded by the peels of the three bananas I'd eaten to calm my nerves, he suggested I write down some of my goals and expectations for the future. He'd been my soccer coach when I played in the rec league, and I recognized the switch in the tone of his voice from Papi to Coach.

"Think of each year as fourths in a game. The game of high school," he said, and winked.

I rolled my eyes as he went on to explain, "No, really. Think of what you want to accomplish. What things will make the coming years unforgettable. Like a map, you see? That way you'll know where you're going. You'll have goals to shoot for."

He ruffled my already messy brown hair and sent me back to bed.

His words made sense. He and my mom always said high school for them had been "a blast." If I followed his advice, what could I lose?

In my mind, I went over the stories my parents told me about meeting in high school, shortly after immigrating from Argentina with their families. I thought about my favorite movies and books, and combining everything, I came up with my bucket list for a memorable high school experience.

The babyish pink ruled paper I ripped off my diary that

night is practically disintegrating, but I know the whole thing by heart anyway. I have no time to waste sitting around, not checking a big thing off my list, but I don't have my car yet, either. So I go back to the empty living room and plop down on the armrest of the white leather sofa. As my heart rate returns to normal, I pull the list out of my bra to read with a mix of nostalgia for the little girl I was and awe for the things I've accomplished. To kill time, why not stroll down memory lane?

After freshman year, when I figured out what high school was really about, I added a few items.

To my credit, I've checked almost every one of the entries, which, by the way, are mostly sports-related. Don't judge.

> Maintain a good GPA (just so I can qualify for teams, mind you). ✓
> Make the soccer team as a freshman. ✓
> Run with the track team as a sophomore. ✓
> Make the boys' JV football team. ✓
> Break the scoring and assisting records on the basketball team. ✓
> Take the softball team to state. ✓
> Make lifelong friends. ✓
> Attend all the official school parties and the unofficial ones, too! ✓
> Date cute boys. ✓

Having goals worked. My dad jokes that I turned into a goal-crushing machine. But the truth is, having those plans and achieving them showed me I could really do anything I set my mind to, even if the odds were stacked against me. Because being a girl, and the daughter of immigrants at that, the odds have been against me.

In the cold, in the heat, suffering period cramps, calf cramps, or parents' lousy looks for taking their son's spot on the team, I trained my ass off and earned my place on nearly every roster to show the world (or at least, all of Chicago) what I can do.

But there's one last thing on my list that's still uncompleted. Like a splinter in the tip of my thumb, I can't seem to get to it.

Tell Kai Hassel that I like him. ?

Turns out, getting someone to like you isn't simple like in the movies. Besides, I never had to *get* anyone to like me before. It just happened.

With Kai, senior cheer team captain, things are different. The odds are *definitely* stacked against me. Last year, I made the stupid mistake of dating his archnemesis, Spencer, a half-back on the football team. In my defense, that fling lasted a couple of months, but I didn't know there was such bad blood between them. That excuse isn't gonna help my case, though.

Kai is either clueless that I caught feelings for him, or, heaven forbid, not interested in me because of my previous romantic choices (aka Spencer. Ugh!).

No one knows I've been obsessed with him since forever. Well, someone knows. As an act of desperation, I wrote to Miss Abby, an unidentified teen love expert for a popular advice column in the school paper. Anonymously, of course. I just asked her what to do when you're afraid to admit your feelings to a guy. She finally replied a couple of weeks ago, all snark, as usual, but her words were the kick in the butt I needed.

*Just tell him to his face. If you are who I think you are, you better explain why you dated his enemy.*

My cheeks still burn in embarrassment every time I think about it. Why would I need to explain anything? It's not like I cheated on either of them. How was I supposed to know any association with Spencer would blacklist me for life with the boy who's consumed my thoughts for months?

High school sports are over. We just have award galas coming up. I didn't want any drama during the football season, and then my softball schedule was so intense. That's why I waited until tonight to go for Kai.

Now it's time for action—no more plans or pep talks.

I'm going to make a move.

The alarm on my watch blares, and I tuck the list back in my bra. At this point, more than a road map, this piece of paper has been a lucky charm. I guess (at least in my case) there's truth to the notion that when you write something down, you manifest it.

When I turn off the alarm on my watch and see the time, I jump from my perch on the sofa to grab my phone, which I left charging by the front door. A tug from my glutes stops me in my tracks. But then I breathe, relieved. Not a cramp this time. Just the fabric of my dress trying to stretch beyond its intended capabilities to fit the extra leg muscles I put on these last few months of conditioning.

I hobble like a penguin, missing the freedom of movement short shorts or sweats allow. Maybe I should just ditch the dress and change into something more casual. But my neighbor and classmate Fantasia left her house in a red sequined miniskirt that will be seen from the space station. She's on the cheer team with Kai and is one of his closest friends. The rest of their squad will dress just like her. Not that I want to call attention to my-self like Savoy in ruined white or Miranda in her *Interview with the Vampire*–inspired outfit. I still can't wrap my mind around their epic fashion showdown, which I've already partly missed because my dad is late. I love a good competition!

My phone buzzes with a new message from DeAndre. There's a bunch of other unread texts.

**DEANDRE:**
Yo, party's going down, where you at fer?

I quickly reply.

**FERNANDA:**
OMW.

I can't help laughing as I scrawl through the missed mes-sages. Surprise and excitement drip from everyone's replies. This is like the third time DeAndre's posted on Trendsettr and judging by all the stories and snaps, his house is beginning to burst at the seams.

At least a hundred people's avatars flash on the screen. When I check Savoy's video, I catch a glimpse of Kai dancing with a girl, not Fantasia or any of the other cheerleaders. Who is she? I don't recognize her from behind. My skin prickles, competi-tiveness bubbling up. Out of habit, I click on his avatar and go to his stories, which follow him from his house to DeAndre's.

He's the most luminous person I know, and it's not only be-cause of his glowing skin. He has this light inside him, and he's kind and sensitive. Tonight he looks better than ever. He got a fresh fade and is wearing a black T-shirt with the collar ripped, showing off his collarbones. The angles of his jawline could cut through ice, but his skin looks so soft my fingers itch to touch his face. Maybe the app's filter is just crazy flattering, but his lips look perfectly moisturized. He glances straight at the camera, his dark eyes daring me to make a move and come see them up close for myself. I press the heart icon on the corner of the screen, and a second too late, I realize I just broke one of my personal rules.

I observe.

I don't engage.

Now I can't take the heart back because his notifications are probably turned on, and it's weirder to unlike something. I'll look indecisive. Like I'm playing games.

Sweat prickles in my armpits. Suddenly I feel parched.

I should've asked Fantasia if I could ride with her. Why didn't I think about that earlier? But I couldn't leave my friend Penny hanging. Not when she's so torn up over her breakup with Jenny and worried about her mom.

I've known Penny since third grade, and a party has never failed to cheer her up.

Maybe this party could do the same for me? This chance with Kai tonight . . . could it be my last one before we graduate?

Unlike in games, where I can strategize ahead of time, with him, I don't have a plan.

Perhaps we can just connect about our culture like we did last fall? That one time on the team bus when we were heading to a football game, back when I was a kicker, we had a *moment*. His mom's from Brazil, and his dad from Argentina, like my parents. That day, he was drinking *mate*—an herbal drink from South America. We started talking, and before we knew it, he was sharing one with me.

I don't know what was in that *mate* that day, but by the time the ride was over, I was completely obsessed with the dimple on his left cheek, and the way he brushed his dark curly hair away from his eyes, and how his dark eyes sparkled with interest when I told him how the soccer season had just ended in time for football. He'd seen my picture in the paper and said I looked cute. I laughed, but secretly, I felt like my heart had exploded inside me. He's always complimenting his friends, but when he said that about me, I felt special.

And when the tops of my used shoes cracked right before I had to go in for a field goal, he produced some duct tape from his backpack and fixed it before any of the coaches knew what was going on. He'd seen my distress and come to help without hesitation.

After that, every time I was around Kai, I felt like he was the sun and I was a sunflower, blooming when he smiled upon me. I know. I know. Cringe.

The night I finally broke up with my then-boyfriend, Spencer, he was giving me a ride home in his Beemer right after a home game loss. The anger he felt must have been unbearable because he asked, "Why do you keep looking at him? Do you like Bi Hassel or what?" A protectiveness came out of me.

"What did you call him?" I shot back. He was too shocked by my tone to say anything, so I continued. "Besides the fact that he's gorgeous, have you seen him on the field? How he lifts the fliers all on his own? He's the strongest person I know, *and* he's a good human. No one cares that he's bi, for your information." Spencer turned green. "Besides, it's not like you don't gawk at the cheerleaders."

"That's different," he said, offended. "I warn you, though,

Kai's not into chicks like you. And Coach doesn't let anyone on the team date cheerleaders. Too much drama."

"How is Coach ever going to enforce that?" I said, hating how he said "chicks." Especially "chicks like you." Was it possible I didn't have a chance with Kai? Or was I letting Spencer psych me out? "And what about you and me? Surely there are rules about members of the same team?"

"This is a . . . unique situation. You're the first girl—"

"You mean to tell me there have never been two or more guys from the same team who got together? Remember Louis Cannon and—what was his name?—oh, Charly Hernandez?"

"Whatever! He's never going to date you. Not with your temper!"

I snort. "The irony is not lost that you're the only one screaming like a baby." Although I'd never admit it, his words dented my armor.

My brain couldn't waste another second on Spencer after that. Instead, because I always have to shoot for impossible things, Kai started starring in my not-so-PG-rated dreams.

He never goes out with anyone, like officially, but he dates a lot. Guys and girls. I've thought about what those people have in common more than once, to determine if I actually have a shot here, but I can't pinpoint what that shared trait is.

A CAR'S ENGINE rumbles in the distance. I glance up from my phone, but I see it's just an old-fashioned camper. It reminds me of the Mystery Machine, sort of. The green and blue on the sides are dull and chipped, and the flower painted in the front looks like it melted a long time ago, like, decades ago. Who would voluntarily drive a clunker like that? Slowly, like every move hurts, it turns into our cul-de-sac and parks in our driveway.

Oh. The person getting out of the camper is my dad.

*What the hell?* I gasp.

My heart pumps fast like I'm trying to catch up with Allyson Felix on the track at the Olympics, but I'm just standing at the open door, staring at the white monstrosity instead of my refurbished Tiffany Blue Fiat 600.

"You gotta be effing kidding me!"

"Fer," my mom warns as she gets out of the van, too. "Watch your mouth."

"Ma! I didn't even swear!"

She walks in and places a cool hand on my overheated skin. "You look lovely." Her words and her touch calm me.

I turn for her to see my undone dress and say, "Can you help me? I'm late! I still need to pick Penny up."

I sigh, relieved by the sound of the zipper going up, but then I realize I can hardly breathe. The dress is so much tighter now that I'm locked inside. At least it fits. Barely.

"Papi, where's my car?" I ask, trying to ration my oxygen supply. Blacking out is something I can't afford to do right now. "It was supposed to be a quick oil change! Do you know what time it is?"

My dad, dressed in running gear, glances at my mom.

"I don't have a watch on, and my phone's dead. Sorry," he finally says.

"It's almost nine," I reply. A voice in the back of my head reminds me the party started an hour ago.

Out of nervousness, I scratch my head but then remember it took hours to get my hair done, so I take my hand down. I bring it to my mouth out of habit, but when I poke my lip with the long acrylic claws, I ball my hand into fists. The nails press against my palms, and the pain brings me back to the moment.

"It's more than an oil change after all. Timing belts, brakes, the whole shebang." My dad shrugs. "They couldn't get the parts on time. At least they gave us a loaner."

"A fun one," Mom chimes.

I must make a face because my dad puts a hand up and says, "In that case, I'll drive you!"

"I'll come along," Mom says cheerfully. She always jumps at the chance of cruising in his new Porsche Panamera.

"Or you can just take the camper," my dad says.

This is a tough choice. Getting a ride as if I was a freshman, but in the coolest car ever, or showing up in a ridiculous van.

The thing is, judging by what I've seen on social media so far, my parents will freak if they behold the chaos of DeAndre's party. If the camper is the only way to get there and stay, then so be it.

As I clench my teeth and swallow the string of swear words crowding in my mouth, my dad shrugs again and says, "Sorry, mi amor. I tried. Here you go!" He tosses me the keys. I catch them in a reflex move. My dad then heads upstairs. I imagine rolling up to the party of the year in a circus camper and decide . . . I'd rather die.

I pull out my phone and try to get an Uber or a Lyft. But our neighborhood is like a dead zone for rideshare service. There's nothing available closer than a five-mile radius. I want to cry. But I never cry. Not even when we lost the state cup semifinal in penalty shots in club soccer last year.

When I go back to my missed messages, I choke on my own spit.

There's one from Kai.

**KAI:**
Are you coming? 😊

My thumb acts before my brain and I heart his message. "Oh no."

"You're going to be okay. I'm sure you won't be the last one to show up," my mom says, totally misinterpreting my reaction. "Let me fix your makeup a little. Your mascara is smearing."

"Perfect. Now I have raccoon eyes, too?"

I let her dab at my eye with the tip of her finger and a tissue she grabs from the little table at the entrance.

"Are you nervous about something?" she asks, sounding so suspicious my whole face warms. She knows me too well.

I've never done this! Tell a boy I like him. Especially when I'm unsure if he's even into me. Kai's too unpredictable to make a game plan, but I'm not completely flying in the dark tonight, either.

"Me? I'm golden!" I say, smiling hard.

I grab the backpack I left beside the door to change later, kiss my mom goodbye, and finally head out.

"HOLY SHIT!" I say at the sight of the cars parked all over the place in DeAndre's cul-de-sac. The music blares all the way to the street, making the windows of the van vibrate.

I bite my lip as I maneuver through the obstacle course in

front of us. If only I could ditch this monster in the middle of the street! Or there was valet parking somewhere.

Penny lowers the music in the car as if silence will help me find a parking spot sooner.

"Thank you," I say, and squeeze her hand, but then I quickly snatch mine back to grab the steering wheel. A car is heading in our direction, and there's not enough room for both of us.

"Hey, James Bond," the guy yells after honking his horn three more times than necessary. "In America, we drive on the right side of the road! Especially in a soccer mom's car!"

I flip him off and Penny says, "Jerk," but she goes back to texting as if someone's life depends on it.

My heart clenches for her and what she's going through with her mom. Penny didn't offer any details when I asked, but it's obvious things aren't good.

"There!" I exclaim, seeing a small gap between a fire hydrant and a motorcycle where this van can fit. I think. There's another car ahead of us, likely ready to back in, but my reflexes are sharp and my need to be kissed is strong. I take the spot before the other driver can react.

"Yay!" Penny and I cheer and high-five each other when the other car keeps driving without a fight.

"It's a miracle," I say.

"What is?"

"Getting parking in this mess!"

She shrugs. "DeAndre wouldn't have minded if you parked in the driveway, but I guess this space is better. We won't be trapped."

I reach for my backpack in the backseat, but Penny stops me and shakes her head.

"You don't want to be carrying that around in this circus,

and besides, if you need to make a quick exit, the backpack will only slow you down."

Something in her voice sets the alarms on fire in my mind.

"Wait, you're not thinking of leaving early, are you?" I ask.

She gives me a knowing smile. I never told her in detail my plan for tonight, but she must have guessed based on my outfit and my nerves. "Don't worry, Fer. Once Kai sees you like this, he won't be able to resist, and you won't need me around. You got this. Let's go."

Penny has more practice than I do walking in high heels. And even though it's dark, I do my best to keep up with her.

That is, until a brown streak runs in front of me.

I yelp. The streak, which is a dog, whacks her tail against my leg, and I lose my balance. I swing my arms around to catch myself, but there's only air.

Penny doesn't seem to hear me. She's still walking, her head down, looking at her phone.

"Careful," a guy in a cowboy getup says as he holds my arm with one hand and a blue leash attached to the dog with the other. "Are you okay?"

For a second, my heart flip-flops because he looks a lot like Kai, but it's not him.

And now that I can take a good look at the dog, I recognize her, too. She belongs to a neighbor. She's grown a lot since the last time I saw her. But then, I've been so busy, I haven't been at DeAndre's in forever.

"Hey, Daisy," I say breathlessly, and the dog flops on her back for me to rub her tummy. But honestly, it's not like I'm going to squat to pet her with this short dress on. A couple of girls who apparently are with the cowboy start petting Daisy, but it's too much noise and excitement for her. The dog jumps back up so fast that her leash slips out of the cowboy's hand, and she gets lost in some shrubs. By the shrieks I hear, she's making more friends.

I'm about to ask the cowboy what his name is when a voice freezes me on the spot.

"Oh, hey, Fer. I wasn't totally sure if you were coming."

I whip around and find myself face to face with Kai.

Kai and that Superman curl on his forehead. Kai and that smile that obliterates the sun. Kai and his strong arms that can catch a flier in midair like she's a feather.

Kai and a girl holding on to him. The girl from Savoy's story.

Her index finger is hooked onto the belt loop of his distressed gray jeans. I don't know her name, but she has that Barbie-doll look of most of the cheerleaders in our school.

Toned, tanned, tiny.

Her flawless brown hair cascades down her back like a waterfall.

"Hey!" Her smile belongs to a toothpaste commercial as she princess-waves at me.

Now, don't get me wrong. I love my body. I never compare myself to other people. Well, hardly ever. But next to him, I'm like a giant. I didn't calculate that with these heels I'd tower over his five-foot-eight frame.

"Yeah, sorry I never texted you back. I'm here," I tell him, smiling.

The corner of his mouth lifts in a tentative smile, and that dimple peeks in his cheek for the flash of a second. "You look . . ." His gaze sweeps over me, and he scratches his hair as if he's trying to pluck the right word out of his brain.

At that moment, a group of girls from the basketball team surrounds me, shrieking.

"Fer! Finally!"

"Where have you been?"

"You look so pretty!"

When my eyes adjust to the dim light, I see my basketball teammates Cynthia, Lucy, Emma, and Trish. More people keep arriving, and I have to either go with the flow or be trampled. The human tide pushes me inside the house, past the foyer, and into the family room, where a DJ has been playing a mix of my favorite songs since I walked up the driveway.

By the time I glance over my shoulder, Kai and the girl are far away from me, still outside, talking intimately. They're looking at a phone, and I realize that I left mine inside my backpack in the car. Maybe because he felt me eyeing him, Kai glances in my direction. He stares at me for a second too long for it to be just a coincidence. But before I can break away from the girls to go back to Kai, the junior cheer squad surrounds him and whisks him away, squeeing about winning at Summit, the ultimate cheerleading competition.

"Here. I saved this for you, Fer," Trish says, handing me a red cup.

Without thinking, I take a sip even though everything might and will be laced with a forbidden substance. I want to be clearheaded, and tomorrow morning, I want to remember every detail, but I could use some liquid courage.

I swallow the alcohol mixed in with the soda, but it almost comes back up when I walk inside the house and see Spencer sitting on a leather couch making out with one of the cheerleaders, Kennedy. She's a senior, too. He opens his eyes midkiss and notices me noticing him. Flustered, he breaks the kiss and whispers something in the girl's ear before they leave the sofa and float away from me and my group.

"You good?" Lucy asks. She must think I'm jealous. If anything, I'm relieved Spencer moved on. It's time I do, too, which is why I'd rather people stopped asking me if I'm okay.

"I'm fine," I say, stretching the word and placing a hand on my heart for emphasis.

Lucy purses her lips. "It looks like you have things to spill."

The sudden scent of pizza makes my stomach growl. I'm not the only one who's caught the siren call of delicious food, judging by the way the head of everyone in the living room swivels toward the poor delivery guy balancing a tower of boxes on his hand and following behind a girl headed to the basement.

"Yes, spill!" Trish says.

Together the girls sweep me away, into the basement, toward the food, away from Kai, who right at that second is walking into the family room. Once again, his eyes lock with mine, and he smiles.

I owe all my wins to my teams. I'll have to enlist them to help me score tonight, too. First, I need fuel.

# PENNY WASHINGTON

## THE POPULAR GIRL

## PART I

THIS PARTY ALREADY SMELLS LIKE BAD DECISIONS.

"Heyyyy, Pennnnyyy!" I'm caught in a whirlwind of hugs and cheek kisses and people yelling my name like it's got a billion syllables. Somebody I swear I don't even know shouts, "Penny Motherfucking Washington!!!" above the cacophony of teenage revelry. And then there's that moment when you enter the party and all the attention shifts your way. There's a high in being looked at, wanted, envied, even if, at times, it makes me want to run and hide.

Let it be known that I have heard all the rumors about myself, and some of them are true. Except the one about a certain former boy band member. Seriously, he just hearted a political post of mine that went low-key viral, and everyone at school took that ball and ran with it. If you're the kind of person who cares about followers, I'm semifamous. About a year ago, I started posting makeup tutorials on TikTok and they took off. Some people think spending time doing your makeup is superficial, or like bowing to the patriarchy or whatever, but I love how you can use makeup to paint a mood, how the right highlight creates a feeling. I know it's not that serious, but maybe everything doesn't have to be. It's a perfect side hustle, and lord knows, my mother and I definitely need the extra income right now.

"You haven't been at one of these things in ages!" Will says. Will is taller than any other person our age. He would make a great baller except he's spectacularly clumsy and "more thespian than Jordan [Michael, duh], but just as bitchy!" His joke, not mine.

He and the rest of the theater kids are on a total high cause they just wrapped up *Romeo and Juliet* tonight, which thank god, because I'm so sick of them yelling *Do you bite your thumb, sir?* in the halls.

Will passes me his Solo cup benevolently. "Fruit punch for our Queen P!" he says.

"Is fruit the only thing in here?"

He shrugs and laughs. "Does it matter?"

Fair point. I chug until the cup's empty. It's the kinda drink that's deceptive, that tastes all sweet like a summer afternoon, and next thing you know you're laid out on somebody's bathroom floor feeling the room spin. Usually I try to avoid getting too sloppy, but tonight I just want to let go. Be normal.

My phone buzzes in my pocket, and I know it's Mama. Likely she has burned down our whole street. Or possibly gotten arrested for public indecency. Or perhaps she's throwing a tantrum because our neighbor Ms. Marta won't let her drive the car that Mama doesn't realize I sold months ago, after Mama started getting lost on her way to the grocery store we've been going to my entire life. These aren't normal things for a kid to have to worry about.

I pull out my phone, ready for whatever emergency has befallen her. Thank god it's just Trendsettr.

Already, new rumors are a-flowing, because no one at Florence Hills High knows how to mind their business. Miranda and Savoy are at each other's throats. Literally everyone seems to be here.

Since I've already got my phone out, I decide to film a little bit of the party, and my look, before I turn into a sweaty mess. My iridescent blue eyeshadow makes me feel like a particularly ethereal space creature, which I've counterbalanced with a pinky-brown nude lip that feels perfect and earthbound. I blow a kiss and kick up my leg in the direction of somebody filming from SAVOY's team, showcasing my brand-new minidress and heels. It's not high-fashion, but I know my legs look great. They're one of my favorite features, thanks to great genes, and further honed by running from my demons.

DeAndre stumbles toward me, arms outstretched. "Pennyyy!!!"

He envelops me in one of his big strong bear hugs. DeAndre gives you the kind of hugs that feel like he means it, that he wants to be close to you, to know you and be known.

"Let in the love! Let out the hate!" he says. Is he high?

"Um, sure . . . ," I say.

"Have my drink," he says, handing me his beer. "You deserve all the drinks and everything good in the whole beautiful world, Penny Washington."

Yup, DeAndre is higher than a motherfucker.

"What up, Florence Hills seniors!" he yells, and all of us in the house go apeshit for a few moments.

"Falcons! Falcons!" A group of jocks surrounding Fernanda start a chant.

"Wait. Where'd my beer go?" DeAndre says, and I burst out laughing. It feels good to be here. The world is losing its hard edges and I feel myself relax a little. Maybe everything will be okay. For tonight, anyway.

After DeAndre stumbles away, some boy approaches as I'm still filming. "Hey, Penny . . . how's it going?"

Everything he's wearing is either a size too big or too small and entirely too formal for this sort of party, like his mom dressed him for his senior photo. He's not exactly one of the nerds, more like one of those floaters, I think. Those kids who belong to everyone and nobody at once. He's got a smatter-ing of freckles across a strong nose, almond eyes, and beautiful dark long curls that hang down his back. It's the kind of ethni-cally ambiguous look that would make some people ask, *What are you?* But that shit's rude, and I have manners.

He lingers, and I just know he's going to ask me out or wants to hook up. Now that I'm newly single, it's like it is open season on yours truly, which honestly feels gross. I'm not some sort of rare Nike drop that has dudes waiting in line for hours.

"So sorry, I need to get another drink," I say, shaking my empty cup.

"Lemme get you one," the boy says.

"Nah, don't worry about it, bro!" Jrue is an absolute lifesaver and the most hilarious person I know.

"I got you!" he whispers into my ear.

We head toward the kitchen, where Dre's cousin, Liam, has made an absolute culinary masterpiece, like we're at a fancy adult dinner party in Lincoln Park, not one where teens are chugging from Solo cups and there's a stolen goat in the garage. I stuff a canapé into my mouth.

"You aight?" Jrue places one of those canned fruity drinks in my hand. Even after all this time, he's remembered that I like pineapple the best. Jrue's good people.

I nod before he leaves me, likely to chase after his ride-or-die Sadie.

"Oh shit, that's good!" I say, and grab another canapé before I've even finished chewing the one in my mouth.

"Slow your roll!" the rando still trying to hit on me says jokingly. "Get it . . . 'cause you're a Penny?"

I roll my eyes. Why is dude following me? He starts to say something else but pauses before he can spit it out. I follow his gaze over to the former love of my life, or at least of like three very important years of high school, Jenny S.

She's got her arm around some girl I don't know, who doesn't go to our school. The girl's got a totally shaved head and she's wearing a cropped tank and baggy jeans. She looks like the kind of girl who is effortlessly cool and confident, but also like she has opinions on what's going down in Afghanistan and the use of the word "Latinx." Smart ones. I bet she doesn't even need to use deodorant.

Jenny sees me staring at the two of them and waves sheepishly. A whole month hasn't even passed since she unceremoniously dumped me. Or has it?

I feel caught off guard. And so I panic. That is the only possible reason for what I do next, which is lean into Rando, laugh like he's said the funniest thing ever, and kiss him. On the mouth. His lips are ever so slightly chapped, and he tastes like beer, which, ugh, but his mouth is actually quite pillowy. He's a legitimately good kisser. He places his hand on the small of my back as we kiss, and somehow, in spite of myself, I audibly moan. Softly, though. I'm not a heathen.

"You high?" He stares at me like he's just woken up from a very good dream. "Just . . . 'cause you know . . . I'm not a creep and . . . consent?"

He's got really kind eyes. I didn't notice those before. And he smells really good. Not in that "I've drenched myself in cologne" sorta way. Just boy good. Like shampoo and nice body wash that his mom probably buys from Lush or something.

"Penny!" The cute girl who was all up on Jenny is somehow right next to me. Did she sprint across the room? Float? Teleport?

"I've heard so much about you! All good things, I promise. I'm Violet. Most people call me V."

Now that I think about it, I do remember Jenny mentioning a V when she was playing in the summer league. I didn't pay much attention back then because it was around the time my mom finally got her diagnosis, and we were swimming in worry and doctors' appointments.

"Omigod, you're stunning!" V says.

"You too!"

I'm always super awkward whenever people comment on my appearance. I know I'm pretty. People have been telling me that ever since I grew into my teeth and grew a pair of Ds in eighth grade, but it's weird. If you acknowledge that you know you're pretty, you're an arrogant asshole, but if you pretend you're not pretty, you're like insincere or, worse yet, insecure. Why do our bodies feel like such a trap sometimes?

"So I know these things are like way awkward, but I just wanted to say no hard feelings. Right?" V says.

"About what?" I say.

"Exactly!" She laughs and touches my arm. It's a lovely girlish laugh, unlike mine, which sometimes sounds like a donkey choking. Normally, I'm not gonna lie, I'm a total flirt, especially with new people. But with V, I can't seem to remember words. Any.

"So nice to meet you . . . ," she says, sticking her hand out toward Rando next to me.

Shit, what is his name? I think he was in one of my classes? Or maybe it was gym? It's Charlie. Or maybe Chris?

"Colin. Pronouns 'he' and 'him,'" he says to her, with what appears to be a firm handshake, but not obnoxiously so.

Oh yes! That's it. I still can't recall where we know each other from, though.

"He's my date," I say. "We're dating."

Why on earth would I say that? Colin nearly chokes on his beer before readjusting himself and grabbing ahold of my hand.

"Well, from what I hear, you must be a lucky dude," V says awkwardly.

"Very!" Colin says a little too enthusiastically. "Definitely! The luckiest . . ."

Jenny swoops in and clocks Colin's almond-colored hand in mine. I can see the gears in her head churning, as she decides whether to say something snarky, nosy, or both. I wrap my arm around his waist. She lifts her eyebrows but says nothing.

"V, there's somebody I'd like you to meet," she says, quickly ushering V away.

"It was lovely meeting you, Penny," V says over her shoulder. I should repeat it back, but I'm not in the mood to be polite right now.

"You okay . . . babe?" Colin says with a smirk. I quickly remove my arm from his person as soon as Jenny's out of sight.

I suppose I owe him some sort of explanation, but before I can answer, I see my phone light up in my purse. I check the caller ID.

"Shit. Hold on . . . it's my mom," I say.

My mother is trying to FaceTime me, which, again, could mean any number of things. Our neighbor, Ms. Marta, came over to watch her while I'm here. Ms. Marta's got gray locs down her back and looks like an artist, but she was actually a badass civil rights lawyer, and Mama's former mentor. Mama says Ms. Marta helped show her the ropes in everything from how to write a kick-ass legal brief to how to get me into a really great preschool, back in the day. She practically raised me. I was always over at her house as a little kid, whenever my mom had to work super late. Now it's Mama she's babysitting.

Last time Ms. Marta came over, Mama called me frantically to tell me, "There's a strange woman in the house, Penny. She seems nice enough, but I don't know who she is. Do you think I should call the police?"

The first time I realized something might be off with my mom, about a year or two back, her glasses were in the fridge and her gardening clogs were in the hall closet with the towels. It didn't seem important, but things like that kept happening. And she started forgetting the words for even basic items, like soap. She would stare at it for a long time as if searching for something she knew she was supposed to know.

Still, Mama is the one who forced me to go to the party, during one of her moments of lucidity.

"Isn't it a Friday?" she asked.

"Yeah."

"And you can't tell me there aren't all kinds of parties in the weeks leading up to graduation?"

"I'm not really in the mood for all that, Mama," I said.

"You're only young once." She took my face in her hands. "Don't you dare stop living your life on my account."

So here I am. Living my life. Yay.

Before I can answer and ask Mama what's up, Nathan Henderson swoops and snatches my phone from me.

"Put your phone down for five seconds and live in the fucking moment!" he says.

Nathan is that guy who thinks he's so nice, and that girls are just superficial idiots who don't like him because he has a glass eye and they only want jocks. But really, it's that he's a pompous dick and that's why nobody wants him. His eye is actually pretty cool. He let me hold it once in eighth grade.

"Give me my phone back!"

"Trust me, I'm helping you!" he yells over his shoulder and starts running. I try to chase after him, but just as he disappears down some hallway, the lights dim. I'm faced with a dilemma. I could continue chasing him, in these heels, in the near dark, only to trip and face-plant, in my minidress, right in front of SAVOY, or somebody else, who would inevitably document the utter social humiliation that would follow. Or I could just hold off until the lights go back up. The internet is forever, so I decide to hold off.

Colin and I stand around awkwardly swilling from our Solo cups and making small talk for what feels like an eternity, until Jrue leads Nathan into the kitchen by the collar like he's been a bad dog.

"I saw him running around and recognized your phone case. I tried to keep up with him," Jrue says, slightly out of breath.

"Where's my shit?" I demand.

"I don't even know, man," Nathan slurs, and I believe him 'cause his eyes are hella glassy, or at least, the one that isn't already actually glass. He probably doesn't know what planet he's on.

I grab another canapé from the tray on the counter and pop it into my mouth.

"Penny, how many of those have you had? They're edibles," Jrue says.

"You couldn't have told me that before?!"

"You'll be fine! Drink water! Don't do anything I wouldn't!" Jrue laughs. Then he looks between me and Colin. "Anyway . . . lemme go check on the goat! Make sure it's not eating through wires and shit!"

Jrue runs off in the direction of the garage.

"To be fair, *I* tried to warn you," Colin says.

"You failed to mention the whole 'they're full of marijuana' part," I say.

"I thought you knew!"

"How the hell am I gonna find my phone if I won't even know my head from my ass in the next five minutes?" I ask.

"I'll help you," he says. "It's the least I can do, being your boyfriend and all . . ."

I roll my eyes.

"All right . . . babe," I say, trying to focus, because all of a sudden, my world feels like the moment right before a beat drops.

# OSCAR GRAHAM

## THE WANNABE RAPPER

### PART I

"TONIGHT'S THE NIGHT."

The other me stares back in the mirror. Not Oscar Graham. My alter ego. IntelleQt.

I smooth imaginary wrinkles from my vintage denim jacket, which has a whole lot of pockets (guess they had to carry a bunch of stuff back in the day), matching jeans, Jordan 4 Breds, and, of course, the face.

Future greatest rapper alive gotta look good!

Bars, baby! Built for this!

Thumping bass shakes the house, vibrating my reflection. I'm one with the music. "This is your moment."

Tonight's goals are simple. One: kill my first live performance. Two: go viral again. (Shouldn't be a problem if number one goes well.) And three: ride that momentum all the way to the bank.

A heavy fist falls on the locked bathroom door. "You okay in there?"

"I'm good, Stasia."

"I told you the coconut shrimp *and* the bloomin' onion was a bad idea."

I crack the door and stare into the concerned brown eyes of my gorgeous girlfriend. Slow strobing party lights drench her in electric blue, then candy red, and those lights should be grateful they get to touch such beauty. I sure am. I say, "My stomach's fine, bae. I'm just getting my head together. Camera's ready, right?"

She lifts the bulky Canon strapped to her neck. "Always."

That camera's a beast. The latest upgrade in the line of rigs she's cycled through since we got together freshman year. Most people are good with their phones, but Stasia's for real for real a visionary when it comes to showing you exactly what you need to see. She does it like the pros, capturing the moments in time that people hang on their walls or rewatch in awe. Ask anybody at Florence Hills High—me included—why they rock with Shakespeare heavy now, and they'll tell you it's because of the version of *Romeo and Juliet* she directed.

Lucky for me, my girlfriend can now use all those incredible skills to capture my come-up. The night a legend is born!

She says, "Think you'll be in there much longer, though? DeAndre wants to keep the bathroom clear. Plus, if the shrimp and the bloomin' onion are bothering you, he'd rather you go upstairs because this is really close to the kitchen—"

"It's not my stomach! Hey, you're not recording this part, right?"

"Nope." She pats the body of her new fav piece of gear. "Only the good stuff on here."

I step outside, and someone slides into the bathroom immediately, slamming the door and flipping on the jet-engine-loud exhaust fan. Me and Stasia swap looks, have a whole silent conversation in the span of a second, and crack up. DeAndre's plan for bathroom integrity is already shot.

She slips a hand into mine and we dive into the growing, buzzing crowd, recognizing everyone so far. We trade daps and hugs with several Florence Hills High friends, associates, acquaintances, and so on while somehow never breaking contact with each other. It's not lost on me that, after graduation in a couple of weeks, I may never see some of them again.

At least they'll have the benefit of saying they knew me way back when.

Fishing my phone from my back pocket, I open my notes app.

Stasia's on her phone, too. "Are you checking the Trendsettr dashboard?"

I'm actually in my "Hottest Verses" document, but the concern in her voice worries me. "Did it crash?"

Swiping away from my rhymes, I log into the back end of the party's official unofficial messaging app, which I created at the request of our classmate Savoy. They wanted a custom audience engagement solution that allowed for voting, real-time Q&A, polling, stories, and so on. There wasn't much lead time, but Savoy provided their own color palette and—admittedly fabulous—graphics. The rest I developed off the spines of several existing apps, then plugged it all into a simple interface. I finished it yesterday, and in theory, it should be fine. But speedy development and stable functionality don't necessarily pair well.

Stasia says, "No. It's working. There are just way more users than I expected."

She isn't wrong. The numbers I'm clocking on the dashboard

are kind of ridiculous. "How many followers does Savoy have across all their social media?"

"A lot, a lot."

Evidently.

Stasia says, "Who has access to this?"

"I gave Savoy an access link to distribute."

"Well, Savoy distributed it to the entire internet. Is it safe?"

"All user data is encrypted, and the app purges everything in thirty hours. I think we're fine, but I'll keep an eye on it."

Stasia smiles sweetly. "I bet you will, Mr. MIT." She squeezes my hand after bringing up MIT for like the twentieth time since she picked me up. I swear she's got like a Spidey sense for topics I'm trying to avoid. I know how big a deal getting into the top STEM university in the country is. How could I not? It's just not the *only* big deal.

I shrug, getting back to my mental checklist. Rhymes on phone. Check. I pat the bulge in my jacket pocket. Good to go there. Drip . . . on a thousand. It's time.

"Let's go holler at Jade, and make sure that camera's rolling."

The living room is loose with people clutching red cups and vibing to the sounds bumping through the house. Thin mist slithers by our ankles, thickening to pea-soup fog the closer we get to the heart of the party. Multicolored lights shift through their spectrum in sync with the increasingly loud music. Cables secured with duct tape snake from corner speakers to the laptop and mixer sitting atop the Dixon family piano. Putting in work is my girl Jade. A blue party light strobing over her brown skin at that moment has her looking like the Goddess of Music.

She's been my people since we were kids. The only other member of the Florence Hills Fringe, as we like to call ourselves.

Her house is across the street from mine and due to some weird voting map getting redrawn when we were in middle school, we ended up on the very edge of the well-off Florence Hills district. If either of us lived just three houses down, we'd be at a different, less-privileged high school. Kids who do live three houses down—former friends in some cases—never let us forget it, either. Can't even blame them. I can't think of one freezing winter day where a Florence Hills classroom didn't have functioning heat.

Anyway . . .

The sticker that used to be on Jade's laptop identifying her as DJ Harley Spin is covered by a plain white label and black Sharpie writing that says *MM/YY*.

"Jade, what up?"

She jumps like I startled her, swiping nervously at the pink hair on the unshaven side of her scalp, then looks over my shoulder, almost . . . *apprehensive?*

I say, "Don't worry about Stasia, we're shooting a little documentary. Wait." I turn to Stasia. "Do we need to get people to sign releases or something? I didn't even think about that."

She peeks over the top of the camera. "We're probably fine."

Then she looks past me to Jade, real intense, and I'm like, "You two okay?"

Quick, jerky nods from both.

To Jade, I say, "You changed your stage name."

"Yeah. The whole Harley Spin thing was supposed to be about chaotic mixes and unpredictability. Turns out people don't love hiring unpredictable DJs—even when we're very cheap. I learned that at my last gig when I faded Nicki Minaj into Kenny Rogers and mixed it with Nine Inch Nails. The bride and groom were not happy. So now I'm MM/YY."

"Like Month-Month-Year-Year?"

"Exactly. That way, I can stay current."

Stasia says, "What if I see that and think of, like, the month and year I was born? Or, the far future? November 3034."

"Then I'm retro. Or I'm futuristic. I'm whatever the audience needs me to be. It's like a Rorschach test and a DJ name."

I don't know if that makes a ton of sense, but since we're discussing needs, I say, "I'm ready to do the thing we talked about."

Jade focuses on her laptop. "Refresh my memory."

"Tuesday. When I was at your house fixing that short in your mixer—how's it working, by the way?"

Jade fades into the next track, eliciting cheers and random twerking from party guests. "It's actually better than when I first bought the thing."

"Good to know. But remember when I was fixing it, and we talked about IntelleQt's world-premiere live performance?"

"What I remember most is we're spelling 'intellect' with a 'q,' which seems like a mixed message, but go on."

"A *deep* message." I dig the flash drive from my pocket. "Anyway, there's a track on here I want you to cue up, then I'mma spit."

Jade shoots another weird look toward Stasia. She must really be camera-shy. We all have our anxieties, I guess. No cap, I'm nervous about tonight's performance, too. But you don't level up if you don't step up. Dudes on my block stay stressing that piece of wisdom. They're always telling stories about how the heroes from this city became legends. D-Wade. Quincy Jones. Common. Derrick Rose. Bernie Mac. Jennifer Hudson. Juice WRLD (may he rest in peace). And on and on. All of them had their moments. I'mma have mine next.

Jade still hasn't taken my flash drive. "We got a problem, Oscar. I—I forgot my good mic. If you use my bum mic, you're going to sound terrible."

"That's why I always come prepared." The bulge in my jacket pocket feels warm to the touch, like some powerful magical object. King Arthur's sword and shit. I unsheathe my weapon of choice.

"Wow," Jade says, "you brought your own mic."

I place my sword, plated in faux gold, $68.70 from Target, next to her laptop. "It's Bluetooth. Should connect real easy."

"So . . . we're doing this." She finally takes my drive and plugs it in. A few taps on the touch pad, and her brow furrows. "Dude, there are like a thousand files on here."

"Yessir!" I wave Stasia closer; she's ready to film. I want a bunch of good footage for my eventual Netflix documentary. "Make sure you get this part."

I sit my phone on the piano bench to free my hands, then squeeze in with Jade so that we all see her screen. I motion to the files. "Go to the one named 'Party.' The reason there's so much fire on this one drive is because I make three beats a day."

Jade asks, "Why?"

"Prime numbers, baby. IntelleQt! I'm about this hip-hop life. Rapper and producer. For anyone who's seen my 'Top to Bottom' video on YouTube, you may not have known that track was all me, beats and rhymes." I pause, make a show of it for the camera. "Top . . . to Bottom."

Then I pose with my right index finger pointing up and my left index finger pointing down. That's going to be my thing. "Top . . . to Bottom," then the fingers. Like how Drake goes "OVO Clique." But with fingers.

Jade says, "Are your hands okay?"

"Is my mic connected?"

She shakes her head, clearly over being recorded. I motion for Stasia to do like we talked about at dinner where she gets a good angle on me and the crowd's reaction at the same time. Jade hands me my mic. "Just hit unmute. Cue me in."

Deep breath. Focus. This is your moment.

"Yo, yo, yo!" I can barely hear me. My pulse is like a water pump in my ears. Swooz-Swooz-Swooz!

Jade shouts over the music again. "Un. Mute."

Oh, right. I toggle the button on the mic handle and piercing feedback stabs the entire party like an ice pick, halting all revels, until it dissipates a moment later and my labored breathing huffs through the speakers. Everyone's looking at me now. The mic feels slick in my hand because my palms are sweaty. My knees are weak. Arms feel like I've been doing curls all day.

I catch a glimpse of Stasia. Her sweet, sweet smile encouraging me. She mouths, *It'll be okay.*

It will be.

Okay. Let's get it!

But when I glance at Jade, DeAndre's in her face yelling about the new Kendrick. Then Kendrick Lamar is playing, and everyone's vibing, and I shrug like *WTF?*

Did I just get preempted?

Jade holds up a wait-a-minute finger and remutes my mic so the crowd doesn't hear me groan.

I guess we'll get it . . . soon.

# SADIE BERNBAUM

## THE SCHOOL PAPER EDITOR; KNOWER OF ALL TEA

## PART I

I AM NOT A PEOPLE PERSON, WHICH IS IRONIC BE-cause I can suck the gossip out of a crowd like a mosquito feasting at a backyard BBQ, then buzz away before anyone even realizes they've been bit. Everyone seems to think that makes me a snitch, but as editor of the *Florence Hills High Gazette,* I simply think it's my job to share breaking news before anyone else. It's not my fault I found my purpose early in life. I can't help that I'm good at what I do. Unlike some kids at our school who post anonymously on the Trendsettr app, I *always* put my name in black-and-white next to what I write. I'm a newspaper-woman through and through, which means I chase truth, and for the first (and last) time in my high school career, I am at a party to bury my own secret (though I won't be mad if I pick up a few).

The truth is: I have never been kissed, and I cannot go to college without popping my makeout cherry. But to make that happen, I have to go inside DeAndre's house, and it would be a lot easier to do that if Jrue, my best and only friend, was by my side. I check my texts to him again:

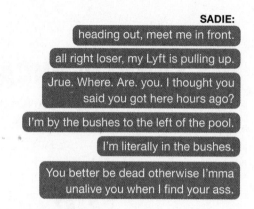

**SADIE:**
heading out, meet me in front.

all right loser, my Lyft is pulling up.

Jrue. Where. Are. you. I thought you said you got here hours ago?

I'm by the bushes to the left of the pool.

I'm literally in the bushes.

You better be dead otherwise I'mma unalive you when I find your ass.

He's probably following Mia around like an NBA star hypnotized by a Kardashian, and while he does that, I'm getting branches stuck in my half top bun.

"Get it together, Bernbaum," I whisper to myself.

I've been in higher-stakes situations than this. I broke into the school cafeteria one weekend to expose the questionable past-due-date mystery meat they were serving. I caught half the lacrosse team forcing freshman recruits to write their midterm papers. I (accidentally) walked in on our valedictorian's mother spread-eagled in the principal's office. I can handle this. I don't need anyone. I just need to shake out my 3C curls in all their glory and walk in there. I throw my phone back into my purse and a sensual groan echoes out of it, interrupting the conversation I am having in my head. I pull my phone back out and find I accidentally hit play on the YouTube compilation of best kisses I have been watching for research. Classmates look with confusion in the direction of my bush as I scramble to turn the video off.

Honestly, this situation tracks. There has never been a more Sadie moment than this one right here, right now, while I watch soft-core porn in DeAndre's bushes as my classmates stream inside without a care in the world. What I need to do is focus. Every good journalist knows you can't go into a news story without a lead, or at the very least, a plan:

**The plan Sadie writes in her notes on her phone once she's positive she's closed the YouTube app:**

1. Go inside.
2. Find someone to kiss.
3. Get out in time to make it home to catch a rerun of *20/20* with Ira Glass guest hosting.

Voices skip over the Olympic-sized pool just as Savoy's minions, Grant, Mirage, and Effie, walk out, making grand gestures and sizing people up based on their outfits. I duck so low, so quickly, that I lose my balance and face-plant—because who doesn't love a shot of mulch? I spit out wood chunks and pray they didn't see me. The last thing I need to start this night off with is the team otherwise known as SAVOY reading me from this shrubbery all the way to Kansas in the name of their leader. (Savoy never forgave me after the review I wrote in the *Gazette* about their sophomore-year self-portrait gallery, but seriously, anyone being honest with themselves would know it was amateur and uninspired. Artists are so damned temperamental; like, don't put your work out there if you can't handle the critique!) I text Jrue again, doing my best to shield the light on my screen so as not to attract SAVOY's attention.

The message-sent swoosh rushes out of my phone like the Nike logo personified just before the screen goes deader than a jean-capri fad. I stuff my phone into my purse.

Wow, utter, unadulterated perfection. Looks like it's on me to get this done. Rolling with numero uno. Hunting down leads and cracking the case on my own. Well, I will be as soon as I climb out of this hydrangea bush.

A couple of people stream out of the house and head straight for the hot tub. What I wouldn't give to just fly across this backyard and jump in; the Illinois late-spring evening has a nip to it, and there's nothing more satisfying than a hot tub when your body is all goose-pimply. I can almost feel the satisfaction as I imagine sinking lower into it and cupping my hands to bring the warm water to splash across my cheeks. The feeling on my face is almost too real to be a dream as heavy breathing interrupts my reverie. My eyes open and my reality becomes immediately clear: a pit bull with its ass in my face, leg up, peeing all over me.

"Aggh, what the fuck?!" I clamp my mouth shut as dog pee dribbles down my forehead.

Perfect. Motherfucking piss-perfect-ion.

Leaves stick to my urine-soaked hair and like a forest demon, I rise from the bushes. People scream, but I rush past them and drop my purse on the ground as I dive into the pit of hot steam. I hold my breath underwater for as long as possible before I let myself break through the surface.

Two sets of eyes meet mine: a sophomore named Tyrone, a cryptocurrency savant who I profiled after he was hired by

*Fortune* 500 CEOs and venture capitalists to advise them on their investments, and Jesse Kaplan, a fellow senior, who usually lives under a marijuana haze so thick I have never seen him make it through an entire class with his eyes open. I couldn't pick two students with less in common, so I lean back against the edge of the tub and stretch my arms out to get comfortable. I can't resist the urge to get the scoop.

"So, nice night, huh?"

Neither of them responds.

"Tyrone, I was thinking of doing a follow-up on our piece, ya know? Where he started, where he's going. Has a nice ring to it, don't you think?"

Still nothing. Weird. These tech guys usually jump at the chance to be on a front cover. I clock a mixture of annoyance and shock on both of their faces, then I notice Jesse's arm around Tyrone's neck, and the dark hickey on Jesse's collarbone, and Tyrone's hand down in Jesse's lap—I jump up. "Stay safe! I mean, enjoy! I mean . . . sorry!"

I climb out of the hot tub, dripping wet, and grab my purse off the ground as I run inside the house. The crowd parts to the squish of my shoes as I rush toward the kitchen and shove some juniors away from the double sink to wring my hair out. The water hits some beer cans in a shrill stream. I look down to see the dog pee–sex–hot tub water falling from my head into a beer pit. I grab a can like that was always my plan and crack it open, then turn around, straight into a warm body.

"Oops—" I find myself face to face with Mia.

Great. The reason Jrue ditched me in the flesh.

"Oh my god!" she shrieks, moving away from me, though it's unclear whether she's more upset about her proximity to me or the beer I just spilled all over her kicks.

I grab a paper towel, roll off the counter, and shove it into her chest. I try to walk around her, but Mia blocks me. She bends down to blot the stain, then rises.

"Sorry," I say, still trying to get past her.

"It's whatever. Have you seen Jrue?" she asks.

Something about Jrue's name in her mouth makes my stomach tighten. Jrue is my best friend. Honestly, despite having more energy than a toddler with a sugar high, he is the best person I know. The only thing wrong with him is that he doesn't know how great he is. So maybe it's the fact that Jrue has been crushing on Mia for years and she's barely acknowledged his existence. Maybe it's the fact that Jrue convinced me to come to this party and hasn't even checked on me. Maybe it's the fact that popular people like Mia expect the rest of us regulars to cater to their every whim. Or maybe I'm just regretting listening to Jrue and believing I could actually have a fun high school night out, and now I'm here, soaking wet, unkissed, and missing Ira "Journalism Bae" Glass on *20/20*. Maybe Mercury is in retrograde or whatever because something in me snaps.

"No, okay? I haven't. I haven't heard from him. I haven't seen him. Is that what you wanted to hear? The headline reads 'Sadie Snitchbaum Ditched by Her Only Friend at the Last Party of High School'! Are you happy now?"

The party goes silent or maybe I've died—either way, I can feel the hordes of tipsy eyes piercing my back. This was a mistake. Mia tries to say something to me, but I back away from her before I make more of a fool of myself and trip over the garbage can.

*Fan-fucking-tastic,* I think as I fall.

I brace myself for the impact, but two hands catch me and drag me around the corner and into a room.

"What the hell?!" I shout to the unidentified stranger pulling me into what may end up being the bowels of hell. A door clicks behind us and I hear a loud vibrating noise as a fluffy towel falls over my face. The person wipes the excess moisture from me, replacing the last hints of eau de dog pee with lavender fabric softener. I pull the towel out of the mystery hands to clear my vision and reveal a laundry room and Merrill Wortham gazing at me like I am coated in rainbows, our noses just an inch apart. She lingers for a second, then turns around so her back is to me.

She speaks in this oddly official tone: "If you disrobe, it should only take a short tumble-dry. I shall guard the space."

I glance over at the fancy-ass dryer, which looks like a spaceship. I put my purse down before quickly pulling my clothes off and throwing them inside. Then I wrap myself up in the towel.

"Thanks, Merrill. You can turn around now."

"It's an honor to assist you." Her voice is as soft and sweet as those tiny marshmallows my mom likes to put on mashed yams at the holidays. She spins around.

Merrill's a recluse. She's always scribbling in her notebook at the back of class, whispering to no one as she furiously erases everything she's written and starts over. She's never shown any interest in other living beings, so it's sort of shocking she's at this party, but I guess most of the people upstairs would say the same about me, especially if they knew why I was here.

"Thank you," I say.

"Of course." Merrill does a little curtsy. She's definitely an odd duck; there was a rumor floating around that she had a collection of hair taped to the back of her journal, which I personally investigated, and while I could not get her to confirm or deny, I also found no proof. I step back to lean against the dryer, but I can't seem to break eye contact with Merrill. She is staring at me, like she's got a view directly into my soul. I've never really looked at Merrill, not closely. To be fair, she is always hiding under her thick, wavy brown hair, but tonight it's pulled up in a tight topknot. She's pretty, striking even. It's her eyes—I can't put my finger on what exactly—there's just . . . an intensity to them that's almost breathtaking. It's funny how you can be in school with someone for four years and never really see them, but I see her now and she sees me. Merrill is glued to my every move. She steps forward, closing the gap I made between us.

"Will you allow me a kiss?" she asks, bold and earnest.

The quick-dry setting has the machine practically levitating, it's moving so fast behind us, and a shock runs through me. Could this really be happening? Could it actually be this easy? I mean, I've imagined kissing Lara Jean as much as I've imagined kissing Peter Kavinsky, but Merrill? Really? Is she the person I want to recount to my grandkids as the person who took my lip virginity? I try to think about what Jrue would say.

*Damn, Merrill Wortham?! Who knew?* I hear Jrue's voice in my head, and I smile.

I wish he was here right now to help me figure out what to do. But he isn't, and that is precisely why I am here . . . maybe that's the only answer I need. Merrill is so close I can feel her breath on my top lip. I guess this is happening, first kiss: Merrill Wortham.

I nod, yes. Let's do this. Maybe I'll be able to sneak out of this party before anyone notices and off everyone's radar. She takes my shoulders in her hands and pulls me toward her to whisper in my ear.

"This might be the only chance I have to taste your magical essence—" Merrill leans in but her lips meet my open palm, which I hold up as a shield between us, because this just took a right turn straight into a weird zone I'm not prepared for.

"Um . . . wait a second," I say, and pull the string hanging from the lightbulb in the ceiling.

In the fluorescent light, I see what I couldn't with only the string lights in the backyard shining in from the windows in this room. Her eyes, well, her pupils to be exact, are bigger than Savoy's ego. Merrill's high. She's floating in outer space.

This past March, I did a huge exposé in the *Gazette* about the dangers of bath salts, which some students blame for the school board implementing a random bag-search policy (which was completely unfair, totally overshadowed the impressive work I did on that piece). If anyone bothered to ask me, I'd say I don't have a problem with experimentation. I mean, Jrue and I have attempted to smoke weed twice, from my dad's stash, but I don't think we did it right because we tried to watch re-runs of *Seinfeld* and the show still wasn't funny.

I dodge Merrill's hand as she reaches out to pet my face. It's not even worth asking her what she's on: shrooms, acid, some new chemical hybrid that doesn't have a street name yet—I doubt she knows at this point. She seems like she's having a great time, and that's fine by me, but I need my first kiss, at the very least, to happen with someone who is on the same planet as me.

"Merrill, I think I need to go," I say, pushing the stop button on the machine and grabbing my surprisingly almost-dry clothes.

I pull my pants on and try to ignore the itch of the slight dampness as I throw my shirt over my head and let the towel

I've been standing in fall to the floor. She drops to one knee and bows her head.

"Of course, Your Majesty, my unicorn queen, you must escape."

People have called me some interesting names as a biracial Black woman, but that's a first. I nod as I open the door.

"Hey, Merrill, can you do something for me?" I ask her, one foot in the hallway.

"Anything, my liege."

"Drink some water, okay?"

"Yes, yes, of course. I will hydrate to continue the quest. Be safe, until we meet again," she says, and then lifts my towel from the floor and inhales deeply from it.

IN THE HALLWAY, I can hear the party raging, and the air in the house is sticky-strong like someone poured a combination of agave and gasoline all over. I face myself in a mirror I almost walk past. Aside from slight shrinkage, which, honestly, makes my curls more defined, everything is somehow still in place. I scan the rest of my face.

Per usual, my dark brown freckles sprayed across my cheekbones, under my light brown eyes, are the only thing on my otherwise Cream of Wheat–colored skin. I never have energy for makeup so there's nothing to touch up. All in all, aside from a few wrinkles in my clothes and a slight detergent smell, which is a massive improvement from dog piss, I'm still looking pretty good. I keep my head down as I make my way to the empty outlet at the far end of the dining room to plug my phone in.

"Sadie! There you are!" Jrue shouts across the room as he

rushes toward me, carrying half the party's gaze along with him. "I've been walking around the yard for like thirty minutes looking for you. I inspected every bush on the property thrice."

He wasn't ignoring me; he went to look for me. Knowing that makes the night already feel a little lighter, like I'm not in this alone. I plug my phone in and hide it behind the long curtains, then stand to give him a hug.

"Sorry. I, um, had a situation . . . I'm sure you heard," I say.

Jrue raises his left eyebrow so high it practically reaches his hairline.

"What the hell does that mean? Did someone mess with you?!"

Maybe people are already getting tipsy enough to forget my grand entrance.

"No, no, it's already looking pretty hopeless to get anyone half sober to kiss me—"

Jrue grabs my elbow, cheesing. "So my little Sadie is on the first-smooch quest, huh?" He shouts this like the *Hunger Games* announcer shouts "May the odds be ever in your favor."

I clamp my hand over his mouth as people look in our direction. "SHHHHH," I hiss, and punch him in the shoulder.

Jrue and I are complete opposites: He gives most people the benefit of the doubt, and I tend to be skeptical until someone proves otherwise. He sucks up the spotlight like Thanos and the energy of the universe, while I like to fade into Earth's darkest corners where no one notices me, collecting secrets. It makes no sense that we're best friends. But somehow, he's the French fry to my vanilla shake, the ham to my pineapple pizza.

"All right, all right." He holds his hands up like he is surrendering. "If it makes you feel any better, you aren't the only one whose lips are about to get a workout. I'm telling you, there's something about tonight, everything just feels like it's falling into place, now I just have to find Mia. Have you seen her around?"

I've never understood his obsession with her, but something about the way he's talking stings. I know Jrue better than anyone, and all he has ever wanted is to be seen. Especially by Mia. I mean, I see him, I always have, but apparently that's not enough.

"Jrue, I've got my own problems. I didn't come here to stalk yours," I snap before I realize what I am doing—What am I doing?

Twenty minutes ago, Mia was in the kitchen asking me about Jrue. The joy that would seep out of him would overpower the cologne he stole from his dad if I told him. But then what? He'd go find her, profess his love, and then they'd ride off into the Chicago skyline? Please. She'd keep him around for the attention to make herself feel better, then drop him the second someone who made more sense on paper came along. I don't want him to be mad at me for lying, but for some reason, the idea of him being with her feels worse.

"Damn, Sadie. What burrowed into your butt and rotted like the Crypt-Keeper?"

"Sorry. I've got a lot on my mind," I say. Plus, I'm protecting him. What he doesn't know can't hurt him . . . right?

"It's okay, let me save you the embarrassment. I know you're just jealous you can't have this!" He sashays to the left like the cha-cha slide just came on, back to his normal routine, aka "making fun of Sadie" at every possible second.

I roll my eyes, which in Sadie/Jrue language means, "Get me a drink and make it strong."

"Come on," he says as he pulls me toward the kitchen. "Now, tell me who's in the running for this first kiss of yours."

"Well, Merrill Wortham actually tried to kiss me." I start to tell him the story, but he interrupts—

"Damn, Merrill Wortham! Who knew?" he says, just like I knew he would.

## FLORENCE HILLS HS TRENDSETTR MESSAGE BOARD

[ANONYMOUS2039]: Overheard in the dining room, Sadie B in search of her first kiss, anyone out there looking to smooch a snitch?

# OSCAR GRAHAM
## THE WANNABE RAPPER

## PART II

"YO, YO, YO!" MY VOICE BOOMS, DRAWING MORE attention my way. "Now I know most of y'all call me Oscar in the halls of Florence Hills High, but in these Chicago streets, I'm better known as IntelleQt. Er, with a 'q.'"

Someone in the back yells, "Where's the 'q' go?"

Shit. Should've brought a sign. Keep going, Oscar. I tip my chin at Jade, and she finally starts my track. It's mid-tempo, so the crowd can concentrate on my wordplay.

"Because you're my people, you're gonna be the first to hear my latest, it's . . ."

My. Heart. Stops.

The crowd's bouncing to my beat. A little. Heads are bobbing. Somewhat. But . . .

Where's my phone?

They're waiting for what I'm promising, but I don't have my phone, my rhymes. My track is almost to the drop. I either gotta tell Jade to run it back to the beginning while I find my phone—vibe-killer—or . . .

Go off top.

I mean, they're my words. I rehearsed. Once. Just gotta let preparation plus perspiration meet the situation, like the old heads at the barbershop be saying. In four . . . three . . . two . . .

*"IntelleQt, meant to wreck*
*Forget your calculator I can split your check . . ."*

No, no, no. That's an old verse. I need my phone.

"By calculator, I mean the app that comes with your phone. Because phones today are . . ."

Chuckles and murmurs in the crowd. I'm losing them. Fall back on a go-to rhyme scheme. Vowel sounds. "A," "E," "I"—got it!

*"Fully loaded, features bloated,*
*You now roll with the kid who codes it*
*And I code fast . . . Kentucky Derby . . ."*

Why'd you say Kentucky Derby?! NOTHING RHYMES WITH KENTUCKY DERBY! What about "fast" things? There's gotta be something there!

*"I'm a racehorse meets Space Force . . ."*

One girl from my history class yells, " 'Racehorse'?"

Other phones point my way, their owners snickering. I'm about to get dragged by everybody! I can fix this. There's still time to recover, I think.

Until I see the dog.

She's a brown-and-white pit bull mix, her leash dangling from her mouth. What the fuck? She's nosing her way to the front of the crowd before she sits. Her head cocks. She's got this whole Scooby-Doo vibe, like I'm confusing her as much as she's confusing me.

I'm upside down now. No bearings. "Wait, wait. That's just an . . . intro! My real rhymes are on my—"

"Booo!"

Where it comes from, I don't know. But somebody else joins in. Then a third. I'm close to getting crushed by an avalanche of my peers' jeers when the music switches abruptly at Jade's prompting. "Ski" by Young Thug blasts through the speakers and the crowd welcomes the energy.

This is supposed to be my moment. They've forgotten me already. Except for Jrue Edwards.

Jrue nudges his way through the crowd looking giddy. He slaps me on the shoulder and says, "Ayyye! Oscar, that was hilarious, bro. Wish I'd thought of it. 'IntelleQt' with a 'q.'" He chuckles. While walking away, he adds, "Jenius. With a 'J.'"

"I—I wasn't joking." But Young Thug is loud, and Jrue's already gone.

Stasia sidles next to me, her shoulder touching mine. "Hey."

It's impossible to muster any lightness in the moment. I motion at the camera with my chin. "All that's on there?"

"Hey," she says again, and tugs me to her for a quick, pain-killing kiss. Her thumb hovers over the delete button. "Doesn't have to be."

Jade leans toward us, my phone in hand. "You're probably looking for this. You left it on the piano bench."

I take it, staring at my reflection in the dark screen.

Stasia says, "Why don't we go outside where it's quieter and look at some footage I shot earlier? It might cheer you up to see—"

"I need a do-over," I say.

Stasia and Jade go completely still.

"Look. I know what you're thinking."

Jade says, "Do you, though?"

"Yeah, you want me to go home. Regroup. But if I let this setback shake me now, I might not ever recover. This is just like when Eminem had to go through it, then defeat Papa Doc and Tha Free World."

Jade says, "You're confusing Eminem with his character in *8 Mile*."

My nose scrunches up. "What do you mean? *8 Mile* was a documentary about Eminem."

"Oh god." Jade yanks my flash drive from her laptop, shoves it into my hand, then tugs her headphones over her ears and tends to her playlist.

Stasia grabs my sleeve. "Let's walk."

She guides me from the living room to a family room where three times the amount of people the wraparound sofa was designed to hold squeeze onto the seats, arms, and back of the furniture. Some sit on the floor, others post on the wall flanking the ninety-inch TV. Scenes from the last Avengers movie flicker on the screen while a couple of juniors run cable from a Switch to the set's HDMI input. A moment later the Nintendo logo displays in 4K.

"You know," I say, "it's probably best that my first live performance of the night didn't go so great. I can only go up from here—"

Stasia waves to Cam Booker, who's chugging a beer on

the other side of the kitchen island. He quick-steps over to us, radiating friendly vibes. "Stasia!" He hugs her with one arm, then tugs me close to be heard over the music. "Oscar, I owe you big, man. Might not have made it out of trigonometry without those mnemonic tricks you put me onto. I told your girl already, but I felt like I needed to say it to you direct. You know?"

I only hear like half of what he says—something about the trig mnemonics I showed him at the beginning of the school year—because "Ski" fades into "Big Paper" by Cardi B and DJ Khaled and the whole party lets out a collective "Ohhhhh!"

That's the "Ohhhhh!" I need.

"Anyway," Cam says, "I'll holla at you two later. Hope you caught my good side, Stasia."

He goes on to greet more of our classmates, and I say, "What'd he mean about getting his good side?"

"You know me." She raises her camera. "I shoot everyone. Wanna get some air?"

There's a traffic jam of people between us and the open patio door. A warm breeze carries notes of chlorine from the pool. We nudge our way closer to the house's exterior.

I say, "The party crowd's really getting thick. More people, more pressure, but I got my phone back, so I won't fumble lyrics again. I got a better beat, too. Something closer to a DJ Khaled track, you know? Or . . ."

Wait a minute. I do a double take on my phone, absorbing the app chatter.

"Yo. Sy Navarro's coming. You know what this could mean, right?"

Stasia's eyes narrow. "Spell it out for me."

"Collabo! Me and There Is No Kevin in Team. Fire!"

"Right. I think it's worth discussing in more detail. Let's find someplace quieter, okay?"

"Okay." Plans are swirling in my head when a wicked cramp slices through my lower abdomen, followed by a gurgle the room could've heard if not for the music.

Stasia notices me rubbing my belly. "The shrimp and the bloomin', huh?"

I nod. "Where's that other bathroom?"

She points at the ceiling. "Upstairs, to the right. DeAndre said be sure to spray before you go."

# MEMI MATSON
## THE ACTOR

---

## PART I

### THE PROLOGUE

GO, GIRL, SEEK HAPPY NIGHTS TO HAPPY DAYS.

It's been five days since the final performance of *Romeo and Juliet*, but my brain still bathes in luminous lines. My own and everyone else's. Immersing yourself in a role requires a noble sacrifice. No longer Memi Matson—an Ojibwe-Lithuanian girl from Chicago; a high school junior; and a spiky-haired lover of makeup, avocados, and tuxedo cats. Someone who cannot carry a tune but has a photographic memory for scripts and an ear for accents. Memi, hardworking and frugal, yet willing to part with her savings to purchase hair extensions for a role, because everything in the wig trunk smells like corn chips.

All to inhabit her.

Juliet from the House of Capulet. Daughter of one of Verona's aristocrats. Naive and innocent (hold for laughter in real life). She falls for Romeo, an (questionably?) older, impulsive, dreamy heartthrob who is equal parts cinnamon-bun sweetness and horny-as-hell teen.

Blake, who's hot in his own right, understands this metamorphosis in the way that only theater geeks can. Not that Blake is a geek. He's the opposite. I explain it to my nontheater friends like this: theater is a universe, and each production is a solar system that revolves around one bright star. Blake Donnelly is the center of Florence Hills's spring-semester staging of *Romeo and Juliet*.

For the past five months, I've yearned for Blake-as-Romeo. He and I would sneak backstage during rehearsals, having discovered a door to the school boiler room beneath the theater. We hid from our director (pretending he was my Capulet father) aided by our closest castmates: my Nurse, his cousin Benvolio, his friend Mercutio, and our dear Friar Lawrence. We delighted in stolen kisses while our fingers explored each other's bodies, barely resisting the temptation to shed caution along with our clothing. We even went to prom together as Romeo and Juliet—wearing our costumes and staying in character the entire time—parting reluctantly at the end of the night. We both understood that the sexual tension added a fiery desperation to our performances. Between passionate moans, we promised to give in after our final performance. Our swan song as Romeo and Juliet.

Instead, everything went to hell.

We didn't know the second-to-last show would be Blake's final turn as Romeo. His agent called a few hours before our final performance on Sunday. Blake needed to screen-test in Los Angeles for the latest Star Trek series reboot, an all-teen version called *Star Trek: Fountain of Youth*. With apologies to our director and to me, Romeo Number One was at O'Hare

Airport by the time the curtain rose with a gobsmacked Romeo Number Two blinking into the stage lights.

The final show was not a swan song but the garbled groaning of a goose that had the audience laughing. Actual, full-on LOL'ing.

So tonight is about closure and I'm not just talking about the wrap party for cast and crew that I just exited. I made a brief appearance and gave an Academy Award–worthy speech on behalf of Blake and myself thanking everyone—except Chance Jackson—for the stellar production of *Romeo and Juliet,* which put to shame Bayside High's horrid spring production. Seriously, what high school is still doing *Wizard of Oz?* Before he authored *Oz,* L. Frank Baum wrote more than one newspaper editorial calling for every Native American to be killed. Seriously! He called us "miserable wretches." So, again, why is anyone still telling his story?

Now it's on to the epic party at DeAndre Dixon's to rendezvous with Blake, who is on his way back from five days of screen tests and various meetings his agent set up for him. It's time to celebrate my leading man.

*Come, night. Come, Romeo. Come, thou day in night.*
*For thou wilt lie upon the wings of night. Give me my Romeo.*
Total cheeseballs, I know. But tonight, I intend to fuck Romeo.

# SY NAVARRO

## THE EMO BAND KID

BY THE TIME I ARRIVE AT DEANDRE'S, I CAN TELL BY the parking situation that the party's already in full swing. The winding road's packed with cars, and I have to land my rickety-ass Honda Civic several blocks away, on a hill steep enough that the emergency brake doesn't inspire much confidence. At least there's a sad-looking *Scooby-Doo* camper out here that makes me feel a bit less embarrassed.

As soon as I step out of my car and onto the pavement, I can hear music pulsing through the night, filling me with nervous excitement. It's only a matter of time until one of the neighbors calls the cops, even if the houses are all separated by huge, manicured lawns that take up more space than the apartment complex where my family lives.

I pull on my backpack full of gear, lift my amp out of the trunk, and grab my guitar case from the backseat. Then I zip up my black hoodie, flip up the hood, and begin my trek uphill, tonguing my lip ring the entire way like I always do when I'm nervous.

By the time I reach the house, I'm mad sweaty and my arms are burning. Wish I'd thought to unload everything right in front of DeAndre's before finding parking, but like my dad says, I don't always use my head.

"If it isn't my favorite Filipino, Sy Navarro!" someone calls as soon as I step onto the driveway. It's a grinning George Nguyen, coming at me with arms wide open, red cup in one hand, a cookie in the other, and eyes glazed over.

Perfect.

"What's up, George?" I say as he wraps his arms around me, reeking of alcohol. When we break apart, I notice he's wearing one of our band's original tees, the one with the logo Asa drew in Studio Ghibli style. "Nice shirt."

"Thanks, dude. I didn't know you ever came to these things!" He takes a bite of this big-ass cookie, then holds it out to me.

I shrug, break off a piece. Chocolate chip. Pretty good.

George notices the gear I'm hauling and does this over-the-top shocked expression, complete with one hand clutching his chest. "Wait—you're playing tonight?"

I shift. "Um, yeah."

He smacks my shoulder with too much familiarity. "I knew it—I've been telling everyone you should go solo. You've got the perfect voice for it."

"Actually," I say, looking around as if to make sure nobody's eavesdropping, "I won't be playing alone."

His eyebrows go up. "You started a new band? How the fuck did I not hear about this shit yet?!"

"Nah, not a new band."

Confusion passes over his face, but then his eyes go even wider as he puts the pieces together. "Shut the fuck up, man—you're telling me There Is No Kevin in Team is rising from the ashes?!"

I nod. Slowly.

The seed has been planted. Time to watch it grow.

"Sick!" He pumps his fists, spilling his drink, while letting out what I can only describe as a primal scream. I had heard George cried when he found out we broke up, and I believe it now. "This is going to be so epic, dude! When did you all start speaking to each other again?"

"A few weeks ago," I lie.

"Damn—it must have taken some apology for them to forgive you."

"Right. But it's just for tonight. One last show."

He hugs me again.

I pry myself free. "Can you do me a favor and not tell anyone else about this yet?" I ask, as if I'm not intentionally leaking the info.

"For sure. A secret show—like back in the day."

"Exactly," I say, because it certainly is secret. So secret I'm the only person in the band who even knows about it yet. But by the time the word's spread, the others won't have any choice but to show up, right?

"Where you setting up?"

I adjust my backpack's straps. "Somewhere."

"And when you going on?"

"Later."

"Can I see your set list? Anything off *Radiation People*?

Forget Sadie's stupid review—that album's definitely not 'insipid and uninspired.' It rocks. Dude, you've got to play 'Cat Café'! If you don't, I will literally kill you." He laughs.

"Cat Café" was the first song Asa and I cowrote. We were jamming after practice had finished up and Sam and Perry had already left. We were in my garage; it was raining. She was wearing my old red flannel. When we stumbled upon the hook, we felt the magic and looked up at each other, grinning. We knew we had something and just kept playing until, like, three in the morning, when we finally cracked it.

Sure enough, "Cat Café" became our best-known track. It's the one that racked up streams and caught the attention of the label. It has this epic part where the song builds, then everyone suddenly goes silent except for Sam keeping a soft, pulsing beat on the drums. After a few measures, Perry's bass line begins and I start gently singing the chorus. Asa takes over, then we sing it together a couple of times. Asa's cello and my guitar start weaving around each other as the energy builds and builds. A beat before the climax, we stop—then I hit a few high, spiraling notes on my guitar and we all come crashing back together, ending with a few driving measures.

"Maybe," I say. "You see the others around?"

George takes a drink and then answers, "Sam's chilling on the couch in the family room, Perry's in the kitchen, and Asa was heading upstairs last I saw."

"That was a really precise answer."

"You're welcome. Anyway, can't wait to hear you guys rock out later, man. I'll be front row, like always!" He flashes the devil's horns and stumbles away, dropping the rest of his big-ass cookie.

IT PAINS ME to part with my gear, but there's no way I'm going to be able to maneuver through the bodies inside the house hauling a guitar case, amp, and backpack full of cords and such. So I make my way into the garage through the side and hit the button to open the door. As it grinds open, the overhead light comes on, startling a couple that's hooking up against one of the cars.

"My bad," I say. After confirming I'm not a cop or someone's dad, they resume devouring each other's faces.

I make my way to the other side, where I find a goat. It looks up at me with those creepy goat eyes, chewing on something.

"My bad," I say again.

"Maa," says the goat.

I stash my stuff in a corner not occupied by a goat or a horny couple ignoring the goat, then head into the house, dodging a crowd of kids smoking, vaping, and drinking all along the wraparound porch. A few people catch sight of me. Someone asks, "Is it true that There Is No Kevin in Team is playing a reunion show tonight?" I shrug and act cool, grateful for George Nguyen's predictably loose lips.

When I finally get inside, it's dark, loud, and hot as hell. The air is pulsing with music and reeks of alcohol, sweat, weed, and Doritos. Kids holding red cups fill the foyer and the staircase. Most are standing around chatting, but a few are bopping to the music or making out.

I review the info George gave me and decide to find Sam first. She's the most laid-back and should be the easiest to convince.

The living room's even more crowded than the foyer. The furniture's been pushed aside and everyone's swaying or grinding or rapping/shouting the lyrics as music blasts from a professional setup, complete with that girl Jade DJ'ing behind a set of turntables framed by big-ass speakers, flashing colored lights, and a fog machine.

I scan for space to slip through, but there are bodies from wall to wall. After taking a deep breath, I enter the crowd like I'm about to go spelunking.

The song's actually pretty good, and it's kind of like being in the mosh pit at a punk show—but much less violent and much more sexual.

Before I know it, I'm past the crowd. In the family room, there's a decidedly more chill vibe. A few people are standing around snacking on chips or drinking, but most sit on or lean against the wraparound couch or the random chairs and beanbags set up in a semicircle facing a big-ass flat-screen TV mounted on the wall, which has nearly everyone's attention because there's a Mario Kart tournament going down.

Sam's at the far end of the couch, sitting up on the back of it with her pink Chuck Taylors on the leather cushions and Switch controller in hand. I sidle up next to her.

"Let me guess," I say, rubbing the back of my neck, "Yoshi?"

She nods without even turning to look at me. Hopefully it's because she's concentrating on holding down first place.

"So . . . about everything that went down," I say, "I'm sorry."

She shrugs. "It's cool."

On-screen, she bumps an item box, gets banana peels, and immediately launches them. Behind her, Bowser hits one and careens off the track, making the kid sitting cross-legged on the floor in front of the TV curse.

"Really?" I say.

"Yeah, man. Pobody's Nerfect." She keeps racing.

"Cool." I continue, "So how would you feel about getting the band back together? Not permanently. Just for tonight."

She raises an eyebrow. "Ah, so the rumors *are* true."

"And?"

"I'm down."

"Oh, okay . . . You're not going to ask why?"

She smirks. "As if I need to."

"That obvious?"

"Always has been."

"Whatever. You have your kit here?"

"Nah, but I can text my mom to bring it by."

"Rad."

"Just let me know when we're going on."

Sam calmly steers Yoshi past the finish line and raises her arms in victory as the other three players groan with frustration and everyone else cheers. She holds her palm up for a high five, so I oblige, and we finally look at each other, smiling like the last few months never happened.

One down, two to go.

"Perry's over in the kitchen if this is, like, your apology tour," she says, reading my mind.

"Thanks," I say. "It kind of is."

DEANDRE'S KITCHEN IS straight out of a magazine—all stainless steel and granite and white tile. There's even a freaking skylight above the sink. But unlike a magazine, there's a keg sitting in a tub of ice in the corner and the island's crowded with bowls of chips, a stack of greasy pizza boxes, and enough liquor bottles to stock a small club.

I spot Perry, sipping a drink in the corner by himself and vibing because he's the kind of dude who never seems out of place, even when he's alone. But before I can reach him, a grinning Oscar Graham steps in front of me, looking fresh in a denim jacket with more pockets than I could pull off.

"Navarro to the Sy. My guy!"

"Oh, hey, you made that rhyme."

He shrugs. "It's what I do."

I try to sidle past Oscar, but he moves with me. "Are the rumors true?"

"What rumors?"

"There Is No Kevin in Team is playing a secret show tonight!"

"Who told you that?"

"George. Sadie. Everyone, bro. Trendsettr is abuzz."

"Great."

"Tonight might be the night for us to finally make it happen, Sy."

"Make what happen?"

"First: Run-DMC met Aerosmith. Then: Kanye met Bon Iver. Now: Oscar Graham—aka IntelleQt—meets There Is No Kevin in Team."

"Oh, right. The collab. And it's actually pronounced 'bone-ee-VARE.'" Back when the band was starting to blow up and we were on the verge of inking the record deal, everyone was giving us their demos and mixtapes, hoping we'd pass it along to the label. Oscar—before he settled on the name IntelleQt—was no exception. He even included a track with him rapping over one of our songs to propose a collaboration. It was . . . not good. Not just that track. All of them. Super smart and nice dude, though.

"Yeah, I don't know, Oscar. Tonight might not be a good time for that."

"What you talking about? It's the perfect night, Sy. Nobody'd see it coming, and everyone would remember it forever!"

"That's for sure."

His smile widens. "So you're down?"

"Sorry, Oscar. Anyway, your stuff is totally better solo, man." Not a lie.

His face falls. "Yeah, okay, I mean, we haven't rehearsed or anything. It'd probably be strong on vibes alone, but I get it."

I pat him on the shoulder as he walks away.

"I was thinking it'd be more like Jay-Z and Linkin Park," Perry says, stepping into the space Oscar left behind with a beer in hand, his boyfriend Marlon with the beautiful hair in tow.

"Oh well, in that case, let me call him back."

We laugh, which is a good sign, right?

But then the laughter passes, and it's mad awkward.

"I'll leave you two alone," Marlon says, then wanders away.

And it stays mad awkward. We stand there bobbing our heads to the music as kids keep scooting past to grab some food or refill a drink.

"Marlon seems cool," I say, finally breaking the noisy silence between us.

"He is."

Our conversation falters. Already.

I know I need to apologize, but for some reason, I don't.

He clears his throat. Gestures toward the keg. "Want a drink?"

"Nah, I'm good. Thanks, though."

"Still on that old-school straight-edge kick, eh?"

"Yup," I say.

"Very punk."

"Yup."

Jade transitions seamlessly into the next track. A group of kids start chanting "Chug! Chug! Chug! Chug!" Someone knocks over a nearby bowl of chips, then walks away without batting an eye.

Perry and I exchange a look signaling our shared lack of faith in humanity. I pick up the bowl, then we both stoop to clean up the mess. And maybe it's because my hands have something to do that I'm finally brave enough to say it: "I'm sorry about how things went down that night, Perry."

He continues brushing chip fragments with his hands into a small pile.

I go on. "I didn't mean any of it."

"I know you didn't, Sy."

"You do?"

He looks up. "You were frustrated, angry, sad. Maybe even grieving the future you'd planned for us, or at least for yourself. Like a lot of people, you didn't know how to express all these emotions, so you projected and took it out on all of us."

"Yeah." It's been so long since we've talked, I forgot how this dude's always able to see right through everyone. "That was super insightful."

"The benefit of having a therapist mom. But, for real, you've got to do better. Get in touch with your emotions."

We combine our chip piles, then I scoop it all up into my palm and dump it into the trash can. "Working on it."

"Good. Toxic masculinity kills."

I brush the crumbs from my hands and raise a fist in

solidarity as we both stand back up. "Yeah, dismantle the patri-archy!"

"It's not a joke, Sy."

I lower my arm. "Yeah, I know. Sorry. Angry outbursts, avoidance, and shitty jokes—I've got defense mechanisms for days."

"That you do. But how've you actually been? Since the band broke up?"

I shrug. "Chillin'."

"For real?"

"No."

Perry nods.

"You know I almost failed, like, two classes?" I say.

"I heard."

"But without the band, I actually had time to get my shit to-gether enough to scrape by. Earned all my credits to graduate."

"I'm glad," he says.

"How about you?"

"I've been all right, actually. I loved No Kevin, but it wasn't my entire life."

*Like it was for you* is the rest of that sentence. But he's smart enough to know I know he's thinking that and kind enough not to say it anyway.

"Maybe you really are working on you," he continues. "After all, you're here and you finally apologized. Even if you did take almost five months."

"Yup."

"I hope this means you're also apologizing to the others?"

"Already apologized to Sam," I say.

"And Asa?"

"Up next."

He takes a drink. "Good luck with that."

"But that's not all, Perry."

"Oh?"

I clear my throat. "Actually, I was hoping to get the band back together."

"I heard that going around. Let me guess: You 'leaked' that rumor in hopes everyone would be so excited we'd have no choice but to play?"

I nod.

"But it can't happen, dude—"

"Not permanently," I explain. "Just for one last show. To-night."

He smirks. "So I'm guessing you've already heard that Asa's leaving right after graduation for that summer backpacking program?"

"I won't deny that that might be a factor in the timing here."

"And you think some big, dumb romantic gesture like getting us together one last time will give you a chance to tell her how you feel?"

"Exactly."

He takes a drink. "It's a terrible plan."

"Wait—what? Why?"

"You'll be using the pressure from everyone expecting us to perform to coerce her into playing. And if you tell her you like her in front of everyone, that'll be like the same thing. But relationships need to be realer, deeper than that, Sy. If you want to start something with Asa, you've got to do it correctly."

"Shit. You're right."

"I know."

"What do I do, Perry? The rumor's running its course as we speak, and people are already expecting us to play."

"Hmm. Maybe think of an even bigger, dumber romantic gesture to top this one?"

"Really?" I ask.

"No, course not. Just talk to her, man. Apologize. Explain everything. Explain how you feel. Then, if she's down with playing, so am I."

I lift Perry off the floor in a bear hug, give him a few shakes, then set him down. "You still keep your bass and your amp in your trunk?"

"Of course."

"Cool. But you really think that'll work—just talking to her?"

"Only one way to find out." He raises his cup.

I tap it with my fist and then peace out of the kitchen, nervous but buzzing.

UP ON THE second floor, it's mad dark because every single door is shut. I scan the bathroom line looking for someone who might know Asa and could point me in her direction and land on this girl Merrill.

"Hey," I say. "You see Asa Rao around?"

She turns to me with wide, glazed eyes and a dreamy smile. "Good sir, is that sloth on your shoulder your steed?"

"What?"

"Perchance may I hug it?"

"She came up here a while ago," someone interjects, saving me. It's the ever-popular Penny Washington, hanging with Colin, a chill dude from class. "Hasn't walked past again, so she must be in one of the rooms."

"Thanks," I say, and start to walk away.

"Does this mean the show's about to start?" Penny asks.

I glance around like I don't want anyone to eavesdrop, then stage-whisper, "Maybe in, like, an hour. But do me a favor and keep it on the DL. I don't want to 'overhype' it."

"Of course," she says, and flashes that winning smile.

I slip away, find the nearest bedroom door, and knock. Nobody answers, so I try again after a few seconds. "Asa, you in there? It's me—Sy."

The music's muffled up here, but it's still loud enough and there's, like, a hundred different conversations going on, so I press my ear to the door. There's the rhythmic shifting of bedsprings accompanied by overenthusiastic grunting.

I back away and go to the next door. This time, it opens after I knock, revealing Olivia Martinez, a girl from my AP Lang class.

"Oh, hey, Sy!" she says, smiling.

"Hey, Olivia. I'm looking for Asa. She in here?"

"Of course you are." She offers an exaggerated wink.

I guess it really is that obvious.

"But nope, sorry." She steps aside so I can see into the well-lit room. There's a group of four other kids sitting on the floor deep into playing some complicated-looking board game. They wave. I nod.

"Care to join us?" Olivia asks. "We could use a sixth. We're beta-testing *Liberators of Catan*. It's this TTG I created that's kind of like a feminist, Marxist, postcolonial send-up of all those old board games our parents love that perpetuate oppressive, racist settler mechanics."

"Thanks, but maybe some other time," I say, having no idea what she's talking about.

"Suit yourself. Good luck finding Asa. Can't wait for the show to start!"

"Right."

That leaves one last bedroom.

I step up to the door and listen for a moment to make sure I'm not interrupting anyone's sexy times. No grunting or moaning. Just the sound of a strumming guitar.

I knock.

The guitar stops. But nobody comes to the door.

I wait. Knock again.

More silence.

But then the door cracks open, and there's Asa Rao. Surprise flashes across her face. And then anger. She crosses her arms over her chest. I don't know if it's because we haven't been face to face in a while or what, but she looks even more beautiful than I remember.

"Asa Rao." I do that pew-pew-pew motion with my fingers for some reason.

She looks down at my finger guns. Doesn't even crack a smile.

I holster them.

"If it isn't Seymour Gutierrez Navarro," she says. "The 'real talent.'"

I cringe at my own words from five months ago being thrown back at me.

She glares. "What do you want?"

"Can we talk?"

"I'm kind of busy."

"I want to apol—"

She pushes me back a little, then slams the door right in my face.

# JRUE EDWARDS

### THE CLASS CLOWN

### Sadie 🤍

FRIDAY, 10:13 P.M.

**JRUE:**
haven't seen you in a bit, guessing you're
hanging out in a closet somewhere lol

**SADIE:**
Um why would I be in a closet? You think I'm
such a party loser I'd hide in a closet??

**JRUE:**
bruh, tf?! no, I meant you're in
a closet getting ur smooch on

**SADIE:**
Ew, smooch sounds like I'm making out with Briana

**JRUE:**
briana?!

**SADIE:**
Um the goat we stole last night, broke into a barn, any of this ringing a bell??

**JRUE:**
brenda

**SADIE:**
Who's Brenda??

**JRUE:**
briana is brenda! Lolol

**SADIE:**
Also, I'm still a kiss virgin, thanks v much for reminding me.

**JRUE:**
hahaha, as if you could forget w ur thirsty ass

**SADIE:**
😐😐😐

🖕

And how's Mission: Make-out and Marry Mia McKenzie going?

**JRUE:**
damn, all those m's huh? It's not going YET. We're texting rn tho so should be scones

soon*

**SADIE:**
Damn, I want a scone now 😭

**JRUE:**
easy, betty crock o' shit

**SADIE:**
Whatever, Dry Fieri. Phone's dying . . .

**JRUE:**
🖕

# Mia

**MIA:**
💥
Hey you, we still gotta talk

**JRUE:**
oh yeah, I got u lol

**MIA:**
Ur cute

**JRUE:**
who, me??

**MIA:**
Oh fuck I thought I was texting the other kid
in my phone who spells drew jrue, sorrrryyyyyy

**JRUE:**
it's a rly common spelling, so I get it lol

**MIA:**
You know what I don't get, why ppl spell it Drew

**JRUE:**
yo that's what I'm saying!! ty!!

**MIA:**
I just feel bad cuz you're never gonna experience the joys of
receiving gas station souvenirs with your name on them

**JRUE:**
yeah we all have our crosses hahaha

mine is knowing I'll never get a plastic
mini-license plate unless it says DREW

**MIA:**

😆

So how do you intro urself

**JRUE:**
huh? wym

**MIA:**
R u like hi I'm drew with a j

**JRUE:**
lmfao I say rue with a j

**MIA:**
Nice to meet you jue

**JRUE:**
ur dumb ugh lol

**MIA:**
Lol if only u knew my friend

Soooo

**JRUE:**
soooo what lol

**MIA:**
When can we talk

**JRUE:**
whenever's cool with me

**MIA:**
Come find me later??

**JRUE:**
for sure

**MIA:**

# CARLA SCHMIDT

## THE COOL MOM

## PART I

*DON'T BE A KAREN.*

I repeat my mantra to myself as I pull in across from the Dixons', which, as my two kids say, is *bumpin'*. Or is it *bussing*? What the fuck is bussing? I barely get into my driveway because some high schoolers are parked past the curb. I should say something. But . . .

*Don't be that kind of mom.*

I'm not a Karen. I'm a Carla. *Just your typical Chicago mom,* I used to say, until Sky told me it was a microaggression to "conflate typicality with your assumed whiteness," which isn't even what I meant, but the way he said it . . . with so much pity. Where do preteens get all that superiority? The internet? I checked a social media site on the internet once, and it was all talking heads trying on makeup. I seriously don't get it, and I guess that's the problem. Which is why it bears repeating to myself:

*Don't be a Karen.*

A confession: my middle name actually *is* Karen. Carla Karen-Anne Schmidt. I know what you're thinking, but I'm not that kind of lady. Not that kind of mom. I'm cool, open to feedback, and *not* the kind of person who calls the cops.

But, really, do they need to have the music up so loud? Why is there so much moaning in modern music? I hustle inside, lyrics expounding upon wet-ass . . . vaginas.

"Sky! Matthew! Help me with the bags!"

My twelve-year-old twins sluggishly emerge from the basement, their eyes glassy from staring at their computers. Another night lost to Minecraft, I guess. I'm past trying to get them to do other stuff like, I don't know, read. Their father never lets them use screens, so I get stuck with zombies on my weekends, but at least they're *my* zombies. They trudge outside but leave the door open, and I yell, "Hey, the door!"

They turn, shrug in unison, and grin. Creepy twin shit that I can never admit is creepy twin shit.

"Daisy got out," Sky says.

"On our walk. She saw D."

DeAndre, Daisy's favorite human outside of our family and I guess mine, too. DeAndre is the one hosting the party across the street. I point at the house, which is practically bouncing with vibes. Is that how you use "vibes"?

"You let Daisy go during a walk?"

The twins shrug, once again in unison.

"And she ran into the Dixons'?"

They shake their heads. Matthew says, "No, a guy in a cowboy hat picked her up and carried her inside."

"You let Daisy get *dognapped*?"

The twins finally crack a mutual, sly grin as I begin to lose my cool. This is precisely when I'd call the ex-husband if this was one year ago, but that's not gonna happen.

"We can go get her," Sky says. Matt adds, "We'll be really quick. DeAndre said we were *always* allowed to come hang out if he was home, remember?"

I clap my hands, ending this charade. "Groceries. Now. I'll handle Daisy. And don't keep the door open."

Inside, I curse under my breath. My ex can't find out about this. I fought hard for Daisy in the divorce, swearing on my thirty-eight years of life that I would take good care of her. She wants for nothing. She eats better than I do. She has a freaking stroller that I don't even bother putting away anymore; it fills up the entryway where everyone's shoes used to live.

And suddenly I'm sad, but I shove that feeling away, like I've learned to do. Focus on Daisy. Really, I should have seen this coming. How does she always run off right before an early-morning visit to the doggy salon? How does she know? I swear, she has informants. I compose myself and dial Mrs. Dixon, but the second she picks up I realize what I'm doing, scream, and throw the phone away from me. What am I *thinking*? I was in high school once, and I threw plenty of parties, and my own parents never knew about any of them until we finally got caught, which was only because someone drove the lawn mower into the pool. I can't expose DeAndre! The twins will never forgive me if I cost them their hero.

Mrs. Dixon, of course, calls back. I answer, voice trembling, and make up a lie about someone stealing Amazon packages. She says she'll make sure to bring them into the house quickly, then rushes off the phone.

*Think, Carla, think.*

I scroll through neighborhood association emails until I find the Dixon landline. I try that, expecting DeAndre to know better than to pick up a phone in the middle of a big party. But someone does pick up.

"Hello, it's me," says a haunted, feminine voice in a bad British accent.

"Adele?" I guess.

The person giggles. "Merrill, actually. A pleasure to meet you."

She's lost the accent. In the background, I hear people shouting and laughing, and music, of course.

I put on my mom voice. My *friendly* mom voice. "Sweetie, hi. Is DeAndre there? He's not in trouble, I promise. I'm just looking for my dog. Her name is Daisy, and she's a brown-and-white pit bull terrier. She ran away on her walk. You see, I'm—" I cut myself off before I admit that I'm a full-fledged adult dialing into what I'm sure is the party of the year.

Merrill, or Adele, or whoever, is giggling.

"O wise voice from beyond, it is a dog-eat-dog world," she says through a fit of giggles.

"Very funny. Have you seen her?"

"Everyone loves Daisy. Everyone just wants to *gobble* her up!"

I laugh, but I'm getting nervous. There's something so strange about this conversation, and I realize it's because half of it is high, and it's certainly not *my* half.

"Merrill, sweetie, do you need help?" I ask. "Did someone give you something? You can tell me. You won't be in trouble. I'm just trying to help and get my dog back."

The girl's voice chokes up with a dramatic sob. "My quest is ruined. My unicorn queen has escaped. The dark star of loss rises over us, and now the maiden Daisy moves beyond the veil!"

The what? I have HBO. I know something bad when I see it. Or hear it. I click into stern-mom mode. The stuff of a PTA veteran who just got through the divorce of a lifetime.

"Merrill, that's enough. I'm going to need you to calm down and tell me exactly where my dog—"

"Daisy! Maiden Daisy! We mourn thee!"

Merrill is getting faint, like she's backing away from the phone. The clamor swallows up her voice, and I'm left yelling, "Don't go! I'm coming over! Don't do anything to my fucking dog, you psychos!"

The line hangs up. A chill rushes over me, and I shiver. What did she mean? Was she on bath salts? Isn't that just a Floridian meme? What do I do? Do teens eat dogs? Is *that* a meme?

I dial:

9

1

1

But my thumb hovers over the green call button. A few years ago, I used to think that was just what you did if you needed help. Not so. Not now. I don't trust the police, and I don't need them making this worse. What I need is . . .

I open my closet, pushing all the way to the back, to the dresses I haven't worn since my stint as an eternal bridesmaid in my late twenties.

Cheetah print.

What I need is cheetah print. I hold my breath as I rush into a slinky, stretchy dress. Then I drag dark liner around my eyes and shake out my hair, which, thank god, is long and curly. Not that typical Karen cut with the helmet-looking bangs and the blown-out back, like they all fell asleep on grenades. God, I can just envision the videos online of those entitled, horrible women. I do whatever I can to make sure I look nothing like them. I grab a big sun hat from the coat closet, big glasses, and a spare lipstick off the cluttered table in the entryway.

"Boys?" I call down to the basement, into silence and the sound of little fingers typing on laptop keyboards. "Mom's going out. Don't answer the door for anyone, don't share identifiable information with strangers on the internet, and . . ."

"Don't invest in cryptocurrency!" they call back, bored.

"Good boys!" I affirm.

I glance at myself one more time in the mirror. I look . . . strange. Not bad, but different, yet also familiar. It takes me a second to identify that I'm feeling the feeling of looking at an old photograph of yourself, wondering where that person faded away to. Except she's back before me, in a party dress I've nearly donated every year for the past eleven years, and she looks *hot*.

And I think: *Mrs. Schmidt decided she would rescue the dog herself.*

And then I catch myself. I'm *Ms.* Schmidt, these days. That stings to keep reminding myself, but there's no time to wallow. *Ms.* Schmidt decided she would rescue the dog herself.

I give my girls a little lift. And by "girls," I mean my boobs, because we use anatomically correct language in this house, and then I'm off across my lawn. The sounds of the party assault me. No, beckon me. I need to adjust my attitude if I'm really going to do this. But who am I kidding? This is like when those adults play kids on TV. Somehow, this might even be worse than Ben Platt looking like a Claymation horror in *Dear Evan Hansen*.

I step into the road, my ankles wobbling in my heels.

*Enough, Carla,* I think. *You don't care about any of this. This isn't about you at all. It's about . . .*

"Daisy's mom," a voice intones from the Dixons' lawn. I halt. Before me is a girl hunched over hands that fold and unfold, like she's anxious. Instantly, I know who I'm speaking to.

"Merrill. Hi, dear. I'm—"

"Daisy's mom. I know. Here, want a cookie?"

She hands me a cookie. Just hands it to me, no platter, no tin, no nothing. It's warm from her hand. To appease the wild stare in her eyes, I take a little nibble. I gag. It tastes like no cookie should taste, and I realize that's because it's probably drugged. You can drug cookies now, I read that on Facebook. I go to drop it in the grass but halt—Daisy or another dog will find it and gobble it up, and then what happens? Facebook has given me shockingly few details on how to handle high dogs. I just hold the cookie and try to look cool, or fresh, or super fly or . . . I don't know. I try to look like anyone other than me, which is a mom living on the edge.

"Come," Merrill says, and she runs into the party.

I should go home. What if I'm high now? The boys shouldn't be on their laptops all night. There are a million things for a mom to do, and none of them are infiltrating a party to rescue a dog that's probably having the time of her life wrestling the body glitter off drunk teenagers.

But tonight, I'm not a regular mom. I'm a *cool* mom. I'm a mom in cheetah print.

Hang on, Daisy, Mama's comin'!

# MEMI MATSON

## THE ACTOR

## PART II

### RISING ACTION

I'M DRINKING A TALLBOY, A CHERRY HARD SELT-zer, and laughing with friends. I accept unanimous rave reviews on my outfit: a sleeveless ivory bodice top with a chiffon cape (courtesy of the incredibly talented Miranda) and faded, vintage boyfriend Levi's. My light bronze skin glows from shimmer body oil.

Blake's signature cologne—Prada Luna Rossa Carbon—arrives three seconds before he wraps his arms around me from behind. He brushes my long copper waves to the side to kiss my neck.

"At last, my Juliet," he purrs into my ear.

My legs go weak. I remain enveloped in Blake's arms. My friends cheer as he leads me toward the makeshift dance area. Oblivious to the fast beats, we sway with my back still pressed against his chest. I turn enough to kiss his freshly shaven cheek.

Beneath the cologne, I detect his deodorant, shampoo, and toothpaste. He smells clean and fresh. I look up at him. Oh. My. God. Blake Donnelly is movie-star gorgeous. My most handsome costar of any production, either in high school or community theater.

His strawberry-blond man-bun is the only version of an updo that works for me. He committed to growing out his hair last December when the *Gazette* first reported that Florence Hills High School would be doing *Romeo and Juliet*. Blake wanted his Romeo to be part Leonardo DiCaprio in Baz Luhrmann's version and part Chris Hemsworth, though more *Rush* than *Thor*. We teased him about filling the house (theater-speak for audience) with thirsty moms. Completely spot-on.

Blake grinds against me. Not in a gross way, but in a slow and sexy way that makes me tingle with anticipation for what will happen between us tonight.

I'm aware of my reputation for showmances—but having an intense relationship with a costar is part of my artistic process. I don't sleep with every actor cast opposite me. What is this, Hollywood circa 1950? It obviously depends on whether I actually like them. Besides, there are different ways to get closure. When we did *Clue,* I adored Max Sato as Professor Plum, and we spent a postproduction day together at Navy Pier. After *Almost, Maine* wrapped, I took Jeff Berkeley (who played East to my Glory) to see Blue Man Group (which he had never experienced) at the Briar Street Theatre. We pregamed hard, spent the entire show drunkenly kissing, and never spoke again. I did have sex last semester with Ron Flint, my *Radium Girls* costar. He was sweet and funny, and hoped for more, but all showmances have an expiration date. I commit myself to the production. I'm talking significant time and energy. And when it's over, I celebrate with the person I bonded most closely with. Then I get my hair extensions removed and that's it. Over and done. Closure. Time to recharge so I am ready for the next opportunity. This summer that means a local community theater. Auditions are coming up for *A Midsummer Night's Dream*.

After another song where we find a slow rhythm hidden within the pulsating beat, Blake walks us over to an oversized recliner. He sits down still holding me and being careful to drape my long chiffon cape over the arm of the chair.

"Memi, what a week! You wouldn't believe the auditions." Blake gazes somewhere beyond the house party, reliving the experience. He proceeds to tell me about each one.

Half listening, I sip my drink and continue to gaze at him, imagining our beautiful swan song together. Tonight.

"—but nothing compares to the first audition. I'm glad we started with the hardest one on Tuesday. Everything else was easier—"

Wait a minute. Tuesday?

"I thought your audition was Monday," I say. "That's why you needed to fly to LA on Sunday."

Blake shifts uncomfortably and, since I'm sitting on his lap, it moves me as well.

"Oh, I needed Monday to get myself in the right headspace. Got some sun. Relaxed. It really helped with the Star Trek audition." He flashes a smile that could be a cosmetic dentistry ad. "I have a good feeling about it, Memi."

"But you left us high and dry on Sunday!" I stand and stare incredulously at Blake.

"Yeah . . . that's why we have understudies," he says.

"While you were flying to LA, Chance Jackson ruined my

final performance." My cape flutters as I gesture wildly. "People fucking laughed at me."

"Sweetheart . . ." Blake holds out his hand. "I'm sorry."

I let him grasp my hand. When he tugs for me to rejoin him in the chair, I remain standing firmly.

"I'm too upset to accept an apology right now. I need some fresh air." I pull away. "Let's talk a little later tonight." What? He might've left me high and dry, but he's still hot.

His eyebrows raise in surprise as I turn and walk away.

I make a brief stop in the kitchen for another tallboy. Plunging my hand into the ice-filled cooler, I feel for a can. Pulling out a Four Loko, I'm about to try for something else, but . . . you know what? Screw it.

I wipe the can with a paper towel and pop the top. Sour grape tastes better than I expected. Drink in hand, I walk outside for fresh air and text Zara. Zara, Miranda, and I are the only lab group in AP Chem. We talk about Miranda and Savoy's fashion fight. I say nothing about Blake Donnelly.

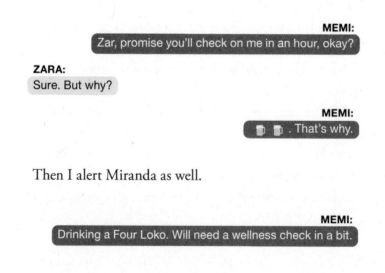

**MEMI:**
Zar, promise you'll check on me in an hour, okay?

**ZARA:**
Sure. But why?

**MEMI:**
🍺 🍺 . That's why.

Then I alert Miranda as well.

**MEMI:**
Drinking a Four Loko. Will need a wellness check in a bit.

While waiting for her reply, I open Trendsettr and get an eyeful of Miranda-versus-Savoy replays. Zara promises to find me in an hour. I chug more of my drink on the front lawn and take deep breaths of the cool evening air. A dog approaches, and I freeze. It's some sort of pit bull mix but with a stubby, wagging tail. The pupper sniffs my dyed jeans. I hold out my hand. Pretend I'm a person who isn't afraid of dogs. This sweetheart licks my fingers, so I respond with some head scratches that have its tail wiggling even faster.

My thoughts go back to Blake. He ditched our final performance on Sunday. He also ditched the wrap party tonight. That's not closure; that's being an inconsiderate asshole. He's been a dream throughout this five-month experience. How could he let me—us—down at the very end? I want to embrace the anger before I let it go. Just immerse myself. Then I can leave it behind and rejoin Blake for our closure, as planned.

I recall the audience laughter from Sunday. Chance brought a different energy to the role than Blake had. It threw me off my game. Then he did something so unexpected that I forgot my lines and went silent for what seemed to be many agonizing minutes. And when I did speak, they all laughed at me. It was worse than a nightmare because there was nothing to wake up from.

A group of people approach DeAndre's house from the street. Familiar voices that become even more lively when they see me.

"Memi!" a few castmates shout in unison.

I shout back, suddenly overjoyed they're here as if it's been days instead of an hour since we last parted. Hugs flow freely. I tell them I'm deep in Four Loko.

Then I spot him. The tall, slender figure with wavy, dark brown hair that, for once, isn't lacquered in product.

Chance Jackson. The other Romeo that I am furious with.

"You," I say venomously.

Chance tells the group to go inside and that he'll look after me.

"Even with this harsh lighting, Mem Matson always glows."

"You," I repeat. "You Potawatomis are always taking short-cuts. It's Memi, not Mem."

"Saves time. Gets us where we want to go faster, aaayyye." The pendant light over the front entrance catches Chance's smile.

I take a step back and cross my arms. With as withering a stare as I can muster, I make a dramatic show of looking Chance up and down. He's wearing button-fly Levi's, vintage like mine. The rest of his fashion choices are hella casual, though: a T-shirt from the Chicago powwow last fall and old Chucks that may have come from a dumpster.

"It irritates me when rich people wear scroungy footwear," I announce. Don't even get me started on Golden Goose sneakers.

"I'm sorry for hanging on to my favorite shoes?" Chance's voice isn't apologetic at all. It sounds like he's mocking me.

"That's the second crappy apology I got today."

"Who's responsible for the first one?" he asks.

"I'm not talking about Blake with you." Each time I say the word "you" to Chance, it seems to lengthen.

"Hmmm. And wherefore art Romeo number one? Full of stories about Hollywood?" Chance looks toward the house. The music is so loud that the bass makes the ground reverberate with tiny earthquake tremors.

" 'Wherefore art' means 'why' in Shakespearean language," I correct.

"Does 'whyfore art' mean 'where'?" He flashes another mischievous grin.

I look away, refusing to interact further. My fingertips smooth my hair from my temples, up to my high half ponytail before I wrap the long red extensions into a makeshift bun.

"What color you gonna try next?" Chance points with his lips toward my hair.

Chance's and mine are not the only Anishinaabe families in town. After all, Chicago has the third-largest Native population in the country. Usually when someone does something that reminds me of my cousins back home on the rez, like pointing with their lips or ending a sentence with an exaggerated aaayyye, it's a comfort.

Not tonight, though. I don't want anything about Chance to be familiar.

"My vote is for blue hair with black tips," he offers. "The blue morpho butterfly's wings are electric blue with black edges. They're rare and larger than life. Like me." He adds a wink.

"My hair choices are not an Insta poll, Chance," I say, despite Miranda having suggested I do exactly that.

The front door opens as a couple leaves. I catch a glimpse of the party inside and decide that's where I'd rather be.

"I am done with youuuu." For some reason, marching away from Chance seems like a better option than walking.

"Whatever you say, Blue Morpho Mem."

### Ten Things I Loathe About Chance Jackson:

1. He knows my routine of trying a new hair color between roles. I don't like him knowing anything about me.
2. It's unfair for a guy to have eyelashes like that. I

overhead him telling my understudy that he wears contacts because his lashes kept brushing against his glasses. Apparently, having long and luxurious eyelashes is burdensome.

3. He behaves unpredictably. I blame his love of improv. Here I expected him to bring up what happened on closing night but instead he says something random about my hair.

4. He shellacs his hair with so much product. It turns his beautiful soft curls into a greasy dark brown helmet.

5. His Potawatomi tribe will pay for him to attend any college, anywhere, for as many degrees as he cares to earn. Okay, so I don't loathe him for this. I'm just hella envious because my tribe's casino operates primarily to keep members employed. My dad jokes that our reservation is so far north and so remote that even the internet gets brought in by dogsled.

6. He's a know-it-all—always mentioning different species of butterflies. Just because my full name, Memingwaans, is Ojibwe for "butterfly," it doesn't mean I want to hear all about them.

7. He is the only person who calls me Mem. Even my brother's nickname for me (Moth) is less annoying.

8. He knows about my dad's least-proud moment. It's the reason why his dad and mine don't talk, even though they were in high school together. I don't like Chance knowing about it and judging my dad.

9. He is responsible for the worst stage performance in FHHS history.

10. He knows I will Google the blue morpho butterfly.

# SAVOY

## THE INFLUENCER

## *PART II*

THE BEST PARTIES TURN US INSIDE OUT. FLIP US around, reverse us. For instance, here I am, Savoy, famously hot (but not dumb), looking decidedly un-hot while rather dumbly making out with my secret girlfriend on the roof of a house containing approximately ninety-nine percent of our high school class.

Whatever. It's magical up here. Because of the nature of my relationship with Miranda, we never get to enjoy time together in public, yet here we are: not in public, but above it. Just two anonymous shadows tucked into the darkness just out of the party's reach. It's thrilling and scandalous and . . . am I turned on?

I know Miranda is. She nearly gets me completely out of my ruined bodysuit, and we both nearly topple right off the roof and into the pool. Then she is laughing, laughing, laughing, and I'm begging her to be quiet as I try to pull my pants back on, but I'm laughing, too. I think I hear someone shout up a question from below—*Hey, who's up there?*—so we flatten ourselves onto the roof and play dead, silently in stitches as we look up at the stars.

The whole scene is a mess, but it's also very us. The flirtation with danger has always been central to how we like to do things, but never has it presented itself as literal danger.

Dressed again, we scoot closer, and kiss one more time. A slow kiss now, a restrained kiss, because that's all you can afford when your whole world balances upon an edge like ours.

"So," I say, breaking the kiss.

"So," Miranda says.

The stuff we haven't said yet fills in the big silence I've triggered.

"This is it," I finally blurt.

"Say what you mean, Savoy."

I blow out a long breath. I can't look at Miranda, so I stare at the Ferris wheel so hard I think I can almost see all the couples making out in those rocking, candy-colored pods. Regular people on regular dates. Not like Miranda and me. Our skyborne kisses lack the safety, the security.

And I'm sick of it.

"Savoy?" she prods me.

We've only got a few more minutes up here before we need to go find our respective camps. I should say exactly what I need to, while I have her.

"You're leaving," I blurt. "In a few weeks you're going to New York, then you've got college and . . . and I hate it."

Miranda sighs. We might be in love, but it's a dramatic, irregular love that connects us. Talking—being honest and vulnerable like this—is not how we do things.

"You've known about my plans since we were kids," Miranda says. "I thought you were proud of me for getting into FIT?"

"Of course I'm proud of you. But that doesn't mean I'm excited for you to leave me behind."

"I can't stay in Florence Hills forever, Savoy. Neither of us can. Isn't that why we do what we do? The rivalry, the act? So that we can build something that'll carry us out of here? So that you can create a career without blowing your mom's savings on college?"

I finally feel the chill of the night on my bare skin. The inch of distance between us suddenly feels like a football field. A football field dotted in land mines. Miranda has money, I don't. It's always impacted the way we run toward our similar goals. And now, as high school ends, our paths are about to split.

"That's not what I'm saying. You've got your plans, and I have mine, and I know all our hard work is going to be so worth it. But . . . it's just . . ."

I close my eyes, surprise tears welling up and causing the Ferris wheel to wobble terribly. I push myself to say what's been pulling at me for a while now.

"Do you ever feel like we're wasting time, not being together openly? I know we both love the drama of it all, but how long are we going to keep this up? Can a rivalry like ours be long-distance?"

Miranda finally understands. I can tell because she doesn't immediately respond with a sassy evasion. After a minute she says, "It's not forever. I'll move to New York and make a million friends. Powerful, gay friends. We'll use them to help get you a job someplace cute, like a boutique. We'll stage a welcome party–bloodbath combo at LaGuardia when you arrive. A runway walk-off in the Guggenheim. A fistfight in Central Park, just in jeans."

I laugh.

Miranda nudges me. "We'll do it right where they park the horses. I've got everything planned."

"Babe, you don't park horses," I laugh, but the laugh turns blue and sad as her words sink in. "Where in your plan does our rivalry end?"

"You're not having fun?"

"I am, but . . ."

My throat closes. My eyes burn with fresh tears, so sudden I almost can't hide them. I'm whispering when I say, "I just want to dance with you."

"In front of everyone?"

"In front of the whole world."

Miranda takes my hand. We keep our eyes ahead, visions of the future turning in my mind.

"That's in my plan, too. Don't you worry," she says.

But I know something now. Miranda doesn't have a plan. There is no end in sight. We will go our separate ways, and our love-hate-whatever-you-call-it will wilt without ever really being allowed to bloom. Her silence confirms this. And something about the eternity that appears before us breaks me. The excitement, the sparks—they fade. I feel a futility that's been waiting there for me, in the far future. It reaches through time and takes ahold of me, here on this roof, with all of Florence Hills High jumping beneath us.

I pull away.

I've been dumb, I realize. I've let this go on for too long, thinking we were building something, but all we've built is a chasm that neither of us can cross without it costing both of us everything.

Miranda finds my hand again and squeezes. I look at her, and I'm surprised to find that sometime in the last few minutes, a tear has carved through her eyeliner. I've never seen her cry.

"Soon," she says. "We'll figure it out. When the timing is right."

"What about tonight?" I propose.

"Tonight?" Miranda's sureness falters. I hate seeing her like this, unsure and stumbling, but I need clarity. If not tonight, when? I can accept tomorrow, or next month. I can even accept never because that would be enough to tell me to move on.

What I can't accept is a lifetime of "not yet."

I hold up my phone, showing her the anonymous message accusing us of faking our feud. In the past hour, it's gotten traction on the app, people speculating about where we've both disappeared to in the aftermath of our fight.

"People are talking," I say. "If we don't expose ourselves, someone else might. And then what will our friends do?"

"Kill us for sure," Miranda says, all grim.

"So? What about tonight?"

It's now or never. Expose ourselves and try, for real, or double down on the fantasy of our feud for good and lose any chance of discovering if we could make this work in reality. Before Miranda can answer, a shout cuts the night around us.

"Savoy? Are you out here?"

Miranda is catlike. She slips down the roof, lying flat on the shingles and holding on to the ridge with just her hands. I scoot to hide her right as a phone flashlight grabs onto me from behind.

"Grant!" I say, a big smile on my face. "You found me!"

Grant lowers the light and peers at me from the edge of the roof we crawled over, where the balcony must be. I'm talking to his floating head.

"You good? We're ready for phase two. You need to get dressed."

He helps me down, no sign in his stern expression that he saw Miranda.

"Needed a minute?" Grant asks before we reenter the bedroom. Effie and Mirage are glued to their phones. A group of girls knock on the bathroom door, but it's still obviously locked from the inside. I make a mental note to fix that later.

"Yeah, sorry for running off. I was pretty heated," I tell Grant.

"I don't blame you. That was dirty, what she did." Grant balls his fists up and there's real anger in his face. I deduce that he doesn't know our secret. He confirms this when he says, "Whatever Miranda's got planned for the rest of the night, I don't think it'll go so well. Two can play at sabotage."

"It's cool, Grant. We got our shots," I remind him.

"But the jacket is ruined."

The jacket, abandoned in the sink, is for sure ruined.

"The good news," Grant says, "is that there's tons of buzz about the fight. Effie went live right after and interviewed a bunch of people who saw it. Mirage said we should give you time to calm down, so we've been scouting out the best—"

"And worst!" Effie adds.

"Yes, the best and *worst* outfits of the night—thank you, Effie—for our spotlight segment."

Grant says this with flair, knowing I normally love to run our spotlights, where we interview partygoers about their outfits and then post them online so that the loyal legions of SAVOY followers can hype them up. But I'm not feeling the hype right now. I'm distracted. Sad. A million miles away, and from that distance, our project seems so small and pointless.

Grant nudges me. "We're just waiting on you. You're still up for our antics, right?"

As if to coax me, Effie says, "Fernanda is wearing a dress for probably the second time ever, after prom, and she looks so hot. I'm *not* missing my chance to tell her."

"And," Mirage adds, "you said for yourself that you wanted to actually, you know . . . party? Hang out? Now's our chance."

They're right. There is so much joy around me. I have no right to ignore it just because my heart is hurting. For all my friends know, I don't even have a heart to break in the first place. Remembering that, I stand up straight and ask Mirage, "Where's my next look?"

AS I PULL on a pair of hyperdistressed overalls, the group gives me updates on what I've missed.

"Blake is back from LA, or wherever he was, and of course Memi was *right* at his side. That said, she looks good. Vintage Levi's, I think?"

"We're not interviewing Memi. She's Team Miranda, remember?"

"Sy was spotted with equipment and there's a rumor on Trendsettr that there's gonna be a No Kevin in Team reunion, so maybe we should get you back in the band T-shirt under the overalls?"

I nod my approval. The shirt is thrown my way, and when I point at a pair of sewing scissors in our supplies, those are passed to me, too.

"Oh! And someone gave Merrill psychedelics and locked her in the linen closet for her own safety before she tried to probe someone's brain with a potato peeler."

"A potato peeler?"

"Vintage Sur La Table. That's what I commented. Funny, right? Anyway, she got out. So let's try not to get probed or peeled, okay?"

I interrupt the gossip and ask, "What about Oscar?" If I can get to him, maybe he can fiddle around with the code of the app and figure out who's trying to expose Miranda and me. Then I can kill the scandal within the scandal for good and leave our act untarnished.

"Oscar?" Effie's eyebrows go up. "He's . . . wearing Oscar clothes. Nothing wild. Why?"

"Let's find him," I say. "Give him some shine, you know? We owe him for building all that techy stuff."

With expert speed, I snip tiny holes into my band T-shirt to give it a more distressed look, faking focus on that so that no one catches on to my real reasons for seeking Oscar.

"Fine," Grant says, jotting down Oscar's name on his tablet, where I guess he's created an agenda. "Shall we start, then?"

There's an art to interviewing people about their clothes, and I daresay SAVOY has perfected it.

First, you find the right subjects. Every party—every time we go out, whether it be to the mall, to the movies, or for bubble tea—we keep an eye out for people who dress with a strong sense of personal style. Miranda would probably scan for labels and brands, but we look for a point of view. That flair or edge that emanates off a person when they feel good in what they've got on, whether it be a ball gown or basketball shorts.

I scan the party for the people on Grant's list, but instead zero in on a flash of cheetah print hiding in the dining room. Perfect. I approach the person, waiting to recognize them, but make it all the way in front of them convinced I've never seen them before.

Oh well. I open my mouth and out comes "Cheetah print! My favorite neutral!"

Second, you gas them up. You don't just tell them what you like, you tell them why you like it. I add, "People who wear cheetah print have the best stories."

The person blinks at me through huge sunglasses, which is, yes, weird for a night ensemble, but whatever. I've worn weirder. I've worn weirder *tonight*.

"Thanks," the person squeaks. They seem to be distracted by the camera in Effie's hands and the spotlight from Grant's phone held up to light us in the room's dimness.

Third—and this is the big one for a good interview—you ask the right questions.

I ask, "Dressed for the hunt tonight? Or simply blending into the wild? What did you envision for the night when you picked this look?"

A common misconception about fashion influencers is that we only care about the clothes. It would be more correct to say we care about taste. When I want to know a person, I don't ask them what they're wearing. I ask them why.

"I envisioned a night of new beginnings. An adventure, like from someone else's life," our new friend says, a bit wistfully. "But I wanted to feel like my old self doing it. I haven't worn this dress in years. I didn't think it would fit but look!"

I take their hand and give them a twirl.

"So somehow in one outfit, you've combined personal history and dreamy potential. That's not easy! Goes to show you that sometimes our closets hold more than we know!"

"Like skeletons," Effie adds, just loud enough for me to catch it. I'm sure the camera picked it up, too. I play her words off like one of the many jokes we sprinkle into our fashion highlights but note the evil twist of Effie's grin visible behind the glare of Grant's light.

"Skeletons would suit the deadly cheetah, but only if it's been well fed," I say quickly, catching hold of the conversation once again. "Tell me, with your old-new attire, do you feel ready to make a catch tonight, or is this kitty keeping solitary?"

We keep the interviews going like this for a bit, picking names from Grant's list and snagging people out of the crowd when we see an outfit choice we love. We end up back in the kitchen, fresh drinks in hand, and every time I take a sip, Effie refills my cup.

"Relaaaax, Savoy," she shouts at one point, misreading my face as I scan for Oscar. "You're doing great. We're getting plenty of good stuff. We can take a break, can't we?"

"I don't want to be sloshed for phase three," I shout back. "And I don't want any of you to be too drunk, either. We've got a job to do, remember?"

Effie cackles. "Weren't you the one making us take swigs of vodka from the bottle like a bunch of pirates? My, how the turns have tabled!" She's playing up her inebriation to get a rise out of me. It's working. Despite the jovial atmosphere, I'm starting to feel the pinch of several potential disasters all converging at once. Someone knows about Miranda and me. Effie is acting weird. Miranda is probably still stranded on the roof. I'm sure I left that sink running in the primary bedroom's locked bathroom. And on and on.

"Chill out, Savoy. We'll find Oscar, I promise," Grant says, arm hanging over Effie's shoulder. Blush fills his cheeks and neck. He's not faking being drunk, like Effie.

"Actually, we won't," Mirage adds. She holds her cup with two hands, like an adorable elf. "He tried to do a performance before, totally bombed, and people are saying he ran upstairs to the bathroom. Door's been closed awhile. Sounds . . . pretty bad."

I almost swear in frustration, but that wouldn't make sense with the lie I've spun with the group, so I just shrug and make a comment about getting changed so we can switch to phase three.

"Oh, and before we do, check this out, babyyyyy." Grant flips around his tablet. "SAVOY is ahead in the poll. By a lot!"

The fucking poll. The content. It's what I should be focused on, but all I can think of is Miranda stranded on the roof, flat on her stomach, gripping the edge with her extra-long, coffin-tipped nails. Clinging to a hiding spot, just like she likes. Suddenly, imagining her like that, I'm mad.

I leave her up there, just like she's going to leave me behind in just a matter of weeks, and I return to the world of Grant's hungry determination.

"Good. Let's move on to phase three, then."

"But first!" Effie shouts. "A drink!"

Her voice is loud enough that the immediate crowd around us hears, cheers, and raises their cups.

"Bottoms up!" Effie calls, and even though I'm already way too tipsy I have no choice but to down the remainder of what I think was once a gin and tonic. I take a huge gulp and that's when Effie leans in real close and says, "I hope you enjoyed your little break. Miranda seemed to need one, too."

I stifle a choke and swipe the burning gin from my chin. Effie grins, satisfied with my shock. Does she know? Could she be the one? Is this particular call for honesty coming from inside the fashion house?

Effie takes my cup and chugs the last inch of my gross drink without breaking our little staring match. And that's how I know.

I'm fucked. We're fucked.

One way or another, SAVOY will die tonight.

# SADIE BERNBAUM

## THE SCHOOL PAPER EDITOR; KNOWER OF ALL TEA

### PART II

COOL COOL COOL. JRUE GOT SWEPT UP IN HIS goat prank madness and without him, I've been back on my bullshit, wandering around and getting into everyone else's business rather than dealing with my own. Normally the constant stream of gossip would burst through my veins like caffeine-fueled adrenaline, but every juicy tidbit I hear about everyone else's hookups is just another reminder of how badly I've failed tonight at being kissed. I push through the crowds toward the dining room to collect my phone and charger. I'm calling an Uber and getting the hell out of here. The dining room cleared out since I was last in here, and I tiptoe around the sticky piles of bottles to the back of the room by the windows and reach behind the curtains where I hid my phone to charge and grab it.

**JRUE:**
Where you at

A selfie of Jrue with Brenda, smiling so big it's a miracle his face doesn't split down the middle, pops up on my screen under his text. Before I can respond, the red low battery warning flashes across the screen before it dies.

"Are you kidding me?" I shout, but when I check the cord from my charger, I bang my knuckles against the empty outlet.

Amazing. Fan-fucking-tastic. Tonight cannot get any worse. I slide down to the floor to will the rapture and Lewis Carmack, one of the basketball team's captains, trips over me.

"Seriously?" I shout at him.

He looks down shocked, like he had no clue there was another human in the room. A loud roar erupts from somewhere above us, and without another word, he double-times it up the stairs. My body moves quicker than it ever has as I follow because commotion = phones and someone has got to have a charger up there. I jog through the house, trying to keep up with Lewis until we make it to a second living room, where chaos abounds. There are so many muscles shouting at each other it's almost as if the house vomited jocks out of the air vents and I can only catch snippets between the bursts of testosterone—words like "sixth," "forfeit," "champions"—but for the first time in my life, I couldn't care less what's going on. I just need to find a way out of here.

"Excuse me." I try to weave my way through the rows of spectators who keep piling in but they push me back, trapping me against the table in the middle of the room. The way people are cramming into the space, I may be trampled.

The headline flashes before my eyes: RUDE PRUDE DIES MIDPARTY, NEVER BEEN KISSED, NOT GOING TO BE MISSED.

Then I see it, a white cord hanging out of a gold cup

centerpiece. Finally, the universe is giving me a break, I think, leaning across the table and grabbing the cup. But then the world goes silent just as my hand closes over the gold cup, just as I look down to see that the cup is not just a cup, but a trophy, and the white cord is not a charger, but a white lanyard with a basketball pendant, just as I realize that tonight can and did get much, much worse.

"Sadie, NOOOOOO!"

I recognize the voice before I face the person it belongs to. Travis Marshall, aka the other cocaptain of the basketball team aka the unfairly attractive combination of Loki and Captain America, perpetually straddling the line between confident and cocky but with enough charm to disarm even the most skeptical aka one of the most popular guys at Florence Hills High aka the worst. Travis takes a sip of his drink, something brown and bubbly, and walks over to me.

"Do you know what this means?" he asks, snatching the trophy from my hands.

Of course I do. Anyone within a hundred-mile radius of Florence Hills would. The basketball team has held the tradition of Beer Olympics at the last house party of the year, every year since house parties started. And like sports traditions, there are superstitions, the most important one being: only those participating in the Olympics touch the trophy.

"It was a mistake!" I shout, and try to slide past him, but he steps to his left, blocking me. I move to the right, but he anticipates my move again.

"Hand it over, Marshall; you're done," Lewis Carmack goads as he walks over, hands outstretched for the gold cup. "I know Jimmy took too many edibles. I just saw him and that weirdo Merrill crawling around the backyard looking for a gnome village on my way up here. Snitchbaum just sealed the deal. You forfeit. I win."

Travis snarls like a wolf who's spotted his dinner, flashing a glimpse of his sparkling white teeth above his perfectly chiseled jawline. "Back up, Carmack!" Travis shouts, and pulls me around to the other side of the table.

"Oh my god. I can wipe the thing down with a Clorox wipe, erase my DNA from it. The basketball gods will never know," I whisper-shout at him.

Travis looks stressed—no, worried—no, pathetic almost. His eyes lock onto mine. "It's not that simple, Sadie. Jimmy never did the tap-in on the trophy, so my team is down one player, which means we can still play, but now . . ."

"Now that I touched it, the player has to be me," I finish his sentence.

Perfect. If I walk away, I ruin one of the main events of this party. If I stick around, I will make a complete fool of myself because even though Jrue and I have had an ongoing one-on-one pong tournament in his basement, I am not exactly champion material and half the party is in here tracking Travis's every move with the same lust as Fernanda does with Kai—wait, that's it!

Lightning strikes me so quickly, my arm hairs sizzle. Proverbial lightning, that is. It's a journalist thing that always happens when I am trying to build a story and find the hook and as it turns out: Travis is the key. Not for the kissing (God no, I can't sell my soul to that devil no matter how desperate I am), but anyone who is anyone is paying attention to him, so if I stay close, all eyes will be on me by association, which means there may still be hope yet for tonight's assignment.

He steps closer so I can practically taste the rum-soaked

desperation. "Please, Sadie." Travis has this golden boy persona, and sure, he can be nice, even charismatic . . . to the people he thinks he can get what he wants out of. But if you don't fit into that category, you end up as the butt of his very basic jokes. I should know. Travis is the person who started the whole "Snitchbaum" nonsense. Plus, I haven't forgotten that in the second grade, he asked me to sit next to him in the cafeteria and then pulled my jorts up and gave me a wedgie in front of our whole class. I know he's expecting me to walk away, everything in me wants to ruin this moment for him, but I can't.

"Save your sob story, Travis, I'm in," I say.

"You are?" he asks, taken aback.

I nod.

He resumes his normal douchey persona and yells across the table to Lewis, "Hope you're ready to get your ass beat by Snitchbaum."

"Oh my g—" I start, but stop myself. I have to play it cool. All eyes are on me and one of those sets of oculi may be inches away from the lips destined to tango with mine.

### Sadie Makes a Plan in Her Head as She Joins the Beer Olympics with the Basketball Team:

1. Move fast.
2. Drink quick.
3. Don't let Travis make a fool of you.

Travis summons the rest of the team with a simple flick of his wrist. Three juniors: Bernard Higgins, who has notoriously terrible breath, rushes over along with Teddy and Toby McMillan, identical twins who, I discovered after using a computer in the library that they forgot to log out of, are set to film a twin dating show on MTV over the summer, and a fellow senior, Marcos, who keeps to himself off court but has been nicknamed the Hammer for how hard he plays on it.

Travis steps to the head of the table. "All right, welcome to the annual Beer Olympics. Per usual, there will be three rounds. Flip cup, beer pong, and shotgun relay. The team with the most wins, wins."

"What impressive alliteration," I say.

The guys on my team look over at me, annoyed and probably confused, but before I can give them a definition of the noun, someone plays the sound of a gym teacher's whistle on their phone, and the teams spring into action.

The first two competitors are the captains, Lewis and Travis. They chug their beers in what seems like a millisecond. Travis finishes his just a hair before Lewis, but Travis stumbles on his first flip and Lewis catches up. He lands his cup facedown on the first try. His team takes the lead, barely.

The next two pairs chug and flip with such coordination you would think they were on a synchronized swimming team rather than opponents. Two more players before me and this game is moving so quickly, I keep having to remind myself to exhale so when my turn comes, I'm ready to drink without choking on carbon dioxide.

The next two are a mess; a junior named Percy chokes on his beer and has to refill what he spit out before. Amateur. Marcos, on our team, chugs like he found water after a drought but then takes a record ten flips before he lands the cup upside down, barely beating the junior, who has recovered, impressively, from his major fumble. Across the table, our rivals continue to lag behind. Meanwhile, next to me, Bernard Higgins keeps the lead, chugging and flipping on the first try.

My turn. The chanting "Go! Go! Go!" drowns my ears as I grab my cup and drink as fast as I can, but from the unfortunately familiar smell of piss water, my stomach starts to feel like it's full of a hot-air balloon halfway through.

By the time I finish, my opponent, Justice Campbell, is completely caught up and we bend down to flip. I can feel the eyes of every person in the room focused on me, but I shut them out and zoom in on the cup, placing it just slightly at an overhang on the end of the table and using the pad of my pointer finger to fly it into the air. Across from me, Justice is doing the same and our cups tumble upward, flipping so many times it makes me dizzy as they both fall onto the table, rolling around, neither landing. We grab them and go at it again. This time, I place the cup a little farther off the table to give it a sturdier flip and we watch them both as they flip twice and head downward, facing in the right direction, two missiles with the same bull's-eye as they crash down. First Justice's, then mine, half a second later.

The whistle blows, Lewis's team ahead 1–0. Travis pulls us together for a huddle as sophomores from the JV team appear in full uniform out of nowhere like Cinderella's mice friends to set up the next game.

"All right, that was close, we need to get them on this next round or it's a wrap. You all know the drill, it's one cup on each side, rapid-fire, knockout. Sade, you are with me, the rest of you pair up however you want."

They clap and roar like they are headed to war. I scan the crowd for Jrue, but of course I don't see him, or Mia. I wonder if he found her—

"Sadie!" Travis waves his hands in my face like I've been hypnotized. "Get your head in the game!"

"All right, baby Zac Efron, relax," I snap.

"Look, hang back and let me take the lead," Travis patronizes as he gives me a feigned gentle squeeze on the shoulder just as the whistle blows.

We face off against Lewis and the junior, already in position, as we scramble to grab our Ping-Pong balls. Prepared, they throw first, but their balls are all over the place and neither comes close. While Lewis sends the junior to collect the balls and dunk them in the water bowl to clean them, Travis throws his at the same time that I throw mine.

"What are you doing?!" he shouts as we watch the balls fly across the table in slow motion.

Both of our Ping-Pong balls barrel downward, Travis's falling slightly before mine, but as they near the cup, Travis's ball starts to go off course, as if pulled toward mine, which is a tad to the left of where it needs to be to land in the center of the cup. The junior from the other team gets into position to throw as our two balls collide just inches over the cup, mine knocking Travis's just enough so it splashes into the beer in front of them. The crowd erupts and Travis throws his arms into the air in triumph and then they are around my waist, lifting me up and spinning me around. I see fire in the eyes of Travis's ex, Tabitha Smart, at the sight of me pushed up against him. A few more people have their brows raised in interest. It's working.

"Looks like you brought in a ringer to pick up the dead weight you were carrying," Lewis trolls Travis from across the table. Truer frenemies have never existed, but I know tonight is deeper for Travis than just the glory of the basketball pendant. I might have been standing outside the college counselor's office when he found out he hadn't been recruited to any colleges; meanwhile Lewis is off to UNC as an alternate, but only after his grandfather made a hefty donation to their new cafeteria.

"Who knows, maybe your grandpa can pay to clean up the mess I make of both of you," I snap back, and Lewis shuts up real quick.

The next two rounds go down just as smoothly: our team sinks all three of the cups, tied game. The whistle blows and Lewis takes the stage one more time as the sophomores sweep in to reset.

"Is this a hazing thing?" I whisper to Travis, pointing at the youths tidying up.

"More like a rite of passage," he whispers back with a wink.

"All right, the last event of the night is shotgun relay. You key your beer, you chug your beer, you turn it upside down to prove it's empty, you pass the key. The team that finishes first wins the whole damned thing!"

Our audience, now double in size, cheers like it's the homecoming game.

I take a deep breath as we are directed to our positions, same order as flip cup, which means it all falls on me. Last time I tried to chug half a cup of beer, I could barely make it. How am I going to survive an entire can? The panic must read on my face because Travis comes up behind me the way Jrue would if he sensed my mounting fears, to calm me down.

"This is easier, you literally don't have to do anything, just let the beer flow." He squeezes my shoulders, this time genuinely, and resumes his position at the front of the table. The whistle blows.

I watch Travis pierce the top of the can with a key and put the hole to his lips before opening the tab; he tilts his head back and in less than a minute, he turns the can upside down and passes the key over. Lewis finishes only seconds after him and does the same. The game stays basically neck and neck until Todrick, the player on the other team the round before me, chokes or hiccups? Some bodily function interferes and beer flies everywhere. I'm talking about water-park levels of liquid. Sophomores rush over with a roll of paper towels and start soaking up the booze from the rug, but the game is still going and while Todrick has to dance around the cleanup crew at his ankles to get fresh beer and start over, Bernard finishes his can and puts the key in my hand.

I take a deep breath and push the point of the key into the can, then put it to my lips and open the tab. The rush of bitter bubbles is quick, but I fight back against the urge to breathe and just do what Travis told me, I let it flow. As soon as the liquid starts sloshing, it stops and I open my eyes to see the entire room, eyes wide, cheering and jumping. I pull the can from my lips and turn it upside down. Nothing. It's empty. Across the table Todrick is finally handing his key to Justice, but it's a wrap. We won. Because of me. And everyone is shouting my name. Marcos is the first to hug me, then Bernard, but I forget to hold my breath and his almost knocks me out. Travis runs over and saves me.

"Come with me," he says, and pulls me out of the growing crowd and into the nearest bedroom.

"I can't believe it. This is such a rush, no wonder athletes have God complexes, this is totally addictive."

I throw myself back onto the bed and look up at the ceiling. That beer has gone straight to my head, and it's hard to tell if the ceiling fan is actually spinning or not.

"Not too shabby, Snitchbau—sorry. Old habit."

Travis lies down next to me, gently. I face him. "Why are you like that? What did I ever do to you?"

He pauses to reflect. "You're so driven, you know exactly who you are, and you don't care that everyone thinks you are a self-involved monster-bitch. It's intimidating, Sade."

"Thank you?"

"I guess I can be a dick sometimes, sorry."

I lie back down and look over at him, beyond the cheekbones and the wavy hair that looks like it's been prepped for a Pantene Pro-V campaign. Maybe I misjudged him. Maybe Travis is just as insecure as the rest of us. Maybe he's not as bad as I thought. He sits up and I follow and almost fall right off the bed.

"Easy there, killer," he says as I sway, trying to keep myself upright.

Travis steadies me, taking my hands in his and turning me toward him.

"Just pick a point on my face and focus on it," he says.

"What, are you a doctor now?"

"Just do it, Sadie."

I roll my eyes but stare at his nose. After a few awkward moments of silence, I have to admit, it works. The beer in me seems to settle into a nice tipsy simmer. Just enough to make me loosen up.

"Thanks," I say quietly, turning my face down to avoid my gaze landing on his lips. But his fingers find my chin, and he pulls me back up. This time, we meet eye to eye.

"I know what you want," he whispers over a full-sparkle-tooth smile.

"Um . . . what do you mean?"

"A kiss."

In shock, I stand up too quickly, and my head spins.

"What? How do you—"

He holds up his phone to show me a page on Trendsettr. My eyes zero in on a message from two hours ago:

[ANONYMOUS2039]: Overheard in the dining room, Sadie B in search of her first kiss, anyone out there looking to smooch a snitch?

"Oh my god!" I can't tell if I'm more upset that someone got the scoop on me quicker than I could make my secret disappear or that Travis has known about my kiss conundrum this whole time and played me for a fool. I stand to march out of the room, but he rises as well. "Sadie, wait."

"Travis—"

"Hey! Chill. It's out there already, nothing you can do, but believe me, you are going to want someone who knows what they're doing."

I wrinkle my nose but he's not wrong. I sit back down.

"Why would you do that for me?"

"Maybe it's my way of saying sorry . . . starting over? Why did you defend me against Lewis?"

I have no clue why I did that. I got swept up in the moment, but maybe this is my chance to start giving people a chance. Maybe this is what Jrue was talking about, how tonight feels different.

"So you're saying you would just kiss me, no strings attached, no jokes . . . just like . . . our little secret?" (I can't believe I am asking Travis this, but a good journalist knows you don't always get the story right the first time around.) I make a quick adjustment to my mental note.

**First kiss:**
~~Merrill Wortham~~
Travis Marshall?!?!

"Yeah, I guess that's what I'm saying. Which is crazy because this would be like . . . a lot of points."

"Points?" I know I'm still pretty drunk, but I definitely missed the part of the conversation where we veered into sportsball. "Travis. What are you talking about?"

He picks at his fingernails as he talks.

"Nothing, it's nothing."

"No, tell me. What do you mean by points?"

"Don't take this the wrong way. It's just the team. We have this competition, who can hook up with the most people tonight, and you check off two boxes."

The surge of adrenaline sobers me enough to jump up and stay steady. I can't believe I started to fall for his nonsense. Travis is exactly who I always thought he was: the human embodiment of the bad place. Even if he has the potential, why would he change? He thrives on mediocrity. For young men like him, it's quite literally the American way.

"That is disgusting . . . 'two boxes'? Do you know how messed up that is?"

"Chill . . . you get an extra point if anything you do is with someone new to the school, like Zara Hussein, or . . . if it's their first time, like you—" Travis goes silent and his face turns purple as my knee barrels into his groin. He slowly slides down to the floor, clutching between his legs like he's just had an accident, a nuts-crushed-into-chunky-peanut-butter-type accident.

"You know, Travis—"

I swing the door open and let it slam into his hamstring, then savor the groan he lets out before I continue, "You are right. I don't care what you think. Because when you are forty and you look back at your pathetic life and realize that tonight was your peak and it was all downhill from here, you are going to remember this monster-bitch and this moment, and Travis?" I pull his chin back up gently the way he did moments ago and get close enough so that all I need to do is whisper, "You are going to regret even thinking you could fuck with me."

The upstairs has pretty much emptied out, but Lewis is passed out on the couch, next to his phone. I use his thumb to unlock it, since mine is dead.

## FLORENCE HILLS HS TRENDSETTR MESSAGE BOARD

> [brotatochip]: Watch out folx, before you get frisky, I have it on good authority that Travis M and the rest of the basketball team are competing to see who can hook up with the most people tonight. Don't just be a notch on their belts.
> XO, snitchbaum

I hit send, throw the phone down, and walk away.

# JRUE EDWARDS

## THE CLASS CLOWN

## INTERLUDE

### Sadie

---

FRIDAY, 11:01 P.M.

**SADIE:**
So fuck Travis Marshall and all his neanderthal friends

**JRUE:**
uh, who's this?

**SADIE:**
Me. I'm using some rando's phone because my phone is dead dead. Anyway, Travis . . .

**JRUE:**
right. shit, you okay?? what happened??

**SADIE:**
I'm okay. But looks like we're both gonna be Drews now

Well Drew and Jrue

**JRUE:**
what are you talking about rn?? u drunk?!

**SADIE:**
Drew Barrymore

**JRUE:**
tf???

**SADIE:**
I'm Drew Barrymore

**JRUE:**
lol uh i got that part. WHYYYY

**SADIE:**
Bc I've never been kissed

**JRUE:**
what??

**SADIE:**
OMG, J, it's a movie she made in the 90s!! Someone clearly sucks at movie trivia!! 😕 it was a joke jesus christ

dude you took way too long getting there lol

**JRUE:**
someone clearly sucks at joke telling!!

**SADIE:**
I hate u

**JRUE:**
aww, boo, thank you so much, I love that

**SADIE:**
😐

**JRUE:**
hey, but fr tho, you rly okay??

**SADIE:**
I'm okay

u sure?? cuz you know I'll bust some heads all up in this mf'er if I have to! nobody fuckin with da homie!!

**SADIE:**

Hahaha you know I bust my own heads lololol but thank you

**JRUE:**

yeah I know u do 😊 and ofc, any time.

i got u!! I'll bury all the bodies for u, gurl haha

**SADIE:**

OMG hahaha but yeah saaaammmeeee. 🩶

Gotta go. This kid "needs" his phone back

# OSCAR GRAHAM

## THE WANNABE RAPPER

**PART III**

PEOPLE ARE STILL ARRIVING, SO I INSIST WE GET some confessional footage of me before this place is too packed to move.

"You spoke to Sy?" Stasia asks.

"Yeah, and, um, you know we've still got details to work out. It'll come together."

Stasia nods. "Uh-huh. Maybe you should take a look at what I've pieced together in camera already."

I put my hand on the small of her back. "And I do want to see it, Stas. I just feel like we should take advantage of this time and get more footage first. We'll have plenty of opportunities to review in edits, right?"

"I suppose, but . . ."

"Cool." I pick a chair that allows me to sort of hunch in a way that looks like I'm not trying to hunch. "I'll sit here, and we can shoot."

"Fine," Stasia sighs. "Just tell me what you told me before."

I reach across the table and trace my fingers along the back of her hand. "That you're incredible, and I love you?"

She perks up a bit. "Well, yes. I'll take that as much as I can get. I mean about your goals, though."

We're at the far side of the pool away from the party noise. I'm lit by the low amber landscaping lights along the perimeter of DeAndre's yard. Stasia sits across from me with her camera resting on a patio table for stability while she adjusts settings that are as complex to me as she says my coding is to her.

"Whenever you're ready," she says.

"Okay. Um. Well, I gotta make it in the rap game. I can't see living some ordinary life when I have skills I can hone that can make me rich and famous."

"Talk more about your skills. When did you transition from casual fan to, er, a practitioner?"

"Honestly, it started accidentally. Little over a year ago, I guess. It was one of those social media challenges. I'd finished a project for this CS camp scholarship I was—"

"CS camp? Explain that. For those who don't know."

"Sorry, computer science camp. I'd coded a simple AI as part of my application for a camp scholarship."

"Nothing about that sounds simple. You ended up getting that really cool, prestigious camp scholarship?"

"For sure."

"Nothing ordinary about that, right?" Her lens whines as it zooms slightly. "Go on."

"After I'd finished my application packet, it was late, and I saw people posting raps to this challenge beat. Most of it was goofy, you know, people having fun. I was buzzing on cranberry Red Bull, had a bunch of code in my head, and the beat triggered something. I wrote sixteen bars that were about code.

Made it funny. *Pour a hot cup of JavaScript, take a bite of Swift, then pop some C-plus-plus for a vita-lift . . .* that sort of thing. Then I posted it. Crashed, slept for twelve hours straight, and woke up to like a hundred thousand views."

There's a squeal and splash as someone goes into the pool. I hear something about "optimal temperature for bad-bitch saturation." That sounds . . . interesting, but I lose track of what's happening in the water when Stasia pulls me back into our interview.

"I recall that viral moment," she says. "That was a big deal. You were very happy."

"Understatement. I stepped outside and the corner boys were looking for me. Usually, that's not great news, but they just wanted to show love. Started comparing me to Reggie Beaumont and shit."

"Reggie Beaumont?"

"Only dude from our neighborhood to ever make it big. Singer from back in the day. Had two platinum albums and won a Grammy. Even my pops be talking about him, on some old 'be nice to get some of that Reggie Beaumont money' type stuff."

"Are wealth and fame the ultimate goal?"

"Yeah. No." I ponder. Those things aren't the same as happiness. But they're like . . . what? I think about the Trendsettr dashboard, the different ways I see stats and know what's working and what isn't. "They're like metrics. That you're doing something right. People respect that."

"By 'people' you mean . . . ?"

"Everyone. Look around." I motion to this incredible house, and incredible yard, and incredible pool where everyone's loving life. "Who wouldn't want this?"

"Rap isn't the only way to get this. Besides, it's just stuff."

I snort. "People with stuff always say stuff like that."

Stasia bristles. She isn't like me and Jade. She grew up comfortably in the center of the Florence Hills school district. Don't get me wrong—I support Black excellence to the fullest. Stasia's doctor mom and finance guy dad own a house they live in, and another vacation house they only go to for like a week in the summer. She's got a college fund. She never stresses about eating at fancy restaurants like Outback Steakhouse. I just can't help but think sometimes that the grass is greener.

Like she can't help being born solidly upper-class. Her and her parents have never ever been assholes about it. The whole reason we started hanging out was because I missed my bus freshman year, and she got her mom to give me a ride home without either of them being scared to drive a Benz into my neighborhood. That's a tiny fraction of the reasons I love her—she's always putting others, me, before herself. But it is what it is. Some things she might not ever get about me, and vice versa. That's okay, though.

She asks, "Have you posted more of your raps?"

I move in my chair. Wonder what the camera sees. "The rap game's tough. There are a lot of haters. So you gotta develop a thick skin. Single-minded focus. That's what all the greats say. Nobody made it without struggling. The lows are like— what's those things Boy Scouts get for accomplishing missions or whatever?"

"Merit badges."

I snap my fingers. "That right there. Going through the lows is like earning your merit badges."

"You don't think you have a ton of merit badges already? From your coding? Your mind for science? You got into MIT. That's a big-ass merit badge."

"Some see it that way. It's a backup plan, I guess."

She lifts her gaze from the camera's display, eyebrow cocked. "Ummm, since when is it a backup plan? My *actual* plan is to be across the river at MassArt, like we've been talking about for two years, Oscar, and it sounds like you're trying to switch up without telling me."

"Stasia, chill. I'm probably still going to MIT. I'm just saying if the music starts looking up, I'mma have to shift my focus."

"Shift your . . ." She trails off. "Is this about the corner boys again? The people on your block? Do you believe they don't respect your academic accomplishments?"

Why the hell we keep coming back to this? "They don't know about my academic accomplishments. That shit'll get your shoes took. I learned a long time ago it was just safer to shut the hell up about my grades, or building robots, or programming languages."

Her expression softens. "Except when you're rapping about it. Rap feels safe, then?"

"I'm not scared of them."

"I didn't say you were."

"Rap is . . . it's . . ." I glance sideways and spot a familiar face weaving through the party. "Yo, is that Savoy?"

"I don't see them."

I stand. "I was thinking, they owe me a favor, right? Me rushing their Trendsettr poll and all. I could perform live on their social media. All those followers. I'm viral tomorrow!"

"Oscar. Wait!" Stasia's gathered her camera like the interview's over and is at my hip. "Let me show you my footage first."

I turn around fast, confused. She's holding the camera one-handed, and my elbow clips the extended lens. It flies loose and remains airborne for what feels like a decade before crunching on the concrete patio, where the body and lens separate like a booster from a space shuttle. Anyone close enough to see winces. Except Stasia. She's a statue.

"Oh shit, Stasia. I'm sorry. I was just trying to—"

"I know what you were trying to do." Her voice is low, but I still hear. "No one wants you to rap, Oscar. You did a fun thing, once, and you've been trying to ride the wave to a destination that doesn't exist. I love you. Probably most of the people here love you. As lovable as you are, you are stubborn and you're not being a good listener right now. Come find me if either of those things changes tonight."

Now I'm the statue. She collects the pieces of her camera and shoves her way toward the front of the house. I lose track of her quickly, and though I know—I KNOW—I'm supposed to go after her, I don't. Because I'm MAD mad.

It feels like whatever direction I look in, everybody turns away. I need to move, but when I do, something scrapes beneath my shoe. Lifting my foot, I spot a thin aluminum ring on the ground. It's a piece from Stasia's camera.

Scooping it up, I hold it an inch or two from my nose. The circumference is smaller than the lens it came from. In a couple of places, rough plastic shards are still affixed from where it broke. Must be part of what mounts the lens to the camera body. I slip the ring in my pocket but still don't chase Stasia.

And people call me a genius.

# FERNANDA MANNING

### THE JOCK

DOWN IN THE BASEMENT, IT'S LIKE AN EPISODE OF *The Twilight Zone* with Truth or Dare Jenga, strip poker, and a combination of Spin the Bottle and Seven Minutes in Heaven going on in different corners. For the record, in the thirty minutes I've been waiting for Kai to come back down to the basement, I obliterated everyone in Jenga.

After my fifth victory in a row, my head kind of throbs. It could also be my nerves, or the loud music from speakers in the ceiling, flashing red and white lights from one of those electronic basketball hoop games that make it seem like we're in a club.

I can hardly see anything, but I catch a glimpse of a new pizza guy running back upstairs as if he's afraid for his life. I'm about to follow him when I hear a chorus of "Fernanda! Don't go!"

I'm surrounded by the girls from the basketball team, but

there's no sign of Penny, DeAndre, or my neighbor Fantasia. And for all I stare at the stairs, there's no sign of Kai.

To calm my growling stomach, I grab a slice of pizza from one of the boxes on the counter. Although it's blissfully warm and my taste buds explode with the spicy cheesy gooeyness of it, after one bite, I know it's the wrong move. If I want my night to end on the perfect note with Kai, I don't want my breath to smell like pepperoni and garlic.

"Are you okay?" Lucy, one of the girls' basketball team captains, asks, probably noticing how I keep looking at the stairs.

"You look kind of sick. Sorry to bring this up, but is it because of Spencer?" Emma asks.

Her words snap me out of my queasiness.

"What? Spencer? Whoa, whoa, whoa," I say, putting the slice of pizza back on the counter to make the time-out gesture. "We've been broken up for a while. Forever, actually. I don't care that he's moved on."

If anything, I'm delighted that our names aren't linked anymore.

"Why did you guys even break up?" Cynthia insists. "He's one of the best-looking guys on the varsity football team."

I don't understand why they're interrogating me like this, but they're all staring at me like my words are a matter of life and death. I shrug, not knowing what to tell them. I mean, I obviously saw the appeal in Spencer, once upon a time. I'm not afraid to admit I liked his Mr. Incredible look. But I now need more than good looks. There's not a lot of substance to Spencer, but I don't want to bash him in front of the girls. In fact, I don't want to talk about him whatsoever.

"It just didn't work out, you know?"

"But you never dated anyone else after him," Lucy says, not giving up.

"Because I don't have time," I say, getting a little exasperated. I don't think most of them are involved in more than one team sport, but even when I was in only one, it was a struggle not to come home from a game and collapse until Monday morning to do it all over again. Aren't they exhausted, too? But then, afraid my words will come back and haunt me, I clarify, "I mean, now that the season's over, things are more chill."

"So, you're on the lookout?" Cynthia asks, her green eyes intent on my face as if trying to figure me out.

Is she scoping for information on someone in particular? My ears buzz as I try to sense the meaning behind her words.

"On the lookout?" I reply, mirroring her smile. "Well, I already—"

A commotion upstairs swallows my words just as I'm about to confess to them that I've had a crush on Kai forever. There's lots of yelling and loud noises like two boulders crashing against each other.

The games go silent for a bit as people try to understand what's going on; then one of the girls from the track team dashes to my group and says, "Kai and Spencer are fighting over one of the cheerleaders."

The one bite of pizza hardens in my stomach.

They're fighting over a girl? My quest is lost before I've had the chance to make a move.

At the sound of the promise of a fight, everyone starts running upstairs to witness the mess as if someone let off a race horn. Not gonna lie. My runner instincts kick off, too, but for different reasons than getting the scoop on the latest scandal.

If Spencer and Kai are duking it out over a girl—a girl who's not me—I need to see it with my own eyes so I can get over Kai before I make a grave mistake.

In these heels, I walk in slow motion, so I kick them off my feet. I'll put them back on later because now speed is of the essence.

"Ouch!" a boy's voice complains. "Whoever threw these knives disguised as shoes, are you trying to kill me?"

The shoes must have accidentally landed on—in?—an innocent bystander.

"Oops," I whisper, not wanting to call attention to myself.

But by the time I follow the girls, they're coming back to the basement, to our spot by the kitchenette counter.

"What happened with Kai?" I ask.

Too late, I realize the girls are led by no other than Kai. Barefoot, we're eye-level, and maybe the top of my dress is too tight, but I feel like I can't breathe.

Even in the semidarkness, I see his cheeks are bright red, just like mine. The body heat radiates off him in waves, and, irrationally, my hands go cold with nerves. I wanted to be cool with him, but I feel the words evaporate from my lips and my brain before I can form a coherent thought.

Good thing none of the other girls are affected by his mere presence. They ask him about the fight all at once, but Cynthia's voice is loudest when she says, "Were you really fighting over a girl?" She holds on to his arm possessively.

Jealousy eats at me, but I'm also grateful that she asked. I lean in to hear over the rising volume of music and voices in the basement.

But before Kai can speak, Emma blurts out, "Yes and no. Spencer yelled at Kennedy for not telling the pizza guy to bring the delivery to him specifically. Someone must've directed the driver to the basement. Kai told him to cut it out, and you know Spencer." She looks at me then, as if I'm the expert on a boy I dated for only two months. We must have been on like five real dates before whatever we had fizzled out. "He didn't like being called out in front of everyone. And he's upset he didn't get to eat his pizza."

"I left a slice on the counter, not that Spencer deserves it," I say, shrugging one shoulder.

In that moment, someone spills a cup of beer all over the counter, soaking the sad-looking slice of pizza.

"Symbolism."

We all start laughing like it's the funniest thing in the world.

"And Kennedy?" I ask when the laughter dies down. "Is she okay?"

Kai's standing next to me now and says, "She's fine. She went out to the hot tub with some of her friends."

I glance at him, trying to see if he wishes he was out there with those girls in the hot tub.

He looks at me, too, but I won't even start to guess what's crossing his mind. I worry I seem too serious, but a current of electricity buzzes between us. I want to hold on to it, stretch it to last all night, and I know if I don't say anything witty or interesting, the spark will be gone.

I realize that my plan of telling him how I feel wasn't a plan at all. It was just a wish because I didn't set out steps to accomplish my goal. I need to get Kai alone. But at this party, with pretty much the whole school around us, how am I going to do that?

Luckily, a couple of guys join our group as I'm pondering. One of them is the cowboy who made fun of me for driving the minivan. He notices me and makes a show of doing a double take.

"I know who you are now," he says. "Fernanda? You were the kicker on the football team this past season. You told me about her once or twice, Kai, right?"

Kai blushes.

If this means what I think it means, then I'm way closer to scoring than I thought. Confidence rushes through me.

"You were talking about me?" I say, smirking at Kai.

Kai turns toward the cowboy, and I don't see the expression on his face, but the cowboy laughs. Then he leans between Kai and me and says, "You looked amazing in the football uniform, but this dress? Wow . . ."

I turn to Kai again, and I see his ears are bright red.

"Heads up!" a girl yells from the basketball arcade game, and instinctively, people cover their heads.

Not me.

I look up and, in my mind's eye, I see the basketball's trajectory from beginning to end.

I raise my hands to grab the basketball and jump. The skirt of my dress hitches, and a part of my mind hopes that tomorrow no one online will make fun of my boy-shorts underwear. My left hand comes down, trying to keep my clothes in place.

But Kai steps in the way, as if he's trying to protect me from the ball. A second before it happens, I know we're going to crash into each other.

It's too late for me to pull back, and instead of grabbing the ball, my right hand falls hard on Kai's face. I know my fake nails don't have nerve endings, but I feel them scrape Kai's perfect face and I cringe.

The ball bounces on the cowboy's head and then gets lost among the people playing strip poker, sending chips all over the place.

"Kai," I say, placing my hand on the angry red scratch on his face as if I had the power to heal it instantly. The adrenaline leaving my body is making me all sweaty. "Are you okay? I'm so sorry."

My eyes prickle with embarrassment. For jumping without thinking about what I'm wearing, for scratching him, for being so damn awkward off court. I pull my hand back. It's wet, so I brush it against my dress. My cream-colored dress.

"It's nothing, Fer."

The way he says my name makes butterflies sing "Alleluia" in my stomach.

"It's hot down here. Let's get drinks," the cowboy cuts in between us. "We'll be right back."

Kai leaves with the cowboy and some other guys, and I stand like a statue trying to analyze what just happened.

When I turn to look at the girls, Cynthia glances at my skirt and winces.

"What?" I ask, self-conscious.

She points down and I see the smudge of blood on my ruined dress.

"Fu—" I groan, but she grabs me by the arm and leads me farther into the basement.

"Where are we going?" I say, hoping I don't stub my toe against a piece of furniture or a wall next.

"To the bathroom," she says over her shoulder.

We step through a door into a bathroom that smells like paint, like it was just remodeled. She turns on the light and closes the door behind her. When I see my reflection in the mirror, I gasp. The curls I spent hours trying to tame are all frizzy. My lipstick is gone from unconsciously licking my lips every few seconds, and worse, there is a tiny piece of oregano from the one bite of pizza stuck in between my front teeth.

I quickly turn on the faucet and wash my hands before I get more blood on my dress.

Someone knocks on the door. "Get lost!" I yell, my frustration reaching a boiling point.

Emma and Lucy say, "It's us! Open up!"

Cynthia glances at me as if asking what I want to do. For a second, I feel unmoored, like I'm playing a game I don't know the rules for. I'm not going to lie, though. I like not being on my own through a situation like this.

I nod, and she smiles as if I passed a friendship test.

"Oh, honey!" Emma says when she comes in and notices the stain on my dress. "We're going to help you. Come over here. We need to rinse the fabric with cold water."

"How do you know that?" I ask, doing what she says regardless.

Lucy whistles. "In eighth grade, when you weren't on the team yet, Emma got her period during a home game. We were wearing white shorts and Coach Vera knew to rinse Emma's in cold water. She wrung them out, and Emma played the game with wet pants."

"But they weren't stained," Emma says, laughing, as she rubs one of the fancy paper guest towels on my dress. I stand on tiptoes as close to the sink as possible, so we won't make a bigger mess. The stain vanishes after a few seconds, but with it goes my determination to go through with my plan to talk to Kai and tell him how I feel.

I look up at our reflection in the mirror, and Cynthia says, "You like him, huh?"

The brief silence that follows is heavy like the dread weighing me down. I should deny it, keep playing it cool, but I know that as soon as I get home, no, as soon as I turn my back on this party and Kai, I'll regret it.

I sigh. "Is it that obvious?" My cheeks are burning.

"We could kind of tell you had a thing for him," Emma says in a soft voice.

"You could?" I sit on the toilet (which has the lid down, of course) and hide my face in my hands. "I'm a mess. And I'm never a mess!"

"He's a special one, that Kai," Lucy says, taking the chance to fix her hair, too.

"Yeah, I like him," I say. "Like, I really really do."

The three girls stare at me, not surprised, but kind of relieved.

"What?" I ask, kind of annoyed. "Say it."

Emma sits on the tub next to me and places a hand on mine. "Not that it's up to us to speak about his feelings, which are valid, but . . . are you just trying to get him to tick something off a list?"

"Why would I do that?"

Cynthia clears her voice as if warning the other two not to say anything. They're driving me nuts. But then, they've known me forever. They know how determined I am to get what—or who—I want.

"You always have to win at everything, Fer," she says. "Love isn't a competition, though."

I know this is different. Kai is different.

"I don't know how to do this another way," I confess.

"Why do you like him?" Emma asks.

I smile just thinking about all the things. What's not to like?

"He's special." I shrug. "He's funny and sweet and just, like, so much more mature and collected than the other boys at FH."

"So why don't you tell him that?" Emma asks, seeming convinced by both the happiness radiating from me when I talk about him and my actual words.

"I don't know how!" I say. "What if he rejects me? What if he doesn't like me that way?"

The girls look at me like I said the wrong thing.

"What?" I ask.

Lucy smiles and shrugs. "Nothing. It's just that you're like . . . unstoppable. You're a machine. Someone we'd never guess gets nervous."

"I get nervous all the time!" I say, ducking my head. "Especially when it comes to Kai, you know? I'm scared that, after my dating Spencer, who is such an asshat to him, he won't give me a chance."

"I guess you'll just have to go out there and see for yourself. You have to tell him just like you told us," Cynthia says, opening the door. This is a challenge I can't turn away from. Not a challenge from them, but from deep inside me.

Before I cross the threshold of the bathroom and head back to the party, I feel like I'm standing on a tiny island of possibility. What if instead of telling him I show him?

When I kiss him, he'll know how I feel, and I won't have to talk about feelings.

In the basement's big room, I first see Kai with a red cup in each hand, standing next to a new group playing Spin the Bottle/Seven Minutes in Heaven. It would be the easy way out to play the game and then go from there. But a quick joke of a kiss isn't what I want. There's depth in Kai Hassel. Will he think there's depth in me, too, or does he think I'm a single-minded jock like Spencer?

Even from a few feet away, Kai's eyes are bright in the darkness, and his dimple flashes in a shy smile.

Cynthia gently nudges me forward.

I step toward him. We weren't that far apart, but by the time I reach him, I feel like I ran up one thousand steps.

"Gossiping in the bathroom?" His voice quivers nervously. A crack in his cool armor.

My armor is shattered by now. There's no way he doesn't know I like him, but I promised myself I'd tell him aloud how I feel about him. I promised myself I'd make my move, even if I have zero guarantees that it's the right one.

I open my mouth to bare my heart in front of everyone, but just then, one of his cheerleader friends pulls him by the hand. "We need you for the pyramid. Come on!"

He looks at me—is that regret in his eyes?—but still follows his friend for a cheerleading routine—or, knowing that enthusiastic bunch, several—by the pool. My breath leaves me in a sigh.

# CARLA SCHMIDT

## THE COOL MOM

$$\boxed{\textit{PART II}}$$

HELL.

I'm in hell.

I don't know what I was thinking, infiltrating this teen party to look for Daisy.

Or, I do know what I was thinking, but it's hard to figure out *why* I thought it was a good idea as I sit here, crammed into a closet in the basement, swathed in another family's ski jackets, having an out-of-body experience.

I had thought: *You've still got it, babe, you can still throw on that old cheetah-print dress and resume your days as a party girl just for an hour. You can show up and be the cool mom for once, get your dog back, and be home in time to rewatch two episodes of* Bridgerton *before bed.*

That all felt so real as I was marching across to the Dixons'. How did this night go so wrong, so quickly?

I've got time. I'm stuck in a closet. Here's how:

First, I entered and immediately lost Merrill in the mosh pit of literal children covering every inch of the Dixons' home. I've been inside their house before but couldn't even remember what it looked like, such was the current mess. I got lost, ending up in a dining room I think, texting my boys back home: *Had to pop out for an errand. Everything okay at home?* That's when the cowboy found me.

"Rawr," he said, clawing the air like a cat. It took me a beat to realize two things. First, that he was talking to me. Second, that he was roaring at me because of my cheetah print.

"I see you, Carole Baskin," he said to me, moving closer. "On the prowl tonight?"

I couldn't figure out what to say so I did the only thing that made sense. I took a bite of the gross cookie Merrill gave me.

"Let me break off a piece," the kid whispered, getting closer and reaching for the rest of the cookie. I crammed the rest into my mouth. Providing drugs to a minor is illegal! I resolved to get out as soon as possible, ride out whatever drug I just ingested, and simply wait for Daisy to come back in the morning. The cowboy had other plans.

"You know, I'm nineteen. Held back on a technicality. And I've always had a love for cougars," he whispered, and that's when I finally broke my silence.

"I'm a *mom*!"

"I can tell."

I adjusted my sunglasses and pulled the brim of my hat down. The aftertaste of the gross cookie was nothing compared to the bile inspired by this kid's smarmy attempts at . . . I don't know . . . conversation? In the awkward silence I checked my phone. No text back from the kids. I thought: *They're fine, but is it so hard to let me know? They're probably staring at their phones anyway.* My heart began to race. Thankfully, a commotion from outside the room pulled the cowboy's attention away long enough for me to slip sideways, to freedom.

Unfortunately, I slipped right into a spotlight. An interview, to be exact. A kid dressed like a rock star sidled up to me and began asking me questions about my outfit while three others held up cameras and bright lights. I was dazzled and dizzy right away, realizing too late that my shock was already being recorded by the cameras.

The kid said something like *People who wear cheetah print have the best stories. What's yours?* I choked down the rest of the cookie in my mouth, thinking I could save this if I could just keep my cool, not make a scene, and leave. Then the kid asked something that actually made me think.

"What did you envision for the night when you picked this look?"

I was determined to not answer but I saw the cowboy past the cameras, looking upon me with disappointment as the interview formed the perfect barrier. I was safe for as long as I could talk.

"I envisioned . . ." I paused for a second, surprised to even hear myself speaking. It was like someone else was talking through me. Someone confident. Someone I buried within myself ages ago, under business and bills and *life*. I found her, down in my depths, grabbed for her, and pulled her up so that she could speak for the first time in years.

I don't remember what she—or what I—said, just that I told the rock-star kid I was going to begin again, start over, try harder not to lose myself this time. Something like that.

And that I was amazed the dress still fit, but what I meant was that *I* still fit. The young me and the old me don't have to be two different people. I've still got what I've always had. The kids twirled me, cheering. At first, I thought they were maybe laughing at me, but there was no cruelty in the way they kept me chatting for their little project. I relaxed, like maybe a little attention wasn't a bad thing once in a while, especially after years of feeling myself slowly vanish. Talking to those kids, I felt the shock of being seen all at once and so honestly, and it was exhilarating.

The interview ended when Merrill darted to my side, guiding me through the house and upstairs toward a raucous crowd around a large table. I recognized beer pong more by the smell than the sight. Everyone was cheering on a girl with her head tipped back, beer dripping over her chin as she chugged, and I was tempted to swat the cup away. Go full-on mom. But Merrill had me in a death grip and was dragging me down—*down?!*—under the table.

"Come, my quester, come!" Merrill screamed over the chanting. Crouching under the table in a mess of crushed cans, Merrill showed me something spectacular.

A crushed-up Ping-Pong ball.

"Treasure," she whispered.

Treasure indeed! I recognized Daisy's chew toy immediately! No human hand could crush a Ping-Pong ball like that. No force on earth except the jaws of an excited, adorable pit bull, who no doubt thought she was playing fetch with the group of kids tossing ball after ball into the crowded oblivion. Balls for her to find, chew, and spit out because she knows better than to eat garbage because she's a *good girl*!

Our hunt was back on. Merrill and I followed the trail of chewed-up balls from room to room until we lost it somewhere in the basement. The Dixons, I discovered, own one of those massive basketball machines you see at carnivals, and as I stared into the flashing white and red lights I realized something: I was high. Or about to be. The cookie was kicking in.

I blinked at the lights. A ball rolled toward me, like the ones Daisy had been chewing except huge, like way too big for a dog, because it was a basketball, and the image of Daisy trying to chew it felt so *funny*. I just burst out laughing and tossed the ball overhead, not even worried about where it might land, and that was funny, too.

And then the cookie kicked my ass.

The rest is a blur.

I was on the couch, playing a video game. I was showing Merrill how to apply lipstick in the mirror of a freshly renovated bathroom, listening to her talk about how her mom never lets her wear makeup because she says it's for sluts and clowns. I was introducing myself as Mother Slut Clown to a taxidermy elk head on the basement's back wall just to make Merrill laugh, to make myself laugh again. I danced. I think I did the worm.

Then we orbited too close to a ring of kids playing some form of Seven Minutes in Heaven, and Merrill got roped in. I could tell right away she was uncomfortable, even as she let the kids spin the bottle for her. Then they led her to the closet, and she gave one last, mournful look at me as the darkness yawned open and some kid with neck pimples named Jimmy eyed her hungrily.

I sprang into action, dashing through the cluster of giggling kids, tossing Merrill and Neck-Pimple Boy aside and throwing myself into the closet first, and shouting, "SORRY, OCCU-PIED!" And slamming the door shut in their faces. No one would be doing anything unsavory against their will. Not tonight! Not in this closet!

Outside, one of the perplexed kids asked, "Who on earth was that?"

"Mother Slut Clown," Merrill intoned, and I smiled hearing the respect in her voice. She's safe, and that's what matters.

But I've been trapped in the closet ever since, waiting to be forgotten about.

And wowsers, I'm high. Like, *high* high.

It's honestly thrilling. The tension between me and the people I imagine staring at the door, willing me to give them back their private space to make out, is electric. I won't do it! I have kissed too many sticky boys in cramped crawl spaces to permit this kind of nonsense. Merrill deserves better. I can tell she's out of her element in a party of this magnitude, and that she doesn't really have anyone to hang out with, but even in the last hour I've watched her confidence blossom as she's led me on this wild-goose chase after Daisy.

Daisy is starting to feel like a serial killer, too. This all feels like a seedy, noir type of show. Like a new Batman movie or something, with Daisy leaving little clues that lead to traps, like this, and she's watching from behind a wall of flickering monitors, observing my every move as she deploys clues, like *Woof, Carla is ready for her next hint, deploy the paw print of salsa on the staircase, woof.*

I stifle a giggle. I'm having fun. Actual fun! Mirth, Merrill would call it, in her strange Arthurian dialect. It seems astounding to me that any of this should be the case since I'm literally a grown-ass woman sitting alone in a closet, but it is.

All the worry I felt on my way home from work today feels so remote. I feel content, like I could hang out here forever.

Have you ever been trapped in a closet when you're high? It's actually kind of nice. If you lean just right, it's like being hugged. I know it's only surplus jackets doing the hugging, but I miss this. Not just the sensation, but the smell of clothes and mothballs and boots—the clutter of another life wrapped around you. You don't really have this when you live by yourself. For so long it's just been me and my stuff. Of course, there's the twins and all their stuff, but they come and go. They take their lives with them when they leave, and it's just me in a house that feels . . . how do I describe this? Like a house that's suddenly too big for all the memories you once envisioned would fill it, that will now never fill it, because life surprises you, and people leave, and things simply . . . change.

A high thought if I've ever heard it. I'm over my ex-husband. The divorce was my idea. I wanted the house. I got it. I paid for it, after all. So why am I so hesitant to go home? Why do the madness of this party and the clutter of another family wrapped around me feel more like home than my actual address, where my actual kids sit unattended, probably not even aware that their mom hasn't returned?

Wait.

The twins!

It's this precise moment of contemplation when my phone goes off and I remember, with the force of being hit by an ice cream truck, that I'm a mother. Are the boys alive? Are they choking to death on LEGO people? Are they Googling body parts? All of these questions race in my mind as I fumble to find my phone—which is somehow in my cleavage—and the screen lights up the entire closet. Maximum mom brightness. I have one text, from Skylar, that just says: *Ya.*

Not much, but his response is enough to assure me they're alive, and that feels incredible. I'm ecstatic. I type out an entire paragraph about how much I love them, how I'm sorry if my divorce ruined their childhoods and they spend their thirties writing essays about me, but then I delete everything. I'm high, and they can never know. If I ever lost visitation, I don't know what I'd do. I catch myself writing a paragraph about that, delete it all, and just send a few heart emojis. Then the phone goes back into my boob tourniquet. In fresh darkness, I'm left to wonder if they miss me, too, when I go? Or have I become someone so invisible in life that it makes no difference if I'm one room away, a house away, or gone for good?

And I have to ask myself: What the fuck am I doing in this fucking closet, still?

I burst out of the closet, tears blurring behind my askew sunglasses. People scream. I have been in here for an hour or three minutes, I don't know, but Merrill and the kissy cherubs of Seven Minutes in Heaven have dispersed. I race through the darkness. I know I'm way too high for any of this because I feel as angry with myself as I do elated to be alive and able to do something about it. I feel like if I just think hard enough, I'll be able to manifest Daisy from thin air, wrap my arms around her wiggling, stocky body, and together we will cannonball out a window and into the night. Cannonball, as a verb.

What was I even doing hiding in a closet, where she couldn't even sniff me out? I need to be out here, arms wide, ready to embrace her and take us both home.

I crash into a man in a pizza delivery uniform somewhere on the first floor.

"HAVE YOU SEEN MY DOG?" I shout. I should add a descriptor. I come up with "SHE'S A GOOD GIRL!"

"I just deliver pizzas, lady!" He shakes his head, terrified, but he's given me an important clue. Daisy *loves* pizza.

"WHERE IS IT?" I shout.

"I don't know where your dog is, lady!"

"THE PIZZA, NOT THE DOG!"

He meekly points and I *run*. Kids group around the open boxes on the counter, steaming slices pulling apart. A few slices are close to the counter edge. So close that—yes!—there's a flash of brown and a pit bull suddenly bobs up from the floor, grabs a slice, and jets off.

"STOP HER!" I wail, digging into the crowd. I trip and fall, slapping my hands onto the floor, but this even feels like destiny because it puts me at eye level with a smear of some kind of sauce along the wall. I know this smear is from Daisy—my house is covered in similar ones, at this exact height, which is the height of her mouth when she's got her head ducked down out of guilt because she's just dragged something off the dining room table.

I crawl like I've never crawled before. I prowl. People jump back, probably shocked to see how great I am at crawling. Probably mistaking me for an actual cheetah because I'm so *fast*. Daisy is in my sights, but just before I can grab her, she dodges sideways. I scamper after her, and suddenly cold air rushes over me. I stand, realizing I'm outside. Kids on the back deck stare at me, struck silent by my sudden appearance. From the way they look at me, they probably know I am not a real cheetah after all. I mean, I *did* just stand up on two legs.

What do I do? I feel my chance of catching Daisy slipping away. In a few moments, my pursuit will end.

What would a cheetah do?

I meow.

The kids erupt in cheers and applause. Part of me marvels about just how high I am, but the rest of my parts just crawl onward. I slink (or at least I think I slink) the length of the deck, down the stairs, and out into a back garden.

"Daisy!" I call out, my human senses coming back to me as the crisp night air sobers me up a bit. "Daisy-girl, it's Mama!"

A crash behind me makes me scream, but when I turn there's no dog. It's . . . Merrill. Merrill, in the bushes. I can't help but let out a groan of disappointment, but I cut it off when I hear her sniffle.

"Are you crying?"

"No," she says. Right away. Not in her strange, fantastical affectation. She sniffles again. She's just a girl crying now.

"Are *you* crying?" she asks.

I wipe at my eyes, remembering that I was crying just a few minutes ago.

"Jinx," I offer with a shrug.

Merrill laughs. She gives another sniff, then turns toward the party. "Come on, Daisy awaits, right?"

"Wait."

She stops, her back to me.

"What's wrong, sweetie?"

She shrugs, still refusing to face me. "Nothing," she says. "Don't you want to go back inside?"

My chance to capture Daisy is slipping away with every second I spend here. So is the high, the prowling sense of adventure, the elation and terror of what I think might have been a momentary ego death in that closet. It all washes off me and what's left is who I am with none of that. Good thing for Merrill, it's who she needs right now.

A mom.

I sit down, right on the cool grass.

"Let's take a break. It's getting too crazy in there for me. The air is nice, right?"

Merrill doesn't sit. She rubs new tears from her face and says, "You don't have to hang out with me, okay? I know I'm not, like, cool or anything. Everyone has made that abundantly clear."

"I don't really agree with that, but I'll listen if you want to talk about it?" I make it a question.

She shakes her head.

I wait.

Waiting works.

Merrill slumps to the ground and starts talking. "You're old. You don't get what it's like."

"So tell me."

"It's like . . ." She puts her head in her hands in a way that is so deeply angsty, I almost smile. "It's like everything matters so much, all the time. My dad is always saying how high school is the best years of my life, how I need to put myself out there, make friends, make it count. But it's not working. It's been four years and by now I'm an expert at putting myself out there. I've tried every club, tried out for every sport. I even tried to get into the school play. I've tried to be so many different versions of myself, but it's always the same. People either think I'm weird, or that I try too hard, or that I try hard to be weird. It just feels like the more people see me, the less they want to be my friend."

"I want to be your friend," I point out.

"You wanted to get your dog back and look like a MILF doing it."

I have got to give it to this girl. For all her wide-eyed whimsicality, she's got my number. That's often the case with the insecure ones. They see all the cracks in everyone, and assume it means everyone sees all their cracks as well.

"True," I say. There's no point patronizing her. "But we became friends anyway, didn't we?"

Merrill shrugs. "Until you get your dog back."

I'm not going to lie by telling her she's wrong. I don't want to be yet another disappointment to this kid, and I can't give her what she's looking for. I've got my own life. She's got hers. There is no forever friendship between us, just a few decades of life experience she'll have to figure out on her own. But . . . she doesn't need me to be her friend forever. She needs me to be her friend right now. And it's just dumb luck that right now, her friend is a mom.

"You know, before this party, and before Daisy, and before I had a family of my own, I was in high school once."

"Ages ago," Merrill snipes.

"Hey, I'm thirty-eight, not three hundred. I swear, you kids think anyone older than twenty-one must have been a passenger on the *Mayflower*."

The joke makes Merrill give a resigned chuckle. I go on.

"I'll be honest with you. I never did any of this shit in high school. Parties and theater and clubs . . . I thought about them all, but never did any of it. I wasn't like you. I never put myself out there. For a long time, I thought I was just shy, but it wasn't that."

I pause to find the right word, and I've got Merrill's attention.

"What was it?"

"Bored," I say. "I was bored. Some people love high school, some people hate it, and some people just wait for it to be over so they can move on to whatever is next. You're just not the high school type, I'm guessing, which is okay. All this talk about the best years of your life? Throw it away. For people like you, the best is yet to come."

Merrill is nodding, but tears well in her eyes. "But I wanted it," she whispers. "I wanted these years to matter. I wanted to have the best friends. I wanted the lifelong memories. I wanted crushes and kisses and breakups and gossip."

I put my arm around her shoulder and let her get her cry on.

"Honey, none of that drama goes away. There's a reason all the teens on TV are played by adults. You haven't missed a thing, I promise."

"It's just . . ." She sniffs. "Everyone else seems so sure of themselves. They have these clear roles, like from a movie. What if I'm stuck as the weird girl forever?"

I laugh.

"If you manage to stay weird forever, you're going to be a blast at every party you go to, I promise."

"Really?"

"Really. I remember going to my reunion a few years ago. My *ten*-year reunion, and people barely recognized me. I had to introduce myself to everyone, all over again, with a picture from the yearbook held up to my face. And they kept saying, 'Carla, wow, you're so fun, we wish we knew in high school!' But the thing is, I wasn't fun in high school. I held back. It took moving on from Florence Hills for me to notice the small box I'd put myself in, step out of it, and find my groove. And I bet you that's true for everyone else, even people you think have it all figured out. When you're young, it's easy to find yourself playing a part. The athlete, the popular girl. You know, archetypes. But after graduation, the athlete's off the team. The popular girl has to start over elsewhere. You grow up, you grow out, and you invent yourself all over again."

Merrill has stopped crying. She's looking at me like I've finally said something that resonates. After a beat she blinks and looks at my dress.

"And you invented this?"

I laugh. Fuck, she's frank.

"Well, to be honest, I'm still learning this lesson. Turns out, you can change anytime you want, for any reason. It doesn't have to take graduation, or a party, or . . . a divorce. You can just change. However many times it takes to fall in love with who you are. But you can't force it. You've just got to follow your heart and let the rest of life catch up."

"Do you love you?" Merrill asks.

"Working on it."

"I think I love me," Merrill says, with a nod.

"Good," I laugh. "You know, it takes a special kind of person to have a blast all by themselves. The best parties are made out of people like you."

"You think so?"

I nod pensively. "Know so."

"So, what do I do?" she asks.

I stand up and dust off my dress. I reach out a hand for Merrill and say, "Well, that's obvious, Merrill. You throw the next party."

Merrill's face breaks into a wide smile, like she finally gets it. She takes my hand and I pull her up, but just as she gets to her feet, something huge tumbles out of the bushes and lands, tail wagging, between us. I scream. So does Merrill. The tumbling thing resolves into the shape of a dog and suddenly Daisy is launching herself into my arms. Mud smears all over me as I try to grab her, but then she's winding between my legs and I end up flat on my ass again. I fumble for the leash, but it's in the grass somewhere! I miss my chance and Daisy darts off.

"Oh no you don't!" Merrill screams. She grabs me and pulls me after her, and the chase is back on. We bust through the gate, into the pool area, which is a riot of color and sound. The tranquility from the garden is instantly replaced by screaming teenagers everywhere—even in the pool!

Oh no.

Daisy *loves* to swim. She thinks every bit of water, even the kiddie pools the neighbors put out for their babies during Chicago's handful of broiling-hot days, are for her. I spot her trotting along the perimeter with a look of pure doggy elation.

Now I'm the one dragging Merrill. We push through a crop of kids I recognize from the school's production of *Romeo and Juliet*. One of them I know is Blake Donnelly, infamous among the moms at PTA, and I apologize to his thousand-watt smile as I shove him aside. Next is that rock-star kid from before. I push his group aside, too. Daisy is only a few feet away, getting ready to jump. I shove forward, almost on top of her, and then I hear the first splash and realize what I've done. But there's no time to apologize for basically tossing a child into the pool. Daisy is inching away, but I'm close enough to ready her leash in a maneuver I've practiced a hundred times. I open the clasp, draw back my arm, and jump at her.

But nothing happens as it should. I trip, or slip, or I don't know what, but suddenly the pavement vanishes and I'm diving over an expanse of blue. The pool. I have just enough time to make eye contact with Daisy—does she look a little evil with the pellucid light of the pool glowing beneath her doggy jowls?—and then I'm underwater.

And cats *hate* water.

# ZARA HUSSEIN

## THE NEW GIRL

**PART I**

THE MOMENT I WALK INSIDE AND HEAR MUSIC, I know coming here was a huge mistake. Okay, that's a lie. I knew this was a mistake as I drove over in a beat-up Volvo—which isn't even MY beater Volvo, but instead borrowed from Mom—and saw the crowd of shiny mega-expensive brand-freaking-new cars. The whole scene screamed: This is Florence Hills. Land of too much money. Land of tons of opportunity.

I mean, that's kind of why Mom had us leave Florence Hills six years ago to move to Oak Hollow, a small town about three hundred miles downstate. It's the kind of town with actual farms and zero chain stores. Mom wanted us to grow up somewhere less . . . glitzy and corporate and commercial. But now, all of a sudden, she's obsessed with Layla and me having the aforementioned opportunity that comes from the "too much money" thing, so we're back.

One semester before I graduate, yanked from my old school and pulled back here. For opportunity. Yeah right.

But let's be honest, the opportunity we really came back to chase is Mom's. Her old friend Sarah May Beth—yes, you need to say all three names—called up Mom and invited her to be the director of the Florence Hills Art Festival.

"It's a huge opportunity," Mom said. "I want to push the festival to showcase more of Florence Hills's diversity."

"Opportunity, right," I said.

"Yes, opportunity," Mom said.

"If you say that word one more time, I swear it's going to be stuck on your face."

"That's a very unkind thing to say," Mom answered.

"I'm happy for you, Mom," Layla said, which, of course, instantly made me feel bad. Layla and I are only seventeen months apart. I love her enough to want to kill her sometimes. In other words, she's my little sister.

I say, "I'm happy for you, too, but—"

And that was that.

So I'm back in Florence Hills. Yay.

But truly, it's not so bad. I finished the second half of senior year. And I've managed to stay pretty invisible. Which is easy enough at a school as big as Florence Hills High.

Head down, survive. Don't make any new attachments that will be hard to break when I'm out of here in less than five months. That's been my motto. But Memi and Miranda kept pushing about this stupid party.

"Zar Zar, you gotta show your face somewhere," Memi said.

"Yeah, Zar Zar, I'm really going to need your support," Miranda piled on.

"No, I really don't," I said while doing our entire lab for us. Memi and Miranda bring the entertainment to our AP Chem efforts. I bring the . . . chemistry. I mean, the real kind. The kind you can actually chart and diagram.

"I don't know," I said.

"Come on! I SERIOUSLY need you. Savoy will no doubt be rallying the troops," Miranda said.

"You so do not." I measured the iridescent mixture in the test tube. "You have like a million friends. I mean, I'm not even, like really, your friend." The truth was I thought of Miranda as my very best friend. And I knew how sad that fact was because we only ever talked during the ninety-minute AP Chem block.

Miranda pretended to be wounded. She dramatically bent at the waist. "Zar Zar, you are my friend."

"You like me because I'm not afraid of the Bunsen burner."

"Yes, and because you are a lovely person and more people should know you."

"I agree with all that. Plus, the party will be fun. But yeah, also the part about people needing to know you," Memi added.

It was my turn to have a theatrical response. I pulled out the jazz hands, but then got nervous at the last moment and bailed to a prayer hand salute. "Gee, thanks." I fiddled with my safety goggles and went back to studying the iridescent mixture.

Anyway, I'd mostly forgotten about that exchange, but then Miranda had texted me, which was the first time she'd ever contacted me outside of that ninety-minute AP Chem block. That combined with the fact that Layla was having all her friends over at our apartment, which made me feel even more like an invisible loser than my normal state.

I guess that's a good philosophical question. Is one an invisible loser if their goal was to be an invisible loser?

But now I'm here. And yes, it's a mistake. I walked past all those big-ass new cars and I'm standing in a big-ass foyer and DeAndre's big-ass staircase is literally vibrating from the music being spun by a DJ. I'm pretty sure the DJ is a girl in our senior class named Jade. But the point still stands. A freaking DJ is in this foyer, playing Kate Bush's "Running Up That Hill."

I've never even met DeAndre, but I know who he is. One of the side superpowers of being an invisible loser is that you notice all kinds of things. Some people would call that creepy. I choose to call it observant.

I wind my way through the foyer, which is full of bodies in a motion I guess some people would describe as dancing. I bump into a couple of shoulders and murmur a "Sorry sorry" as I push through.

Then I reach another massive room that is full of couches. People are sprawled all around, talking, and drinking out of red Solo cups. Despite my best efforts in AP Chem, I'm not like a professional scientist, but I feel pretty good about my hypothesis that those cups are filled with more than water.

This room also contains the biggest television I've ever seen in my whole life. A Mario Kart race streams across it as people yell and chant at the screen. A girl named Sam from the local band There Is No Kevin in Team has her pink Converse on the table and her controller in hand as if the tournament is no sweat. If I was a different person in another life, I might want to play. I mean, I kind of like Mario Kart.

But no. I need to find Miranda, show my support, and then make my exit.

"Hussein?"

I freeze. I swear it sounds like someone is calling my last name. Which doesn't make any sense because I don't know anyone here except for Miranda and Memi and that's neither of their voices and they never call me by my last name—

"Hussein?" the voice says again.

I turn to the left and there he is.

Liam Freaking Richardson-Ito. Okay, his middle name isn't Freaking. It's Scott. Yeah, file that knowledge under either creepy or observant. Your call.

But you see, the thing is, I've been in love with Liam Freaking Richardson-Ito since I was six years old and we were in first grade together and he presented his show-and-tell on making the perfect peanut butter and jelly sandwich, and I don't even like peanut butter, but that was enough for me. And don't tell me that six years old is too early to be in love because this is a flame that I have carried—and oh my god, he is walking toward me.

"Hussein?" he says for the third time. "I sent you a message when I heard you moved back, but you never answered, and I thought maybe I'd gotten my info mixed up. But look. Here you are!" He spreads his arms out.

Wait. Is he trying to hug me? Or is he just expressing his feelings? A statistical study of his Instagram would lead me to believe that Liam Freaking Richardson-Ito does fall into the subspecies of humans that likes a hug. But also the kind that makes dramatic gestures with his arms. He has a whole series of photos with very loud, exaggerated poses.

Holy shit, he's walking even closer to me. His arms are now down, though. Not sure if that should make me feel better or disappointed. What is even happening?

My heart pounds in my ears. Or maybe I'm just hearing the loud-ass music. Either way, I'm pretty sure I'm about to vomit. I look again at Liam. His face is a mixture of confusion and amusement, which makes the hurling feeling inside me stronger.

So I do what any normal functioning human being would do, I bolt. I should run all the way back to my Volvo, but I'm not breathing that well, so I collapse onto one of the Adirondack chairs that are on DeAndre's big-ass wraparound porch.

# PENNY WASHINGTON
## THE POPULAR GIRL

## PART II

"OKAY. GIMME YOUR NUMBER," COLIN SAYS. I HESitate for a moment, which I guess he notices because he totally rolls his eyes at me.

"Dude. So I can dial it . . . to help you find your phone. Asking around while taking dance breaks isn't working," he says.

"It's on silent, though," I say, ignoring the last bit. If the phone wasn't on silent, I would've suggested this an hour ago, or at least after I fully came down from my high.

"Challenge accepted," he laughs.

So I give him my number. Let's find this damn phone.

" 'Here we gooo!' " I say in perfect imitation of the Mario game, which keeps pouring in from the tournament in the other room.

"That was dorky. I liked it. Are you actually a secret dork, Penny Washington?"

"I'm just a woman of many hidden talents."

I put my hand on Colin's arm to make sure we stay together through the people talking and laughing and drinking and slobbering on each other's faces in the near dark.

"What's up, Penny?" Sophie B. intercepts us near the staircase. She's the queen bee of the sophomore popular kids and clearly riding high after being nominated for Prom Princess, even though she's too young to go. I'm fairly certain she and her friends bullied half the juniors into voting for her, but it doesn't much matter, does it? Not really. Maybe when I was her age I might've cared, too, but now I've got much more important things to worry about, like my mother. Not to mention my future.

"Fucking Nathan took my phone," I tell her.

Focus. I need to focus. Mama's gonna be so worried if she tries to get ahold of me and I don't answer. Never mind that she's the one who told me to go out tonight. Or what if Ms. Marta needs to know something about Mama's meds? Or Mama gets into one of her moods and Ms. Marta's not able to get ahold of me to help her talk Mama down. For a very brief moment, some small, horrible piece of me feels relieved that dealing with Mama isn't my problem for however long it takes to find this phone.

"Yo, we gotta find Penny's phone!" Sophie B. shouts at her minions, and suddenly I have a whole search party, though I'm certain in about ten minutes they won't remember what they were even searching for.

"We'll take the basement!" Sophie B. says.

As Colin and I head up the stairs, we pass photos of De-Andre and his baby sister growing taller along the wall. A family portrait in matching white button-downs. Kendra at kindergarten graduation. DeAndre in Pop Warner football. There's even a picture with me and DeAndre from homecoming freshman year. Colin seems to linger on that one for a half second longer than the rest.

"He's a good dude for the most part," I say, looking at DeAndre. "He means well, anyway."

"Mhmm," Colin says, and I swear I detect a hint of jealousy. "Did you hear Mia broke up with him?"

"I know. Poor Dre, it's no wonder he's all messed up," I say.

"Love is dead . . . ," Colin says dryly.

And suddenly, I realize where I know Colin from!

"AP Euro!" I shout.

"What?" Colin says.

"You were in my class, right?"

"We fell in love over the Defenestration of Prague . . . I'm hurt you don't remember." He laughs.

"That class was so damn early in the morning. I was half asleep through most of it."

"You and everyone else," he says as we start our search in the first room to the right.

Last time I was in here, DeAndre's sister's bedroom was covered in like preschool-type toys, big and plastic in primary colors. Lots of LEGOs. Now Kendra seems to be into those American Girl dolls. A doll that looks just like her rests in the middle of her bed. She's also got a big ole iMac atop a lovely vintage desk overlooking the backyard, where there are shenanigans going on around the pool. And a fancy gaming chair. Seriously, who gets a gaming chair for a seven-year-old?

"So . . . where are you going to school next year?"

He waits for me to respond, but instead I stare out the

window as Todd Harris attempts a skateboard trick into the pool and just narrowly avoids cracking his head open.

"Seven out of ten!" somebody shouts from the pool chairs.

"I'm not sure yet . . . it's complicated." I sit down on Kendra's twin bed and grab ahold of her doll for comfort. The doll's hair is so soft, I keep stroking it against my cheek.

Colin sifts through a bunch of tiny accessories. He lifts up a tiny doll phone in triumph. "Aha!"

"My hero!" I laugh.

"Dude! This shit is surprisingly realistic?! I mean, look at this camping set! This doll seriously has itty-bitty granola bars in her backpack!"

"I've never been camping," I say.

"My parents and I used to go all the time up to Starved Rock . . ." He drifts off for a moment. "When I was a little kid, I used to get so excited by the waterfalls, even though I'd seen them a billion times already. And we would all argue as my dad pitched the tent, 'cause we were tired from hiking all day, but after that we'd sit by the fire and laugh, and stuff ourselves with s'mores, and it was the best fucking time . . ."

"Why'd you stop?" I say.

"My mom died. Cancer . . . ," he says.

"It happens," I say before freezing.

Omigod, did I just say that? I shouldn't have just said that. This poor boy is pouring out his heart to me, and this is how I respond?! I don't know that I've ever said anything so heinous in my life. My brain isn't working right. Like it's completely short-circuited. System Failure. Red Alert.

"I honestly don't know why I just said that!" I say. "I'm so so sorry."

He's going to think I'm a complete asshole. *I* think I'm a complete asshole!

Instead, he starts to laugh.

"My dad's dead, too, is what I meant," I offer quickly. "Also cancer."

"It happens," he says, and starts to laugh harder. I hit him with one of Kendra's pillows.

"How old were you when it happened?" I ask.

"Last year," he says. "It was rough. I dunno . . . School seemed pointless at the time. Dances. I was angry, or sad, or both, and listening to people bitch about SAT scores or like who they had a crush on . . . anyway, I ditched a lot."

"I can imagine," I say. But I don't have to imagine at all. That's how I've been feeling all year, ever since Ms. Marta recognized the signs and recommended we take Mom to visit a specialist for a mental acuity test.

"How old were you?" he says.

"I was just a baby. I don't really remember him at all . . . ," I explain. "My mom says I look just like him, though."

"He must've been . . . h—" he says, and then catches himself abruptly.

"Were you about to call my dead dad hot?"

"I was gonna say handsome!" He looks sufficiently mortified. "You're not the only one who's had a few tonight!"

"It happens," I say.

We continue down the hall to DeAndre's room. Inside, DeAndre is passed the fuck out on the bed.

"Yo, Dre?" I ask.

He mumbles in response.

"Did Nathan Henderson come in here?" Colin asks.

DeAndre grunts. I can't tell if it's a yes or a no. Colin dials the number. We turn over every stack of junk and crawl around on the floor, checking for a lit screen. Dre really should've cleaned his room better before a party. Even with Colin and me going full Indiana Jones in his bedroom, Dre doesn't so much as budge. I start humming the Indiana Jones theme song (second-best ride at Disneyland behind Space Mountain—I made my mother go three times in a row when we visited California) while we search, and at some point, drunk-ass Dre starts to hum it, too, from the bed, which makes Colin and me laugh our asses off.

"So . . . why did you kiss me earlier? Other than my boyish good looks and natural charm?"

"Is that what we're calling this?" I laugh and gesture at his face.

"Hey, I'm doing something right! Rumor has it I'm now dating the most popular girl in school!"

"I just . . . panicked," I say. "I mean, Jenny broke up with me over text! After almost three years."

"She's an absolute idiot. Who with half a brain would let you go? You're so smart and you're funny and . . ." He trails off, looking at me so intently that I have to look away.

"You're gonna give me a big head," I say.

"It's nothing your bajillion followers don't say every day."

"That's not real life . . . ," I counter. I feel an involuntary full-body flush. "Anyway . . . I'm a lot right now, I guess. She didn't want to deal with it. My life. It's messy."

Colin searches my eyes for more. It's like he's trying to stare into me. It makes me feel naked, vulnerable, like every emotion is just under the surface. Like at any moment this boy could reach out and touch my fear, sadness, guilt, or even joy. He's shared so much of himself, maybe I should tell him about

Mama. But what's happening with Mama is such an ongoing hurt, even pressing at it a little might make me come undone.

"Do you want to talk about it?" he says gently.

"Absolutely not."

I didn't come here for a therapy session. I came to this party to not feel anything.

"Mia!!!" DeAndre groans theatrically from the bed. "Mi-aaaa! Why???"

COLIN AND I move on to the next bedroom, where somebody is hooking up hard-core. Like stripping off clothes and everything, which is totally cool for them, but I really need this phone. I definitely feel like a creeper entering a room where other people are hooking up, but like, I don't want to stop them and ask *Excuse me, have you seen my phone? No? Carry on!* either?

Colin begins a *Mission: Impossible*–style crawl across the floor, and I get down and follow his lead, doing my best not to make eye contact with the couple. The whole thing is definitely absurd, but kinda fun. A wayward bra actually lands on his head, and I can't help laughing out loud.

"What the fuck, Penny?"

The lights quickly turn on, and there are Jenny and V. Again.

V sits up and covers her chest. She doesn't have much of one, but she's taut and lean like an athlete. Much more androgynous than I am, which makes me feel both good and bad about myself at the same time. Maybe V is more Jenny's type.

"Oh boy," Colin mumbles.

"I'm just . . . I'm looking for my phone," I say. It sounds like a lie, I know. I stand there frozen.

"Get out!" Jenny yells at Colin, who looks over at me.

"Can you do me a really big favor?" I ask her. "Can you just check your phone and see if my mother's texted you? Nathan took my phone and you know how she is . . . please. Please."

"Yeah, all right." Jenny softens. "One sec."

"Turn around!" she growls at Colin.

Sure enough, there's several messages from Mama from twenty minutes ago.

**MAMA:**

Is Penny with you?

Are you girls all right?

Please text me when you see this. I can't get ahold of Penny.

"I'll let her know you're safe," Jenny says gently.

"Thank you," I say.

I know I should turn and leave it at that, but I can't. "Did you guys . . . Was this happening when we were together?"

"No . . . I mean we kinda liked each other—"

"But we didn't do anything!" V interjects.

"And now you have Conrad!" Jenny says with a hint of jealousy.

"Actually, it's Col—" Colin starts.

But before he can finish, because I have impeccable timing, I throw up all over myself. Colin quickly grabs my hair for me as I do it again. My puke tastes like rancid pineapple and herb.

"Omigod, are you okay?" V says.

I need to get out of here ASAP.

And because I'm on the floor, and mortified, and kind of afraid of puking again if I stand, I decide to slow-crawl across the floor out of the bedroom. And Colin, god bless him, decides to crawl behind me.

"You didn't have to crawl, too," I say when we get far enough away and Jenny slams the door behind us.

"Solidarity," he says, and laughs.

I peek down at my soiled dress. "I'm disgusting."

"Never," Colin says. "Not even possible."

First the spilled alcohol, now this. How many indignities must I be expected to suffer in one night? Colin starts to lift up his shirt. "Wear this instead!" he says.

His undershirt rides up, exposing just a bit of his nascent happy trail. Dude is surprisingly ripped under there.

"What are you doing? Put your shirt back down, you drunk," I laugh.

"I'm not the one with vomit all over myself."

"Touché . . ."

"That was so shitty. I'm sorry, Penny. About that girl and Jenny."

"It's all right. I'm over her," I say, and I think I actually mean it.

"You are?" He stares at me.

"Why? Do you want me to be?" I poke him in his stomach, and it comes out flirtier than I mean it to be.

"BRB, gonna try to wash this shit off my dress," I say to Colin, who's blushing hard.

# JRUE EDWARDS

## THE CLASS CLOWN

## PART II

THE PARTY IS IN FULL FORCE AT THIS POINT. Sadie's whirling around her camera, Savoy and Miranda are off wardrobe-changing, and Jade's DJ'ing and spinning the kinds of songs that make everyone dance. Kendrick's "Die Hard" blending into the Marías' "Calling U Back" mixing into Chayla's "Falling." Even the kids who normally stay posted on the walls get sucked into the vibe for a few tracks, weed is in the air, and love, too (or at least *like*) as kids smush lips together.

Oh, there's also a dog on the loose—Daisy, I think—roaming from friend group to clique to random in-progress hookups, kids instantly showing her mad petting love; whoever the dog belongs to, though, I swear she's got a bone for DeAndre. Every time I spot her, she's jumping up DeAndre's back, dropping her paws onto either side of his waist, and swaying her doggy hips to the bass line.

And not to be upstaged, a kid bumps into me from behind and I look over my shoulder and see . . . an actual kid . . .

As in the family farm variety.

Okay, damn, I was trying to cleverly say *goat*, that Brenda, our unofficial mascot, is no longer in the garage but is now solidly in the middle of the party and yet it's all working.

Everything feels right.

Maybe even kinda meant to be.

But I've still got a couple Mia-centric objectives to check off before tonight's all the way perfect.

A quick recap of my party agenda:

1. ACTION ITEM #3B: Confess feelings to Mia.
2. ACTION ITEM #4: Maybe make out with Mia?

But it's like every time Mia and I are almost next to each other, something or someone's dragging us back apart. Classic rom-com shit, I guess.

Right on cue, Mia and I meet eyes from across the room and she gives me a little wave, cuffs her hands around her mouth like a megaphone, and yells something I can't quite make out.

I shake my head, my eyebrows sliding upward like *What?*

She tries in vain a few more times and then takes her hands away. She overemphasizes each word so I can read her lips.

*Are you having fun?*

*Yes, what about you?* I shoot back, except either I'm not as good at telegraphing my words or she stinks at lip-reading because then my phone buzzes and it's a text . . . from Mia.

**MIA:**
Sorry lip-syncing isn't my jam

I didn't even realize she had my phone number.

I mean, I guess I knew she had it, because I have hers, but I guess I didn't think *she knew* she had it, if that makes sense? My phone buzzes thrice more in rapid succession.

**MIA:**

Ugh

Lip-reading*

Wanna dance?

I type *Yes* but then decide that a gif would be better. Because let's be clear: nothing says I want you, I care about you, you're perfect for me, you're my person, quite like the perfect gif. One that's thoughtful but also funny. Charming but also flirtatious. And I'm the kind of person who likes to send gifs you probably have never seen before because I feel like it makes it mean more, you know?

I hold up a *one sec* finger in Mia's direction as my other hand quickly scrolls through gifs ranging from *overused* to *cute but not quite* and I can feel the pull. I'm so close to the right one. And boom, I find it—except I make the mistake of scrolling a bit more, and I see another perfect one. And another. And now it's like what do I do? Send all three? Nope, too thirsty. Send the best two out of three? No, just pick *one*, Jrue, I tell myself. Just one, dude. And I've all but narrowed it down when—

The front doors explode open.

And there, in the living room or family room—or whatever really rich people call their front sitting room—stand three kids from Bayside, our rival school. One lanky redhead, a muscly blond, and their ringleader, aka the only athlete in the county who might be as talented as DeAndre—

Bryson Baller.

No, that is not his street name, or his clever sports nick-name, you know, on account of him balling so hard.

Nope, his last name is really Baller.

And actually, he really does ball so hard.

"We're here for Brenda, and we're not leaving without her!" Bryson bellows as one of the Bayside kids makes his way to Jade, prompting her to cut the music. She flips him off.

"Booooo," all the partygoers say in surprisingly near-perfect unison, which is dope considering no one's like *on the count of three* . . .

"Bayside sucks!" someone yells from the back.

"Get the hell out!" another kid barks, sparking another se-ries of boos, each louder than the last.

But Bryson isn't budging.

And based on his very chiseled frame and impeccably su-perb posture, he doesn't seem to be any closer to getting the hell out.

But then a blast of electronic feedback sends everyone cov-ering their ears as DeAndre grabs a mic. And now everyone is quiet, a hush rushing through the big-ass house, spilling out onto the front and back lawns, as everyone awaits DeAndre's voice. He commands attention, even with dried-up sleep drool on his face.

"Listen, even under normal circumstances, we wouldn't wanna chill with the enemy. But in my house? This isn't some Disney movie where the rivals kiss and make up. Not happen-ing," he booms.

"You wish," Bryson says, smirking, as he folds his arms across his impressively toned chest.

And I get that you guys are like, *Damn, Jrue, you're really into this Bryson dude,* but it's not that, I swear. I'm just trying to set the whole scene.

Anyway, DeAndre goes on. "So you say you're here for Brenda, but I'm not sure most of us know any Brendas. Do you guys know any Brendas?" he asks, playing to the crowd.

"Noooooo," the crowd replies.

"But you know who might know a Brenda? My man, and the funniest dude in all of Florence Hills, Jrue Edwards. Jrue, get your ass over here, man."

And okay, a part of me wants to not go, to run out of the room or at least drop to the floor and duck everyone, but I can't do that. Not now. Because this is it. This is what I've wanted. My chance at cementing my legacy as not just one of the funniest kids at Florence Hills (ever!), but the best prankster our school's ever seen. Yep, it's time for GOAT status.

I make my way through the crowd until I'm standing next to DeAndre, and he wraps his arm around my shoulder. "Now we're not saying we *took* your Brenda, but supposing we were to stumble across her, her being lost and all, well then in that case, you can be sure we'll take great care of her, treat her like one of our own, because you know, we love all animals here at Florence, amirite?"

The crowd goes wild.

"Because we're animals, amirite?" DeAndre asks.

And now everyone's in a frenzy as DeAndre hands the mic to me.

"Tell them what they gotta do if they wanna walk outta here with Brenda, Jrue."

I nod as kids shout out all kinds of crazy tasks.

"Make them streak through the neighborhood. Take it all off, Bryson!"

"Make them throw the next game so maybe we actually win for once!"

And I raise my hand instinctively, and everyone quiets enough for me to say, "This is what it's gonna take to get Brenda back, and you'll find it's not only *not* problematic, you get to keep your clothes on, guys, don't worry, but it's also a display of incredible sportsmanship, don't you think, DeAndre?"

DeAndre leans into the mic. "Cosigned."

"All you have to do, Bayside, is put on a little costume and sing two little songs."

"Fuck off," Bryson says, unmoved. "For it to be a rivalry, you'd actually have to give us a challenge, right?"

The crowd jeers, but DeAndre settles them back down. "No, no, that's well within our *rival's* right. We haven't beaten them on the field. But off the field, well, from where I'm standing, looks to be a different story."

"We love you, D!" someone screams from the backyard, followed by whoops and catcalls.

"I love y'all, too," DeAndre says, grinning. "But okay, let's be real. They don't have to honor our request . . . as long as they know they're not walking outta here with Brenda until they do."

And that's how it happens.

That's how it goes down.

Ten minutes later, Bryson and his two buds are rocking three homemade goat costumes and singing "The Three Billy Goats Gruff" before very begrudgingly launching into a not-very-awesome rendition of our Florence Hills High fight song.

Every second captured by a hundred phones.

The Bayside Trio's trending locally on every social even before we hand over the leash.

"Bye, Brenda, I'm gonna miss you," I say, petting her one last time.

"You're welcome back anytime," DeAndre adds. "Don't be a stranger. You're one of us now."

"BAAAAAAAAAA," Brenda says in response.

"Wait a minute," I say, grabbing the mic. "This isn't how we roll. We can't send them off without at least a drink or two, right, guys?"

And all the partygoers, my classmates and a good chunk of the rest of the Florence Hills student body, cheer.

"Baaaaaaaad Light for everyone," I yell into the mic. "Let's go, DJ!"

And a bottle of beer materializes before Bryson and he stares at it a beat, the air buzzing with suspense, and then shakes his head.

"What the hell, right?" Bryson says, snatching the beer and sinking his teeth into the side of the can, shotgunning it.

And now there are more cheers mixed in with shouts of *You the man, Jrue, you rock, bro,* floating through the near-summer Friday night, as Jade moves her dials, pushes her sliders, sending a wave of music slamming back into us, thumping from the monstrous speakers, jolting everyone into full party mode.

Bryson and DeAndre go note for note in the center of the room, one epic lip-sync battle that no one asked for but all of us needed, fake-belting out "The Boy Is Mine," Bryson holding down Brandy's verses while DeAndre's conjuring Monica.

Oh, and okay, maybe me inviting them to stay and kick it might've been me stalling so I could carry out the last part of ACTION ITEM #5 . . .

As I shake the cans of temporary paint and spray all of our glad tidings and heartfelt sentiments that have been bottled up in us for the last four years all over Bryson's beautiful red Range Rover . . .

**FLORENCE HILLS are the REAL CHAMPS**

**HONK if you think this car is making up for my inadequacies**

**FHHS is the TRUE GOAT**

**Help eradicate bro-ism! Adopt a Baysider today!**

Because, you know, what good is a prank unless you share it with everyone?

I'M THROWING THE paint can evidence in the trash when a voice behind me says my name.

"Hey," I say.

"Finally, I found you. I see you did it," Sadie says, nodding toward the paint. "Congrats."

"Thanks," I say. "I couldn't have done it without you."

Sadie half smiles. "Eh, probably not, but you still would've tried."

And it's weird because I suddenly realize we're standing in DeAndre's garage, but with so much space between us. Almost like there are tractor beams keeping us physically apart. I take a step closer. Then another.

"Does it feel as good as you hoped?" Sadie asks.

"What part?"

"Being the best practical joker in Florence Hills history."

I shrug. "Honestly? It feels better to know I made a few people laugh. That feels good." I take another step closer. "All that history stuff? I think that's probably for someone else to decide."

Sadie nods, the moonlight slanting into the garage behind her, half her face brighter than the other. "So now what?"

"I don't know," I say back. Because it's true. I don't know. I don't have any special objectives to complete beyond tonight. Or even beyond ACTION ITEM #5. But maybe I should work on that.

"Have you talked to Mia?"

"We've texted, but that's it so far."

"You know what you're gonna say?"

"What's in my heart, I guess? I know that sounds super corny but . . . it's what I got."

"It does sound super corny, but that doesn't mean it's not right."

And somehow the gap between us has been cut in half, so that if I wanted to, I could reach out and graze her with the tip of my fingers.

"Are you just saying that because you're kinda corny, too?"

Sadie laughs. "Your corny and my corny are not the same, okay?"

I smile. "Whatever. That's what you think." My phone vibrates and I check the screen.

"Fairy godfather telling you it's time to go home?"

"It's Mia, actually."

Sadie leans toward my screen, the way she always does, the way we always do, trading gossip or watching a video, or . . . anything. The point is, it's not a big deal.

"Oooh, she's asking where you are. Saying she needs to talk to you still."

I nod.

"Well, what are you standing here for? Go find her."

I take a step to the side because I don't know, something feels . . . off. "We're good, right?"

"Huh?"

"You and me, we're good?"

"What?" Sadie laughs, not super convincingly. "Why would we not be good? We're always good, right?"

"Yeah," I agree. "Always, even when we're not, it's like we're always on our way back to good."

"Okay, you really are super corny. How did I not see just how chronic your condition was until right now?"

I laugh. "It's all your fault, see?"

And then my brain does something weird and we're not in DeAndre's massive garage anymore, we're backward in time, less than twenty-four hours ago, sneaking into Sugar Ridge Groves, a little ranchlike setup, where people rent stalls to house their large animals—mostly horses.

Except a few days prior, when I was still trying to brainstorm a prank worthy of the Florence Hills High Hall of Fame, I'd gotten a tip that a certain rival's four-legged furry friend boarded there, too, and then it was on . . .

Well, almost.

Naturally, I needed backup. And who better to back me

up than the one person who'd consistently had my back since day one?

"What do goats even eat?" Sadie kept asking, until she was one ask away from the *If you value your life, please don't ask again.*

"Hmmm . . ." I stroked my chin hairs with the hand *not* currently clutching the inside of the stall as I lowered myself down into hay and shit pebbles. "If only there was a quick and convenient way to find answers . . ."

"I really hate you," she snapped back as she fished her phone from her pocket. "Hey, Siri, what do goats eat?"

*"I'm sorry, I cannot help you right now."*

And I couldn't fight off a laugh as I dropped into the stall.

"See?" Sadie said, firing me a look. "So much for quick and convenient. Wait, do you hear footsteps?" she said at the precise moment I was hearing footsteps.

My face twisted and my stomach dropped. "Oh shoot, someone's coming! Hide!"

"Hide?" Sadie shook her head. "Hide where?!"

"Here," I said, grabbing her by the arms and lifting her over the five-foot wall, except I lost my footing, sending us both crashing into the mud. At least we hoped it was only mud.

And we saw a flashlight moving from stall to stall, sweeping across the long barn corridor, and we knew we were caught, except Sadie, always smart on her feet, got the bright idea we should bury ourselves in the straw. Which we did, diving into the hay together, wiggling and trying to keep from giggling as we stuffed ourselves deep into the scratchy glorified yellow grass.

Of course, the flashlight never made it deep enough into

the stalls to even glimpse us. Fact, the only light other than the moon, this same moon now just behind Sadie's shoulder, that we saw was the flash of our phones as we posed together, long reeds of hay poking from our hair; me breaking one in half and us putting them in our mouths, like "real farmers." It's a wonder we even got Brenda in my Town & Country, but we did. Because that's how we rolled together. We made shit work. No, we made shit do more than just work. We made shit magic.

And now I'm back in the garage, Sadie in front of me, tucking a few stray curls behind her ear, smiling at me in a way that makes her dimples pop. Only I can't read my best friend's eyes, and I stuff my hands into my pockets because suddenly it feels weird to have arms.

She bumps my shoulder with her own. "Some friend I am, I guess."

"Yeah," I agree. "Some friend you are."

# PENNY WASHINGTON

## THE POPULAR GIRL

I SEARCH THROUGH DEANDRE'S MOM'S CLOTHES to find something to replace my puke dress. I decide on a pullover leather-look black sports bra and a pair of perfectly worn baggy jeans at the farthest end of her closet that look like she's had them since the nineties. Colin patiently waits outside like a puppy tied up to a bicycle rack outside a store. He's got the loveliest eyes with these super-long lashes. They're kinda sleepy in the best way.

"Outfit change! I love it. Total icon move, Penny," one of Sophie B.'s minions says as they stumble past.

"We're working on a few leads for your phone! I think we're close!" they shout as they miss two steps on the stairs and grab onto the railing for dear life.

"Shall we continue, m'lady?" Colin says, and I just raise my eyebrows at him 'cause are we in *Game of Thrones* or something? Though I guess high school is kinda like that—everybody's horny and vying for power, and it seems super important until one day it all ends abruptly and you're like, *Hmm, okay, not sure what that was. Now what?*

Which is definitely how I'm feeling right now about my entire damn life.

As Colin and I continue searching through the house, we find out we have a stupid number of things in common, not limited to the fact that (a) we were born in the same hospital, only three days apart, (b) our mothers are both named Katherine, (c) we both love Korean horror films, and (d) we both vehemently hate zoos ("cruel!") as well as the TV show *Friends*.

"Like that episode with Chandler's dad?! WTF? And where are all the Black and brown folks? In New York? Seriously, why did people love that show? They should've left that shit in the nineties where it belongs," Colin says.

"Jennifer Aniston's nipples," I say. "I'm sure that was like half of their ratings right there."

Colin blushes furiously at the mention of the word "nipples."

"Are you blushing?" I tease. "'Nipples' did it. Didn't it? Don't be embarrassed, we all have them."

"Omigod, stop!" He's beet-red.

"Nipples. Nipples. Hard nipples!" I yell out that last one and he goes to shush me.

"You're sooo not what I thought you'd be," he says.

"Better, I hope," I say.

"You know, my mother says the American fear of the nipple ended Janet Jackson's career," he says.

"Omigod, my mama loves herself some Janet! I used to wake up on Saturday to her blaring 'If' and telling me to get up, it was time to clean the house. Which was definitely not the most appropriate song for a small child, now that I think about it."

"Your mother also forced you to listen to Janet? I thought I was the only one! Must be a Black-mama-of-a-certain-age thing," he says.

We both start to sing along to the chorus, *"If I was your girl, oh, the things I'd do to you . . ."*

Which then gets me thinking, just momentarily, about what a good kisser he was, and what other things that maybe it wouldn't be so awful to do with him. He's got the slightest gap between his two front teeth that's super cute when he smiles.

"How did we never talk before this?" I wonder aloud.

"You're Penny Washington." He shrugs. "And I'm nobody. I'm like practically invisible here."

"Don't say that," I say. "Besides, what made you come up to me tonight?"

He shrugs. "It's the last month of senior year. Why not?"

"Well. I'm glad you did," I say.

"Yeah. Me too . . . bae." He smirks.

I groan. "Ugh, no. Not bae."

"Lover?!"

"You're really entertaining yourself, aren't you?" I say.

"Wait . . . I got it, honeybuns!"

We end up bumping into Fernanda.

"Oh, Penny, do you think you'd be able to find another ride home?" she says, grinning. "Unless you really need me."

"Tell me you didn't get back with Spencer, please," I say. I'm the worst. I totally should've checked in with her sooner.

"Hell no! I'll tell you everything later! I'm getting closer to Kai," she says with a slight nod of her head toward him.

"Omigod, finally!!!!!" I squeal.

"You okay?" she asks.

"Hell yeah!" I add a little too emphatically. I mean, I'm

definitely pretty certain that tonight is definitely not my night, but I'm genuinely happy for Fernanda.

"Drink up, honeybuns," Colin says, and passes me a Solo cup full of water.

"What and who is this?" Fernanda says, lifting her eyebrows and eyeing Colin as he places his hand on the small of my back on cue.

"It's . . . nothing," I say, wriggling away from him. "He's just helping me search for my phone."

I wish I could take it back as soon as I say it. Poor Colin looks like I kicked a puppy. "If you say so . . . ," she says with a wink, not even pretending to be subtle, before heading in Kai's general direction.

"Sorry about that . . . I thought you needed me to . . . ," Colin says.

"Nonono, it's cool! I know you were trying to help," I say. But I can tell I've hurt his feelings 'cause he grows super quiet. I don't know why I did that. Colin's not Jenny, or Dre or even Jrue. He's not popular in the slightest. Zero social standing. But he's kind, and he's funny, and I genuinely haven't had this much fun with somebody in ages. Besides, what does any of that popularity shit even matter when you're about to graduate? What did it ever really matter? And why am I still clinging to it?

In the basement, a couple of sophomores drink DeAndre's parents' good wine straight from the bottle. He's gonna be in sooo much trouble come Sunday. He's about to be grounded until he heads off to Howard!

"We found it! We found it!" Sophie B. presents my phone to me like it's a crown. It looks like it's been good and trampled on. Fuck.

"I think the goat stepped on it," she says, making a sad face. "Sorry."

And I can't help but start to laugh—who gets their phone ruined by a goat?

"Want a sip?" One of her minions passes me a very French, very fancy bottle that says it's from the actual year I was born. I take a sip, 'cause at this point, why not?

"I'm going to kick Nathan's ass," I say, also taking my phone from Sophie B.

"You want us to destroy him for you?" Sophie B. says. "Just say the word."

Damn, Sophie B. Chill.

"No need for the nuclear option," I say. "Thanks, though."

"Um . . . well, now you have your phone . . . I guess I should let you get back to your friends," Colin says.

"Aren't we friends?" I say.

"I'm 'nothing,' remember?" he mumbles. "Anyway. I guess I'll see you around, Penny."

"Colin, wait!"

But he's already disappeared into the crowd.

A broken phone means I'll have to use my laptop to record and edit my videos, and it's old and the video quality isn't as good. Plus, I can't get the same angles that I can with my phone. It's definitely not even remotely as portable. My iCloud has been full for ages, so I know I'm going to have lost some of my photos. Which means losing memories of high school, but most importantly, with my mom. There's also our last trip to visit my grandmother in Missouri, before she died, not to mention our trip to Iceland early last year. Mama said she wanted to cross seeing the northern lights off her bucket list, but I wonder if maybe she knew something was wrong, even then. And now

I've gone and messed things up with Colin, who feels like the first person who's really actually seen me in forever. I start to tear up.

"What the hell did you give her?" I hear somebody say to Sophie's minion, who drunkenly slurs, "It's from France!"

# FERNANDA MANNING

## THE JOCK

$$\boxed{\textbf{\textit{PART III}}}$$

EVENTUALLY, AFTER A SHOT OF TEQUILA THAT sends a jolt through me and a boost from Penny, I muster up some courage and walk over to Kai. The cheer routines are gratefully over. "I want to talk to you," I say. "Can we go somewhere quiet?"

A smile teases Kai's lips as he nods, takes my hand, and leads me to a room at the end of the hallway on the first floor. I don't think we're supposed to be here, but at this point, I don't care.

The room turns out to be a kind of catchall, full of discarded things that don't match the stylish upstairs. It's dark, but with the blinds open, enough light reaches us from the pool area and the neighbor's floodlights that I can tell just enough of our surroundings.

There's an old daybed shoved against a wall, and a china cabinet with old ceramic dolls.

"Yikes," I say, stepping away from them.

Kai chuckles and walks to the window, where I catch a glimpse of a curly-haired girl outside. She's petite and shy. Zara, I remember her name is. We have study hall together. She looks like she's seen a ghost.

But I don't have time to wonder about anyone else but Kai.

"Sorry about the scratch again. I'm usually not that clumsy," I say, my voice small and thin. At least the bleeding stopped.

Kai brushes a hand on his cheek adorably and laughs. "I told you it's not a big deal. Besides, that's what I get for standing between you and a ball to slam!"

I'm flattered that he thinks I'm so driven, but also, I'm a little worried that he thinks that's all that I am.

I playfully shove him with my open hand on his chest. It's not the best idea I ever had. Or maybe it's the most brilliant? Because when I rest it over his heart, I can tell how fast it's beating, and how his breath hitches in his throat.

"I've been wanting to tell you something for ages," I say.

"What?" he asks.

He's not making things easy for me, either. Telling him that I like him is like I'm undressing in front of him. The image this paints in my mind makes me bold and shy all at the same time.

Kai takes my hands and squeezes them softly. Encouragingly. I guess it's the cheerleader in him, spreading courage all around.

Right this second, I want to tell him that I like him, I really want him to know. What better way than to kiss him? And I want this kiss to mean something. He's not a trophy like I was to Spencer or just another for my shelf.

"Can I kiss you?" I ask, my lips a hair away from his.

He cocks his head to the side, and for a second, I think

he's going to leave this storage room and go back to the party. Maybe that's not what he expected me to say. But then he closes that crucial distance and kisses me.

His lips are soft, and they taste just like I imagined.

Kai sighs against my lips and wraps his arms around me like the music is a whirlpool and he has to hold on to me to stay safe. I break off the kiss first and say, "I've wanted to do *this* for ages," and when I kiss him again, he's smiling as he kisses me back, whispering, "God, you're beautiful," into my ear. I wrap my arms around him, and he pushes me against the wall as we try to make up for lost time not being honest about our feelings. He kisses his way down my neck and back to my mouth.

Turns out, I have no idea how long we go at it. Neither one of us is keeping track of time, but then when he slides his hand across my chest, a crinkly sound startles us so hard, we bump foreheads.

"What was that sound?" he asks.

I groan, then pause. The paper in my bra! I don't want him to think I filled my bra with paper to pretend to be who I'm not. If I've learned anything tonight, it's to be vulnerable and honest.

Without considering what it looks like, I take the bucket list out of my bra and give it to him.

"You really had paper stashed in your bra?" he jokes.

"You're going to die when you see the last line."

He takes the paper from my hand. He's still smiling, which has to be a good sign, right?

But then my phone chimes with a text.

**CYNTHIA:**
Have you scored with Kai yet? Is that why we can't find you?

I laugh, paraphrasing it for him, but he doesn't even smile.

"What's wrong?" I ask, already wishing I could turn back time.

"The bucket list is kind of cute. But . . . score? Am I another trophy you can win like everything else? Typical jock behavior, huh? You're no better than the guys on the football team."

"What?" I say, unable to find the words to explain that I feel the exact opposite.

The magic, the chemistry between us, is gone. I ruined it all by telling him the wrong thing.

"It's not what you think . . . My friends, like, it's just a phrase." Words are my enemy. Nothing I say tonight is coming out the right way. I can tell by the stony expression on his face, so I stop before I make things worse.

"Fer, this isn't how I wanted things to go with you, you know? A kiss in a storage room at a crazy party. I thought there was a real connection. I thought there was depth, and now I know it was all a game for you. Another accomplishment to check off."

Kai walks out of the room and leaves me in the dark on my own, the warmth of his lips already fading from mine.

# OSCAR GRAHAM

## THE WANNABE RAPPER

## PART IV

*NO ONE WANTS YOU TO RAP, OSCAR.*

Seriously? The fuck?

I've been moving through the party like a dejected zombie, replaying the night's events in my head. I'm back in the foggy living room, where Jade's playing the new Vince Staples song. She sees me coming and slips the headphone cup off her right ear. "Dude, that dog snatched your mic. Must've mistaken it for a bone. I don't know where it is."

"For real, Jade. You too?"

"Me too what?"

"Stasia snapped on me and said no one wants me to rap. I figured she was mad, but wow . . . one of my best friends is also on Team Hater."

She shakes her head slow and holds up a halting finger while she fades into some Lil Nas X. With the new track set, she tugs her headphones all the way off and levels with me. "Oscar, in a way, I get why you might be a little mad. We should've been straight up with you sooner. But you get like obsessively deranged when you get an idea in your head, and when you're like that, it's hard to get through to you."

"Obsessively deranged. Tell me how you really feel, Jade."

"Don't play victim. I'm not saying you're a serial killer who eats baby toes."

"Wait. There's somebody like that?" I shudder.

"I'm saying most of the time your tunnel vision is not a bad thing. You're like if Adderall was a person. It's the reason you're able to zero in on all your coding and do stuff in hours that would take most people—hell, forever. Most people could never do what you do. Savoy's been telling the whole planet to get on that fire app you made. That's not good enough for you, though. You gotta be a rapper. Hello, Black Dude Stereotype!"

"You're literally doing music, too." I smack the DJ MM/YY sign on her laptop. "This you?"

"For. Fun. Ninety-five percent chance, this is my last gig. I'm not taking any of this gear to college. I'm going to be a podiatrist."

"A foot doctor?"

"Yeah."

How did I not know that was what Jade wanted to do? "Hold on, you brought up a serial killer who eats toes, and you want to be a foot doctor. That's way more overlap than I'm comfortable with."

"My point is," she says, stabbing her index finger into my chest, "you're confusing what we tell the streets and what's real. Everyone on our block be posing when we have to. Music is safe. Sports are safe. You say that shit and no one rips into you because they understand. How long Jaylen Monroe been saying he's going to the NBA? You ever see dude even touch a basketball?"

I consider. "He is five foot one."

She motions to the mixer, and the speakers, and the lights. "For me, all this is a fun distraction. But you got a little online clout and took it serious. You shouldn't have."

What I'm hearing, I don't like, and a petty part points my irritation back to my girlfriend. "I always support Stasia's stuff no matter what! The photography. The theater."

"As you should. Because she's *good* good and you know it. You support her with your honesty. Get it?"

Damn. I—

Damn.

Jade says, "If you're mad about what I'm saying, cool. I can take that. We'll play some 2K over the weekend and it'll be squashed. If you're mad at Stasia, I'm almost certain you're dead wrong. That girl's been down from day one."

"Why she didn't just tell me what she thought before, though?"

"Obsessive. Deranged. Add in 'boy' and you might as well not have ears when she's talking sense to you."

A moment of silence kills the vibe. Partygoers become meerkats staring Jade down. She scrambles, gets another track going, then retrieves my gold mic from the guts of the piano. "Here. The dog didn't take it."

I snatch it. "I knew the dog didn't take it."

"Oh, go be salty somewhere else! You over here looking like a sad-faced clown is distracting me."

"Kiss my ass, Jade."

She says, "I love you, too," then gets back to mixing.

I stomp back into the crowd. Still mad. No plan. And I'm hurting.

That's what the truth does sometimes, right?

Trudging back into the family room, I spot a rare gap on the wraparound sofa. I flop down, sinking into the cushions, and get momentarily caught up in the intense Mario Kart tournament that now has a pool of money, two iPhones, and actual car keys on the floor between the trash-talking competitors.

The person sitting next to me leaves, and the seat is immediately taken by Isabel Pham, a fellow senior. "Oscar, hey, glad I caught up with you."

"What up, Izzy."

"My bad for not connecting with Stasia earlier this week, but I wanted to tell you directly how awesome you are."

Twisting so I'm facing her, I say, "Huh?"

"Look, that day my car wouldn't start after school and no one wanted to give me a jump, the way you rigged those half-dead batteries from the robotics lab together to get me going. You were like real-life Tony Stark or something. Thank you."

"No thanks necessary. If I can help, I help."

"You don't understand. I had an interview for a summer internship that afternoon. You got me there just in time. The reason I couldn't catch up with Stasia was because I was at my gig. First steps toward the future, Oscar! Don't ever stop being you." She pops up, jubilant. Does a couple of high-knees like she's warming up for a track meet. "Also, I'm really high right now."

Isabel sprints into the party, leaving me . . . not so mad anymore.

I gotta find Stasia.

Getting through the crowd is work. Even when I make it to the pool, I can barely move; so many people are here. When I ask if anyone's seen her, some girls point me to the driveway.

I leave DeAndre's yard completely and find Stasia's Prius still parked on the hill. The engine's off and the window's open. Her phone's propped on the dashboard with a video playing while she looks down. "Shit, shit, shit."

Circling around to the passenger door, I see the camera and lens in her lap, still separated. The phone video is a frizzy-haired lady holding a similar camera and lens, talking about emergency fixes. I gently knock on the passenger door. "Cool if I get in?"

She taps her phone, pausing the video. "Not yet. Stand right there and convince me it's cool."

Heavy sigh. "Fair enough. I'm a dick. Who's probably not such a great rapper."

"You're probably not moving the thermometer right now, Oscar."

"You want me to say I suck, Stasia?"

"I want you to not drag rap into every conversation with me tonight. If you're going to apologize, do it. If not, get one of your fans to take you home."

I laugh a little. "The vibe I'm getting, I'd be walking."

She shakes her head.

"I'm sorry. I was rude, self-centered, and a bad listener. You've been trying to show me something all night and I wouldn't give you the opportunity."

"Wait, wait. Don't forget I also tried to save you from having nasty bubble guts and being the dude who takes a shit at a party."

"Really, Stasia?" My head whips, checking for eavesdroppers. "All right, all right. I'm sorry I didn't take your advice about the bloomin' onion."

She mulls it over. "It is now cool for you to get into the car."

As I'm climbing in, my mic jostles from the jacket pocket and thunks onto the center console. Stasia mean-mugs it like I dropped a bag of the mystery dog's poop. I don't bother picking it up and instead reach for her lens. "How bad is it?"

"No broken glass, but it won't mount to my camera."

Digging in my hip pocket, I retrieve the metal ring I picked up off the floor. "This might help."

"Shit, Oscar! How do you have that?"

"I paid attention. For once." I press the busted mount to the lens. "It fits. A little epoxy should fix it."

"You can do that?"

"Sure. Trip to the hardware store. Easy. First, can I see what you've been trying to show me all night?"

She crosses her arms and gets pouty. "I don't know if we're that cool yet."

I lean toward her, plant a kiss on her cheek, then produce a strawberry Nutri-Grain bar I just swiped from the pantry because I noticed the food was getting low. "I come bearing gifts."

"You so know my Kryptonite." She snatches the bar, then brings up a saved video on her phone. She settles on a midshot of herself, then says, "When I said one of your fans could drive you home, I wasn't talking about IntelleQt."

Stasia taps play, and I see exactly what she means . . .

"This is an appreciation video—"

Jade shouts off-camera, "Say 'intervention'!"

"—for my awesome, genius, loving boyfriend, Oscar

Graham. Maybe we all need reminders of what we're great at from time to time. Here's yours . . ."

The video cuts to Sierra Shepherd, a junior who once came to me with a laptop problem. "I click on everything! It's like, the internet, it knows my soul. Anyway, my PC had a bunch of viruses, and I thought I'd lost this big-deal midterm paper I'd bought from this site that sells solid B-plus papers. Went to Oscar, he did what he does, and boom, paper's back. That paper got flagged by Mr. Grisham's plagiarism software, though, so I got a zero. But whatever Oscar did to my machine made it so I can also write my own papers without getting a bunch of porn pop-ups, so it's still all good. Thanks, Oscar!"

Cam Booker, who I tutored in math for like thirty seconds once, was next. Stasia got his good side. He says, "My dad always told me skilled people make hard stuff look easy. That's Oscar. Dude really should be teaching my trig class because he helped me understand in an afternoon what's been confusing for months. Everyone knows that, though. You need that brain work, you hit up the man. Certified genius. Thanks, Oscar!"

The video goes on with more people and shorter clips. From the full-breath testimonials to quick callouts of the things I've done for them.

"Broke down how molecular weight works with, like, actual weights in the football team's training room."

"Wired custom lights for the school musical."

"Fixed my tuba."

Most of it I'd forgotten because I don't keep receipts—I like helping. It's something to see people I've helped like this. By the end, I've counted fifteen classmates. Then the video cuts back to Stasia.

"Oscar, this is who we could get on short notice. I hope you know we could've gotten way more. You're the smartest, most generous person I know. A gift to everyone you come in contact with. I wanna give you a gift back. I hope you see it comes from a place of love. Say no to rap."

Jade: "Say no to rap."

Sierra Shepherd: "Say no to rap."

Cam Booker: "Say no to rap."

A clip of Savoy cuts in with different, fabulous lighting and a low cinematic score. I get the impression they shot this. Always extra. "Oscar, Boo-Boo, you know your rhymes are trash. Please say hell no to rap."

It goes down the line of everyone who sang my praises a moment before. By the eighth person I'm like, "Okay. I get it. Damn."

Stasia taps the screen, freezing my "intervention." She says, "I hope that wasn't too painful."

The truth stings. Not gonna lie. "More than anything, I'm a little embarrassed I couldn't get to that conclusion on my own."

She takes my hand. "You don't have to do anything on your own. That's my point. I got you. Always."

"I'm going to do better at returning the favor." I lean in for a kiss and she meets me halfway.

There may be things about each other that we never quite understand. But there are things about us, together, that the world's gonna have to watch out for. I've always felt it, but more now than ever. Saying no to rap is a small sacrifice if it means saying yes to her.

We break, and I ask, "You feel like partying more, or . . ."

"Yes!" Stasia just about kicks her door open. "Finally! Let's have some actual fun."

I secure her camera and lens in the center console, making a mental checklist of all I'll need to fix it tomorrow, then join her on the hill.

"Wait, almost forgot something." She half dives back into the car and returns with my mic.

"What are you going to do with that?"

"Just because you aren't rapping anymore doesn't mean I can't try my hand at some BARS!"

"You serious?"

"Hell no. I'm throwing this shit in the pool."

Looping my arm over her shoulder, I kiss her on the temple and say, "Lead the way."

This is our moment.

# MEMI MATSON

## THE ACTOR

## PART III

### MIDPOINT REVEAL

THE PARTY'S BEEN RAGING FOR A WHILE NOW. I need to go to the bathroom. I spy two doors next to the kitchen. Behind one is a laundry room where a couple yells for me to get the fuck out. The other door is locked. I search for a different bathroom.

The elaborate dual staircase in the foyer has a landing that reminds me of the balcony onstage. Why did that boy have to ruin my last performance? Closing a show on a high note feels finished. When it's a less-than-perfect ending, you want another chance . . . I mean, a shot, do-over, whatever.

Holding up the wall, I steady myself in the long line for the bathroom. Some girls compliment my look and ask who I'm wearing. Most ooh and aah when I mention my top was created by Miranda. I catch one or two side-eyeing me. My anger is with the Romeos, not with #TeamSavoy.

"You were fantastic in the play," a girl behind me says.

I turn and smile at my fangirl. "Thank you so much."

We inch forward with the rest of the line. She continues the conversation.

"I was there Friday and again on Sunday when my mom could go." Before I can apologize to my fangirl for that last performance, she adds, "Sunday was my favorite."

"Really?" Shock takes my voice up an octave.

"For sure. I mean, Blake was great, but I never knew Chance Jackson could act like that. Like he was Romeo for real."

The party fades, replaced by the memory of last Sunday, when I was onstage being kissed by the Romeo understudy. He had pulled away and smiled bashfully.

"Thus from my lips, by thine, my sin is purged," he said.

I froze. My photographic memory evaporated. All I could do was stare at that boy.

"Just breathe, Mem," he whispered. Not as Romeo, but as Chance Jackson.

He improvised the next line. "Give me my sin again that you may sweetly purge again and again," said the understudy who thought he could do better than William Shakespeare.

Then he kissed me once more. So softly that our lips barely touched. As if he was showing a shy virgin how tender a kiss could be.

Despite the heat from the stage lighting, a delicious shiver ran through me.

His next kiss was an invitation to play. I felt his smile upon my lips. He left a trail of kisses on my cheeks, forehead, the tip of my nose, each earlobe, and down my neck.

My entire body tingled. Every inch of my skin had goose pimples except for the places his lips touched. My fingers acted of their own accord to rake through his silky brown wavy curls. My hands pulled him to me. My tongue crossed the threshold of his lips.

I was not kissing Romeo as some sort of Method acting experience. I was kissing Chance. And I had no intention of stopping. Until . . .

I remembered that my dad was in the audience. At that point, I didn't know the full story between Chance's dad and mine. Only that they had graduated the same year from Flandreau Indian boarding school in South Dakota but were most definitely not friends.

I pushed Chance away. My next line, when it eventually came, was flat.

"You kiss by the book."

Someone in the audience hooted at that. Actually LOL'd. It was contagious. The entire auditorium filled with laughter and cheers.

I'd gone on autopilot then. I said my lines the way Siri would have narrated Juliet. Emerged from a fog toward the end of a scene because those lines seemed like a cosmic joke.

"My only love sprung from my only hate! Too early seen unknown and known too late! Prodigious birth of love it is to me, that I must love a loathed enemy."

My fangirl gives me a gentle nudge to keep moving forward. I take one step but the wall tilts next to me. I steady myself by holding on to the nearest person in front of me. They push me away, and I struggle to keep my balance.

"You okay?" my fangirl asks.

I laugh. "You saw my final performance. You should know I'm not okay."

"Wait, are you talking about Sunday? I was asking about now."

"I was messed up then," I say. "But I'm fine now." The bathroom line moves again, but this time I take tiny steps that feel safer. "Blake Donnelly is waiting for me downstairs."

# ZARA HUSSEIN

## THE NEW GIRL

## PART II

PEOPLE STREAM BY, SHOULDERING THEIR WAY into the party, ignoring me. I breathe in and out. I am invisible again. The pounding goes away a little.

Out of the corner of my eye, I see a girl I recognize from AP Lit. I think her name is Asa. I see her watching me, taking in my shaky breathing, which is thankfully slowing.

"You okay?" Asa asks.

I manage an unsteady nod.

Asa's eyes narrow sympathetically. "You sure?"

Before I can answer, a group of Bayside athletes barge out of the house.

"Wait," I say. "Are they shouting about a goat?"

Asa laughs. "Sure sounded like it."

She gives me another knowing look, and I can tell she's about to ask me again about before, but then another voice says, "There she is."

"Yeah. See? I told you. I knew she'd come out here."

I look up and Liam Freaking Richardson-Ito is standing right next to Sadie Bernbaum, who is beaming like she just solved a decades-long cold case—the kind they make viral podcasts about.

I've probably only been hiding away for twenty or so minutes.

Seeing that I'm no longer alone, Asa heads back inside, humming a tune I've never heard.

Liam's lips twist into a gentle smile. It's different from his twenty-four-karat Instagram smile. This one reminds me of how he used to smile back when we were younger. Like, for example, he gave me this same smile the day we trapped this beautiful grasshopper and spent the whole afternoon making a habitat for it—even though neither of us could quite pronounce the word "habitat" right with our little-kid voices and missing front teeth. I squeeze my eyes shut for a second and take a deep breath.

"You okay, Hussein? You disappeared for a bit."

Back when we were little, Liam always called me by my last name. It takes me a moment to realize he's talking to me, even though he literally said my own last name. But before I can say anything, Sadie Bernbaum answers for me.

"I think she's maybe taking a mental break. You know—"

"Sadie, it's okay," Liam says. "Why don't we give her some space?"

"I don't think it's a good idea to just leave her."

I'm not even sure why Sadie Bernbaum cares at all. I'm a literal nobody. I'm not sure what kind of gossip she thinks she's going to get out of me. But as I watch her eyes scanning Liam,

I start to connect the dots. She thinks there's a story between us. The only story, though, is one of my extreme adolescent embarrassment.

Remembering that day—the last day I saw Liam before we moved away—when I was twelve and—ugh. It's too mortifying to even think about. My breathing grows more rapid—I'm full-on hyperventilating now. This can't be happening.

"Maybe I'll stay, and you could go back to the party?" Liam says.

Even with the pounding and pulsing, the shaky breathing, and the overall feeling of WTF, I register appreciation of Liam's insane chill.

Sensing Sadie's hesitation, he adds, "Really. I've got this. Good luck on your own . . . mission." Then he winks.

Sadie shoves him playfully before slinking off. But I'm not convinced she's really gone. I don't know Sadie well, but I wouldn't put it past her to spy on us from around the corner. I'm almost positive she's the one behind the Miss Abby love advice column in the school paper; she lives for this stuff.

Liam's quiet, and I sort of wish he would go away, too, which is a very confusing feeling to have about someone I've been keeping not-so-low-key tabs on for years online. People stroll by, streaming in and out of the massive front door. Some nod at Liam. Some raise their Solo cups in his direction. No one really says anything to me. Invisible status holding strong.

"So," Liam says. "You are back."

I scratch the skin between my eyebrows. I know it's not an attractive gesture, but it's a soothing one. "Yeah. We moved back right after winter break."

Liam tilts his head a little. "You never answered my message.

And I thought I saw you in the hall a few months ago—I called out to you."

He's not wrong. And I know it's starting to make me look like some unkind, cold monster, but the truth is, I just couldn't reopen the box with Liam. Because I knew it would lead to . . .

Well, it might lead to something as embarrassing as the situation I find myself in now.

I struggle to come up with an answer, but my brain is like an overheated lightbulb, and all I manage to get out is "Uh, yeah, I guess." Which doesn't make any sense because what he said is factually accurate, and there's no guesswork needed.

He hooks his thumbs through the belt loops of his jeans. I lift my eyes and let myself really look at him for the first time all night. He's wearing a faded T-shirt of some band that I know the name of but don't really know their music. His dark hair has grown out enough that it has a slight curl, and his brown skin has a touch of red like he spent all day in the sun. My stomach does the same flip it always does when I let myself really take in Liam Freaking Richardson-Ito.

"Well, Hussein, I want to hear what you've been up to." He holds out his hand to me. "Want to get out of here?"

I squint at him. "You mean, leave the party?"

He tilts his head back and laughs. "Yeah. DeAndre wants me to pick up some snacks for the party. People are getting hungry again." Another soft smile. "Might be easier to catch up away from all this noise?"

DeAndre is Liam's cousin by marriage, and the latter's always been reliable, so this does sound like a plausible request. "Okay." I take his hand and a current of energy surges through me. It makes my breath even more unsteady, but in a sort of enjoyable way as opposed to the nauseous feeling from before.

Liam keeps hold of my hand as we stroll toward the elaborate flower garden that's to the side of the wraparound porch. We pass by some of the biggest rosebushes I've ever seen in my entire life. We also pass by several gorgeous flowering plants that I have no idea what the names for them are.

"This is some garden," I say.

Liam laughs. "Yeah, it is. I thought it'd be easier to leave this way. So we didn't have to fight the crowd in the front."

I smile a little. He's still thoughtful.

"Do DeAndre's parents do this all themselves?" I ask.

Liam makes a face, and it's my turn to laugh.

"But I know the garden is really special to his mom. She cares about it a lot," Liam adds.

"That's nice." My mom isn't much of a gardener, though we've never lived somewhere we've had a yard that belongs to us. At our current apartment complex, the manager pays for someone to mow the lawn and cut back the sad-looking bushes.

The stone path narrows, and Liam's shoulder bumps mine. "Man, I can't believe I haven't run into you until now."

"Because I'm invisible."

"What?"

That's when I realize I said the invisible part out loud. "Uh," I say. "That's my joke." I think about trying to do the jazz hands move that I couldn't quite pull off in AP Chem class with Miranda and Memi but decide against it. I drop his hand, though, and I swear I see something pass on his face, but I'm not sure what.

"Like that's my thing. Being invisible. You know? Like not being seen? I mean—" I stop talking.

Liam stares at me. There's an intensity to his gaze. "Yeah, yeah. I know the definition of 'invisible.'"

"Of course." I glance down at my sneakers.

"But you, Hussein, are not invisible."

I pick my head up.

"Yeah, okay," I say, and maneuver to pass him on the narrow path. My fingers brush against the tiger lilies as I lean to keep my balance.

"Really," he says, and his footsteps quicken, matching my pace. "But why didn't you answer my message? And what made you guys move back? Must've been something big for Sana to pull you before the end of your senior year."

Sana is my mom. Liam remembers her name. This shouldn't make me as happy as it does, but my heart flutters a little inside my chest. I try to laugh, but it comes out like a nervous cough.

"What?" Liam asks.

"It's just . . . I'm surprised you're so interested."

A wounded expression spreads across his face. "I mean, I was the one who messaged YOU, remember?"

I shrug.

What I don't say, per usual, is: *Of course I read your message. I read it like five million times. I applied Sherlock Holmes–level decoding to that shit. I've social media stalked you for the last four years, but I was never delusional enough to think it was mutual. But wait: Was it mutual?*

No, it definitely wasn't mutual, because of what happened right before I moved. Has he forgotten?

"Uh," I say. "I don't know. We weren't really friends . . . when I moved."

The wounded look deepens. "We definitely were."

"Liam, we didn't talk for like all of sixth grade." I don't say: *And also, on my last day, you basically humiliated me.*

His nose wrinkles up like he's thinking about it. "We didn't have any of the same classes."

"Yeah," I say slowly. "Hence, why I said we weren't really friends."

"It was just middle school."

I stare at him. "It was just middle school" is the kind of phrase only people like Liam Freaking Richardson-Ito would use. People who, somehow, even in middle school, even in the years of hormones, growth spurts, pimples, sweaty underarms desperately in need of deodorant, manage to stay good-looking and well-liked, able to navigate each and every social group.

In elementary school, Liam and I were always in the same class, and would often hang out in the classroom, choosing to be at the same station, or both playing on the monkey bars at recess. But by middle school, our orbits changed. There was never a conversation about it. We just . . . drifted. By fifth grade, I was already mastering my invisibility skills, and Liam was doing whatever the opposite of that is.

"Just middle school," I finally deadpan.

He holds his hands up by his face, all sheepish.

"Liam—do you remember my last day?"

Liam's eyes dart all around. We've almost reached the end of the flower garden. In the distance, sounds from the party—the thump of the bass, an occasional super-loud yelp, fast footsteps—can faintly be heard, but it also feels like we're in an entirely different world.

"Yeah—about that—"

"About that," I say.

"I was a kid. And I was nervous. You were moving."

"Liam, I wrote you a letter. I poured my guts out to you. And you shared the whole thing with your brother, who started reading it on his little megaphone for the whole neighborhood to hear."

Liam puts up his hands. "Okay, no one heard except me and you—"

"Uhhh, the WHOLE neighborhood heard it. Including all of your brother's friends. AND MY MOM. Do you know how humiliating that was?"

Liam furrows his eyebrows. "You're right. It was a total clown move of me to share your letter with my brother, but the truth is, I didn't know what to do. I was so . . . excited."

I freeze. A shiver runs through me. "Excited?"

"Yeah, I'd, like—" He reaches up and touches his hair. I can't help but wonder if it feels as soft as it looks. "I'd been into you . . . for like . . . forever. And then I thought you'd forgotten about me after you left because you went all silent and whatever . . ." He shoves his hands into his pockets.

"I didn't forget about you," I say quietly.

"Well, I never forgot about you, either." He flashes me his smile. The real one.

And just then, we hear a click. And then, all of a sudden, water is spraying all around us.

"The sprinklers," Liam and I say at the same time, and take off sprinting. We run through the water, trying to dodge the sprayers but frequently getting pelted in the face.

By the time we reach the garden exit, we're pretty soaked. Liam's dark curls are matted to his forehead, and his T-shirt is

wet and clingy. I try not to stare but fail. He's still the same adorable Liam I remember. But he's grown-up. In a really good way.

He gives me a lopsided grin and we both burst out laughing.

"Ready to get snacks?"

"Yup," I say.

On the walk to his car, he says, "Can we forget about my
clown moment, please?"

"You mean the moment when you trampled my heart like a
bull in a china shop?"

"Oof. Yeah. That."

"Okay. I guess we can let it drop," I say, and then add,
"For now."

Liam laughs again. "No, seriously. Tell me? I want to know
how you're here." At a stop sign, he looks over at me, and I feel
my heart race.

We reach his car. I open the door and get in. Liam hops
behind the wheel and turns on the car. "We're back 'cause of
my mom."

"She wanted to move back?"

"She got offered a job as director of the art festival."

Liam smiles again, even wider. It's big and bright. Like
the kind he always posts on Instagram. "No way, dude. That's
major! I'm so psyched for your mom. She was always so talented."

I squint at him. "My mom?"

"Remember in fourth grade she came into our class and
taught us all about mixed-media art projects?"

I laugh a little and nod. "Oh yeah. That's right."

"You're so lucky you have a mom that, like . . . gets it."

"Gets it?"

We're stopped at a red light. Liam cranes his neck to look up at the sky, which is dark. In the far distance, you can spot the exhaust of a plane taking off. I wonder where it's going. When we were little, Liam and I would lie outside at night sometimes and look up at the planes and make up stories about the passengers on them.

I'm about to ask him if he remembers that when he says, "You know, like, she's an artist. You're lucky, Zara."

"Maybe."

"No, Zara, you are."

The use of my first name gets my attention. Liam, in all the years I've known him, has never called me by my first name. "What? Do your parents not appreciate art?"

I don't know Liam's parents well. I have foggy memories of them showing up for our fourth-grade graduation. His mom, a petite Black woman wearing a flower-print sundress, and his dad, an Asian man in a well-fitted gray suit. I know Liam's mom was born in Jamaica, and his dad was born in Japan, and we would sometimes talk about having immigrant parents—my mom was born in Lebanon—but our conversations about it were brief and breezy, never anything deep.

"My parents think I don't have the luxury of pursuing my passion. They want me to be a doctor. Like my mom."

"Well, what's your passion?"

Liam jokingly frowns. "Oh. So that's how it is? You'll only believe in me if you think it's something good?"

I reach over to lightly pat his shoulder. Another unexpected jolt runs through me. I hadn't meant to touch him, but now all I can think about is doing it again. "I mean, yeah," I joke. "It could be super corny like Pokémon."

"Whoa, whoa. First off, Pokémon is not super corny. But also, how does one pursue a Pokémon passion, career-wise?"

Liam pulls the car into the parking lot of a Whole Foods. All the lights are off. It's clearly closed.

"Um, I hate to break it to you but it's almost midnight. I don't think Whole Paycheck is staying open at these hours."

Liam snorts. "You're right. But where are we going to get snacks?"

"Are you serious right now?"

"I mean, I need good ingredients if I'm going to whip up some—"

I try to stifle a laugh. "Wait. You're going to *make* the snacks?"

Liam turns in the driver's seat to face me. His seat belt stretches against his chest. "Yeah. That's kind of my . . . thing."

"Your passion is . . . snacks?"

He flashes me a broad smile. "Well, yes. Food in general. Cooking, to be specific."

This tracks now that I think about it. Liam's Insta feed is filled with photos of delicious and elaborate meals. I'd always assumed this was a flex about all the fancy places he'd gone to eat (and the presumably fancy people he'd gone to eat with), but now I'm starting to wonder if I misread the situation.

I sneak a side glance at Liam's profile. It's easy to see his sixth-grade self, but he's also obviously changed. Grown. He's both familiar and a mystery. More of a mystery than I realized.

I wonder how I seem to him. If he still sees me as that shy little girl who wrote him the letter or . . .

"Nothing?" Liam says. He lets out a light laugh, but I think I detect a little hurt in it. My heart squeezes.

"Sorry . . . I just . . ."

He drums his hand against the steering wheel and looks out the window at the empty parking lot. "It's whatever. My parents might be right. Being a chef is like . . . a pipe dream. Everyone these days wants to open a restaurant."

"I don't know," I say, finding my voice. "You're not . . . everyone."

A soft smile crosses his face. It's one I've never seen on his Instagram. I've never seen it period. My stomach flips.

"You really think so, Hussein?"

"Yeah, Liam. I do."

The fluttering feeling in my stomach stays. He looks at me, his lips twitching like he might say something else, but then he pulls the car out of the parking lot. "I guess I'm going to have to pick up whatever I can find from, like, 7-Eleven or something."

"Well, I'll definitely believe in you if you end up creating something mad delicious with your only ingredients being pre-packaged snack foods from 7-Eleven."

"Oh, I'm going to elevate the hell out of some Fritos. You just wait and see."

I laugh. "Okay, okay. But wait, what were you planning to make if Whole Foods had been open?"

"Err, I don't know. I was thinking maybe some Gruyère-cheese-and-beef tourtières. Delicious but accessible. Who doesn't love cheese when they're drunk? And maybe also some small biscuit snacks with smoked salmon and herbed cream cheese. Or maybe steak-and-blue-cheese bruschetta. What do you think?"

"Damn," I say. "Now I'm hungry."

His eyes linger on me. For the first time, I don't flinch and glance away. I meet his gaze.

"Zara?" he says.

"Yeah?"

"You'll have to let me cook for you sometime."

"I'd like that," I say softly.

"But for now, we've got to see what we can possibly find at 7-Eleven."

On the drive to the convenience store, Liam asks me about my time away from Florence Hills. I keep dodging questions, answering with simple, nondescript responses, but he presses, nudging me to expand and dig deeper.

I've already laid out for him that I was pretty much a low-key nerd. Not good enough at school to be one of those flashy nerds that everyone starts to put their hopes and dreams for the community into, but I was definitely on the quiet, bookish side. Have two best friends—Anna Beth and Nawal. Both of them are headed to University of Illinois next year. I'm technically headed there, too—we're supposed to room together—but I'm not so sure about it.

"I just don't know what I want to do."

"You'll figure it out."

"Maybe," I say.

"You will, Hussein."

"And you?" I ask, even though I already know he's heading to Stanford. Liam is one of those people who would be easy to hate for his symmetrical face plus top-notch brain if it wasn't so hard to dislike someone with his face and top-notch brain.

"Stanford," he says.

"You don't sound too pumped. Aren't your parents thrilled?"

He presses down on the brakes hard as we pull into a parking spot in front of 7-Eleven. "Oh, THEY are freaking over the moon. Me, I don't know."

"I'm guessing Stanford doesn't exactly have a culinary arts program?"

He gets out and opens my door for me. "You are correct."

"Man, then you shouldn't go."

He touches my shoulder. The electric current is back. "You really think so?"

"I think you should do what you want. It's your life."

He lets go of my shoulder, but the warmth from his touch lingers. "You're the best, Hussein. But now I'm really feeling the pressure to make these snacks an A-plus."

I laugh. "Well, yeah. You should definitely feel the pressure. Drunk teens are known to be food snobs."

He laughs, but he keeps looking at me.

"What?" I finally say.

"You were always cute," he says. "But now you're beautiful."

My whole face flushes red. "Come on. I already told you I think you can make it as a chef. You don't have to flatter me."

He touches my shoulder again. "I'm just being honest."

I grin a little and surprise myself by saying, "Yeah, well, you're not so bad-looking yourself."

That makes him laugh. We head into the store and scour it for anything we can find. All of a sudden, I'm starving. I fill up our basket with every type of crunchy snack you can imagine—BBQ potato chips, cheese puffs, salt-and-vinegar potato chips, tortilla chips. And, of course, I grab tons of sweet stuff, too—Oreos, a bag of Reese's Pieces, a huge-ass bag of Skittles.

Liam is grabbing some things that maybe make a bit more sense, like the few sad-ass spices 7-Eleven sells, and one particularly funky-looking apple.

I point at his basket. "That's your plan for elevating the snacks?"

He shrugs, a sheepish (and absolutely adorable) smile on his face. "The plan is fluid right now. But you want me to let you in on what is going to be my secret to success?"

I smile back. "Sure."

He motions for me to come closer to him so he can whisper in my ear. "DeAndre gave me some special seasoning to add to some of these snacks, if you get what I mean."

I shake my head, laughing. "Seems like you've got an ace up your sleeve, then."

"Definitely."

We stand there for a few seconds. Me pressed up close to him, post-whisper. And I swear something might be about to happen, but then our phones buzz at the exact same time.

We both look at each other. I slide mine out of my pocket first. "It's Miranda," I say. I hold out my phone screen. "Updates from her battle with Savoy."

"Ah," Liam says. "I got the same update from Trendsettr. Plus, I have about a hundred frantic texts from DeAndre. Shit seems to be getting even wilder over there. He's hoping snacks will help people chill out some before the cops are called. I mean, it was pretty out of control." He raises his eyebrows playfully. "I don't know if the party will be able to handle your energy when you get back in there, party animal."

I playfully swat at him before I realize what I'm doing. But it's like we crossed some kind of line before, and now I'm looking for any excuse to touch him again. "Then you better hurry up. You're needed."

"Those people can wait. I'm having a great time here. Who knew my favorite moment of senior year would take place in a 7-Eleven?"

"Your favorite moment of senior year?" My voice is a bit quivery when I say that, and I kind of feel like an idiot because my knees are buckling, but also there's another feeling that's a decidedly good one.

Liam drops his basket of items to the side and leans toward me. "Well, it's almost the best moment."

We lock eyes. I lean in.

And then he kisses me. Liam Freaking Richardson-Ito is kissing me in this 7-Eleven. His lips press against mine, and I swear to god I understand now every single fireworks metaphor I've ever read in a romance novel before.

When he pulls away, he says, "Now, that was officially the best moment."

"Yeah," I say, the confidence in my voice back. "I definitely agree."

He takes my hand, and we walk up to the checkout counter together. Once everything is paid for and bagged, we load up his Jeep Wrangler and head back to DeAndre's. Liam's phone keeps buzzing. I get one more text from Miranda, which I respond to with a bunch of random-ass emojis because I can't quite think straight since I literally just kissed Liam Freaking Richardson-Ito!

We're mostly quiet on the drive and I start to worry it's because Liam regrets what happened or at least wants to backpedal on it, but then when we pull onto DeAndre's street he says, "I mean, I'm excited to go back to the party, but I don't want to lose this feeling, you know? Like it's just me and you."

"I get that." I take a deep breath. Now's my chance. "Liam?"

"Yeah?"

"You do know that I've basically been in"—my throat feels tight, but I push the words out—"in love with you since forever."

He beams. "The feeling is mutual, Hussein. I've basically been in love with you since forever, too."

"Wait, what?" My heart is doing a serious amount of Olympic-level somersaults.

"For real. I have," Liam says. "I feel like I missed out on so much time with you—"

"Let's not think about that. Let's think about now. And this summer," I say, leaning over to kiss him again. This kiss, if possible, is even better than the first one.

"We can do this for months on end," I say.

When the kiss ends, there's a huge grin on his face.

"Okay, Hussein, you're right. We've got this summer and beyond."

I make an imaginary toast. "To the summer and beyond."

"Now let's go get some real drinks for that toast and whip up these snacks."

We gather the bags and walk back through the garden to the house. I hear Whitney Houston. Liam holds my hand the entire way. I can feel people staring at us, probably wondering if I even go to FHHS, but that's okay.

Maybe I'm ready to not be invisible anymore. Better late than never, right?

Here's to the summer and beyond.

# SAVOY

## THE INFLUENCER

## PART III

MIRAGE UNZIPS A FRESH GARMENT BAG WITH flair. We, all of us, the hive mind known as SAVOY, gasp. A gown of slithering organza spills out, and phase three of our plan to entomb Miranda in a sarcophagus of obscurity begins.

We snap into our jobs. Mirage powers up the steamer, Grant drafts several posts so that we can just pop the content we shoot into them and *whoosh,* release them onto both Trendsettr and our other socials. I'll be in that gown in moments, and Effie's getting dressed up, too.

In scuba equipment.

"Ready for a swim?" she says, holding up a snorkel in one hand and the bottle of Grey Goose in the other. My head spins just looking at her, and I have to lean on Mirage as she helps me into the gown.

"Ready." I smile.

Effie thrusts the bottle at me. A challenge. I drink and pass it back, then pose for a behind-the-scenes shot while enveloped in a cloud of steam as Mirage works out the wrinkles in my skirts.

"Gorgeous, Savoy," Grant says, snapping the shots on my phone.

"It fits," Mirage says.

"I'm gonna die," Effie moans. "I will die photographing this, and all our efforts will be worth it, right, Savoy?"

Maybe I'm imagining things, but it sounds like Effie's threatening me. Like she's saying: *Do not mess this up. If you sink this ship, we all drown together. Right, Savoy?*

Despite the alcohol warming my blood, chills spread over my exposed skin. I shake them off—I could be reading Effie all wrong, it could be the paranoia I've had all night or my desperate hope to be free of this charade or just the alcohol clouding my judgment, I need to focus on the now, I need to focus, I need—

"Savoy, you in there?" Grant waves a hand in front of my face. I force myself to concentrate on being present. Like loyal courtesans, my three friends pluck and pull at me in the gown we've created, which is now on my body. It's a masterpiece, an extravaganza of jewel-tone organza in sapphire blue, aquamarine, and opalescent rainbow. It's oversized, enveloping me so that I, Savoy, am barely visible. But that'll change as soon as I'm submerged.

Which is, of course, the next step. DeAndre's pool has probably seen a lot in the last few hours, but it's about to see a lot more. My ass, to be specific. The slit of this gown goes all the way to my ribs, the colors picked to contrast with my skin. The shoot will be tasteful, of course, but we're going for shock here.

Shock is plentiful as we make our way through the party. People back away from me instinctively, like the weightless tendrils of my gown might try to eat them. The party is wild, the crowd wobbling as one giant entity around us. In the heat and the noise, I'm caught in the realization that this—this right now, this right here—is a monumental moment. A night we will all remember forever. A living myth rushing past us, which I need to grab ahold of and appreciate no matter the cost.

We get outside, to the patio, and the fresh air stings my lungs. People I barely know are coming up to me, complimenting my gown, asking for photos. I pose and smile, turning so that we're facing the house. And so that I can peer up through the trees, at the roof.

I do not see my trans goth Barbie. She probably got down a while ago. Which means she's got to be around here somewhere. I wonder if, in her descent, she realized that sometimes plans are good.

Effie starts up another interview segment, and I tell her camera about the pieces of my look. Where I got what. How I matched what to what. The silhouette. The color. Every choice needs to be dissected in real time for my followers, the people who take their cues off my trend predictions.

I treat the analysis like science, but fashion is mostly magic, I've learned. When a look works, it's not because of measurements and calculus. It's because clothing creates art out of armor. That's magic, if you ask me.

"We've got a problem," Grant reports, shooing away an errant group of sophomores I was posing with. "She beat us to it."

My heart drops. My heart flutters. My heart . . . sings? The warring emotions threaten to overwhelm me as I push through the people milling near the pool and see it all for myself.

Picture this: partygoers in the pool, eyes slick with melting makeup, clothes sucking to skin as they laugh and splash and play. The water churns with their energy, creating a cerulean whirlpool around the pool's center. There, a wobbling mountain of pink, jewel-clear plastic. A giant flotation device shaped like a pair of lips and, sprawled across it like a wagging tongue, a girl sheathed in a crimson velvet dress. Despite the splashing, the drops don't touch her. A malevolent aura pushes out from her as she poses for shot after shot on the swollen lips, like she's a goddess of the underworld and this—this party, this pool—is her personal playground.

"Fuck," I say. I am so horribly, achingly in love with that bitch.

Effie swears, too, but out of anger. She marches right over to Miranda's photographer and in a flash, they're bickering. Grant joins in. Even Mirage is on the verge of wading into the upcoming brawl. But I can't move to get in the middle of it—this dress is too cumbersome. Miranda watches everything from the pool, never disrupting her luxurious posing. Then she sees me, and the sight wipes the slick confidence from her lips. I look away, feeling a new feeling. Shame, about what we've created. So much anger and vitriol as the result of our diabolical love affair. And if it's not even fun anymore for her, because I've ruined that, too, with my need for a conclusion, what's the point?

A yelp from the pool draws me back. Effie has somehow gotten ahold of the pool skimmer and is swatting at Miranda, luring her closer to the edge. Miranda twists away, trying to stay balanced, but her heels catch on the plastic. There's a barely audible puncture sound and then, quite distinctly, the puffed lips crinkle.

Miranda feels it right away, going rigid on the deflating float, and the pool skimmer clunks the back of her head. Hard enough that I practically see stars. Then—horribly, slowly—Miranda goes under.

"Effie, no!" I scream, pushing my way into the fight.

Picture this: complete chaos.

Then picture this: a huge splash.

Warm as it is, the water comes as a shock as it closes over me. One second, I had a hand around Effie's waist, pulling her away, the next there was simply no stone where I was stepping. And then there was only water. Water, water, everywhere, and soaking organza wrapping around me.

I kick and squirm, breaching the surface and pulling in huge breaths of chlorinated air. Effie is already swimming to the edge beside me, camera in hand, looking like a drowned rat. My gown is heavy, a million pounds pulling me down as I swim to the pool's center, where the wreckage of the float sinks like a candied iceberg.

"Miranda!" I shout, tearing through the people splashing and playing, mistaking the crisis for just another fun prank. Then I see a flash of brown skin in the depths. A hand, punching through the blue, leading down to a scarlet blur trapped below.

I dive, dragging my dress down with me.

I keep my eyes open even though it stings.

I find her, but when I try to pull us up, she pulls me down. I realize in underwater slo-mo: she's not drowning. It's an act. A lure. To get me right where she wants me. Down here, in the glimmering dark, with her.

Lungs aching for a breath, I smile.

We fold into our familiar, strange embrace, down in the depths of the pool, fabric and plastic drifting around us like living sculptures. The underwater lights pulse, the music above muffles into a distant throb. The party surges on the other side of our upside-down reflections, just past the surface, but if there's one thing Miranda and I know about parties, it's that the most private moments happen right in the middle of everything.

I forget breathing. I forget air.

Picture this: two people drifting in a pale blue sky—their mouths pressing together creates the only tension in the shot. Otherwise, it's all softness. It's all floating. It's rippling fabric and pink plastic glinting like liquefied light. It's bubbles, everywhere, like discarded diamonds. It's a picture of a moment that has no end; that must end right away.

Because our moments always end too soon.

Then it happens, too quick to stop. Miranda kicks off the pool floor and we surge toward the surface, still locked in our kiss.

*No!* I think. *Everyone will see!*

The sounds above sharpen. We are inches away from exposure, from ruin. Miranda won't let me go. She's going to show us to everyone.

*Oh, maybe she did have a plan all along,* I think, brain sluggish from a lack of air or a surplus of love, I don't know which.

We break through the mirror, up into the real world, the party, the public. We arrive in reality not as warring rivals, not as Miranda and Savoy, but as one. A statement, made.

Except, no one sees it. Because somewhere in the last few inches of water, the world has gone dark.

"BLACKOUT!" someone screams.

# MEMI MATSON

## THE ACTOR

## PART IV

### DARK NIGHT OF THE SOUL

MY IMMEDIATE PROBLEM—TOO MANY TALLBOYS—
has me in a world of hurt. I am next in line for the bathroom
again and the person in there is taking too damn long. The
lights go out suddenly. People laugh and shout. And somehow,
the blackout makes my urgent need to pee even more urgent. It
even impedes my ability to converse with a boy who I assumed
was fanboying me, but only wants to talk about Chance. I
mean, did everyone attend on Sunday?

"I heard Chance Jackson was accepted into Juilliard," the
fanboy says. "Makes sense, seeing what he could do onstage."

Chance is going to Juilliard? That rich fucker. Juilliard is
a dream I cannot entertain. My family's financial situation is
very different from Chance Jackson's.

His dad is an executive at HILL-IONS, the nearest amusement park. His mom was in an all-girl folk-rock band called

the Betty Kittens, and she still gets royalties from their one huge hit. My dad is a postal worker, and my mom works the deli counter at a Jewel-Osco. She also has a side hustle making cepelinai for Lithuanian celebrations. They're taking out a second mortgage for my brother's room and board when he transfers to an engineering school next fall. Our parents want him focused on classes rather than a part-time job. Dad says I should go to Haskell Indian Nations University because they give decent financial aid. When I tell him Haskell doesn't have a drama program, he says maybe that's for the best.

Mom says first-generation college students don't have the luxury of picking any major. Nothing that my parents would consider a hobby. Which is why Migizii is transferring to an electrical engineering program when all he really wants is to teach history and make it interesting for students.

"About damn time," I say when it's my turn in the bathroom. Shutting the door barely muffles the house party sounds. After I zhiishiig and wash my hands, I stare at my reflection in the mirror. Two reflections, actually. The Four Loko is messing with my vision.

After Sunday's production, I arrived back home positively fuming. Chance had thrown me off my game. My final performance was horrible. I wasn't Juliet onstage. I was Memi, staring at Chance Jackson. Curious and furious at the same time.

My dad was sitting at the kitchen table. We ate poppy seed cookies while I grumbled about how awful Chance Jackson was. I told my dad I didn't know the reason for the feud between him and Chance's dad but, whatever the reason, it was my feud now, too.

"Memingwaans," my dad said. "Charlie Jackson was my friend at Flandreau. We had a band with some other guys.

Charlie was the lead singer. He was really good. The summer before senior year, we were going to drive around looking for gigs instead of going back to our reservations. Charlie said no. He wanted to attend a precollege intensive seminar. Take classes all summer to prepare for college entrance exams."

Dad looked down at the crumbs and when he met my eyes, I saw he was ashamed.

"We . . . I told him he was a sellout. I said other things, too. Ignorant things. It doesn't make an Anishinaabe any less Nish to pursue an education. I was jealous and hurt. Without him, we didn't have much going for our band."

I held Dad's hand in mine. We sat in silence for a while before he spoke again.

"You were very good in the play. You have talent. I can see that. But an artist's life is a hard one. So much uncertainty. Charlie Jackson was smart to choose college over our band. Look at him. He works with entertainers at that park but as the boss. He lives in a big house with four garage bays. I think he has a car just for hot, sunny days. His boy can become an actor because Charlie provided a safety net."

Dad looked away. I've never heard his voice sound so small.

"Your mom and I work hard, but we don't have a nest egg like the Jacksons. Mama wants you to have a steady paycheck, with benefits and regular raises. She's been running that deli for ten years but the fast-food places are advertising starting wages for new employees that are the same as what she makes."

Someone knocks on the door.

"Memi, are you okay?" It's the fanboy from the line.

"I'm good," I call out. I watch the two Memis in the bathroom mirror. One for each Romeo. I giggle. Two Memis plus two Romeos equals Four Loko.

My smile fades as I turn away. Blake Donnelly is somewhere downstairs, waiting for me. Tonight is about getting closure and moving on, for both of us. Blake, Chance, and the other seniors will graduate. Blake will return to Los Angeles. Chance will go to Juilliard. I'll audition for my senior-year productions. It will be my last chance to be part of theater life. Then I'll pick a university and a major that will lead to a solid job.

It's like a script. And I've always been great at following the script.

# SY NAVARRO

## THE EMO BAND KID

$$\boxed{\textbf{PART II}}$$

"YEAH, THAT'S ABOUT WHAT I EXPECTED," PERRY says after I finish telling him, Sam, and Perry's boyfriend Marlon with the beautiful hair about Asa shutting the door in my face, the series of long texts I sent afterward apologizing and pouring out my heart—and the radio silence that's followed ever since.

We've just been sitting out back on the patio, catching up. A lot I missed in five months. I heard Jrue's trying to get the power back up, so it's still mostly dark since the generator is apparently decades old, and it's finally kind of quiet. Except George Nguyen and all these other kids have gathered in the backyard and keep shooting us expectant glances. A lot of them go to our school, but I recognize several from the underground scene. James Tercero—this elder millennial hipster indie music blogger—is even here.

"Who's going to break it to them?" I ask. "Would've been rad to play with you guys one last time, though."

"For sure," Sam says.

Perry nods.

"Cool to know our music still means something to people," I say.

"A lot of people," Perry says. "'Cat Café' is almost at a million streams."

"Damn," I say, as if I didn't already know. "We had something good going."

"But all good things come to an end," Marlon says.

"They don't have to," I say, my bitterness rearing its head.

Perry says, "They do when the band member who's the cellist, co-singer, and co-songwriter graduates and plans to go to college on the other side of the country."

"Yeah," I say, "but it was shitty of the label to tell us they wouldn't sign us without her."

"If I recall," says Perry, shaking his head, "that wasn't the only reason they retracted the offer."

"What do you mean?" Marlon asks, since he wasn't there and apparently never read Sadie's article.

"Sy here kept demanding more and more money."

I lean forward, resting my elbows on my knees and clasping my hands together. "It's called negotiating."

"It's called being greedy and delusional."

"The label—" I start to say, but Perry interrupts me.

"Was it the label who failed to show up when we were supposed to open for Japanese Breakfast at the freaking House of Blues?"

I look down.

"Was it the label who then didn't answer any texts or calls so we all thought he was freaking dead or dying in a ditch somewhere since there was no way he'd miss a show that big?"

I stay quiet, shame coursing through me.

"Was it the label who threw a freaking tantrum the next day, yelled at all of us, called Asa selfish and conceited, said he was 'the real talent,' then insisted we break up right then and there instead of playing together for a few more months?"

"No." I sigh. "It wasn't the label."

"Damn right it wasn't," Perry says, shaking his head.

"It was Sy," Sam stage-whispers to Marlon.

"I said I'm sorry," I say. "At least, I've tried to."

We fall quiet. And it's like when I'm standing in front of a crowd and can sense I'm losing them. I tongue my lip ring for a few seconds, then clear my throat. "Trying to get us to play one last show together wasn't just about trying to set the stage for me to tell Asa how I feel . . . I missed us. Not just the band. But *us*. Our friendship."

They wait for me to say more.

I take a deep breath. "When we started to get big, I forgot all about that. I got so focused on what we could be, where we could go, that everything in my life became about There Is No Kevin in Team. I spent all my time practicing and writing and promoting and planning. There was no more room in my life for school or college apps—or any of you, if it wasn't about the band."

"Yeah, dude," Sam says. "You got scary intense."

"Once we fell apart, there was like this big void in my life. Almost like someone had died and I was grieving."

"So, what changed?" Perry asks.

I lean back in my chair. "I let myself grieve, I guess. I let myself move on, like everyone. And when I looked back on everything, I realized that I'd been a shitty bandmate and a shitty friend to all of you. Just because we were going to stop playing music together didn't mean we had to stop being friends—until I made it that way."

Perry and Sam nod.

"So I'm thankful I got you two back," I say. "I've been mad lonely. But I guess Asa's a lost cause."

Perry squeezes my shoulder. "Two out of three's not bad."

I smile. "Definitely not."

"Maybe it's not over yet," Sam says.

"What do you mean?" I ask, leaning forward.

Sam gazes off into the distance for a while. "I don't know. Seemed like the thing to say."

I sink into my chair.

But Perry's eyes shift to the windows above us. "You said she was in one of the bedrooms when you saw her earlier, right?"

"Yeah."

"Go see if she's still up there."

"Why?"

Perry rolls his eyes. "So you can talk to her."

I run a hand through my hair. "Yeah, I don't know, man. Not sure that's a great idea."

"I don't get it—you said you wanted to."

"But what if I make everything worse? Seems to be my MO."

"You have to at least try."

I don't say anything or move a muscle.

Perry sighs, stands, and leaves.

"Where you going?" I call after him.

But he's already gone.

# PENNY WASHINGTON

## THE POPULAR GIRL

COLIN DANCES LIKE ONE OF THOSE WAVY PLAS-tic guys at a car dealership to some throwback nineties jams that Jade, the DJ, is playing on her iPhone to keep the party going. I can't tell if it's because he's drunk, or if these are his actual moves, but it kinda works for him. Then, as if by fate, or maybe just because she's a nineties essential, the playlist starts playing Janet Jackson's "If."

I join in and copy Colin so both of us are waving around to the music like lunatics.

He turns when he sees me and starts to head away.

"Wait," I say, and grab his arm. "Please . . . I just . . . My mother has early-onset Alzheimer's," I blurt out. "She's only in her forties."

And then it tumbles out, everything going on with my mother. All the stress and frustration of watching her slowly disappear and feeling powerless to stop it.

". . . You know, several months ago we got our water and

power shut off in the same month because my mother forgot to pay the bills? So I've been doing it ever since. Shit like that happens all the time now. I'm so mad at her, but mostly I'm just scared. My mom was supposed to have years left with me. Other people take their parents for granted or bitch and moan about how strict they are, and . . ."

"It's not fair," he says knowingly.

"No. It's not."

"So, you're blaming your mother's Alzheimer's for what exactly?" he says.

"I've just . . . I've gotten really used to keeping things secret. Hidden. Even from my best friend. From everyone," I explain. "When Jenny and I broke up, you know what she said? After months of watching me stress out trying to get my mother help? She said I wasn't the girl she used to know. And that she just wanted to be in 'a normal relationship.'"

Colin pulls me in closer to him, and at first I think he's gonna kiss me, but he's just pulling me away from Sophie B., who keeps sloshing her drink here, there, and everywhere.

"Jenny fucking sucks," he says. "You can do way better. But you have no idea what it's like to feel like nobody at this fucking school notices you exist. You didn't even remember my name at first, and I sat next to you for a whole year in AP Chem. Plus, you just made me feel super shitty tonight."

"I'm really sorry," I say. I choose my next words as carefully as I can. "And you're wrong. I mean, I know it's different, but I do know what it's like to feel like nobody really sees you. Tonight, with you, was the first time in forever that . . ."

I've gotten so used to keeping everything buried so far inside, but with Colin it's like I've got emotional diarrhea. "Anyway, you're not nothing." I stumble over my words.

"Gee, thanks," he says.

"You're something, Colin. To me."

I hear myself sounding like the kind of movies my mom and I used to curl up and watch back when I was little. When the world was just the two of us, and happy endings still made sense to me.

"Mmhmm," he murmurs.

I wrap my arms around his neck and press my forehead to his. "Forgive me."

"Somebody might see us," he whispers. It's dark in the room save for a few phone flashlights making it so we all don't trip over each other. But even if the lights were on, I wouldn't care. Not now.

"Let them . . . ," I say. It feels comforting, the two of us leaning against each other like this.

"I have an idea," Colin says.

The purloined mascot wanders around the front yard, bleating, hopping, doing goat shit. On the wraparound porch, our classmates are dancing, making out, vomiting, doing teenage shit. When he sees the two of us, the goat heads over our way. At least, I think it's a he? Gender is a construct, and I'm not about to double-check. Colin drops down to his level.

"What did my phone ever do to you, little dude?" I say to the goat.

"Hey, Brenda," Colin says, just as the goat promptly butts him. Colin falls back, laughing, his body awkwardly splaying out on the lawn. I thought the Baysiders retrieved Brenda already? Maybe in the chaos of everything, after their little dance-off, the goat escaped?

Colin takes off his socks and shoes and sits up in the grass as the party rages on behind us.

"Watch out for vomit," I say. "And goat poop."

"Take off your shoes," he says.

"Did you miss what I said about goat shit?"

He laughs. "Standing in grass is supposed to reduce swelling and inflammation. Plus, it's grounding."

"Grounding?"

"My mom was into that sort of thing." He shrugs. "She was willing to try anything that could help even a little bit toward the end. . . . Try it. Maybe it'll work."

I take off my shoes and let my bare feet sink into the grass before I close my eyes. I don't have any swelling or inflammation. I just need a moment before I eventually head back home, to whatever awaits me there. I guess I need some . . . grounding. I say a little prayer to the universe. For what, I'm not sure. "Please . . . ," I say, and leave it at that.

"It's not as good as camping. But it's something," he says.

"Thank you for . . . for everything," I say, my eyes still closed.

"Penny, I'm here for you, you know," he says. "I've had the biggest crush on you since freshman year. I know I'm not popular like DeAndre, or funny like Jrue, but . . . Anyway, I promise I just mean . . . like as a friend? If you need one. Which . . . of course you don't 'cause you're Penny Washington . . ."

I sit down next to him and reach over to grab his hand. For real this time. The blades of grass are super itchy against my skin, and the goat wanders around the two of us smelling exactly like the funky farm animal he is. Still, I can't remember the last time I was this happy, this at ease. Colin gazes upward at the stars. Or at least whatever we can see through all the light pollution.

"Do you believe in God?" he says. "Or gods? Or Allah, or fate, or whatever."

"I'm not sure," I say. "But I believe in the stars, and the trees, and this itchy-ass grass. The universe. This moment. I think maybe that's enough for me. For now."

This is how I've learned to live with my mother. A dance of memory and forgetting from one moment to the next. But even when Mama forgets, she comes back, even if it's just for a little while, and in those moments, I feel so very deeply loved. That's what I hold on to. What I'll keep of her, even as the rest slowly smudges away.

Colin squeezes my hand.

I feel my busted phone start to vibrate in my pocket.

"Oh shit! It still works!" I shout. "How the hell does it still work?"

"The universe works in mysterious ways!" Colin smiles. "Go on! Answer it!"

My mother starts talking a mile a minute and pacing, while in the background, Ms. Marta apologizes for the interruption and tells Mama to get off the phone and let me live. I'm not surprised Mama's still up. Before, she used to stay up all hours working, but recently she's started sundowning, which is when people with Alzheimer's don't sleep well and get extra confused and restless at night.

"Mama, you wanna meet my friend, Colin?" I point the phone over so that she can see him.

"Hi, Colin!" she excitedly shouts, and momentarily stops her pacing.

"Hi, Ms. Washington!"

"Oh, he's a cutie patootie!" she says.

"Is he single? Asking for a friend," Ms. Marta leans over and says with a smirk.

Colin starts laughing.

"You guys, he's still right next to me."

"Child, why is there a goat behind you?" Mama says.

"It's a long story. Anyway, I'm gonna get off this thing, but I'll be home in a little bit. Don't worry. I'm good, Mama," I say. "I promise."

And, for tonight, I am. I really am.

# FERNANDA MANNING

## THE JOCK

**PART IV**

I'M HEARTBROKEN ABOUT WHAT HAPPENED EAR-lier but too prideful to follow Kai around for the rest of the night, begging for the chance to explain. I even put my phone on Do Not Disturb. Foolishly, I tell myself I'm giving him some time and space to cool off. The thing is, I need the time to cool off, too.

I walk out to the flower garden. It isn't even that hot yet, but if there's even one mosquito in a five-mile radius, it will find me, feed on my ankles, and bring the whole swarm of friends for a buffet dinner.

I slap my leg and feel a couple of mosquitoes squashed under my hand. I wipe it on my dress, and when I realize it's left a gross brown smear on the exact spot that Emma carefully scrubbed for me, I groan.

The bucket list is in my hand. I rip it to pieces. When each section is smaller than confetti, I cup them in my palm, and I blow the paper away.

I did what I set out to do tonight, and it didn't work out. But I don't regret kissing Kai or showing him the note. I just regret not really telling him how I still feel about him.

The girls from my teams are dancing on the stone pavers outside on the patio. The DJ is playing a Bad Bunny song, and the lyrics are beautiful and heartbreaking. I can't explain what it felt like when Kai walked away from me, but this music says it all. The girls look at me with a thousand questions in their eyes, but they don't interrogate me like before. Maybe Kai already texted them. At least they're not judging me or pushing me away. Instead, they make space for me to join them, and barefoot, I let the music take me.

I'm not a ballerina, but I let my body move with the sound without caring what people will say. There isn't a ball to catch or to throw or to score. It's just the music and my body becoming one with the universe. I close my eyes and sway, until I lose my balance.

Someone catches me.

When I open my eyes, I see Kai's face.

"You," I say, stupidly.

His eyes blazing, he replies, "Me."

"You're here?" But then the ego in me wakes up again, hurt. "Why did you leave me before I could explain?"

He lowers his eyes and presses his lips in that bashful way that makes my heartbeat thrum all the way to my fingertips. "Because I have never been so afraid in my life."

"Afraid of me?"

He nods.

"Okay . . . So why did you come back?"

"Because my friends wouldn't ever forgive me if I didn't give myself the chance to hear what you wanted to tell me. Scratch that—I wouldn't forgive me."

I take a deep breath, and before I lose my courage, I say, "My team is like my family, you know? Just like the cheer squad is yours. They weren't challenging me to kiss you. They were encouraging me."

"Encouraging you?"

I bite my lip but reach for his hand. "I like you. Not just as a bucket list item to cross off. I've liked you forever," I say. "And I'm not high or drunk, I promise."

But I'm lying. I'm high and drunk on life. On the night. On being young and strong and beautiful. On the possibilities that have opened up for us because I told him how I felt, even though I was scared.

"Dance with me?"

A part of me, the part that still remembers I don't really know how to dance, rears its head, but the other part of me, the one that wants to live in the moment, even if I look ridiculous, stomps on said head.

I nod.

Kai takes my hand and places his other one on my waist.

I have no rhythm, but I follow his lead, and I don't do too bad, for not being a dancer.

He whispers in my ear, "I like you, too."

His lips and mine are completely aligned. My mouth is dry with nerves. But I know that if I don't kiss him again, I'll regret it.

So I kiss him in front of everyone, and they explode into cheers.

Turns out, the night is just getting started, and we dance to Bad Bunny with abandon.

# SAVOY

## THE INFLUENCER

I'M A BIT UNCLEAR ON HOW I GOT OUT OF THE pool. One second I'm clinging to Miranda in the deep end, and the next I'm washed up against the stairs in the shallows, alone. That's where Mirage finds me.

Thank god it's Mirage, too. In only a few blinks she finds the zipper on my gown and is peeling the soaked garment off me. All around the pool, wet people are screaming. Some are laughing, some are crying. All of it is overloud in the suddenly music-less darkness.

"Grant!" I shout, spotting a shadow that's about his height. It pushes through the crowd as people use their phones for flashlights. Ghostly glows resolve into Grant and Effie, and Effie is pissed. Soaked, and pissed.

"Sabotage!" she's screaming. "Call the fashion police!"

"Police?" A girl near us whips around.

"No—" I try to stop her, but it's too late.

"Police!" the girl screams, and with that, the dark crowd catches with invisible fire. I cling to Mirage as we duck for cover, going for the deck. Somehow, we get shoved inside, and past a knot of people in the family room making an extra-loud commotion. They're calling for buckets, for hats, for anything to catch. . . .

Is that water?

Yes. Streaming through several of the light fixtures is a murky, pink water. People are rushing to shove cups and buckets under the deluge. Others are moving electrical equipment out from beneath it. I put together that this is probably what caused the blackout—a blown fuse, or something caused by the flooding. But how did all that water get upstairs?

And then I figure that out, too.

Picture this: a primary bedroom's en suite bathroom, thick with steam, locked from the inside. A sink, overflowing with pink water. A drain, clogged up by a soggy, stained denim coat, shoved there and then promptly forgotten by yours fucking truly.

I run. Up the stairs, down the hall, through the crowd gathered around the primary bedroom door. I'm out on the balcony and then crawling in through the window into the pitch-black bathroom. I land in a few inches of water. Hot water. I ignore the prickling heat, groping around until I finally find the faucet and shut it off. I don't know what else to do, or how to fix this, but I've had enough lying for tonight. I open the door to the bathroom, ready to face DeAndre and explain what happened.

Instead, I'm facing Effie. Water floods past us, making a swamp out of the primary bedroom.

"What. Is. This."

She's not talking about the mess. She flips her camera around. The screen is cracked but still clear enough to see the last photo she took, right before the blackout.

I see a composition of blue light, pink plastic, and scarlet fabric. I see two bodies, floating in their own mysterious gravity, in an embrace of unmistakable tenderness.

"You—you kissed Miranda. I g-got the whole thing in high definition," Effie stammers.

There's nothing I can do about this photo. This proof. I take a big breath of the steamy bathroom air, and I say, "Yes. I did."

"But you hate Miranda," Grant scoffs behind her.

"No," Effie says, studying me. "They don't. I knew it. I freaking knew it."

Effie turns and dashes for the door. We all follow, the conversation erupting into shouts as we pinball down the dark, crowded halls.

"Effie! I'm sorry!" I plead. "I'll fix this. I just have to . . ."

Have to what? I don't even know what I'm saying, or what I'm begging for. But I've never seen Effie so mad. Finally, I catch her in the living room, right before she gets back outside.

"Effie, please! I'm sorry I lied. It's messed up, I know, but give me a little more time to talk to Miranda. Then we can tell everyone. No more lying."

"Are you kidding me?" Effie scares me backward with her sudden reversal. I bump into Mirage. "Absolutely not. Your rivalry with Miranda is legendary. Do you think any of us would have half the amount of exposure if it wasn't for the two of you going for each other's jugulars every few months? There's a freaking poll at the party of the year to decide which of you is the true icon! It's trending on Twitter, Savoy! Some of the big gossip accounts are talking about it already. You want to give that up?"

"You're . . . not mad about the lying?"

Effie presses us into a corner. "Oh, I'm mad about the lying. But this has always been about manufacturing fame, so at least I can respect what you're trying to do. It's helped us. I can admit that. But what I don't understand is how willing you are to burn it all down, for all of us, so you can kiss her."

I'm stunned. Speechless. She doesn't even care about my happiness.

Effie's right in my face, her voice nearly lost in all the screaming around us, so no one hears what she says next.

"To influence people, you have to have their trust. If people find out the fighting with Miranda is fake, it all falls apart, Savoy. The jig is up. The show is over. Our brand is bankrupt. So we will change nothing. Our followers hate Miranda because we hate Miranda. And we will *keep* hating her."

I'm stunned. I turn to Grant and Mirage. Grant has his strategy face on.

"Effie is right," he says. "We're better off just burying this. And you'll keep up your fake fighting. It's a huge draw to our brand."

"She's leaving, anyway," Mirage adds. "In a few weeks, she won't even be here."

"Good, you'll just stay away from her until then," Effie says. "And it'll be like none of this ever happened."

Like none of this ever happened? They don't mean this fight—I'll never live this down with them. They mean the kiss. The moment Miranda finally had the guts to break free from the secrecy we trapped ourselves in. Our joy and freedom—they want it exterminated.

"Someone knows," I say, thinking of the comment on the video. "Sadie, or someone else, commented on our fight—"

"It's handled," Grant says. "I deleted all those comments. Admin privileges, remember?"

Effie backs up so Grant and Mirage flank her. She lifts her chin.

"Now, promise."

The lights flicker, like someone is flipping circuits, trying to find the right one for the pool. People laugh and scream like they're in a haunted house, but the sound warps into a stretched roar in my ears. Effie's eyes bore into mine.

"Promise," she demands. When I again hesitate, Effie gets even closer.

"Think about it. SAVOY isn't just about you. It's all of us. You can't do this alone. You're nothing without us, and you know it. Is she really worth losing everything?"

The lights buzz back on all around the house, the party breaking into song and laughter. And across the living room, I see Miranda. She sees me. She must see the anger surrounding me. I expect her to flinch away and vanish into her own comfy posse, but instead she takes a deep breath and slips toward me. Alone, she advances through the party. Somewhere the DJ strikes up another song.

I look at Effie. She barely holds my gaze. I see the regret in her eyes already, but I can't let this go unchecked.

"I'm hot, Effie, not dumb," I say, a fire blooming in my chest. "Remember that the next time you try to convince me I'm nothing."

"She didn't mean it," Grant cuts in.

"I know. She's mad. I lied to you guys. I made a mess of

your trust and jeopardized all of our hard work. I understand the anger, okay?"

I put out a hand for Effie to take. Pouting, she finally relents, taking it.

I squeeze. "We're all a little messed up in our own way, but that's no reason to ruin a party. We got our shots, didn't we? And if people loved the fighting, they're gonna scream about what happens next. Let me do what I do best: make a scene. Tomorrow we can figure out the spin together. Okay?"

Effie finally meets my gaze. Through her anger I see relief, a path forward for us. Mutual forgiveness, I hope. She finally nods.

Grant and Mirage nod, too.

"Good," I say. I grab Effie's camera and hold it up to her until she takes it. "Now, if you'll indulge me for one more shoot, I have a scandal to cause."

I leave my crew behind. Miranda and I meet in a throng of bodies that have taken up the DJ's beat. I'm in just my underwear. Miranda is in an oversized shirt, probably stolen from the discarded clothes on the pool deck.

"They know," I tell her.

Shadows cross her face as someone slides the lights down low. It's like I can see her doubts, like she wears them like a veil. But through them, she smiles, and the shadows drift away. She takes my hand.

"Just as I planned," she says.

Something clicks in my head. If Effie wasn't the anonymous poster, then . . .

"You posted that comment? You tried to expose us?"

Miranda's grin is sly and mysterious. It's the face of many

secrets all rolling around in that genius head of hers. She doesn't say yes or no, but her hesitation is answer enough.

The lights change again, but this time it's the track lighting Grant set up for our runway shoot. They throb a romantic scarlet. I turn back to my friends, and sure enough Grant has his trusty tablet up, programming the perfect lighting for the shot. Effie's got her camera at the ready. Mirage subtly bumps people out of the way to compose the shot.

Team SAVOY, at it again, forever making something out of nothing. My heart swells. This is how I know things will be okay. Miranda sees them getting ready, too. She drapes her arms over my shoulders and lets her forehead rest against mine.

"Hey," she says. "I heard a rumor. That you wanted . . . to dance with me?"

I pull back to see if she's serious. I look for that playful smirk, that arched eyebrow that tells the world what a joke she thinks it all is. And the playfulness is there, but she's being sincere. She means this. She wants this.

"I'd love to dance with you," I tell her. And I mean it. So much.

We join together, her arms over my shoulders, my hands on her hips. Vaguely, I register the flash of Effie's camera. Then many more phones buzzing around us. People are noticing what's happening. People are seeing us.

Seeing us.

I don't really care about the photos, though. I don't think about what they'll show, how they'll look, the composition or the clever captions or any of it.

I don't have to picture anything at all because I've got what I want right here. Right in front of me.

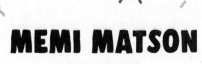

# MEMI MATSON

## THE ACTOR

### PART V

## CLIMAX AND RESOLUTION

AS IF PROVING MY POINT THAT ANYTHING CAN happen, the lights are back on now. It's a good thing, too, because navigating stairs by flashlight in a haze would not end well.

When I reach the dual staircase, Blake is waiting at the bottom of the left side. He smiles up at me. I smile back.

I glance at the other side. Chance is there. And I have the sudden urge to try improv.

Gripping the railing as if my (love) life depends on it, which I suppose it does, I descend slowly. Finally, I stand in front of Chance and reach for his hand. I lead him to the dance floor just as a club edit of Brooke Simpson's "Perfect" kicks up.

He grins before launching into the practiced steps, spins, and swoops of a powwow fancy dancer mixed with standard hip-hop moves. Laughing at my pursed-lip appraisal of his dancing, he motions for me to join him. His mouth moves and I see rather than hear, "C'mon, Mem."

I'm about to scowl at him but settle for an amused eye roll. He takes it as a challenge.

Seriously? He isn't . . . Oh yes, he is. Chance Jackson crouches low to the floor, pretending to peer around a non-existent obstacle. His right hand shields his gaze from an imaginary sun. Finally rising, he stomps his feet to the bass beats coming from someone's playlist and makes his way toward me. Chance's face is shiny with sweat. It kind of makes him glow.

The grinning fool is doing a powwow sneak-up dance. I shake my head with an exaggerated slowness. I wanted to dance with him, but not like this. There is no way I'm taking the bait.

Chance is such a goofball. Annoying, silly, and—fuck it—irresistible.

I spread my arms to hold my imaginary shawl and skip dance steps around him. As the crowd cheers, I add spins and lightning-fast footwork.

My classmates have never seen an Anishinaabe dance battle. Chance and I do not hang out together. When I was cast as the lead Juliet and he as the Romeo understudy, no one at FHHS knew it was kind of, well, history-making. And our Sunday performance? An Indigenous Juliet AND an Indigenous Romeo? It went unheralded. That should've been front-page news, Sadie!

We circle each other, matching moves and quickening the pace. I spin like a tornado until the exact moment the song ends, and I strike a pose on the final beat. The room continues to spin. I focus on Chance. He looks confident and proud. I guess he hit his final pose, too.

The circle of people around us erupts in applause.

While I'm reveling in the adoration, a tap on my shoulder brings me face to face with Blake.

"Memi, do you think we can go somewhere to talk?" He sidesteps Chance.

I nod. Blake laces our fingers together and walks me away from the dance floor.

"You were right, Memi," he says. "It was a dick move to ditch the last performance and the wrap party tonight." After a beat, he continues, "Can we get out of here and go somewhere quiet?"

I pull him close. He responds by lightly kissing my neck and telling me how he wants to celebrate tonight. It's everything I wanted at the beginning of the party. Everything I've wanted since our first week of rehearsals. And yet . . .

"Blake," I say, breaking away to meet his eyes. "We're good."

He unleashes his megawatt smile and holds me closer.

I stand tippy-toe to reach his face. I plant a kiss on his smooth cheek before pulling away.

"But I'm not done celebrating with everyone."

"Everyone, meaning Chance?" He nods over my shoulder.

"Yes."

"I fucked up," Blake huffs. "Guess I opened the window of opportunity for my understudy to upstage me, huh? Again."

I lean into him and whisper in his ear.

"I hope you get the Star Trek reboot, Blake. I will always be your biggest fan. Thank you for everything." My goodbye kiss is soft and sweet on his lips. "Adieu, my handsome Romeo. Parting is such sweet sorrow."

He mirrors my kiss before letting me go. He looks around and over to our castmates, who have formed a new dance circle around Chance. Blake nudges me toward them.

"Go. Seek happy nights to happy days."

I join the dance circle, where Chance Jackson is living his best life. He challenges each dancer. He dips Marni Jones, who played the part of my nurse. Wesley Varma, also known as Mercutio, wants to twirl. After Chance obliges, I jump in for my turn.

"Go, Memi! Go, Memi!" my castmates shout.

"What do you say we show everyone how to two-step, hey?" I say to Chance.

Beaming, he takes my hand and raises it high.

"Lead the way, Mem."

# SY NAVARRO

## THE EMO BAND KID

**PART III**

WHEN I FINALLY FIND DEANDRE TO ASK IF IT'S cool if we play a quick set, he gives me a semiconscious thumbs-up from where he's embracing the toilet in the first-floor bathroom.

Sam collects her drum kit from her mom's minivan idling out front; Perry grabs his bass and amp from his car; I retrieve my guitar, amp, and backpack full of cords, mics, and pedals from where I stashed everything in the garage with Bayside's goat. And, just in time, Marlon returns from picking up Asa's cello like I asked him to.

Now that Savoy's fashion-off has wrapped up and Jrue's fixed the power situation, we set up everything in the backyard next to the pool. Jade agreed to take a break from spinning, so there's just the conversation of the crowd, vibrating with excitement. Besides the kids gathered around outside, they're also spilling out the doorways and sitting on the roof. People even pop out the screens in the windows and lean over the frames.

Only one window remains shut tight, curtains drawn. As we tune and do a brief sound check, I keep glancing up at that window.

There's a bunch of people checking the time on their phones and casting confused glances at Asa's cello, which is to my right sans Asa.

"You think she'll come down?" I ask Perry.

He shrugs. "We had a good talk and she said she'd think about it. So maybe it's fifty-fifty? But, Sy, you're the one she really needs to hear from."

"Okay, thanks, man."

Perry tunes his bass. Sam twirls her sticks. There's nothing left to do but begin.

"Ready?"

They nod.

I take off my hoodie, revealing my black T-shirt with a broken heart over the chest. I step up to the mic and brush hair out of my eyes. The crowd roars.

I wait for it to quiet down, but they keep going. They keep clapping and shouting and whistling. There's even a dog barking somewhere.

I step back from the mic, and—I'm not gonna lie—my eyes well up with tears because is there anything more beautiful than translating your soul into sound and having so many people connect with it, than asking to be seen, and then, being seen?

This might be There Is No Kevin in Team's final show, but I know this isn't the last time I'll be playing music for people. I won't survive without this feeling.

I wipe my eyes and exchange smiles with Perry and Sam as we collectively drink in everyone's love. Even if she doesn't forgive me, I hope Asa's savoring it, too.

Eventually, the noise fades. I turn to face everyone and step back up to the mic. But I don't say anything. Every good musician knows the silence is part of the sound. I honor it, give it space to grow anticipation.

Then, before it goes on a second too long, I say, "Hi. We're There Is No Kevin in Team."

Sam strikes a four-count with her sticks, and we're off.

We launch right into "Orange of Discord," which has the driving energy that always gets people moving right away. Sure enough, the kids gathered closest to us start hopping around, bouncing off each other. And when the catchy-as-hell hook comes around, so many people start singing along that I can barely hear my own voice.

Though we're making the best of it with Perry singing Asa's parts, a sick feeling lingers in the pit of my stomach as I keep strumming and singing. It's not the same without Asa's cello weaving through my guitar riffs, without our harmonizing voices. It's not the same without Asa. I keep glancing at the window for any sign of her, but it remains empty.

We transition into "Dead Weasleys" next. It's not as catchy as "Orange," but the timing and key match, so it keeps the energy up. There's still no sign of Asa by the time it ends, so we go right into "Skeleton Crown." It's a slightly slower tune with more emotional lyrics. A perfect setup.

Finally, it's time to play "Cat Café," the song that's apparently been streamed almost one million times. The one that got the label's attention. The one people have been shouting the name of ever since we pulled out our instruments. The first one that Asa and I cowrote.

Our song.

Perry nods at me and steps away from the second mic. I

hope this works. It's filled with dueling vocals, so if Asa doesn't join us, it's going to feel flat as hell.

I keep my eyes locked on the window and pluck the slow opening notes as I tongue my lip ring. The crowd lights up and loses their shit because they instantly know it's THE song.

When we get through the intro, I signal for Perry and Sam to run through it again to buy us some time. The crowd seems confused, but they roll with it. At least, until we repeat it for a third time. Sensing we're about to lose them, I go ahead and start singing the first verse, no idea what to do about Asa's lines.

When I get to the first one, I'm about to just sing it myself—but the crowd takes over. It's amazing; the song transforms into this electric call-and-response between me and, like, one or two hundred people who know all the lyrics. And they're loving the hell out of it.

But then we reach the quiet part. The part where everyone suddenly stops playing except for Sam keeping a quiet, pulsing beat. I check the window again.

When you play with the same people enough, you get to know each other inside and out. You learn to read each other's body language, eyes, and moods, practically developing a kind of ESP connection so you can have entire silent conversations over the music. That's what happens next as Sam keeps the beat going . . .

The three of us converse through telepathy.

*Sam: What do you want to do?*

*Me: I don't know. She's not coming, dude.*

*Perry: The audience has been great. It'll work if we just move on.*

*Me: But I don't want to give up yet.*

*Sam: I can't just keep playing this beat forever. It's getting super awkward.*

*Perry: Yeah, crowd's getting restless. And there's a bunch of people recording this on their phones, so . . .*

*Me: I know . . .*

*Perry: It's now or never.*

Now or never.

"Asa!" I say—not sing—into the mic as Sam keeps the beat. "Asa! I know you're in there!"

Everyone's confused at first, but then they follow my gaze up to the window and realize what's going on.

"I'm sorry about what went down . . . about what I did."

The curtains remain drawn.

I go on, hitting the highlights of the texts I sent her earlier. "I was stupid and selfish. I made it all about me. Thinking about what I wanted, about the future I saw for myself, without considering what Sam or Perry or you wanted."

Nothing.

Except people start shouting up at the window.

"Come on, Asa!"

"Listen to him!"

People start chanting, "Forgive him! Forgive him! Forgive him!"

Suddenly, the curtains pull back.

And there's Asa at the window. Like a South Asian Juliet.

She slides it open, and everyone cheers. I smile.

She leans out, cups her hands around her mouth, and shouts, "You're a complete asshat, Sy Navarro."

A few people boo.

"Nah, stop with that," I tell them. "She's right, everyone. She's right. I am an asshat. A colossal asshat. But I'm trying not to be anymore."

"We love you, Sy!" someone shouts.

"Even if you are an asshat!" someone else shouts, and the crowd laughs together.

"We're all asshats!" another person shouts, eliciting more laughter.

I go on. "Asa, I'm sorry. I shouldn't have gotten all defensive and angry that night. I shouldn't have called you selfish—"

"And conceited."

"Right, and conceited. I should have respected your decision to do something else with your life, and I should have told you all how I was feeling instead of bottling it up until I burst. See, recently I realized—"

"Yeah, yeah, I know," Asa interrupts.

"You do?"

"I read your texts, and I overheard you talking to Sam and Perry. You were sitting right under this window, idiot."

"Oh," I say, surprised but glad I don't have to put my vulnerability completely on public display. "And?"

"And didn't you read my replies?"

I stop playing long enough to check my phone, but it won't come on. "Oh." I hold it up. "It's dead."

"Well, I already said I forgive you."

I smile. "Thank you, Asa Rao."

The crowd cheers.

I'm also mad curious about how she feels about the part of the texts where I confessed that I like her as more than a friend. I'm about to bring that up when I remember what Perry said about public pressure, about starting things off right. Instead, I ask, "But if you forgave me, then why aren't you down here playing with us?"

"If you'd charged your phone, you'd know that I've been in this room all night working on a new song."

Everyone cheers again.

"YES!" George Nguyen bellows. "A NEW NO KEVIN SONG!"

"Nah, this one's my own," Asa says.

"And I can't wait to hear it when you're ready to play it," I say. "But first, will you please grace us with your beautiful cello and sonorous voice for 'Cat Café' one last time?"

Asa nods, disappears from the window, then reappears downstairs and makes her way through a packed crowd that can't stop giving her high fives and fist bumps.

When she finally reaches me, I shift my guitar to my back, and we wrap our arms around each other, and for the first time in nearly half a year, everything feels right.

"I'm sorry," I say again, this time just for her.

"I know. I forgive you," she says, this time just for me.

Then she moves over to her cello and quickly makes sure it's tuned. When she picks up the bow, resting it against the strings, all four of us can't stop smiling at each other.

Sam starts building the beat.

After a few measures, Perry comes in on bass.

I sing the chorus once by myself.

Then Asa sings by herself.

Then we sing together, my guitar and her cello and our voices spiraling around each other in a way that always makes me feel like the morning after a thunderstorm. And when we lock eyes, I know there's also something new happening here. Something we can figure out later.

The song builds and builds and builds—we hit the hard stop—there's a beat of silence—then we all come crashing back together.

# SADIE BERNBAUM

## THE SCHOOL PAPER EDITOR; KNOWER OF ALL TEA

## PART III

HOW LONG IS TOO LONG TO HIDE IN A CLOSET? This isn't metaphorical. I have been in DeAndre's parents' massive walk-in closet for what feels like a lifetime. While I've been hiding behind an impressive wall of hanging faux-fur coats, two different couples have hooked up, including power couple on- and clearly now offstage Memi Matson and Chance Jackson. Ever since reporting on the cast list, I knew he would make a much better match for her than hot but surface Blake Donnelly. Damn, I wish they could have timed their connection to make it into the review in the final paper. People love a stage-to-streets romance.

Static from a speaker outside ricochets up the walls of the house and I hear Sy trying to end the There Is No Kevin in Team miniconcert and the crowd demanding an encore. The perfect distraction to help me sneak out undetected, never to be seen again. At this point, I'd rather walk the ten miles home than spend another second at this party.

FUTURE PULITZER PRIZE—WINNING JOURNALIST CAN LAND A
STORY BUT NOT A KISS.

I tiptoe through the dark room as the sounds of a drum countdown vibrate and Sy's voice sails through the estate. Damn, they're good—I did them dirty with that review I gave them, it had been a bad week and Sy really pissed me off throwing me under the bus for neglecting a group project in American history because I had a deadline for a huge profile piece about the Florence Hills mayor. But a real journalist knows there are only two rules: write the truth and don't make it personal. If I could go back in time and issue a retraction for articles I've written, that review would be at the top of the list, so I boosted his reunion show to as many people here tonight as I could as an apology.

The house is empty as I make my way through—aside from the random passed-out body here and there, everyone is enjoying the show. Final-fucking-ly something is actually working out for me tonight.

"Where have you been?" Jrue stands a few feet away from me, blocking the front door with a look on his face like I ditched him this entire night.

"Where have I been? Where have YOU been?" I take five giant steps and poke him hard in the chest. "You completely ditched me, Jrue. Sure, we had the garage debrief that was all about you and the Baysiders' car, which was actually very impressive but not the point! The headline literally reads 'Best Friend Abandoned for a Literal Goat and Then a Girl Who Barely Knows You Exist.'"

He throws his arms up like he surrenders and steps back.

"Chill, my bad. Sorry I couldn't hold your hand the entire night, Sadie, but it's not like you've been by my side, either. You were hanging out with the basketball team, remember? They are, like, more jockstrap than human, Sadie. Travis Marshall? You let Travis Marshall almost play you? When you've spent the last year plotting his untimely death by poison followed by leaving his body in the woods for bear meat, but then you go into a bedroom with him? Talk about hypocritical. Since when are those your people?"

Mad doesn't come close. Rage. Demon-wrath. Those are closer but barely cover one-tenth of the anger that I am feeling in this moment. Jrue and I have never fought. Not really. The closest was when we were fourteen after trick-or-treating and he lied about how many KitKats he got because he didn't want to stick to the trade deal we made and end up with that many Twizzlers. But maybe after ten years of friendship, you need to say the things you haven't said.

"You have no idea what I've been through tonight because you've been chasing either laughs or Mia McKenzie. She barely looked in your direction before this party. But now that she's single, you are suddenly worthy of her time. News flash: I'm your best friend. YOU are supposed to be my person, Jrue!"

Jrue's face drops, and I know he knows he went too far, so he does what he always does, he tries to make this a joke.

"Damn! Sadie, did you just *Grey's Anatomy* me? It's like that?"

Like this is funny. Like we aren't about to graduate in a few days. Like I'm not leaving Florence Hills to complete an early semester at Dartmouth before orientation while Jrue travels the world after getting his plumbing certification. We'll hardly ever see each other. Tonight was supposed to mean something, that's what he said to get me to come to this stupid party, but while I've been needing him, he's been too busy needing everyone else. I can feel the tears trying to crawl out of my eyes, but crying is another thing we've never done in our friendship and I'm not starting now.

"Sadie—" he starts to say, his voice softer, but I turn and run up the stairs, away from him.

# JRUE EDWARDS

## THE CLASS CLOWN

### PART III

*I'M SADIE'S PERSON?*

I say that not because I'm surprised to hear those words—Sadie and I have been holding each other down since forever.

Like, if you were talking shit about one of us, everyone knows you better not do it within earshot of the other, because we'd instantly go attack dog on your ass. Is Sadie a bit of a know-it-all? Yep. Since day one. But I've never understood why someone knowing it all is a bad thing? Isn't the annoying part someone telling us they know everything? And the thing that people always get wrong about Sadie is that yes, she knows everyone's business. Yes, she's nosy as hell. But does she throw everyone's secrets all over the internet? Only sometimes—but rarely to be messy. Does she blackmail people, threatening to air all their super-funky, frequently gross laundry, unless they give her a quote? Nope, never. That's not her style.

She's more like walk around cheesing like a cat with a canary in its mouth, but when you're all, *Okay, I'll bite, what's up, what scintillating tidbit did you learn now,* she's all, *I'm a journalist, Jrue. I don't just disclose sensitive info for fun, okay? I report the news. I'm a professional.*

And I'm like, *Okay, never mind then, sorry I—*

And then she's all, *Wait, wait, guess, you have to guess . . .*

Because this is what we do.

Because this is who we are together.

A kind of easy magic.

Sadie's the first person I go to when I'm excited, or sad, or frustrated. After our family's chocolate Lab, Pippi, died and I legit lost my whole mind for months, how many nights did Sadie fall asleep next to me in my bed, holding my hand while I played with her hair? How many times did her horrendous, not-cute, hairball-stuck-in-my-throat snoring make me smile, and laugh, when feeling even an ounce of happiness felt impossible? And when she'd wake up in the dead of night, probably hearing her own snoring (haha), and she'd reach out for me in the dark, her fingers stretching across the queen-sized bed, across the mountain of sheets and twisted blankets, because she also slept like a crazy person, she'd squeeze my fingers, stroke my wrist, roll or scoot closer to me, and say, *You okay? Have you slept yet? Crap, I'm so sorry, I'm supposed to be helping you sleep but instead I'm the one passing out.*

And I'd say something like *You have a lot going on.*

And she'd shake her head. *You're what I have going on. Everything else is irrelevant. But if me being here is keeping you awake, maybe I should . . .*

But I never let her say those two letters . . . *go.*

*Nah, if it's cool, I want you to . . . can you please stay, Sadie . . . ?*

And she'd smile, her trademark smile, brighter than all our favorite roller coasters' neon night lights combined. And I don't know, it's like for a second, everything felt okay. No, Pippi wasn't coming back. She was never coming back. No, I wasn't suddenly fine with that. But it's like I could cope while Sadie was next to me. I could leapfrog from one sad lily pad to the next, slightly less sad lily pad. As if all the extra shit that weighs us all down was falling off my shoulders and I could take the breath I needed. I could breathe. And sometimes, when you have the kind of pain that makes time stop, the kind of pain that makes everything bright and bold about the world fade to black like you're wearing permanent sunglasses that you never wanted, that you never asked for—sometimes, taking a breath, the simple, mostly forgettable act of inhaling and exhaling, feels revolutionary; and knowing there's another breath coming right behind it, a miracle.

But here's the thing—the person who you feel safest with is also the person who can hurt you the most, the person who you love is the person who could destroy you . . . but they don't, they wouldn't.

I'm not just Sadie's person . . . Sadie's my person, too.

And maybe if I didn't have my head shoved so far up my ass, I probably would've realized that, and understood what it means to love and be loved, a long time ago.

But it's not too late! There's still enough time to add and complete ACTION ITEM #6: TELL YOUR BEST FRIEND WHAT YOU SHOULD'VE SAID A LONG TIME AGO.

I race upstairs, taking the steps two at a time. I've just gotta find S—

# SADIE BERNBAUM

## THE SCHOOL PAPER EDITOR; KNOWER OF ALL TEA

## PART IV

I RUN UP THE STAIRS AND DOWN THE HALLWAY and open the first door I see so I can ugly cry in peace.

"Don't you knock?" Penny Washington yells from a toilet.

"Oh my god! Oh my god!" I turn the knob to leave.

"Can you not open the door right now? I'm literally still peeing," she says between tinkles.

"I'm sorry. This whole night has just been so awful. Everyone is the worst. If there was some way to summon the rapture, I would," I sob into the towels on the door, wiping my eyes and nose on them between wails.

"Why are you here?" Penny asks.

I begin to turn around, but she motions for me to face the wall again, as she is midwipe.

"Sorry." I face the wall again, then ask, "What do you mean?"

"I mean, if you hate everyone, why are you at this party?"

"I don't hate everyone," I explain. "I just don't want to have to change who I am for people to like me. I tell the truth. Why is that so bad?"

Penny flushes and I hear the sink turn on, so I figure it's safe to turn around.

"Weren't you wearing something different earlier?" I ask.

"What, are you working with SAVOY now?" she asks.

"It's my job to notice things."

"There was a puke situation. There have been a lot of situations," Penny says casually.

"I heard. But, for what it's worth, you are a way better catch than V, plus Colin seems like a really viable love connection—"

Penny looks at me like I just performed an exorcism.

I shrug. "I'm good at what I do."

She snorts. "Well, I heard something about you, too. Sophie B. is so messy." Penny purses her lips and blows an air kiss. "I would ask how it's going but based on your general state of despair, I'm going to guess not great."

The tears start again, I can't help it. "I just wanted to get my first kiss over with. I don't need, like . . . fireworks, but apparently the only people who want to kiss me either think I'm mystical animal royalty or want to use me to get extra points in some gross hookup competition."

Penny considers something. "Have you seriously never been kissed?"

"We can't all be popular and gorgeous."

She waves me off. "Didn't you ever go to slumber parties in middle school and practice?"

I shake my head. "I spent every weekend of middle school with my aunt Gertie watching soaps and crocheting," I answer.

"Well, that explains a lot."

I slide down to the floor. I can see the headline now: SADIE SEEN SOBBING IN THE BATHROOM, STILL NEVER BEEN KISSED. And a subheading that reads, PATHETIC LOSER MIGHT AS WELL STICK HEAD IN TOILET. There have been weak editors vying for my position at the *Florence Hills High Gazette* since I started. That'd be my send-off.

"Damn, are you always this . . ." Penny can't find the words, so she holds out her hands and shakes like she is being electrocuted.

"I mean . . . I'm Jewish, anxiety is my blood type," I say, lifting my head up.

"Come here," she says, motioning for me to join her by the sink.

I rise from the floor and check my reflection, assuming my face is covered in dried mucus, but aside from my eyes being puffy and red, I'm mostly okay. I look again at Penny, who is still waiting for me.

"Lock the door and come over here," she says again.

"Lock the . . . ? Why?"

Penny huffs past me and clicks the lock on the door. She turns to me. Somehow, even with the faint hint of vomit on her skin, she's still stunning.

"Sadie, I get it. You have your whole 'I'm not giving in to the status quo, no one matters, grumpy is my state of being' vibe, but the reason you haven't been kissed isn't because everyone hates you, it's because you never shut up! You never let anyone in. I don't know how Jrue puts up with you. You haven't been kissed because you spend so much time focused on your goals and making sure everyone knows you don't care what they think that you don't see what's right in front of you. Do you know what kissing someone who isn't in the moment is like? It's like your face is getting licked by a feral llama! There are far worse people out there at this party who have done a whole lot more than kissing, and do you know why? It's because they are open to it. Now get over here."

All of a sudden, I understand what Penny is saying. Could this finally be my first kiss:

~~Merrill Wortham~~
~~Travis Marshall?!?!~~
Penny Washington 🫦

"Really? Are you . . . sure? I don't want to ruin your night with a llama kiss." I cup my hand in front of my mouth and smell.

"Oh no!" Penny laughs. "Sorry, I didn't mean—" She laughs so hard she snorts and can't speak. She bends over laughing and holds on to her knees to catch her breath. After what feels like hours of a laughing fit, she runs back over to the toilet and pees again.

"The idea of kissing me makes you laugh until you pee. Wow." I head for the door. Tonight was a mistake. Everything has been a mistake.

"No. No!" She snorts. "Stop!" she shouts. "Edibles, Sadie. Colin and I just had edibles. I'm not laughing at you, I promise. I am laughing because you think *I* am the best option when the answer has literally been right there the entire time!"

I stare intently at the floor between us where she is pointing but I don't see anything. "Umm, Penny, are you . . . hallucinating or . . . you know, never mind, I should let you enjoy whatever it is you are experiencing . . ."

"Sadie, wait." She takes some deep breaths. "I know you think you know everything but what you don't know is my mom is sick, okay? She's sick, and I don't know what that means for the future. I don't know if I'll ever be able to do anything without worrying about her. This entire night I've been wanting to have fun and enjoy myself and I can't fully because I'm worried about her, even though a really great guy has been trying his hardest to distract me."

Penny is always attached to her phone. I've judged her for what I thought was a social media obsession. I assumed, considering her popularity status and friend group, that she was living for the likes. "I'm sorry. I didn't know."

She gets up to wash her hands. "It is what it is, but Sadie?"

"Yeah?"

"Can you just come over here?"

Despite my head protesting, my body moves toward her. I had a plan. So far that plan has failed. A good journalist knows that sometimes the only way to move forward is to start over with a blank page. A new prompt. A different angle.

"Close your eyes," she says.

I stand before her, eyes wide open. Nothing good has ever happened when one person tells another to close their eyes.

Penny lets out a loud, weary sigh and cocks her head to the side. "I'm waiting."

"Fine," I grunt, and let my eyelids settle down onto each other.

"I want you to imagine lips," Penny says.

Is she for real? I crack open my left eyelid to make sure this isn't just another side effect of the edibles, but she snaps her fingers in my face and practically pinches my eye shut again.

"Do you want my help or not?"

"I mean technically I didn't ask for your help—"

"JUST DO IT, BERNBAUM. You're messing with the vibe!"

I close my eyes. The exercise seems ridiculous but now that I know everything Penny is dealing with, I don't want to make her life any harder. I take a deep slow breath and squeeze my eyes tight. "Okay . . ."

"Concentrate."

At first I just see darkness, but then I see them materialize, soft and supple, coming toward me in the darkness.

"Okay, I see them," I whisper.

"Now I want you to kiss them."

I lean into the fantasy. The thing I have been chasing all night, and when the lips meet mine, they aren't lips anymore but two halves of a locket, fitting together like they are supposed to. They are familiar, these lips, moving in a way that guides me to move, too. Like it's a conversation I've had for years, I anticipate each pause, I flow with each transition. Like flower petals opening to the sun, they keep going that way until I am confident enough to take the lead. And when I do it is familiar, this new thing that I have had in me and never figured out how to use until now. When I stop, it's easy. Just the end of a conversation. Just a bee that's had its fill of nectar and is ready to head home to sleep.

"Look at them one more time, the lips." Penny's voice is airy and about four octaves higher than it was moments ago. If I didn't know any better, I would think I had been transported to some overpriced yoga retreat, but whatever she's doing is working. "Now look up," she says.

I steady my breath, let it slow, then I do and there it is.

The same dumb smile that has kept me company for the past decade. The same lips I've been sitting next to this whole time. The same person I have been wishing I was with all night. I see Jrue. And suddenly I know, for sure now, who my first kiss is supposed to be with:

~~Merrill Wortham~~
~~Travis Marshall?!?!~~
~~Penny Washington~~
Jrue Edwards

Wow, Penny just hot-girl-therapied me. Damn she's good!

I open my eyes and Penny says, "There. Now you'll kiss like a tamed llama."

"You know, maybe you are actually as cool as they say."

She smiles. "Thanks. And Sadie? I think, if you get over yourself, it could still happen tonight, and there could be real fireworks. Everyone deserves THAT type of kiss in high school." She winks at me. "You just have to stop getting in your own way."

Penny walks past me and out the door. I wonder for a second if things could have been different, if I could have gotten over myself, if maybe Penny and I might have been friends over the last four years. The idea pulls a laugh from so deep inside me I snort. Not possible, she's way too cool. Plus, I have a friend. Jrue. I wonder what he's doing, if he's okay. If he will even listen to what I just realized. If he will forgive me for our fight. If he feels the same way.

"All right, people, time to break it up! You have five minutes to vacate the premises."

Holy shit. The party is getting broken up. The police are here. It's nearly one in the morning. I have to find Jrue. If I've learned anything tonight, it's that you've got to take the moments as they come, and I came here to get my first kiss, so I'm leaving with it.

# JRUE EDWARDS

## THE CLASS CLOWN

YOU KNOW THAT THING OLD PEOPLE TRY TO TELL you, something like: when you stop chasing the thing, it'll start chasing you. I'm paraphrasing, obvi, but—

"Hey," a voice says, tapping my shoulder.

I turn around, surprised to see Mia, even though this is exactly the person I've wanted to see most of all. She smiles brighter than ultralight and I feel woozy; and I resist looking behind me to confirm it's me she's smiling at, because confidence, Jrue, confidence. "I've been looking for you," she says.

And for some reason, I feel like I should be leaning on something. Or maybe just that my arm should be draped around something. You know, extra casual-like.

"Mind if we go someplace quiet?"

After I mop up the puddle I've melted into off Mia's mint Air Force Ones, I manage to nod yes. She smiles again, takes me by the hand, and guides me through a sea of familiar faces, as the Neighbourhood's "Stargazing" plays in the background. And

I could get used to this—being led away by Mia McKenzie. And if I didn't know better, I'd say I'm the one being pranked.

Mia closes the bedroom door behind us and suddenly, eyeing the king-sized bed posted up against a bank of picture windows, I'm wheezing like I've just now come down with asthma.

Because somehow, I'm alone in a bedroom with Mia McKenzie.

She sets her hand on my back. "Are you okay?"

Again, no, I'm not okay because somehow, I'm alone in a bedroom with Mia McKenzie.

"Me? I'm perf. Just, you know, parched," I assure her as I try not to hyperventilate. Is spontaneous asthma really a thing?

Mia walks into the adjoining bathroom and comes back with a paper cup of water.

"Go slow," she says as I tilt the water into my mouth. "Better?"

I nod. "Much."

"Good," she says, belly flopping onto the bed and slapping the empty mattress space beside her. "Come. Lie."

And I do. Because this is the rom-com moment I've been waiting for—Mia's adorable face framed by her hands and propped up by her elbows. Me, sprawled beside her, wondering how loud your heart can beat before it's audible to other human beings.

"So you probably heard me and DeAndre broke up a few weeks back," she announces.

"Oh, right, yeah, I heard about that, I think," I squeak out. "Does it feel weird? You guys were together since, like, sophomore year. You were everyone's 'It Couple.'"

"Ugh, I hate that." Mia sighs, shakes her head. "Don't get me wrong. I still love him. I'll always love him. But I finally admitted to myself that I've secretly been into someone else, only I've been too afraid to tell them."

Wait, is Mia McKenzie confessing her love to me? No, it can't be. She would've said I'm afraid to tell *him,* or *you,* not *them.* Right?

Also, did she just say she's afraid to tell someone she's into them?

I try to act shocked, which isn't hard because I'm in actual shock.

"Why are you afraid?" I ask her, digging deep and accessing my most baritone voice.

"Rejection, duh," she says, laughing.

"No one's dumb enough to reject you," I hear myself say in my true voice.

"Why are you so sweet? That's one thing I regret about high school. I wish we'd kicked it more. Why didn't we?"

I shrug like *beats me* even though we both know it's because for four years we've spun in completely different orbits.

"You really mean that?" Mia asks, her cheeks bunched in a shy grin. "That rejecting me would be dumb?"

I nod like a super-agreeable bobblehead. "The dumbest."

"Hey, you," Mia says softly, giggling as she slides closer toward my side of the bed. Closer to . . . me. "So, listen, I had this really great idea, Jrue. Wanna hear it?"

I nod, words caught in my throat, because can I be honest, this isn't what I thought was gonna happen. Sure, I daydreamed about it, regular dreamed about it, but this is Mia McKenzie we're talking about. It's a minor miracle her eyes even physically allow her to see me.

That's not me shitting on myself. That's just honesty. That's just real.

And I say that because, I don't know, maybe that made me like her *more*, you know? Like, knowing that there was less than zero possibility that she would ever reciprocate my vibe, it was easy to keep the fantasy alive. To think of it that way, as some far-flung dream that had about as much of a chance as winning the megamillions lottery or getting smacked by an asteroid.

She beams. "You sure? You don't seem excited by my idea, Jrue . . ."

I hit her with my widest smile. "No, I am. I, uh, I really wanna know your idea."

And she scoots a bit more so that now her face is a handful of inches away from mine, as it has been in so many of my dreams.

"Well, I'm single now for the first time in forever and I'm enjoying it, I am. It's given me a lot of time to just . . . think. To think about what I really want. *Who* I really want. And I . . . I've been afraid to say this but now I'm just gonna because I feel like maybe you feel it, too?"

I tilt my head slightly, careful not to move too much, because our lips might touch, because at the very least we'd knock foreheads, that's how close we are now.

Mia takes a deep breath and exhales slowly, and I feel every bit of her warm, sweet air press into my face, my cheeks hotter now, my lips falling the slightest bit open.

"Okay, here goes, I'm gonna say it. I want my last summer in Florence Hills to be something I never forget . . . and I thought what if we did that together, Jrue? Me and you? What if . . . we spent our last summer together, driving into Chicago to see the Cubbies, bonfires on the beach where you successfully moon the moon, falling asleep in each other's arms. I was thinking about this. I haven't seen your bedroom since fifth grade, I think. But you live two doors down from me, that's weird, right?"

And I can't confirm if I'm nodding my head or shaking my head because the room is spinning. Because this conversation, this moment is mad dizzying, mad disorienting—

Except not quite how I imagined it would be.

This isn't dizzy in love.

I know because I've felt a bit of that before—only the real thing isn't at all disorienting, the room isn't spinning out of control like suddenly you have no concept of space.

The real thing feels like you're spinning *into* control.

Like you've been lost in space but now suddenly here is your true orbit.

Here is your gravity.

Your world finally rotating right.

And I nearly see it too late—Mia's lips puckering.

"Mia, wait, I—"

Mia's lips pause just in front of mine, like a shuttle waiting to dock.

"I'm so so sorry," I tell her. "I really like you. I've liked you since second grade. And honestly, the idea of us spending a summer together sounds awesome . . . but I think I just realized, when you said *our last summer,* that in the end, as cool as that would be, it would probably really be the last thing we did together, you know? We're not the two people who end up together. You'd go off to college and I'd do my plumbing thing and that would probably be the end. I mean, maybe we try to keep in touch on Insta or whatever, liking each other's stories, but . . . we both deserve more. Or maybe what I'm realizing but have been too afraid to say aloud is, *I* deserve more. If this summer turns out to be my last whatever, that's cool. But I'd rather it be the start of something. I'd rather it be the summer of firsts. And as incredibly lucky as I would be to spend any amount of time with you, Mia McKenzie, I think you're just a few years too late because . . . because I'm . . ." I pause, the words rolling around my cheeks but not quite rolling off my tongue . . . And what does that mean if I can't even say it to someone else? If I can't summon the courage to finally admit to myself, admit to *her,* that—

"I'm already in love with someone."

And I see the surprise flare in Mia's eyes, and it's like staring into a mirror, both of us a little stunned. "Well . . . ," she starts. "I can't say I'm not disappointed. But also, I get it. I mean, you've been right under my nose all this time, it's not fair for me to think I could just waltz in at the last second and *presto chango* this shit into something it's not."

I nod. "I'm sorry for being so awkward and flirting with you and for making you feel any kind of way. All those feelings were real. Are real. It's just that . . ."

Mia laughs. "You're not gonna keep sitting here telling me you're in love with someone else, are you? Because I gotta be honest, even being pleasantly rejected still feels not the best."

I shake my head. "No, you're right, sorry, I—"

"Does she know?"

"No? Yes? I think so. I don't know."

"So go tell her."

And then Mia's leaning back toward me again, her lips at long last closing the distance that's lived between us this whole time, even though only one of us probably ever felt it . . .

And she plants a kiss square on my . . . forehead.

And then I'm squeezing her hand and Mia's hopping off the

bed, smoothing the wrinkles from her shirt, gliding her fingers through her hair—and damn, she's gorgeous. But also, equally as cool inside. Omigod, I'm cheesy.

Mia turns the doorknob and with her free hand, she motions for me to join her. "You coming?"

I wave her onward. "Actually, I think I'm gonna hang back for a minute."

She makes a face.

And I stretch my arms like I'm just waking from a million-year nap. "I might catch a few zzz's. I kinda had a long night last night."

Mia smiles. "That's right. Brenda. Jrue Edwards, Thee Best Prankster in all the Midwest."

I smile back, feeling like the universe checked off the last box, officially.

ACTION ITEM #5: SECURE GOAT STATUS.

And okay, maybe I'm not *THEE* GOAT, but I'm in the discussion. My name's in the running.

"I like making people laugh."

She nods. "It's one of the things I love most about you," she says.

And I don't know why I say it. I definitely mean it, though. It's one of those moments where everything in the universe converges for a split second and something clicks inside you; suddenly you realize, understand, something central to who you are. "I guess it's something I love about me, too," I hear myself say loud enough to count as aloud but quiet enough I don't know if Mia hears me.

"Thanks for being a decent dude all these years," Mia says, stepping out into the hallway and pulling the door closed behind her, and I'm . . . alone.

But then the door reverses directions and Mia pokes her head back in. "Just do me a favor?"

I meet her eyes. "What's up?"

"Just don't be a little bitch and keep all your rom-com vibes to yourself, okay? Tell Sadie, yeah?"

"I will."

"But like *now*."

I nod. "Deal."

Mia grins. "Also, for what it's worth, I think it's cool you're postponing college to be an international plumber. While the rest of us are stuck in Stupid Shit 101, you're gonna be exploring and changing the world. Fucking awesome."

I nod again. "Um, thanks. That's really cool of you to say."

"It's partly because I suck at leaving rooms, can you tell?" Mia asks.

Before I can reply, the door clicks shut and I'm, once again, a clown at a house party in a bedroom that Mia McKenzie left, alone.

But also, I'm in love.

# CARLA SCHMIDT

### THE COOL MOM

## PART III

### AT A CERTAIN POINT, YOU JUST GOTTA GIVE UP.

At a certain point, some things are just too dangerous to try to hold on to.

Like this party.

Somehow, I did not drown in the pool. A miracle named Merrill dragged me from the chaos. I wrung out my dress and I was so glad I was soaking wet because I was sobbing. Great, frustrated sobs that went completely unnoticed as the kids around us screamed.

Merrill noticed, though. We found some discarded towels, but they barely kept away the shivers. And they didn't help with the shock, anger, or embarrassment. I just kept thinking: *How on earth did I dive into a pool by accident?*

Daisy. That's how.

And with that, I stood up and told Merrill I was going home.

"You're giving up?" she asked.

"I'm giving in. Daisy wins."

High as I might've been, the cold had sobered the part of my brain that knows I'm not a kid and I don't need to make kid choices. I can give up and not hate myself forever for it, can't I? Failure is not just an option, but sometimes the right answer. Still, I feel bad. Merrill deserved an explanation but I was too shocked to mutter more than a quick apology. Then the blackout hit, and I thought, *That's your cue, Carla, you can't keep up with all this chaos.*

Back at my house, still dripping, I call downstairs to the twins. "All good?"

A meek response follows among the clatter of some action movie on the TV, and I relax. Upstairs, I strip, shower, and change into fresh clothes. Not a cheetah dress but jeans and an old T-shirt. No elaborate makeup, no disguising glasses. Just my damp hair in a ponytail, some moisturizer. When I'm done, the house is quiet. So quiet I can hear the party. I ignore it and venture back to the basement door.

"Boys?" I call. "Bedtime, maybe?"

There's no response. Maybe it's the leftover THC, but paranoia leaps at me from the dark of my mind. Are they okay? Did they go looking for Daisy? Did I even hear them before, or did I just imagine it?

"Boys?"

Nothing. I descend into the dark basement, fending off the urge to snap on the lights, and lo and behold my worries were for nothing. My boys are asleep, game controllers still clutched in their hands, as the TV flashes the bloody words:

# GAME OVER.

## START OVER?
### *Yes or No*

"Mom?" Turning, I see Skylar sitting up. He inspects me, the light from the TV shining in his sleepy eyes. "Why is your hair all wet?"

"I was working out," I lie quickly, although I guess there's also some truth to that. "Getting my sweat on."

"Oh." Skylar rubs his eyes, then asks, "Did you have fun at the party?"

*Maybe,* I think, *they aren't as zombified as I thought.* "Yeah, I did have fun," I admit. I feel guilty now, knowing I left Merrill on her own.

"Did you get Daisy?"

The answer is no, but I don't give it right away. There's a difference between *no* and *not yet.* Skylar's questions are so full of earnest belief. A sleepy, childlike hope that flattens the elaborate saga of rescuing the dog into such a simple task, and I'm amazed I messed this up so badly. I look at the TV screen, and the glowing words ask me if I'm ready to start over, or if GAME OVER is something I'm willing to accept.

"Not yet," I tell him. Then I usher the twins up to their rooms. Content that they're down for the night, I put on some tightly laced sneakers.

"Round two, Daisy," I say to myself as I step back out my front door, facing down the Dixons'. The lights are coming back on. Good. There's no escaping me this time.

Paying zero attention to the kids hanging around the front

door, I dive back into the crowd, but only a few steps in and I'm halted. By Merrill.

"Stop!" Merrill yells. She looks at my normal outfit, horrified. "You've . . . you've *changed*."

"Fun's over!" I yell over the crowd.

"Stop chasing her!" she yells back. "Nothing bad is going to happen to her! Let her be free, and free yourself. You can't force it. Isn't that what you told me?"

This takes the fire out of me. What did I tell her? Some mom bullshit probably.

"You—you follow your heart, and l-let the rest of life catch up," Merrill stammers.

Follow my heart?

Merrill is looking at me like all that matters is this moment. I realize it's because I told her something that resonated, and even though our problems are completely different, this is my chance to prove something to her. To show this young girl that people can choose to change. And I realize that by my choosing to stay with her instead of chasing my dog, she will know that someone in this party has finally chosen to be her friend.

So I let go of Daisy. The *idea* of Daisy. I give her up to the party, just like Merrill said when I spoke with her on the phone, which feels like a lifetime ago. I choose to trust Merrill and the vision she has of me as someone who can be free. I let myself go, too, and I hope that what I'm meant to have will find me.

I think all these lofty things about this moment, but the reality is not as poetic. What actually happens is the DJ cues up some Taylor Swift, and I realize that I recognize the song. Kids are screaming lyrics that *I know*. Merrill sees me perk up, and I'm being dragged onto a dance floor. And then I'm being cheered on. Not in a cruel way. In a *Go, lady, go!* way.

So I guess it would be more accurate to say that the party makes me let go, and it's soon after that when I catch up and decide it's all right.

Whatever. I don't think about any of this as I quickly lose my breath giving these dances my all. The kids show me what to do and how to do it, and they scream when I finally nail the steps. When a band comes on, I jump and shout along to the lyrics I've never even heard.

And I make sure Merrill is by my side for it, joining in on the game of finally being part of something.

WHEN THE MUSIC finally slows and the dance floor empties, I don't want to leave. My feet move on their own. I haven't had this much fun in so long, and I'm not ready to let it all go. I keep myself spinning, not worrying about the embarrassment of being the last one on the dance floor, until I collide quite suddenly with an adult man.

"Oh, I'm so sorry," I say over the music. I check and yes, this is a real-life adult before me on the dance floor. Handsome. Amused.

"You the adult here?"

"Who's asking?" I say with a wink. Subtly, he's started to move to my rhythm. We're dancing. He puts out a hand and I take it, more for dramatics than anything else, but the sudden spark at our fingertips makes me shiver.

"Another adult," he says, spinning me. I'm breathless again, like I've only just surfaced from the pool. Even though the cheetah dress is long gone, and my makeup has melted away, and I'm just a thirtysomething in jeans and sneakers, I feel pretty in the gaze of this stranger. It's been a while since I've felt any excitement like this, and this is the last place I would have expected to find it, yet stranger things have happened to-night, right?

He pulls me closer.

"So, this isn't your house, miss?"

I roll my eyes, more at the *miss* than anything else. A clear *no* to both.

"So, what're you, a concerned citizen?" he asks. "Neighbor-hood patrol gone off the rails?"

"I'm no Karen," I say slyly, spinning again. He looks at me like he agrees. But he's got more questions.

"So, then, what are you doing here?"

"What does it look like I'm doing here?"

"Dancing."

"We could be dancing not at a high school party, you know," he says. A subtle offer. I realize that his hand has been in mine this whole time. He gives it a little squeeze, for emphasis.

"Actually," I say, stepping away a bit but not letting go, "I'm here looking for my dog. She got out and she's been running from me all night."

The man laughs and cocks his head. "That dog?"

At the very edge of the room, near the doors leading out-side, I spot Merrill surrounded by a small group of new friends. She catches my eye and gives me a big, cheesy thumbs-up, like she's cheering me on in this impromptu flirtation. Next to her, patiently sitting with her leash in her mouth, is Daisy. She's watching me, too. I can't be sure, but I think she's smiling.

I jump away from the man, finally self-conscious about how

sparse the dance floor has become. When did the lights get turned up all the way to party-ending brightness? I almost give in to the urge to hide myself, but what's to hide? Having given up, or given in, I'm part of the party now.

I put my hands on my hips and scan the man, who is grinning as he watches me. He's dressed funny.

"Why are you in a cop costume?" I ask. "Are you a stripper?"

"I'm not a stripper. And I'm not in a costume."

"Oh, please," I snap, thinking of the cowboy from earlier. I bet there's a fireman here, too, somewhere. "No real cop would just be having fun at a high school party."

"I guess it's a good thing I'm not a cop, then." He laughs. "I'm an EMT. They tend to bring us along to break up these big parties, especially around graduation. You never know if someone might need some medical assistance after their first attempt at a keg stand."

"Wait." I back away farther, horrified. I glance at Merrill again and her thumbs-up has wilted, perhaps as she reads the stricken expression on my face. To the man I ask, "The *real* cops are here? And you're a *real* EMT?"

"Depends. Are you in need of medical assistance?"

"No. What? Why?"

He takes out a little penlight and gets real close, shining it in my eye. "Have you had any substances tonight, ma'am?"

"N-no," I stutter, trapped between my confused attraction and the instinct to run. "No. I mean yes, but no—and don't call me ma'am."

"What should I call you, then?" he asks.

"Carla Schmidt," I blurt out, aware I've made a mistake immediately.

"And Carla," he says, studying me. Every step backward

I take, he closes with a big stride. "If I asked you for your telephone number, could you recite it?"

"I'm fine," I insist. "I could do it."

He studies me, then breaks into a smile. Next thing I know, he's got out his phone. "Great, because I'd love to see you outside of work sometime, Carla Schmidt."

I blush. I blush all over, head to toe. Was this . . . a ruse? An act of flirtation? Am I so out of practice I didn't even realize it? I'm a mess of glee and horror, and I blurt out the first thing that pops into my head, which, of course, is about my kids.

"I'm a mom."

The EMT winces. Why? Because he hates moms? Or because I basically just yelled this at him?

"But, like. A *cool* mom," I specify, trying to take the edge off.

"Ah." He nods, re-understanding me and my presence at this party. "So I take it you're only in the market for equally cool dads?"

I'm out of my depth with this level of flirtation, to the point that I'm not even sure if we're still flirting. It's gotten too weird. I *made* it weird. I have the urge to power through, like I've been doing all night, but the moment passes. The EMT takes my awkward silence as a shutdown.

"Bummer." He gives a polite smile, like I rejected him. "Nice to meet you, Carla. If you'll excuse me, I'm gonna check on"—he scans the leftover teens sprinkled around the room— "that one over there."

He's pointing at Merrill. Oh god. If she's half as high as I am, she's screwed. I race after the EMT, trying to cut in front of him, but he's fast. He's *running* for some reason. Right at Merrill! And then she's running to *him*. I question my sanity as they embrace. The other kids are staring, too.

"Carla," Merrill says, letting the EMT go, "I want you to meet my very single, not very cool dad."

"We've met," the EMT says, smiling at me.

What.

WHAT?

The EMT—Merrill's *father?*—glances at Merrill, who gives a big thumbs-up back, and I replay the moments before in my head. Merrill's earlier thumbs-up wasn't for me, it was for *him*. She gave him the green light to ask me out.

Daisy whines at my feet, and I impress myself with how cool I pretend to be as I grab her leash from her jaws and rub the top of her head.

"Shift ends in an hour," Merrill's dad says. "How are you getting home, Mer-bear?"

Staying is clearly not an option, with the cops here, and looking around, I wonder if any of these kids can drive. I hope they decided on rideshares and designated drivers.

"I'm across the street," I say before Merrill can respond. "She can stay with me."

"What about the rest of you?" Merrill's dad asks, his deep voice booming toward the crowd of lingering kids.

Merrill's new friends shuffle their feet, no one looking the man in the eye. Merrill goes red as her dad goes into Dad Mode. Whatever rapport she has with these kids, it's evaporating before her very eyes.

"They're coming with me, too," I say. Very cool. Very matter-of-fact.

Everyone gasps. Everyone looks at me. "What? You can all call your parents or whoever and get picked up, but this way no one gets hurt or in trouble."

"Really?" Merrill asks, eyes shining with gratitude. "You're throwing the after-party? Shit, Carla. You *are* cool."

"Absolutely not," I scold. Clearly, so Merrill's dad hears every word I say. "There will be no imbibing or consumption of illicit substances. Not on my watch." The kids all droop a little, so I add, "But I do have a freezer full of pizza rolls that we can heat up."

Almost in unison, the small group shouts: "PIZZA ROLLS?"

I can't help but fire off a playful wink.

"Duh, I'm a mom."

Cheering. Chanting. *Go, Carla, go!* I rally my small new troop and lead them away from the sticky Dixon house. Before I go, I turn to give the mess one last, loving glance, and somehow the EMT is right behind me.

"See you in an hour?" he asks. The flirtation is still in his voice.

"Look," I say, making sure Merrill and the others have moved on. "I'm flattered, but I wasn't kidding. I *am* a mom."

"I'm a dad." He grins. "You know my daughter, I see." That proud-dad look enters his eyes. The one that always chokes me up. He watches Merrill from the doorway with me, and I think I see a note of relief mixed into his pride. I realize he probably knew she was here tonight. Maybe he encouraged her to come, to keep trying. Maybe he was worried about her this whole time. Maybe he's been worried about Merrill for a long time.

"She really is something special," I tell him.

He blinks away the glazed look that I swear meant he was close to crying. His flirtatious smile is back. "So you noticed?"

"Oh boy, did I," I laugh.

He laughs, too, then steps back into the house. "We're in

agreement, then. Wow, already so much in common, Carla Schmidt. I look forward to learning more, say . . . Monday night? You got plans?"

I picture my calendar, all freed up after I send the twins off with their dad on Sunday night. Monday night, like every night alone, holds a taunting blankness. An emptiness I've been so scared to mar with actual effort.

"Nope," I say. "No plans."

"You do now. Have a good rest of your night, then."

He gives me a tip of some invisible hat and leaves me there, holding Daisy's leash, blushing. From the lawn I hear Merrill shouting, asking if I'm coming or not. In response, Daisy lurches forward, her leash flying from my hands, and I chase her all the way home.

# JRUE EDWARDS

## THE CLASS CLOWN

$$\boxed{\textit{INTERLUDE}}$$

## Sadie 🤍

SATURDAY, 12:11 A.M.

**SADIE:**
Hey wya

Hellooooo?!

SATURDAY, 12:37 A.M.

**SADIE:**
JRUEEEEEE WHERE R U?!? COPS ARE HERE!!!!

**JRUE:**
yo my bad, i just saw these lol

wya i need to see you rn

**SADIE:**
OMGGG ABOUT TIME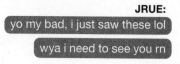

**JRUE:**
just talked to Mia

**SADIE:**
What happened?? All the vibes?!?

**JRUE:**
nope lol

**SADIE:**
No??!?

**JRUE:**
but also YES lolol

**SADIE:**
What are you talking about?! Just spit it out already!!

**JRUE:**
still thirsty, huh hahaha

wya 👀

i need to tell you sumthin f2f

**SADIE:**
Bruh.

if y'all hooked up, just say it, you don't gotta see my fave for that

🫠 🙃

Face* for that

**JRUE:**
bruh what do those emojis even mean

fr where you at lol

🙄

guess i gotta walk around til I c u 🧑‍🦱

**SADIE:**
Jrue

**JRUE:**
Sadie

**SADIE:**
How was it vibes AND no vibes

**JRUE:**

**SADIE:**
So how's that novel coming

**JRUE:**

**SADIE:**
JRUE just say it!! You're killing me dude!!

**JRUE:**
i don't wanna say over text

i'm killing you?! haha SADIE seriously WYAAAAA

**SADIE:**
Um where are you??

**JRUE:**
you know what, nvm. you ain't gotta tell me

**SADIE:**
Huh? What you mean?!

**JRUE:**

**SADIE:**
JRUE QUIT PLAYING

**JRUE:**
who's playing??

also why are you yelling

**SADIE:**
BC YOU'RE FRUSTRATING ME

**JRUE:**
well you don't have to yell

turn around

**SADIE:**
STOP TELLING ME WHAT TO DO

**JRUE:**
dude lolol

**SADIE:**
WHAT?!

**JRUE:**
i'm right behind u

# JRUE EDWARDS

## THE CLASS CLOWN

I HEAR A BOOMING FEMALE VOICE BEHIND ME, not far from the space downstairs I just vacated, shout: "All right, people, time to break it up. You've got five minutes to vacate the premises or we're throwing you in the paddy wagon."

Wait. *Paddy wagon*? Um, 1920 called, and it wants its word back.

Okay, Jrue, focus, man. You got this. Your mission is now twofold:

1. Don't get paddy-wagoned.
2. Talk to Sadie.

Seems I'm pretty good at completing tasks, because I found Sadie mere minutes after deciding I needed to talk to her. And by found, I mean I watched as she came flying out of what I think is a bathroom.

"It was 'vibes and no vibes' because it turns out Mia McKenzie was kinda into me."

"Oh. Okay. Well, then . . ." Sadie slowly turns around to face me. ". . . how was it 'no vibes'?"

I grin. "That *is* the 'no vibes' part."

"What?" Sadie shakes her head. "Make it make sense."

"Okay, well, it's like . . ." Suddenly, inexplicably, it feels weird having my arms at my sides, just dangling mega-awkwardly. So I stuff my hands in my pockets, which feels equally strange, so I take one hand out and leave the other in. Ah, that's . . . better?

I clear my throat. "It was 'no vibes' because—"

A stampede of kids racing for the stairs rushes by, and we slide left and right to dodge them.

I start again. "I mean, Mia's great. Smart and gorgeous and funny, like . . ."

Sadie groans impatiently. "Ugh, we get it already. Mia's amazing. Ten out of ten."

I laugh, because fair. Because this isn't about Mia. Because this is about . . . Sadie. It's always been Sadie.

"It was 'no vibes' because I realized I don't like Mia that way, not anymore. Honestly, I'm not sure I ever did."

Sadie's face wrinkles. "So you're saying you turned down Mia?"

I nod.

Sadie shakes her head. "*The* Mia McKenzie? Are you crazy?"

I nod again.

"Hold up." Sadie's voice drops just the slightest. "So how was it 'vibes,' then?"

"It was 'vibes' because I also realized that the reason I'm not into Mia is because I'm . . . umm . . . I'm kinda sorta . . . No, that's not right. I mean, it's because I'm *really* into—"

"Is anybody up there?" The booming voice is back and clearly a lot closer now, the cop likely standing at the bottom of the stairs. "Come on down now. The party's over!"

Sadie shakes her head. "We should go. Before the cops come looking for us."

"That doesn't matter. What I'm—"

She starts tugging me along. "Um, it definitely matters. We've got futures to protect, Jrue. We can finish this conversation when we—"

"Sadie, the cops are gonna have to wait because this can't. I've already wasted too much time," I say, trying to sound smooth because this feels like that kind of moment. The way my heart is racing—and not just because of the cops—and my mouth has suddenly gone dryer than beef jerky, I know this is gonna be one of those memories we talk about every few months, that we happily relive to anyone who will listen, because it's the moment I realized Sadie Bernbaum isn't just my person. She's my best friend. She's the owner of the best laugh I've ever heard. She's walking, talking sunshine. She's sitting with me in bed after I sit next to her for a gazillion hours in the curbside pickup for D'Angelos (home to the best deep-dish pie you've ever tasted), because sitting together, in the car, on the bed, at school . . . shit, just being together, period . . . makes everything better.

Sadie stops in her tracks. "What . . . can't . . . wait?"

"Sadie," I say, suddenly wishing I'd put on ChapStick.

Sadie's face twists like how it does when she's sniffing a story unfolding. "Uh-oh, what's going on?"

I stammer. "What, what's, uh, nothing . . ."

"Hello? Anybody still up there? Don't make me come upstairs. No, really, please don't make me. It's been a long night."

"Jrue, whatever you have to say, you can tell me when we—"

"I love you, Sadie Bernbaum."

Her face wrinkles. "I know. I love you, too, weirdo."

"No," I say, shaking my head. "No. I'm fucking in love . . . with you . . ."

I watch the words sink into her brain and the unexpected happens for maybe the first time ever—

Sadie Bernbaum is . . . speechle—

"I . . . I . . ." I lean in slower than I want to, to give her time to object, and for a second, I imagine her head suddenly jerking backward, a *What the hell are you doing, dude?* look in her eyes—

But she doesn't move, or flinch, or pull away.

Actually, she does move, but only to tilt her chin so that our lips press together, and then her mouth is opening, and her tongue is playing with my tongue, and there are freaking weird things happening in my stomach. Like, really weird things.

But we keep kissing.

Even when we hear the cops start belting "I'm Every Woman" downstairs, we don't stop kissing. We open our eyes and exchange knowing glances, of course.

Because that's what we do.

Because this is who we are.

"If I'd known stuff like this could happen, I would've gone to more house parties," Sadie says, grinning, when we finally come up for air.

And I'm cheesing at her hard enough to make everyone within a three-mile radius's cheeks hurt. "I think you did it right."

"Oh, I did, did I?"

"Yep," I say as I lean in again, our lips already puckering for round two. "This party? It's gotta be worth at least ten normal house parties combined."

"I feel like you just made up that equation . . ."

Our lips brush. "As usual, your powers of observation are spot-on . . ."

"I love you, Jrue."

"I love you, Sa—"

She pulls my face into hers, her fingers locked around the back of my neck, in a way that feels like this kiss could continue in this hallway at this house party forever.

Or, you know, at least until we pass out from lack of oxygen. Although I'm not even sure that would stop us.

Because who needs air when you've got love?

IT WAS **HER**! AND JUST LIKE THAT, THE WORST PARTY OF MY LIFE BECAME THE **BEST** PARTY OF MY LIFE. A LIFE THAT, SADLY, MAY END PREMATURELY BECAUSE I MISSED MY CURFEW...

BUT THAT'S BESIDE THE POINT. RIGHT NOW I'M JUST THINKING ABOUT HOW A NIGHT WHERE EVERYTHING WENT WRONG ENDED UP TRULY BEING ONE OF THE **GREATEST OF ALL TIME!**

# OKAY, COOL, COOL, BUT WHERE ARE THEY NOW?!?

## FIVE YEARS LATER...

### SADIE BERNBAUM

Sadie spent the remaining weeks before she left for early semester at Dartmouth attached to Jrue's face like a succubus. They kissed until their lips were chapped and they had to stop to drink some water because hydration is key. Once their raging hormones were satiated, they decided that maintaining a long-distance relationship as they both started their new adventures as legal adults didn't make sense, so, for now, their love story is "to be continued" and their best-friendship is stronger than ever.

When Sadie started her summer semester at Dartmouth, she had a list of things she wanted to accomplish (per usual):

1. cozy up to the editors of the school paper, the *Dartmouth*
2. get on staff
3. world/journalistic domination

The first night as she laid out the past decade's worth of yearbooks to research former Dartmouth journalists, she overheard people talking in the hallway about a party. Unlike the old Sadie, she decided to roll through. Within moments of arriving, her unexpected drinking-game skillz were unveiled and she completely annihilated the beer pong table and rode that social high all the way to the dance floor. After a week of making up for all the lost partying time she spent working in high school, Sadie decided to take a sabbatical from journalism and explore other interests. After being invited to join an underground social society (where she learned she was just as good at keeping secrets as she was at sharing them), Sadie decided to put her deft communication skills to different use and majored in creative writing. She is currently working on a memoir in essays.

## JRUE EDWARDS

Jrue "Class Clown" Edwards skipped college to pursue a plumber's certification. To date, he's designed irrigation systems in seven countries and counting and regularly volunteers for Water Works, an organization dedicated to supplying clean drinking water in low-income communities at no cost to the occupants. Jrue and Sadie have exchanged 345 long-form heartfelt and hilarious emails and plan to meet to watch the northern lights in the spring. He's still a sucker for a good laugh, especially hers.

## OSCAR "INTELLEQT" GRAHAM

Oscar retired IntelleQt—for a while—and impressed several MIT professors with the speed and efficiency of his coding. During his sophomore year, he rebranded his old rap name as an app. "inTELLect" helped people list and curate the most positive service and retail experiences in their local area, with an emphasis on shouting out the good people who made it happen. During his junior year, he sold "inTELLect" for like ten million dollars and asked Stasia to marry him. She agreed, and they're currently building her new media empire together. On his old block, it's not unusual to hear the corner boys dreaming about making "Oscar Graham money" someday. On the low, he continues to make three beats a day.

## ZARA HUSSEIN

Zara ditched the idea of the University of Illinois and swapped it for a move to New York City. For the first year, she worked a series of odd jobs—bookshop clerk, clothing store attendant, and hostess at a chain restaurant near Times Square. During her second year, she enrolled in the Fashion Institute of Technology's Art History and Museum Professions program with the hope she might someday be able to work in a museum.

Liam also ended up in New York. Much to his parents' dismay, he went to CIA (Culinary Institute of America), so he didn't live in the city, but he took the train to visit Zara every weekend. After Liam graduated, he moved to the city and took a job at a VERY fancy and well-known restaurant working as a line cook. His parents still don't understand what he's doing, but Zara does, and he's never been happier.

The two of them are plotting a possible move to Paris, where Zara might do some graduate-level studies with a specific focus on paintings from the era of the French Revolution, and Liam plans to work in a restaurant there, getting more experience and exposure.

## CAMERON JACOBS

"Well, I'm happy to say that Denise and I are still a couple. I mean, we didn't date immediately, it took us a while in the beginning. It was hard at first, being that she graduated from high school and I still had a year left. Plus, I was grounded for like a gazillion years!!! But we ended up going to the same art college, which made things soooo much easier. She even got used to being picked up in a minivan. Thanks for nothing, Mom and Dad!

"But where we REALLY connect is with our art. In fact, we're currently working on a graphic novel about our college experience (she graduated last year). We'll start it as a weekly web comic, then see if we can get it published in book form. The good news is that my friends (who you met) and I are still as close as ever. But sadly, I never heard from Daisy or Brenda again. (I feel so used!)

"In the end, the thing that I'll always remember about DeAndre's house party is that's where I finally got to meet the girl of my dreams. She's an amazing artist, and an even better person. And apparently, she thinks I'm pretty okay, too. In fact, the only reason why I even went to that party was on the slim chance that I would get a chance to talk to her. Which obviously wasn't DeAndre's diabolical plan at all. #SeniorPranks. But in the end, I guess you can say that Denise and I were just 'drawn together.'"

## FERNANDA MANNING

Fernanda and Kai both went to UCLA. She joined the softball team, and he was part of the cheer squad. They moved in together. She's expecting a call to represent the US women's team in the next summer Olympics. She never tires of telling Kai that she loves him. He makes life beautiful. And he never gets tired of seeing her dance to the sound of their favorite bands on the rooftop of their overpriced apartment building (even if her movements are jerky and uncoordinated). If she stumbles, he can always catch her.

## MEMI MATSON

Memi and Chance dated and danced together until he left for Juilliard. It was her idea to end their romance rather than continue anything long-distance. Soon after Memi arrived at the Institute of American Indian Arts for her freshman year, she became homesick for Lake Michigan and the smell of water in the air. She thought about crying but someone sat behind her and spoke softly: "Just breathe, Mem."

Memi and Chance (who transferred after his freshman year) graduated from IAIA—she with a degree in performing arts and a certificate in business entrepreneurship; he with a degree in creative writing. Perfect timing as the film industry sought to increase representation of Native American creatives. Chance joined the all-Native writers' room on a popular comedy-drama series while also working on his own play script about two former friends who confront the reason behind their falling-out when their teen children fall in love. Memi was cast as the nemesis of the lead character in a Netflix series adapted from her favorite novel and set on an Indian reservation. They live in Vancouver with a tuxedo cat named Juliet.

## SY NAVARRO

There Is No Kevin in Team's secret show at DeAndre's became legendary. A video recording of their rendition of "Cat Café" that night immediately went viral, while millions continue to stream their music.

Sam currently travels the world, playing drums as the only

living member of an otherwise holographic Dashboard Confessional. Perry followed in his mother's footsteps and became a therapist, specializing in helping adolescent boys find healthy ways to process and express their emotions. Asa and Sy now run a successful independent bookstore/community pantry/cat café/underground music venue in Austin, Texas. Even though that night would truly prove to be There Is No Kevin in Team's final show, the former band members remain friends to this day. They play *Liberators of Catan* online together every Monday night.

## SAVOY

Five years later and SAVOY is dead. Not Savoy, the person, but SAVOY, the collective. After the party, the scandal between House of SAVOY and Miranda rocketed the teens into internet infamy. The individuals within each decided to work on their own solo projects. Mirage opened a design studio in Brooklyn. Grant and Effie paired up to create a buzz blog covering influencer scandals, and a matching podcast with a cultish following. Miranda pursued costume design in New York City, her work catching the eye of drag queens and celebrities. And Savoy took on full-time responsibilities as SAVOY, the influencer, creating a small empire of fashion-forward content, until one day, it all vanished. All of it gone, on the eve of the Met Gala.

Officially, no one knows what happened to Savoy. What's clear—at least to those familiar with this group's antics—is that something big is about to happen. A plan is coming to fruition. A plan that has perhaps been in the works ever since a certain group of teens learned firsthand what a little scandal can get you if it happens at the right party.

## CARLA SCHMIDT

Carla nearly canceled her date with Merrill's cute paramedic dad due to yet another impromptu escape by Daisy (freshly groomed). But he showed up at her house anyway, put the bouquet of flowers he'd brought with him down on her stoop, and the two adults spent the evening laughing and chasing Daisy through the neighborhood. Five years later, Carla and the paramedic got married in a backyard ceremony. Merrill, now a rising star in the reality-TV space (live-action role-playing, of all things), officiated the ceremony while the twins held a wriggling Daisy down in the front row. Daisy wore a beautiful white dress that she then ruined minutes later by belly flopping into the cupcake bar. Pizza rolls were served in lieu of the intended dessert.

## PENNY WASHINGTON

Penny and Colin started dating that summer after graduation. Colin held her hand through her having to put her mother in a home. They had a very short-lived breakup due to growing pains, during which Penny dated a super-hot up-and-coming pop star with major nineties Janet Jackson vibes, and during which Colin could no longer listen to any of their favorite songs together. Colin held Penny's hand yet again as they walked down the aisle together—at graduation (geez, slow your roll, Penny's not the marrying kind, at least not just yet). She studied gerontology and wants to get her Master of Public Health with a focus on hospital administration so she can open compassionate-care homes for early-onset dementia patients. Colin double-majored in English and history and still isn't quite sure he knows what he wants to do, just that he wants to do it all with her by his side.

# JADE'S HOUSE PARTY PLAYLIST

- "Gimme! Gimme! Gimme!" by ABBA

- "Rumors" by Lizzo ft. Cardi B

- "Ski" by Young Thug

- "Big Paper" by DJ Khaled ft. Cardi B

- "I Heard It Through the Grapevine" by Marvin Gaye

- "Walk This Way" by RUN-DMC ft. Aerosmith

- "Lost in the World" by Kanye West ft. Bon Iver

- "Numb" by Linkin Park ft. Jay-Z

- "Buss It Down" by Big Shaq

- "Running Up That Hill" by Kate Bush

- "Magic" by Vince Staples ft. Mustard

- "Industry Baby" by Lil Nas X ft. Jack Harlow

- "Die Hard" by Kendrick Lamar ft. Amanda Reifer & Blxst

- "Calling U Back" by the Marías
- "Falling" by Chayla Hope
- "The Boy Is Mine" by Brandy & Monica
- "If" by Janet Jackson
- "Ojitos Lindos" by Bad Bunny & Bomba Estéreo
- "I Want to Dance with Somebody" by Whitney Houston
- "Shake It Off" by Taylor Swift
- "WAP" by Cardi B ft. Megan Thee Stallion
- "Be Sweet" by Japanese Breakfast
- "Stargazing" by the Neighbourhood
- "Perfect" by Brooke Simpson
- "I'm Every Woman" by Whitney Houston
- "I'd Die Without You" by P.M. Dawn

# ABOUT THE AUTHORS

## THE ACTOR

Angeline Boulley, an enrolled member of the Sault Ste. Marie Tribe of Chippewa Indians, is a storyteller who writes about her Ojibwe community in Michigan's Upper Peninsula. She is a former director of the Office of Indian Education at the US Department of Education. Angeline lives in southwest Michigan, but her home will always be on Sugar Island. *Firekeeper's Daughter* was her debut—a *New York Times* bestseller and the winner of the Michael L. Printz Award and the William C. Morris Award.

angelineboulley.com

## THE ARTIST

Jerry Craft is a number one *New York Times* bestselling author-illustrator who has worked on numerous picture books, graphic novels, and middle-grade novels, including the Newbery Medal–winning graphic novel *New Kid* and its companion,

*Class Act. New Kid* is also the winner of the Coretta Scott King Author Award and the *Kirkus* Prize. Jerry is the creator of *Mama's Boyz,* an award-winning syndicated comic strip. He has won five African American Literary Awards and is a cofounder of the Schomburg Center's Annual Black Comic Book Festival. He received his BFA from the School of Visual Arts and lives in Connecticut.

jerrycraft.com
𝕏 ⓕ ⓘ

## THE SCHOOL PAPER EDITOR;
## KNOWER OF ALL TEA

Natasha Díaz is a born-and-raised New Yorker, author and screenwriter, and current resident of Brooklyn, NY, along with her family. Natasha's scripts have placed as a quarterfinalist in the Austin Film Festival and a finalist for both the NALIP Diverse Women in Media Fellowship and the Sundance Episodic Story Lab. Anthologies featuring her contributions include *Wild Tongues Can't Be Tamed* and Walter Dean Myers's *145th Street* anniversary edition. Natasha's first novel, *Color Me In,* won Best Young Adult Novel in the International Latino Book Awards.

natashaerikadiaz.com
𝕏 ⓕ ⓘ

## THE WANNABE RAPPER

Lamar Giles writes for teens and adults across multiple genres, with work appearing on numerous Best Of lists each and every year. He is the author of the acclaimed novels *Fake ID, Endangered, Overturned, Spin, The Last Last-Day-of-Summer, The Last Mirror on the Left, Not So Pure and Simple,* and *The Getaway,* as well as numerous pieces of short fiction. He is a founding member of We Need Diverse Books and resides in Virginia with his family.

lamargiles.com

🐦 📘 📷

## THE POPULAR GIRL

Christina Hammonds Reed, a native of the Los Angeles area, holds an MFA from the University of Southern California's School of Cinematic Arts. Her work has appeared in the *Santa Monica Review, One Teen Story,* and *Elle.* Her debut novel, *The Black Kids,* was a *New York Times* bestseller, a William C. Morris Award Finalist, a Silver Medalist for the California Book Awards, and an ALAN Amelia Elizabeth Walden Finalist, among other accolades.

📷

## THE INFLUENCER/THE COOL MOM

Ryan La Sala writes about surreal things happening to queer people. He is the author of the wildly imaginative *Reverie,* which was selected as a Barnes & Noble book club pick, a Kids' Indie Next List pick, and an Amazon Best Book of the Month; the crafty breakup romance *Be Dazzled* (also a Kids' Indie Next List pick), and his young adult horror novel, *The Honeys.* He has been featured in *Entertainment Weekly,* on NPR, and at

Tor.com, and one time Shangela from *RuPaul's Drag Race* called him cute. Ryan resides in New York City.

**ryanlasala.com**

🐦 📷 ▶️ ♪

## THE JOCK

Yamile Saied Méndez is a fútbol-obsessed Argentine American Pura Belpré gold medal–winning author. An inaugural Walter Dean Myers Grant recipient, she's also a graduate of Voices of Our Nations and the Vermont College of Fine Arts MFA Writing for Children's and Young Adult program. She writes picture books (*Where Are You From?*), middle-grade fiction (*Horse Country*), young adult fiction (*Furia*), and adult romance (*Twice a Quinceañera*). She lives in Utah with her husband and their five kids, two adorable dogs, and one majestic cat.

**yamilesmendez.com**

🐦 📷 ♪

## THE CLASS CLOWN

justin a. reynolds has always wanted to be a writer. *Opposite of Always,* his debut YA novel, was an Indies Introduce Top Ten Debut Title and a *School Library Journal* Best Book of the Year, was translated into nineteen languages, is being developed for film by Paramount Players, and was recently adapted into a popular Webtoon. His second YA novel, *Early Departures,* published to critical acclaim and was a *Kirkus Reviews* Best Teen Book of the Year. His Marvel graphic novel debut, *Miles Morales: Shock Waves,* featuring Brooklyn's Spider-Man, was an ABA Indie Bestseller. justin is also the cofounder of the CLE Reads Book Festival, a Cleveland Book Festival for middle-grade and young adult writers. He happily hangs out in northeastern Ohio.

justinareynolds.com

### THE EMO BAND KID

Randy Ribay was born in the Philippines and raised in the Midwest. He's the author of *An Infinite Number of Parallel Universes, After the Shot Drops,* and *Patron Saints of Nothing.* The last was selected as a Freeman Book Award winner and as a finalist for the National Book Award, the *LA Times* Book Prize, and the Edgar Award for Best Young Adult Mystery, among other accolades. Randy earned his BA in English literature from the University of Colorado at Boulder and his master's degree in language and literacy from the Harvard Graduate School of Education. He lives in the San Francisco Bay Area with his wife, son, and catlike dog.

randyribay.com

### THE NEW GIRL

Jasmine Warga is the *New York Times* bestselling, award-winning author of the middle-grade novels *Other Words for Home, The Shape of Thunder,* and *A Rover's Story.* She also penned the young adult books *Here We Are Now* and *My Heart and Other Black Holes,* which has been translated into more than twenty languages. Jasmine currently teaches in the MFA program at Vermont College of Fine Arts. Originally from Cincinnati, she now lives in the Chicago area with her family in a house filled with books.

**jasminewarga.com**